The
Prince of Warwood
and the King's Key

To Aunt Susie & Uncle Marty,
Love, J. Noel Clinton

J. Noel Clinton

C² Publishing

PRINCE OF WARWOOD AND THE KING'S KEY

ISBN 0-9773115-1-1

Library of Congress Control Number: 2005908347

Cover design by Toby Mikle
Artwork by J. Noel Clinton and Toby Mikle
Type set Arial and Tempus San ITC

First printing (paperback), January 2006

C^2 Publishing
P.O. Box 5269
Vienna, WV 26105

www.princeofwarwood.com

TO JILL,
YOU'VE ALWAYS BEEN MY STRENGTH AND COURAGE.

THANKS CRAIG, FOR "PUTTING YOUR MONEY WHERE
YOUR MOUTH IS."

FINALLY, THANK YOU TO THE STUDENTS AND STAFF AT
JEFFERSON ELEMENTARY CENTER FOR BEING MY
GUINUEA PIGS.

CONTENTS

Chapter 1
The First Power
★ ★ ★ ★ ★

Xavier stood, shivering, in a garden with a mist surrounding him like a cool blanket. Although it was calm and peaceful, he couldn't help but feel uneasy. The area was in such disarray that it looked more like a garbage compost than a garden. The stone walkway was uneven and decrepit, and the flowerbed walls were sunken and had long since collapsed. Brown, dried stalks stood tall and stiff like skeletons. The bushes were bare and decaying and the air smelled faintly sweet, not fresh air and springtime sweet but rotting, deathly sweet.

When Xavier turned to find his way out of this garden of death, a noise stopped him. He squinted into the fog and found a large shape moving in the veiled whiteness. His breath caught in his throat as he realized the shape was moving toward him. A midnight stallion emerged from the whiteness and trotted toward him. It whinnied and pawed at the ground with a snort.

Xavier expelled a sigh of relief. "It's okay. Don't be afraid," he coaxed.

The stallion danced toward him, and Xavier reached out to touch it. With another snort, the horse shied away from him and reared up agitatedly.

"Whoa, boy. Whoa," he whispered, stepping backwards. "It's all right. I promise; I'm a friend. I won't hurt you." The horse quieted with only its ears twitching. "Easy, boy. Easy," he continued to soothe as he inched closer to the animal.

Xavier's hand was inches from the horse when everything around him dissolved away, and he found himself in a long, stone corridor. Small lanterns cast dancing ghosts of light along the length of the cobble walls, and a humming noise drifted toward him from a red door at the end of the passage. As if his feet had wills of their own, Xavier stumbled toward it. He didn't understand why, but he was drawn to it; it was as if there was a force pulling him to the door and the growing noises within. A sense of urgency grasped at him. He had to get beyond the door and warn …warn who? He had no idea. Ten feet from the door, six feet, two… something, a sound, a voice, something, stirred him from his dream.

Xavier opened his gray eyes to the soft light that filtered through his bedroom window. He wasn't sure what woke him, only that it had been a sound of some kind. He closed his eyes and concentrated on the brief memory of the sound, but the sound toyed with him, refusing to materialize into something recognizable. He could only surmise that the sound had been human; it had been a voice.

With a groan of frustration, he raked his fingers through the long, white curls tousled on top his head. Xavier Wells was a very unusual looking boy. It was because of his hair that bullies sought him out to torment him, and it didn't help matters that he was small for his age. He had overheard his grandparents refer to him as an albino once, but that wasn't accurate. From what he had read about albinos, their skins are as pale as their hair. This was not true of Xavier for his complexion was rich and creamy, not pale and sallow. But this much was certain; he looked very little like his dark-haired, dark-eyed mother, which could only mean that he favored his father.

Xavier Wells had never known his father and had no memory of him. When he was eight years old, Xavier had searched his mother's room for anything that would tell him something about his father. He was disappointed to find that there wasn't a single picture of him, not one. There was no evidence that he even had a father; it was as if his father never existed. When Xavier had mustered up the courage to ask his mother about him, she hadn't answered, but her gaze darted to Grandmother's abominable face. Then, with despair glimmering in her eyes, she walked out of the room without a word. Guilt gnawed at Xavier's gut as he watched her leave.

Then, without warning, Grandmother turned to Xavier and struck him across the jaw, sending him tumbling out of his chair and onto the floor.

"Don't you ever mention that good for nothing father of yours to her again! Do you understand me, you little bastard?" she blared, glaring down at him. "Your father was nothing more than a hoodlum that took advantage of a poor, unsuspecting, vulnerable girl. He coerced your mother into marrying him, and when she became pregnant with *you*, he revealed his true, deviant nature and left her to raise you on her own." She surveyed him with contempt. "And, it appears that you're going to be the spitting image of that monster in every conceivable way. You're thoughtless and cruel. You think of no one but yourself! You're definitely no grandson of mine!"

Xavier thought she would strike him again, but she turned and stormed out of the room. He never questioned about his father again.

"Boy! Boy! Get up, boy! I'm not driving you to school if you're late so get a move on," a gruff voice remarked from outside his door.

"Yes, Grandfather. I'm up," Xavier called, listening as his grandfather shuffled down the hall muttering to himself.

With a noisy yawn, Xavier threw back the covers and stood. After rummaging through the dirty clothes spread across the floor and pulling on a pair of jeans and a very wrinkled t-shirt, he stumbled down the stairs and into the kitchen. His mother sat quietly at the table drinking coffee and reading the morning paper.

"Morning, Mother," Xavier mumbled, kissing her cheek. His grandmother continued scrambling eggs without glancing at him. Xavier hated scrambled eggs and made a face as he crossed the kitchen to the cereal cupboard.

"Hello, honey. Sleep well?" his mother spoke from behind the newspaper.

"Yep," Xavier replied and flopped himself at the table with a box of Apple Jacks.

Finally, Grandmother turned from the stove wiping her hands on an apron tied around her waist and surveyed Xavier with disgust.

"Boy! Don't you have any decent clothes to wear to school? You look like a common thug! Where are the clothes I bought you last week, hmmm?"

"Ah, well..."

"Well, you will not be leaving this house until you have respectable clothing on your back. Now, go and change those clothes," Grandmother spat, glaring down at him and pointing to the stairs.

"I'm not wearing those clothes!" he insisted.

"Excuse me?" Grandmother stormed over to him and yanked him to his feet by his ear. "You *will* wear those clothes when you leave this house even if I have to dress you myself. Now, get up those stairs and change this instant!" She shoved him toward the door and slapped the back of his head.

Rubbing his ear, Xavier looked to his mother for a sign, any sign, of support, but she continued to stare at the newspaper and did not say a word. With a frustrated groan, Xavier trudged through the door and up the stairs.

"Oh, great! As if I don't stand out enough at school; now I have to wear those choir boy clothes," Xavier growled.

Once he was dressed in navy slacks, a powder blue

shirt, patent leather shoes, and, with the insistence from his grandmother, a plaid tie that was almost nauseating to look at, Xavier only had time to grab his schoolbooks and bag before running off to the bus stop.

"Oh, look everyone! It's Wonder Bread. How's it going dork?" taunted a gangly boy with a wide freckled face and a mangle of black hair.

"Leave him be, Donald," growled a petite girl with spiked, brown hair as she pulled Xavier through the crowd of adolescents waiting in a stupor at the bus stop. "Just ignore him X. He's such an idiot. No one listens to him, anyway," she told him, her dark eyes doe-like with sympathy.

"Unfortunately, no one has to, Robbie. Everyone already thinks that I am a dork," Xavier sulked.

"Well, maybe we could jazz up your image a little bit. I mean, why do you always wear church clothes to school? They make you look like a geek or something," Robbie said, wrinkling up her nose as she surveyed his appearance.

"Don't I know it! I can't help it. Grandmother won't let me leave for school until I'm 'appropriately dressed'," Xavier imitated his grandmother's shrill voice.

"We'll just have to fix that, now; won't we?" Robbie whispered with grin. "Okay, X, this is what I'm going to do for you. Tomorrow morning, after you're dressed to your grandmother's liking, come to my house before the bus stop. You can change clothes there before and after school. Your grandmother won't be the wiser."

"Thanks, Robbie, it's a plan," Xavier replied as the school bus pulled up to the curb.

* * * * *

Following history, Xavier and Robbie fought their way toward their second period class through the throngs of students milling about in the hall. A particularly large eighth grader bumped into Xavier and sent him stumbling into Robbie, and they both nearly went sprawling to the floor. So, they slid to the side and walked along the wall to avoid the constant jostling and scrambling through the crowded hallway. As they drew closer to the science and technology wing, the hall thinned out, and they continued to walk in a comfortable silence until someone spoke from behind them.

"Yo! Pus head!" said a taunting, gruff voice.

When Xavier spun around, he confronted a fat, straw-haired boy. Mark Hopkins had a face that surely only his mother could love. Aside from having a greasy, pimply complexion, Mark's body odor made Xavier's eyes water and his head pound.

"You would have thought I could have smelled him coming," Xavier thought, but he didn't dare say it aloud to Mark's face. Though Mark was in the same year as Xavier, he looked much older. He was nearly a foot taller, and he had the beginnings of a thin mustache. And, he was mean; quite simply, he was a bully.

"Watch it, Mark! I'm not in a particularly good mood to put up with your mouth today," Xavier muttered.

"Ah, is mama's little boy having a bad day?" he cooed wickedly and smacked kisses at him.

"Cut it out!" Xavier shoved him away, anger burning on his face.

"Is there a problem here?" an adult's voice called from beyond the crowd of children clustered around them. Mr. Sims fought his way through the onlookers.

"Later, pimple head," Mark growled.

"Pimple head? Me? Look in the mirror!" Xavier grumbled as he watched Mark waddle away.

The crowd began to disperse from the area, and Mr. Sims approached Xavier and Robbie.

"Ah, Xavier Wells, why am I not surprised? What's going on here?" he asked.

"Nothing, Mr. Sims," he muttered.

"Really, now? I can see that," he responded, looking around at the still departing crowd. He looked back at Xavier suspiciously. "You know that fighting is strictly forbidden. Those involved can find themselves in a lot of trouble and possibly even suspended."

"They weren't fighting Mr. Sims," Robbie interrupted. "They were just talking; that's all."

Mr. Sims was unconvinced and fixed her with a piercing stare. "Well, in any case, you two better get a move on or you'll be late for class, and as it turns out that would be my class."

Robbie and Xavier ducked past Mr. Sims and walked the short distance down the hall to the computer lab; most of the class was already present. As they slid to the rear of the room and took their customary seats next to one another, Xavier felt several pairs of eyes watching him.

"Ladies and gentlemen," Mr. Sims called as he entered and stalked to the front of the room. "Your assignment should be in front of you. In this assignment, we will be applying the skills we learned yesterday. It's due at the end of the period, so I'd suggest that you get to work and not waste your time by talking."

The room erupted in a chattering of keyboards, but Xavier sat motionless staring at the blank IBM screen. Anger was still churning and gnawing at him. Why did others find him such an easy target for their jokes and teasing? Why couldn't they just leave him alone? What did he ever do to them? Nothing! That's what! He had done absolutely nothing to them!

"Mr. Wells?" Xavier jerked his head up to find Mr. Sims watching him. "I highly suggest that you get started on your work. This assignment is worth fifty points, and I don't think your grade could withstand another substandard score."

Xavier's anger consumed him, and humiliation burned on his cheeks. With a growl, he slammed his hands onto the keyboard. Instantly, sparks jumped and danced like fireflies from the machine. Then, one by one every computer, every light, every electrical device in the room exploded in a shower of sparks. Chaos ruptured and chairs squealed as students scrambled out of their seats, screaming. The class exited the room in a thundering mob, but Xavier sat staring at the computer, his hands still on the keyboard.

"Come on, X," Robbie hissed in his ear. She dragged him out of the chair and into the hallway.

The computer lab wasn't the only classroom experiencing electrical difficulty. The entire school had emptied into the hall when the fire alarm blared. The students herded themselves outdoors babbling. Robbie led Xavier out with the other children, throwing him troubled looks.

"Are you okay?" she asked finally.

"Yeah, but that was weird!" he said, shaking his head. "I had just touched my keyboard when all those sparks flew. What do you reckon happened?" He turned and looked at her, but Robbie did not meet his eyes. She continued to stare toward the school and shrugged.

The all-clear bell rang nearly thirty minutes later allowing the students to re-enter the school. Gossip began flooding the school hallways over what could have caused the blackout. Only half the school's electrical system was functional; the custodial staff had managed to restore power to the kitchens and most classrooms. However, the gym, the auditorium, the science labs, and the computer labs were all still in the dark. It was all so very weird.

Xavier nearly made it through the rest of the day without another mishap or a thug encounter. Unfortunately, Donald and Mark were only two of many who found Xavier their favorite target for taunts and jokes. Matt Windom, a burly eighth grader, found "ghost-hunting", as he liked to call it, a very enjoyable pastime at moments of boredom. Matt was the type of person that everyone else wanted to be like. So, he was popular, and people seemed to follow him in whatever he did. It wasn't until Xavier was waiting for his bus at the end of the day that Matt finally tracked him down.

"Where've you been, Ghostie? I missed you today," Matt taunted from behind him. Xavier spun on his heal and stared into Matt's sneering face. "How's the little powder puff? Did you have a good day, little girl?"

"Stop it, Matt!" Robbie yelled.

"Ah, look everyone. The flour head has a girlfriend. Isn't that sweet," Matt chided, pinching Xavier's cheek with contrived affection. The group that had formed around them to watch the confrontation chortled. "Do you always let your girlfriend fight your battles for you? Oh, wait a minute," Matt's smile fell, and he studied Robbie before looking back at Xavier. "Maybe she's not your girlfriend after all. I mean her name is Robbie. Is she your boyfriend? Is that it q-tip head?" The giggles grew louder.

"Shut up, Matt!" Xavier hissed, feeling his face grow hot.

"What did you say to me, you little twerp?" Matt challenged, bumping into him and sending him tumbling to the muddy ground.

Xavier sprang to his feet, never taking his eyes off Matt. He'd had enough. He was tired of the stares, the jokes, the teasing, and it was all going to end, now. Anger stirred in his gut with such intensity that his entire body shook and his eyes blurred.

"Are you going to cry, baby powder?" Matt goaded. "Go ahead, cry baby, cry!"

Seething, Xavier simply reacted. Before he knew what he was doing, he punched Matt across the jaw and sent him stumbling backwards and over the bike rack.

"You little..." Matt growled, rubbing his cheek. He staggered to his feet and lunged at Xavier, but Xavier was ready. As Matt's hands clutched his shirt, Xavier spun out of his grasp, swung his leg around, and sent Matt tumbling hard to the ground.

"I'm going to kill you, powder puff!" Matt spat, climbing to his feet and swelling with fury.

This time Matt anticipated Xavier's countermove. When Xavier spun and swung his leg around to trip Matt, Matt simply stepped aside, caught Xavier off-balanced, and slammed him to the ground. Xavier's head spun and before he could regain his senses, Matt had his hands around

15

Xavier's neck. He was choking him! Xavier gasped for air, but he couldn't breathe. Panicking, he clawed desperately at Matt's arms, but everything was quickly growing dim.

* * * * *

That was the last memory Xavier had before he woke up in the nurse's office. His grandparents stood at the other end of the room, arguing with the school principal, Mr. Wildt. His mother was seated next to him, holding a cool compress to his forehead and watching her parents.

"Of course he started it!" Grandmother bellowed. Xavier felt a surge of relief that his grandmother was standing up for him. However, his relief evaporated by her next words. "I live with the boy! You can't tell me that he doesn't have deviant tendencies."

"Xavier?" his mother was looking at him now. "How do you feel sweetheart?"

"Don't coddle the boy, Julia! I dare to say, that is why he's in this predicament to begin with! You're too soft on him," Grandmother snarled. Then, she rounded on Xavier, grabbing him roughly. "You better fess up, boy. We'll go easier on you if you do. Now, what did you do to that poor Windom boy?"

"I...I," Xavier hadn't the foggiest idea what she was talking about. He peered around the room at each expectant, anxious face.

"Come on, out with it!" Grandmother snapped as she shook him.

"I don't know. What are you talking about? What happened to Matt?" Xavier asked.

"What happened? What happened?" She released him, throwing her hands into the air with exasperation. "If you don't stop playing games, I'll smack the truth out of you," Grandmother spat, raising her hand readily.

"Now, Mrs. Menes, please calm down. This kind of talk isn't going to help anyone uncover the truth," Mr. Wildt responded patiently before looking down at Xavier. "Xavier, can you tell us what you remember before you fainted."

"I...I fainted?" Xavier asked.

Grandmother was beside herself at this point. She gestured wildly and stormed out of the room, muttering.

After the door to the office slammed shut, Mr. Wildt continued. "Please, Xavier. Whatever you can remember."

"Ah, I was waiting for my bus. Matt came up to me...and ... we were talking. And, the next thing I knew I woke up in here," Xavier said.

"Then, you don't remember anything about what happened to Matthew?" Mr. Wildt asked.

"No," he insisted. "What happened to Matt? Is there something wrong with him?"

"Apparently, he received a high voltage shock and had to be rushed to the hospital. The paramedics were able to restore his breathing, but we haven't heard any word on his prognoses," the nurse replied.

"Shocked? But, how?" Xavier grilled.

"That's what we were hoping you could tell us," Mr. Wildt replied.

"But, there were others there! Any of them could tell you what happened," Xavier proclaimed.

"Ah, well, only one student claims to be present when it all happened, Roberta Minnows. She says that Matthew was choking you during an argument when suddenly he collapsed. Does this ring a bell?" Mr. Wildt asked, studying Xavier.

Xavier turned his head toward the wall. *"Great! So, everyone knows that Matt Windom embarrassed me in front of a crowd of people. What's worse, my grandparents know!'* Xavier thought despondently.

"Xavier? Is this what happened?" Mr. Wildt asked again.

Xavier felt his face flush. He continued to stare at the wall and nodded.

"I see. Do you know what happened to Matthew to make him collapse the way he did?" he pressed.

Xavier turned his head toward Mr. Wildt but didn't

look at him. "No. I don't know what happened to Matt. I passed out before I could see," Xavier mumbled.

Mr. Wildt studied Xavier for a moment before looking at his mother. "Well, there's nothing else to be done today. You may take him home, Ms. Wells."

Xavier sat in silence for the ride home. Although his grandmother had plenty to say on what she believed to be more evidence of his delinquent nature, Xavier was too wrapped up in the mystery of Matt's injury to hear a word of her ranting.

When they finally arrived home, Grandmother sent Xavier to his room without dinner, which was fine by him. He didn't feel like sitting through another lecture directed toward him on being nothing more than a thug, and then toward his mother on how she was a failure as a mother. He drifted up the stairs and into his room without a backward glance to the rampant bellows coming from his grandmother. He threw himself onto the bed and stared at the ceiling.

What had happened to Matt? How could he have been electrocuted when Xavier's neck was the only thing he had in his hands? And, if he had been shocked, why hadn't Xavier? Too many questions and not enough answers sent him in a restless, dream-filled sleep.

* * * * *

Xavier found himself in a forest. The earthen floor was covered in a thick wooly moss dappled in sunlight, and a pleasant breeze drifted across his face. Unlike the dream of the stone passageway that filled him with tension and dread, he felt utterly at peace here. He continued through the forest tossing a small golden ball from hand to hand. A tingling sensation drew his attention to the hand that held the ball. He scarcely had time to assimilate that the object in his hand was not a ball at all but a swirling sphere of light when suddenly it exploded into a glittering electrical current that tingled up his arm and throughout his body.

Xavier jumped awake. He looked wildly down at his hands but found them empty. Panting, he ran his hands

18

through his pale hair and glanced at the alarm clock on his bedside stand. It was only 3:18 in the morning. Even though he had been in bed since he'd gotten home from school, he was still exhausted. Xavier fell back into his pillows, stared at the ceiling, and sighed. His stomach rumbled, and he felt the hunger that he had ignored when he'd first returned home from school.

Xavier crept out of bed and padded down the steps and into the kitchen. He snatched up a couple cold drumsticks, a roll, a glass of milk, and returned to his room. He ate greedily as he stood looking out his window onto the dark moistened lawn below. In no time, he had both chicken legs gnawed down to the bone, and half of the roll stuffed into his mouth. Xavier turned back toward his bed when his eye caught movement just at the edge of the property near the woods. His stomach lurched with alarm, and he studied the area closely. Nothing. Finally deciding he must have imagined it, he flopped sleepily onto his bed and almost immediately fell off to sleep.

Chapter 2
The Presence
★ ★ ★ ★ ★

The next morning, Xavier, dressed in slacks and a navy dress shirt, stomped down the steps and into the kitchen. Grandmother scanned his appearance and seemed disheartened that he gave her no cause to criticize him. She hastily turned back to preparing breakfast, but his mother was nowhere in sight.

"Where's Mom?" Xavier asked.

"She's still in bed. All the trouble you caused yesterday wore her to a frazzle," Grandmother remarked without turning.

"I bet," Xavier muttered under his breath. "You probably kept her up half the night griping at her."

Xavier downed his cereal in a matter of minutes and raced up the stairs to gather his schoolbooks and an extra pair of clothes to change into at Robbie's.

Then, he clambered down the stairs and stormed out the door. "See ya," he called, letting the storm door slam behind him.

Xavier hurried to Robbie's house where Robbie met him at the door.

"Not here. Follow me into the barn. If my parents find out, they'll ask a bunch of questions," Robbie rattled off as she stepped past him and walked toward the barn. "Come on, X. We don't want to miss the bus."

Minutes later, he emerged from the barn wearing faded jeans and a T-shirt. He stuffed his slacks and dress shirt into his backpack, and the two children walked toward the bus stop.

"Robbie?" Xavier tentatively broke the pregnant silence between them. "What happened to Matt after I passed out? They told me that he'd been electrocuted. How did that happen?"

Robbie glanced at him with dread. "I'm not really sure," she said unconvincingly, walking ahead of him.

"Come on, Robbie! I need to know! I didn't sleep very well last night because of it. I kept having weird dreams. Please, tell me," he pleaded, stumbling after her.

"You've been having weird dreams? What were they about?" Robbie asked, stopping so suddenly that Xavier nearly ran into her.

"It's not important. But, what happened to Matt is. Robbie, why are you trying to keep it from me?"

"I...I'm not!" Robbie denied. "I...it's just that," she sighed. "Okay, I'll tell you, but let's walk, or we'll miss the bus," she said as she turned and continued toward the bus stop. As Xavier stepped into stride beside her, she gave him an anxious glance before beginning.

"When Matt came at you and began to strangle you, I tried to pull him off, but he knocked me to the ground." She lowered her voice and continued, "That's when it happened. You already had your eyes closed and sort of went limp in his grasp, but he wasn't stopping. I swear, I think he really was trying to kill you. Then, a strange sort of golden light appeared and hovered over you both. It swarmed around you, gathering speed, and then, it struck Matt. He went limp and fell to the ground, and the light just evaporated."

Xavier stopped suddenly and stared at Robbie. "A

light? But, where did the light come from? Was it a transformer blowing or something?"

"No," Robbie faced him in all earnestness. "Xavier, the light... the light seemed to have come from you as if it were protecting you."

"What? You're crazy," he gasped. "Robbie, that can't be right! I mean, what you're talking about is, well, it's supernatural. It's superman stuff. It can't be true. Can it?"

"It's what I saw, X. I swear on my life, it's the truth," Robbie insisted. Robbie walked on toward the crowd of kids preparing to board the school bus.

Xavier followed, pouring over what she told him. It just couldn't be true! It was something that could only be found in science fiction novels and comic books. How could it be true?

The moment Xavier boarded the bus, he knew that his life had changed permanently. No one prodded him, giggled at him, or tried to trip him as he walked down the center aisle of the bus. Instead, several kids nodded to him, and many looked at him with renewed interest and respect.

"Yo, Xavier! How's it going?" Donald bellowed from the back of the bus.

"Hey, X. Cool threads," said another boy.

Xavier could only smile at all the attention he was receiving. He was puzzled. Surely, a change of clothes wouldn't cause this sort of reaction. Then, that only left the schoolyard incident with Matt.

Although life seemed to have gotten easier for Xavier at school, he found that he could not keep his mind on his studies. The scenario Robbie had given him about what happened to Matt continued to play over and over in his mind. He couldn't stop thinking about it. How was it possible that he, Xavier, had the ability to conjure up a... a light that would protect him? And, why hadn't it appeared before at times when he was threatened?

"Mr. Wells?" a voice demanded, pulling him from his troubled thoughts. "Do you mind returning from LaLa Land

22

and please pay attention," his math teacher snarled.

"Sorry, Ms. Pickering," Xavier replied.

"Now, as I was saying, can you tell us the solution to 3 factorial?" the teacher asked.

"Six," he responded quickly.

The teacher nodded and turned her attention to another daydreaming student.

By lunchtime, Xavier was so preoccupied that he got his lunch tray, sat down next to Robbie, and ate half his lunch without remembering having done it.

"Look, X. The reason I was hesitant in telling you the truth about what happened yesterday was because I knew you'd react this way!" Robbie exasperated.

"React what way?" he asked.

"Oh, I don't know," she said sarcastically. "Freak out. Spend all your time thinking about it so that you ignore everything and everyone else!"

"Oh, I'm sorry Robbie. I didn't mean to ignore you. It's just that...well, you have to admit it is a bit far fetched!" Xavier said.

"I know. But, maybe it's not that freaky. I mean, I've read about people in mortal danger who could lift entire cars off themselves and stuff like that," Robbie shrugged.

"Lifting cars off of people is not the same as creating an electrical force to zap anyone who gives you trouble. Is it?" Xavier muttered.

"Okay, I'll give you that, but do you realize that a large part of the human brain is never used?" Robbie continued. "I read about it in *The Science Probe*. Scientists are unsure what a particular section of the brain is for. So, for all we know, you could have just tapped into the unused part of your brain. Which in your case, it would be the entire thing."

"Shut up," he laughed, tossing a fry at his best friend.

Xavier considered her theory. It seemed preposterous, but it was a better explanation than what he was able to come up with. Her explanation put his mind at ease, and he smiled.

"Okay, Robbie. I'll let it drop," Xavier told her.

"Good," Robbie blurted.

"For now," Xavier added.

Robbie eyed him warily. Then, after deciding that it was the best she would get from him, she nodded.

The remainder of the day went very well for Xavier. Not one person called him ghost or Q-tip head. And, by the end of the day, Xavier was in such high spirits that he nearly forgot the unusual incident with Matt until Mr. Wildt called him into his office just before his bus was due to arrive.

"Xavier, I thought you might want to know that Matthew's doctors report that he is recovering well. He should be as good as new in a week or so," he told him.

"Oh, good. I'm glad he's going to be okay," Xavier gushed with relief.

"Now," Mr. Wildt continued, "can you remember anything else from yesterday that you'd like to tell me?"

"Ah," Xavier felt his body tense, "no. I really don't remember anything."

Mr. Wildt studied him a moment in silence and then nodded. "All right, then. Off you go. You don't want to miss your bus."

Xavier nodded. "Thank you, Mr. Wildt," he murmured and quickly left the office.

When Xavier exited the school, Robbie was waiting for him. "Where have you been? You nearly missed the bus," she blurted.

"Mr. Wildt's office," he told her as they jogged toward the line of buses parked in front of the school.

Her eyebrows rose as she looked at him. They clambered onto the bus and found seats in the back where they could talk without being disturbed.

"What did he want?" she asked.

"I guess he wanted to tell me that Matt's going to be okay. But, he also wanted to know if I remembered anything more from yesterday," Xavier told her unconcerned.

24

"What?" Robbie yelped. "What did you tell him? You didn't tell him what I told you, did you?"

Xavier stared bewilderedly at her worried face. "No. But, why would you care if I did or not? It wouldn't affect you."

Robbie opened her mouth but said nothing, and for the rest of the ride home, she stared out the window and didn't talk to Xavier.

Xavier changed back into his dress slacks and shirt in Robbie's barn before heading home. Robbie still seemed to be doing her best to avoid him and went into her house without a backward glance. She had behaved quite oddly. Xavier contemplated her peculiar behavior as he cut through the woods toward home. Why would she be so concerned whether or not he told Mr. Wildt about the light? It made no sense. Not that he would, but it really had nothing to do with her, unless she made it all up and was afraid of getting caught. No. He had believed her when she told him what had happened to Matt, and he still did. Okay, so she was telling the truth, but then why... His thoughts strayed.

Suddenly, an intense, peculiar feeling dropped over Xavier like a heavy cloak. Someone was watching him. He stopped and looked around him, but the only thing he saw was dense forest. The sounds of wildlife were all around him, and a fly buzzed annoyingly close to his ear. Although Xavier saw nothing out of the ordinary, he couldn't shake the feeling. Then, like an invisible conductor leading an orchestra, the woods were cut into a profound silence. Xavier had no doubt now; he was not alone. A shallow wind breathed lightly down his neck, and a prickling sensation waved over his body as every hair stood on end. His stomach twisted itself into knots, and he held his breath, trying to calm his erratic breathing.

"Robbie? Is that you?" he called out. Xavier knew it wasn't Robbie even before he had spoken her name. It was something, someone else.

"Hello?" he called again.

No answer greeted him, but something was there. He knew it with utter certainty. And, he knew that whoever, whatever it was did not intend to safely walk him home. It meant him harm. It was, well, evil. And, this evil seemed to be stalking *him*.

Xavier began to walk again more hurriedly this time. Still, the feeling of being watched followed him and became more persistent with every step he took.

"Hello?" he called again, his voice cracking with fear. A large black bird cawed a warning above him and took flight, its wings yelping as it flew away.

'Run, boy. Run,' a voice warned with such clarity that Xavier thought someone had spoken from behind him, and he jumped, spinning around. He saw no one, but the voice came again even stronger this time, *'A man is stalking you. Go boy! Now!'*

Unnerved by the bodiless voice, Xavier raced for the clearing of his grandparents' backyard. Behind him, he heard footsteps crashing through the foliage, and he felt someone pulling at his backpack. Xavier shrugged off the bag and kept running. He threw a look over his shoulder as he emerged from the woods and stepped onto his grandparents' property. His bag lingered in the air for a brief moment before dropping to the ground. But still, he saw no one.

Xavier ran to the back door, tore it opened, stepped inside, and slammed the door shut behind him. He leaned against the door panting, trying to steady his leaping heart. What in the world had happened? He looked out the window toward the backyard only to find it empty and peaceful. Was he losing his mind? Maybe, the story Robbie had told him had made him paranoid. Yeah, that was it. What else could it have been? Shaking his head in disgust with himself, Xavier walked into the kitchen to find it unusually empty. Feeling more relief than concern, he snatched an apple out of the fruit bowl from the table and climbed the stairs to his room. He immediately stripped out of his good clothes and pulled on clean jeans and a t-shirt. Feeling more comfortable, Xavier threw himself onto his bed to contemplate his day, but the extreme silence of the house pounded at his ears. He sat up. Where was everybody?

Xavier stood and went to the door. He opened it slowly and listened for signs of his mother or, more dreadfully, his grandparents. The only thing that greeted him was silence.

He peered into the hallway and called out, "Hello?" But, no one answered, and fear consumed him once more.

With tremendous anxiety, Xavier crept to his mother's room and peered in. The sheets and blankets were askew on her bed, and her bureau was open and empty. Fear rose from the pit of his gut, and he raced into the other rooms of the house only to find that the entire house was deserted. Perhaps they went out for a spell and left him a note on the kitchen counter. Grasping at that sliver of hope, he raced back into the kitchen, but there was no note.

A pandemonium of confusion and fear threatened to overtake him, and Xavier found himself stumbling toward the kitchen window. He grasped the cool surface of the counter as a powerful presence slipped inconspicuously into his mind and took control. The force pulled his gaze to the edge of the woods, and his breath caught painfully in his chest. A man stood just inside the tree line beyond the neatly trimmed lawn of his grandparents' yard. Although the dense foliage mostly concealed his face, Xavier could still see a broad masculine chin and a thin mouth. The man's presence and raw supremacy resounded across the yard and into the house. Xavier's heart thudded madly in his chest, and panic closed its icy fingers around his heart. Sharp pains sliced through Xavier's lungs, and he gulped desperately for air. He couldn't seem to breathe properly as though there was a great invisible hand strangling the air from his lungs. Xavier was not asthmatic, nor did he know what it felt like to have an asthma attack, but he was fairly certain that he was having one now, and that the man at the edge of the woods was the catalyst for the attack. Just when Xavier thought he couldn't bare the searing pain a moment longer, the man smiled triumphantly and, methodically, pulled back into the forest and disappeared.

Xavier slid to the linoleum floor, gasping and feeling nauseous. Who was the man in the woods? What did he want? Why was he following him? And, where were his grandparents and mother? Did the man in the woods have something to do with their disappearance? Had something happened to them? Suddenly, the phone rang, nearly sending Xavier to the ceiling.

He struggled to his feet and snatched up the phone. "Hello?" he blurted.

"X? It's Robbie. Are you okay?" she strained.

"Yeah, well, my grandparents and my mother aren't here, and I don't know where they could be! There's no note or anything. And, my mo... Mother's room... all her things are missing," he rattled.

"Xavier, stay where you are! My father is on his way right now. Don't move, okay?" Robbie commanded.

"All right," he told her and hung up. It never occurred to Xavier to question how she knew he was distraught and to call him.

In a matter of seconds, Mr. Minnows arrived at the house. He slammed through the front door without knocking. "Xavier? Xavier? Where are you boy?" he called out urgently.

"Here, Mr. Minnows. I'm here, in the kitchen." Xavier answered.

He rushed into the kitchen and grabbed him by the shoulders. "Are you all right?" he asked, his dark eyes searching Xavier's with concern.

"Yeah, I'm fine. I just don't know where everyone's gone. My mother's clothes, all her things are missing. I just..." The slamming front door interrupted him.

Mr. Minnows released Xavier and positioned himself between the boy and whoever had entered the house. But, at the sight of Xavier's grandparents, Mr. Minnows relaxed.

"Where's my mother?" Xavier asked, storming past Mr. Minnows toward his grandparents.

"On her way to Boston. She had business there, and I don't think I like the tone you're choosing to use, boy," his grandmother snapped, glaring at him.

"Xavier, would you please excuse us. I need to have a word or two with your grandparents," Mr. Minnows asked, patting his shoulder, his thin face set with anger.

His grandparents' glare drifted to Mr. Minnows as if just seeing him, and his grandmother's contempt flickered.

Xavier hesitated.

"Please, Xavier. I need to speak to them alone," Mr. Minnows repeated firmly.

Xavier met Mr. Minnows's unwavering stare, an argument on his tongue, but finally, he nodded and left the room. Xavier was halfway up the stairs when his grandmother's voice made him freeze.

"What do you want? I believe the arrangement we had was that the boy could stay here if you people would stay away. Julia ran away because you people broke your promise!"

So, his mother wasn't on a business trip after all. She had run away.

"I'm afraid I don't have any idea what you're talking about, Mrs. Menes," Mr. Minnows replied. "And, I'd warn you to keep your voice down, or the boy might overhear us."

"Oh, please! Don't tell me to keep my voice down in my own home!" his grandmother yelled. "Julia has been aggravated all week muttering that she felt a presence. I told her it was nonsense and her imagination was just running away from her."

"Julia said she felt a presence?" Mr. Minnows questioned anxiously. "Where is she, Mrs. Menes?"

"Why would I tell you? She needs peace and quiet! You tell..." Mrs. Menes's voice grew thick with fear and quivered, "you tell your boss that! You tell him to keep his people away! That poor Windom boy at *his* school was nearly electrocuted to death! It's obvious it had to be one of your kind responsible for it."

"Mrs. Menes, the electro force that occurred that day was indeed from one of my people, but not in the way you believe. Your grandson, Xavier, produced the force. He is, after all, one of us, as you have known from the beginning when you so reluctantly agreed to take him in. And, it seems that you may also need reminding of the other terms to that agreement," Mr. Minnows's voice grew harsh. "You are not to leave that boy without supervision! As in the past, you must inform my wife or me anytime you have to leave the boy home alone. Must I remind you of what could happen to him if left unguarded? Now, more than ever, he must be protected. Or, maybe I should remind you of what the Premier will do to *you* if one hair on that boy's head is harmed!" Mr. Minnows finished angrily. There was a long silence before Mr. Minnows began again, more calmly, "Now, let's just..."

But, suddenly he stopped speaking, and Xavier heard footsteps coming toward him. For a brief moment, he considered bolting up the stairs and hiding, but somehow he knew that wouldn't work so he waited, fidgeting. Mr. Minnows appeared at the foot of the stairs and stared up at him.

"Xavier? You haven't been eavesdropping, now, have you?" he asked surprisingly amused.

"No," Xavier lied. "I...I thought you had left, and I was hungry."

"Oh, is that what you were doing?" he said with a smile that told Xavier that he didn't at all believe his story. "Well, you can come on down now. I believe your grandmother will fix you up some dinner as soon as I go." He waved Xavier down to him. "Now," he continued, lowering his voice, "if you're ever left at home alone again, I want you to call me. Do you understand?"

"Okay, Mr. Minnows," Xavier nodded.

Although he was relieved that Mr. Minnows showed up at the house when he did, he found his over-protectiveness disturbing. The last forty-eight hours had been outlandish and peculiar, to say the least, and Xavier had many unanswered questions. Why did Mr. Minnows feel it was his responsibility to protect him? And, what had Mr. Minnows and his grandparents been arguing about? Who was this Premier Mr. Minnows spoke of and his grandparents seemed to fear? How is it that he, Xavier Wells, had the ability to create a ball of light to protect himself? Whose voice had he hear in the woods? Who was the man following him in the woods? Xavier felt like he was stumbling through a maze, and no one would tell him the way through. He was beginning to believe that everyone around him knew something that he did not.

Mr. Minnows was watching him with a creased brow. "Xavier, did something else happen to you today? I mean, apart from finding an empty house when you got home?"

Xavier had not anticipated the sudden question and faltered. "Ah, I..."

"What happened? Tell me boy, no matter how silly or insignificant it may seem to you. I promise I will not judge or laugh," Mr. Minnows interrupted, knowing that there was something.

So, Xavier told him about the walk through the woods, the feelings that overwhelmed him, and the voice that told him to run. Mr. Minnows did not laugh as he promised he wouldn't. Instead, he listened in silence and look gravely at Xavier.

"And, did you see anyone at all?" he asked.

Xavier paused. He wasn't ready to share the circumstances involving the man in the woods and his freakish asthma attack. He was still trying to grapple with what had actually happened. He was certain that the man had been toying with him, taunting him, but it had also been more than that, and he needed more time to figure it out. "No," Xavier finally answered. "I'm sure I just imagined it.

It's no big deal. Really, Mr. Minnows."

Mr. Minnows's eyes narrowed on him. He knew he was lying, Xavier realized. "You could be right, but from now on you're not to set foot off your grandparents' property. And, the woods are off limits. Got it?" he said with finality.

"Yeah," Xavier answered.

"Good, boy," he sighed. "I'll tell Robbie all is well here; I'm sure she's gotten herself into a right tizzy." He patted Xavier on the shoulder and turned to the Meneses who stood unmoving at the door, still wearing their jackets, and looking uneasy. "Mr. and Mrs. Menes, I hope our little talk has clarified some neglected issues. I will have to inform the Premier of this little incident. I dare say from the information I've gathered, this could've been quite serious. I imagine he'll want to speak with you personally about this matter." He glared pointedly at them. His grandparents nodded with a look of pure terror. "Good, now that we understand one another, I'll leave. Don't worry, I'll show myself out. Please tell your daughter when you speak to her next that the Premier will be in touch; I'm sure he'll want to talk to her as well. Goodbye, Xavier." Mr. Minnows nodded toward Xavier and walked out the door, humming.

Chapter 3
Kidnapped
★ ★ ★ ★ ★

The next morning Xavier awoke with a start. He had dreamt of the stallion again, but this time he recognized the animal. The horse was Brewster's Coal. Brewster was a magnificent jet-black stallion. He had once been a racing horse, but when his manager retired him, Xavier's mother had received him as a pet. Xavier had fond memories with his mother and Brewster's Coal. Before his grandparents had insisted that his mother get a job to help pay bills and support the family, they used to go horseback riding together everyday after he got home from school. Xavier loved that horse.

However, Xavier's thoughts didn't linger on the dream, but went directly to the overheard conversation between Mr. Minnows and his grandparents. The same questions flooded his mind. The conversation didn't make any sense. What the heck had they been talking about? His grandparents and Mr. Minnows spoke about Xavier as if he was an alien or something. "He is, after all, one of us..." What, exactly, was he one of?

Xavier had never seen his grandparents afraid

before. In his company, they had always been solid and strong, but they had seemed positively petrified when Mr. Minnows mentioned the Premier. Who was the Premier, and what connection did he have to Xavier? Strange things seemed to be happening around him lately, and no one would tell him anything about any of it. He needed answers! A brisk knock on the door drew his attention away from his troubling thoughts.

"Get a move on, boy. Your mother wants you to tend to that ruddy horse while she's gone," his grandfather's voice called from beyond the door.

"Yes, Grandfather," Xavier yawned.

It was Saturday! No school! No jokes, no teasing! No strange, secretive looks! No feeling like he was under a microscope. Relief poured over him, and he stretched, feeling content and yawning noisily. Then, he hopped out of bed, pulled on jeans and a T-shirt, rushed down the stairs, and settled at the kitchen table with a bowl of cereal. His grandparents were unusually quiet and didn't even acknowledge his presence. He wasn't sure why, but this bothered him. When the phone rang, Grandmother jumped and Grandfather became rigid and stared accusingly at the phone.

"I'll get it," Xavier said, feeling a bit rattled by their behavior as he moved toward the phone and picked up the receiver. "Hello?" he answered.

"Hey, X. How's it going?" It was Robbie.

"Okay, I guess. Look, Robbie, why don't you come over this morning? I have a lot to talk to you about. I'll be in the barn mucking out Brewster's stable," he told her.

"That sounds like fun!" she said sarcastically. "See ya in fifteen minutes."

Desperate to get away from his grandparents' uneasiness, Xavier quickly finished his cereal, grabbed an apple from the fruit basket, and raced out the back door toward the stables. The cool, thick fog that had settled over the land sent goose bumps over his body, and the dew-

34

moistened lawn had his sneakers soaked in no time. When he reached the stable, he found Brewster in the back corner of his stall lazily grazing hay.

"Hi, ya, Brewster!" Xavier blurted out to the animal. The horse twitched its ears at the sound of Xavier's voice and looked at him sheepishly. "I brought you a treat." Xavier held the apple out so that Brewster could see it.

Eyeing the apple, the animal trotted to the stall door. Brewster gingerly plucked the apple from the boy's palm and ate noisily.

"That' a boy," Xavier whispered, stroking the horse's neck.

Brewster looked terrible. His winter coat had begun to shed, leaving thick matted patches of hair sporadically covering his body, and his fur was covered in muck and mud. His eyes were watery and runny. Flies had already manifested themselves all over his ears biting them raw and bloody. The stall itself looked as if it hadn't been cleaned out in couple of weeks and wreaked of manure and urine. No wonder the horse was in poor shape! When was the last time his mother cared for him, cleaned him, or rode him?

"It's all right boy. I'll take care of ya from now on. I'll have you looking as good as new," he reassured, patting the horse.

Xavier couldn't help but think of his dream. Could Brewster have been communicating with him through his dreams? Had he been trying to call to Xavier for help? It was a silly thing to think, but Xavier couldn't help but wonder if there was some connection between Brewster and his dreams. He studied the horse closely. The animal stared back and continued to grind the apple. Slowly, a peculiar chill swallowed over Xavier as if a cool breeze had passed through his body. He closed his eyes and concentrated on the soft murmuring in his subconscious. The murmur began to clarify into a barely audible voice.

'Xavier, where's Julia? Why hasn't she come to me?' the voice asked.

35

Xavier's eyes snapped open. "Was that you?" he asked incredulously. "That *was* you, wasn't it?"

"Do you often talk to yourself when you're in the barn?" Robbie's voice came from behind him.

Xavier spun around to find Robbie leaning against a post.

"I mean, really X, you're losing it if the only person you can talk to is yourself!" She grinned.

"Ha, ha, really funny," he huffed. "Come on and help me. Poor Brewster needs some attention. Just look at him! I don't know why Mom let him get like this. No wonder his health is bad." Xavier reached for a harness hanging on the barn wall. He leashed up the stallion, led him outside the barn to the corral, and tied him to a post.

"Robbie," he called back into the barn, pointing, "grab the bucket, brush, and shampoo there on that shelf."

Robbie emerged from the barn and plopped the items onto the ground beside him. "It's an absolute wreck in there! No animal could live in there in the condition it's in. What do you want me to do?"

"Why don't you find one of the other stalls that's clean and put fresh hay in it for him? That way after I bathe and groom him, he'll have a nice clean stall to go to while we concentrate on his old stall. It'll take us a while to clean that out," he replied despondently.

Robbie nodded and was off.

Xavier concentrated on bathing Brewster and brushing out the old winter coat. Nearly an hour later the children had a freshly cleaned horse in a freshly clean stall grazing happily. By mid-afternoon, the barn and all its stalls were mucked out and fresh hay carpeted the earthen floor. Dirty and grimy, the children lay in the loft sipping Kool-Aid nearly exhausted.

"So," Robbie began lazily, "what was it that you wanted to talk to me about? Or did you just make that up to get me over here to help you clean out manure from your barn?"

Xavier laughed, sitting up. "Well," he began, growing serious. "I just don't know how to put it." He looked at Robbie expectantly. "I know something is happening to me. I mean, there've been all these weird things happening. My grandparents know something. I can tell by the way they've been acting since your dad came over here and yelled at them for leaving me home alone. And, your father knows something, too."

Robbie squirmed under his intense, questioning stare.

"Hang on! You...you know what's going on, don't you? Robbie you do! I know you do!" He stared at her as she unwillingly met his eyes. "Tell me!" he hissed. "Please, Robbie. With all the strange things that have been happening lately, I think I might be losing my mind."

"You're not losing your mind, X," she told him. "There's nothing to worry about, really."

"Then, tell me!" he begged.

"I can't. I can't tell you. It's not my place to do so. Please Xavier, I wish I could but...I can tell you this much: the answers will be given to you soon. I heard my father say so. I wish I could tell you more than that, but I'm sworn not to. I'm sorry, X. Really."

"What do you mean, you're sworn not to? Sworn by who?" he asked.

"I...I can't tell you," she muttered despondently.

"Well, thanks for nothing then!" he spat, jumping to his feet. He stomped to the ladder. "You better go home. I've got to take a shower and clean up before dinner." He climbed down the ladder and stormed off toward the house without another word to Robbie.

"Xavier! Xavier, wait!" Robbie called after him, but he continued toward the house and didn't look back.

The shower may have cleaned the grime from Xavier's body, but it did very little to wash away the agitation surging inside him. Xavier was extremely irritated and paced around his room like a madman. It was obvious that everyone around him was keeping something from him. His mother, his grandparents, Mr. Minnows, Robbie, everyone! He threw himself onto the bed with a frustrated groan.

"I've had enough of this!" he grumbled. "I've got to know what's going on, or I'll go crazy!"

Later that evening, Xavier made up his mind to interrogate his grandparents. He knew it was suicide to attempt it, but maybe they'd let something slip about what was going on. He had no choice. No one was willing to tell him the truth. So, that night at dinner he put his plan into effect.

His grandparents sat eating without speaking, which was how they preferred to eat their evening meals. Xavier picked at his food and tried to find the courage for what he was about to do.

"Stop playing with your food, boy! Eat!" his grandmother growled.

Finally, Xavier took a deep breath and blurted, "Grandfather, I have a problem." He watched his grandfather closely.

"Hmm?" his grandfather responded, without looking up from his dinner plate and shoveled a spoonful of peas into his mouth.

"Well, I just don't know who to turn to. You see, I've been experiencing strange things lately. I've been having strange dreams."

At these words, his grandfather choked and peered over at him with a mingling of curiosity and anxiety. "What are you talking about, boy? I don't think I want to hear about your peculiar dreams!"

"Okay," Xavier responded thoughtfully. "Well, then, there are these strange things that have been happening. I mean how was that boy at my school electrocuted when there wasn't an electrical source anywhere around where it happened? And, there are these voices I keep hearing. I heard a voice in the woods yesterday, and today, I could have sworn I heard a voice in the barn!"

"That is enough!" his grandmother boomed, slamming her fists onto the table and glaring at him.

"There's no need to tell us about your strange ideas!" Grandfather hissed angrily. "We know all about them! How could you not be anything else with a father like yours! You and your kind should be locked up, if you ask me. You're nothing but evil seeds, the whole lot of ya."

"Anthony," his grandmother growled pointedly, "that's enough!"

However, his grandfather did not need to say another word for a peculiar coolness engulfed Xavier's body once again, and his head began to swim with thoughts he couldn't seem to control. The voices sounded like a poorly tuned radio and were marbled and broken up. But, suddenly the thoughts became clear and vivid.

'The boy doesn't need to be provoked. He may decide to electrocute us next. It's no wonder the boy is what he is; how could he not be? His father was the same kind of freak. I don't know why Julia just didn't leave the boy and run away from the lot of them. They keep such an annoyingly close watch on all of us. We might as well be in a prison. I'm sick and tired of all of this. If they want the boy protected, why don't they just do it themselves?'

"Who watches us? In danger from what?" Xavier mumbled, shaking his head vigorously as if trying to dislodge an answer from his thoughts.

"What did you say?" Grandmother said in a controlled whisper.

Xavier looked at his grandmother in stupefaction and saw her fearful, wide-eyed face.

'How did he know what I was thinking? He can't, his kind can't read minds, can they?' the voice crowded into his mind again.

Xavier's stomach dropped to the floor as the realization hit him. The thoughts swarming in his mind were not his thoughts! They were his grandmother's, and his grandmother seemed to realize this as well.

39

"I... I," Xavier stuttered.

"Get out!" she spat. "Get out of my house, you evil creature. I am through with you and your peculiar ways."

"Grandmother, please," Xavier stood at the table. "I didn't mean to do anything. It just happened."

"I said, get out," she said again dangerously slow.

Xavier opened his mouth to speak but fell silent unable to think of anything that he could say to alleviate the problem.

"Now! Get out! Get out! Get out!" Grandmother screeched in near hysterics, slamming her fists repeatedly onto the table.

Xavier fled the kitchen and bounded up the stairs to his room. He grabbed a duffle bag (his backpack lost since the woods incident) and began throwing clothes into it. The whispering thoughts still rattled in his mind, but he pushed them back, trying to ignore them. He threw the bag onto his shoulder, grabbed his jacket, and stormed out of the house.

Xavier stomped a few yards into the woods when a thought so strong consumed his mind that he froze, physically incapable of taking another step. His temples began to throb with the vibration of the thought, and he fell to his knees clutching his head with a groan. His body shivered violently. It was as if someone or something was trying to drill their way inside his brain.

'Xavier, do NOT leave your grandparent's home. It is not safe at this time. Go back now,' a man's voice resonated in his mind.

"Stop, please," he groaned, rubbing his temples.

'Now, boy! Go back to your grandparents,' the voice demanded more intensely.

"Enough!" Xavier yelled into the darkness. "I've had enough! What is wrong with me?" Panting furiously, Xavier knelt for several minutes, trying to keep control of his sanity.

At long last, Xavier was beginning to feel a sense of calm. Slowly, he stood staring into the darkness. The silence around him was so profound that it pounded at his ears. Something wasn't right!

'The woods shouldn't be this quiet,' he thought, his heart racing.

Then, a twig snapped. Xavier stiffened and goose pimples prickled over his body. Suddenly, he knew that he was no longer alone in the woods. But, oddly, his newly found ability seemed to be silent. He scanned the darkness, searching for any signs of movement, but there was none.

Someone was there. Xavier could sense it; he could feel it. He held his breath while his heart thundered madly in his chest. Then, ever so slowly, he knelt back to the forest floor. Not a sound could be heard, yet someone was there. He waited and listened. A soft breeze rustled the leafing foliage overhead. Then, out the corner of his eye, he saw a shadow to his right moved. Xavier had no time to react as a pair of hands seized him and lifted him from the ground, covering his mouth with a strange smelling cloth. Within seconds, Xavier was unconscious.

Chapter 4
The Institute
★ ★ ★ ★ ★

In what seemed like a moment later, Xavier opened his eyes to find himself in a small circular room with drab gray washed walls. The room was empty except for the lumpy, bare mattress he rested on and one battered, metal folding chair. Above his head, two sets of fluorescent lights buzzed in the eerie silence.

"Where am I?" he wondered aloud.

He sat up and instantly regretted such a sudden move; the pounding pain in his head was nearly nauseating. He closed his eyes hoping that it was all a dream, but, when he opened his eyes again, he found that his surroundings had not changed. Gingerly and moving slowly, Xavier climbed from the mattress and circled the room in just a dozen steps. There were no windows, no mirrors, nothing but a single, white, metal door. With a sigh, Xavier sank back down onto the mattress. Why was he here? Why did the man in the woods take him? What did he want? Xavier didn't think he'd ever wish to be back in his grandparents' home, but he wished it now.

Then, faint masculine laughter floated into the room from beyond the door. Maybe if he'd try to listen in, he'd figure out what they wanted and how to get out. Xavier closed his eyes and, not knowing exactly what to do, tried to reach out with his newly discovered gift. For several seconds, he heard absolutely nothing. Finally, faint, incoherent voices crowded into his mind, and then, simply went silent again.

Xavier opened his eyes, feeling short of breath, and clutched his thumping head with a moan. Why had it happened so easily the last time? He hadn't even tried to hear his grandmother's thoughts; they just came to him. That was it! He was trying too hard. Xavier closed his eyes again, and after a moment of breathing deeply and succinctly, the pain lessened, and he was able to try once more. At first, the voices were still muddled together and impossible to understand, but within a couple of minutes of Xavier relaxing his mind and breathing evenly, the voices cleared and became comprehensible.

'Do we know the new one's ability?' a young masculine voice questioned.

'Master would not say,' a high nasal voice responded.

'Do you think this one's the one, the Chosen?' the first guard asked.

'You don't really believe in all those superstitious stories, do ya?' the second guard chided. 'Besides, the Chosen, if there is one, may not have even been born yet, and if Master thought this boy was the Chosen, he'd be dead, wouldn't he?'

'Has the boy awoken yet?' a deep, smooth voice questioned, sending a shudder through Xavier.

'Master, sir! We didn't expect you here so soon,' the second guard quavered.

'Is he awake?' the deep voice asked again.

'I don't think so sir, but he should be waking any time now,' the first guard responded timidly.

'Good. Lewis, go and bring Danson to the boy's chamber. He can begin the assessment as soon as the lad awakens,' the smooth voice ordered.

'Yes, sir. Master, what is the boy's ability?' the second guard, Lewis, asked hesitantly.

'He has the ability to conjure electro forces. That is all we know for sure,' he responded.

There was a brief silence, as the man with the deep voice faded from Xavier's thoughts, and only the guards' thoughts remained.

'Told ya. He's not the Chosen. He's just another weapon Master will use against Warwood and the Premier,' Lewis chided. 'You stay here and stand guard. I'll go after Danson. With his telepathy abilities, Danson will be able to tell us what other abilities, if any, the boy has.'

Xavier withdrew his concentration. The pain in his head had intensified, and he rubbed his temples with a moan. Wherever he was, he was not in a safe place to make his abilities known. He didn't like the sound of these people using him as some kind of weapon. Quickly, Xavier began to create a plan. He would have to keep this Danson character from discovering his abilities. It would be hard, but he could do it. He had to do it. His gut told him that if they knew the truth about him, his life would be in danger. He didn't know how he knew this, but he did. With that known and certain, Xavier began the task of clearing his mind of all the peculiar events from the past week and replacing those memories with unproblematic juvenile thoughts.

Moments later, a short plump man with strawberry blond hair, freckles, and a thin mustache perambulated into the room followed by a tall, lanky man with chestnut hair and pocked-marked scars speckling his face. The second of the two studied Xavier with small, dark, watery eyes. Xavier felt a cold shiver pass through him, and he quickly shifted his thoughts to playing football for his middle school team next year. He thought about Brewster and how much fun it was to ride him.

"Stop that boy," the man said greasily as he crossed the room, adjusted the chair next to Xavier, and sat down.

Xavier looked innocently up at him. "Stop what?" he

asked, mocking confusion. Xavier knew that in order to keep this man from discovering just how deep his abilities went, he would not only have to pretend he was normal, he would have to believe he was normal.

"Don't you think I know what you're trying to do, boy? Enough games! We know you have the ability to conjure electro forces. Is that your only ability?" he interrogated smoothly.

"I really don't know what you're talking about!" Xavier pleaded. "A boy was electrocuted at my school, but I didn't see anything! I was unconscious on the ground!"

"Just who do you think you're talking to, kid? Don't you know where you are?" the man said coolly as he brought his face inches from Xavier's.

Xavier felt fear crawl from every part of his body and form a knot in his abdomen. His throat suddenly felt thick and dry. *Think normal thoughts, think normal thoughts, think...*

A smile sneaked across the man's face as he stared intently at Xavier. "But, you're not normal. Are you?" he whispered.

They stared at one another for quite some time in silence. The man staring and attempting to break through the mental blockade Xavier had built around the knowledge of his abilities, and Xavier, his forehead beading with perspiration, filling his mind with silly little boy thoughts. They stayed in this mesmerized position for nearly fifteen minutes.

"Damn, it, boy! Enough of these games! I know you have the ability to conjure electro forces! What other powers do you have?" the man seemed to be unraveling and losing his concentration. Xavier was succeeding!

"I told you, I don't know what you're talking about! I don't remember anything that happened that day. I passed out!" he told the man again.

"Look, kid. I don't have all day! If you won't stop playing games and tell me your abilities then there are more... *painful* ways to get it out of you," he snarled as a white film of spittle coated the corners of his mouth.

Xavier shivered. He knew this man had the ability to hurt children without a single shred of remorse. He knew he had to give him something, or he'd face mortal danger.

"That's right. You're placing yourself in great peril," the man hissed menacingly and smirked. "And, I actually enjoy torturing little boys." He glared at Xavier with wild eyes.

"Okay," Xavier resounded. "I'll tell the truth. I really don't remember what happened. One moment, that boy was strangling me, and the next, I woke up in the nurse's office. I didn't even know that he had been electrocuted until the principal told me. But, a friend of mine told me that I had somehow conjured up a ball of electric that protected me from him." Xavier paused, watching the sallow man closely.

The man studied Xavier and seemed to be contemplating his confession. Xavier concentrated on keeping his thoughts on the story and the uneasiness he felt toward the man. It was obvious that he wasn't going to completely fool him, but maybe with a little bit of the truth, he could throw him off the scent of the whole story.

"You don't remember a thing about how you conjured it?" the man asked quietly.

"No," he replied shakily.

There was another drawn out silence. The man's eyes continued to dissect him like an insect, and Xavier squirmed uncomfortably under his stare.

"I swear it! It's the truth! That's all I know!" Xavier proclaimed.

The man sneered as he watched Xavier shift in distress for several minutes. Finally, he sighed lightly and stood. "Okay, boy. I'll accept your answer for now, but I know there's more to this story than you're telling me. We will find out what you're hiding. You can be sure of that."

"I don't know what you're talking about. I've told you everything I know," Xavier pleaded, avoiding the man's dark

46

eyes. "I swear!"

"That remains to be seen," the man whispered knowingly. Then, he turned and strode out of the room. The fat man followed, closing the door behind them.

Xavier sighed, relieved to be alone again. However, his reprieve did not last long. A few moments later, the fat man returned followed by a younger man with long greasy brown hair.

"Okay, kid. Grab your stuff. You're being transferred to the residential wing of the facility," the fat man announced nasally. "Come on, come on, I haven't got all day," he snapped.

Xavier stood, turned to the bed, and grabbed his bag and jacket. Then, he turned and faced the men apprehensively. "Where exactly are you taking me? Why am I here? What is this place?" The questions came out in a rush.

The man gave a nicotine stained smile. "It's not for me to tell you. Stop asking questions and let's go."

"No! I'm not going anywhere until someone tells me what the heck is going on," Xavier spat.

The man's smiling face fell into a shadow of anger. "You'll find out when Master is good and ready to tell you and not a moment before. Now, do as your told!"

"NO! And, you can't make me!" Xavier said mulishly.

The man stomped toward him, fuming. Xavier was reminded of a charging hippopotamus, and he could've sworn that he felt the concrete floor shimmy. The fat man grabbed him roughly by the arm.

"Shut your mouth, kid and get going!" he snarled, spraying Xavier in spit. Then, he yanked Xavier off his feet and threw him toward the door.

Xavier fell hard onto the floor and his head slammed against the metal door jam. For an instant, everything around him went black, and the room spun.

"Stop dawdling, boy. Get to your feet and get moving!" the man snapped as he yanked Xavier to his feet, nearly giving him whiplash, and shoved him through the doorway.

Xavier staggered into the hall, collided with a massive guard, and crumpled to the floor in a heap. He peered up at the unforgiving barrier of a man standing in front of him, and his mouth dropped open. The guard had to be at least six and a half feet tall! The bare forearms crossed over his massive chest could rival most men's biceps. The man was solid bulk, and stamina busted from every part of him. He had to be the biggest and possibly the strongest man Xavier had ever seen.

The guard glanced down at him with mild interest. Then, oddly, he jerked his gaze back to Xavier and stared as recognition stole across his face and his brow furrowed. The man looked...fearful, there was no other word to describe it. Finally, with a shake of his head, the guard masked his shock with indifference and turned his gaze once more toward the door.

The fat man squeezed himself through the doorway, and when his eyes fell upon the guard and the three additional guards behind him, puzzlement contorted his fat face. "Why are you here?" he demanded.

The big man raised an eyebrow and considered him severely. "Lewis, I do not believe a subordinate is permitted to speak to his superior in such a way. Do you care to restate your question in a more appropriate manner?" his voice was hard and challenging.

Lewis's face sagged with submission almost immediately. "Sir, I apologize. The boy was being..."

"Don't blame your lack of professionalism on the boy's behavior! He's only a child, and you're a man. Deal with it!" the man replied stonily.

"Y...Yes, sir. Sorry sir," he muttered.

"Now, to answer your question, Master thinks that it's best if the boy has additional security. That is why we are here," he replied matter-of-factly.

"Additional security?" Lewis replied blinking slowly.

"Why? Wait a minute..."

"It is neither your place or mine to question his orders, Lewis. Let's not continue such discussions with the boy present, shall we?" the guard interrupted, eyeing the obese man with contempt.

"Ah, yes. Yes, sir. You're right. How thoughtless of me," Lewis sputtered.

The guard dropped his gaze to Xavier who had not moved from the floor. His eyes were almost kind as he surveyed the boy. His mouth lifted at the corners in a near smile as he stooped down and lifted Xavier to his feet. "Been causing some mayhem, boy?"

Xavier could only stare.

The guard's smile dropped into a frown when he saw evidence of Lewis's brutal treatment. Scarlet marks stood out vividly on Xavier's forearm and a nasty looking knot was beginning to swell on his forehead.

"What the hell..." the guard's eyes darted to Lewis again.

"I was trying to tell you!" Lewis blurted defensively. "The boy was really cheeky and disrespectful. I had to force him from the room!"

A muscle rolled across the guard's jaw. "Fine. But, I'll take it from here. You may check out early for today, Lewis," the guard said thickly. "Stan, you may remain and assist us on the transfer," he added addressing the younger man for the first time.

"Yes, sir," Stan replied, straightening to stand taller.

Lewis opened his mouth to protest but thought better of it and simply left.

"Well, then, are you ready to get settled in your new room, boy?" the guard asked, although it wasn't really a question he expected an answer to because he instantly steered Xavier by the shoulder toward a set of double doors at the end of the hall.

Xavier tried to remember the path as the guards took him to his new room, but by the umpteenth turn, he lost track and simply allowed himself to be led.   Finally, they entered a sterile-looking, white hallway lined with pale gray doors, each with its own observation window.   While the rest of the guards waited just inside the hallway doors, the large guard led Xavier to one of the gray doors, leafed through an enormous key ring until he found the key he needed, and opened the door.   His large hand grasped Xavier by the nape of the neck and lured him inside. After a quick nod to the other men, he entered the room and closed the door.

The sound of the door thudding shut sent Xavier's heart plummeting as if he were on a steep decline of a roller coaster, and he quickly turned to face the man. He felt very near to tears.   He was frightened.   He had never been so frightened in his life.   His entire body prickled with it. Swallowing the hard lump that had formed in his throat, he tried to speak, but couldn't.   A violent shivering began to accumulate in his gut, and he felt his jaw quiver.   He clenched his jaw together, but the more he fought back the fear, the more it sought to come out until he had no control over the sporadic quivering that overtook his body.

The man studied him weightily.   Then, after a moment, he slowly crossed the room, pulled out a metal chair from the small circular table, and, adjusting the sheathed sword attached to his waist, sat down.   He looked at the boy standing so rigid with his little hands balled into tight fists.

"Sit down, boy. There's no need to fear me. Sit," he said in a soft voice.   Slowly, Xavier sat on the edge of the bed, his hands still bound tightly.   The man's mouth twitched, and he asked lightly, "Not planning on punching me, are you boy?"

It took every ounce of control Xavier could muster to unclamp his hands.   "Ah," he cleared his throat. "Why...why am I here? What do you want with me?" Xavier's voice was small and pathetic.

"Well, my boss has learned that you have a special ability, and he wants to help you learn to use it," the guard responded, trying to conceal the sarcasm he felt.

This was not the entire truth, but it was all he could tell the boy. By the way the boy's eyes darted away and avoided him, it was apparent that he knew it wasn't the truth as well.

"My name is Loren. I'm the superintendent of this facility and the security here. This means, it's my job to make sure the guards here keep you... safe," the guard said.

Xavier nodded knowing very well what Loren truly meant; his job was to make sure he stayed there and didn't run away. He felt his muscles contract, and the shivering began to increase. Shamefully, he felt tears tickle the edges of his eyes, and as he fought them back, he sprang to his feet. He turned and crossed the room so the guard wouldn't see him crying.

"Safe?" he muttered hollowly. "Safe?" He hastily rubbed the tears from his cheeks and turned to face the guard. *'Loren, was that what he said his name was? Did it really matter,'* he thought bitterly. He felt his fear being shoved aside by a darker emotion. "Safe?" he repeated flatly and more stoutly. "Safe? Don't you mean imprisoned?"

Loren observed the boy's alteration from a scared little boy into an angry young man in a matter of seconds. He felt a swelling of admiration in his chest and smiled at him. "What's your name, boy?"

"Xavier," he told him truthfully, not seeing how his name would cause any problems. He immediately regretted giving it when Loren hissed a string of profanity, stood, and walked to the door rubbing his face. Without thinking or trying, Xavier felt the cold rush as his abilities took control, and the guard's voice resonated clearly in his mind.

'Dear, God Almighty! It is Jeremiah's son. I knew it! He's the spitting image of him! He must not realize the danger he's in here. Stop it, Loren! You're going to blow your cover.' Loren shook his head slightly and peered across the room at Xavier. The boy's troubled eyes

unfalteringly met his. He knew! Loren looked pointedly at the boy. *'You can read minds, can't you?'* Loren didn't speak the question, but it couldn't have been any clearer to Xavier if he had. Xavier nodded, staring at Loren with disbelieve and confusion.

"Can you?" he asked aloud.

Loren did not speak but answered through his thoughts. *'No. My abilities are not so subtle. Does Danson know?'*

Xavier shook his head ever so slightly.

'Good, keep it that way if you can. And, for God's sake, don't tell him your name. Don't tell anyone! And, be careful what you say in this room; it's bugged. However it's sealed with lead so you should be safe...'

"What does that mean?" Xavier asked aloud.

'The empowered can't use their abilities through lead. It has unique properties that isolates and neutralizes energy. It's not clear on why or how, but lead acts as a barricade for abilities,' Loren explained wordlessly.

"The empowered? Who are you?" Xavier asked aloud.

"I told you. Loren, head of security in this building," Loren answered lightly, but the forewarning on his face made Xavier bite back all other questions. Then, once again, Loren's thoughts pushed into Xavier's mind. *'What did I just tell you, boy? There are bugs, listening devices. It's serious enough that they may have heard your name. Besides, it's best if you don't know anything about me. It's safer for both you and me.'* Loren's face relaxed, and he asked aloud, "What did you say your name was?"

"Ah, Chad, Chad Pennington," he said quickly.

"Pennington, huh? Aren't you the quarterback for the NY Jets?" Loren chuckled. "Well, Master will be in after lunch to talk to you about your residency here. So, get some rest; lunch is in an hour." He patted Xavier on the head and exited the room.

Xavier surveyed the room nervously. He approached

and peered into a two-way mirror that spread half the length of the west wall, but he saw nothing. He closed his eyes and tried "reaching out" with his mind before he remembered what Loren had told him about the room being sealed with lead. So, he was safe as long as he controlled his mind when he had company in the room.

Xavier sighed and turned to face the room. It was plain with very little furniture: a bed with white linens and a baby blue blanket, a table with two chairs, a metal dresser, and a narrow door at the opposite end of the room. He crossed the room in just six long strides and opened the door. It was a bathroom with a small sink and a stand-up shower. The white walls and polished chrome fixtures gave the room a clean, almost sterile appearance, but it gave Xavier the creeps! Xavier returned to the main room and looked around again. Panic and claustrophobia mounted in him like a growing stampede. He walked across the room, flinging his jacket and bag to the floor with a growl, and propelled himself face first onto the bed. He let the tears come then. Tears that didn't change or solve anything, but he cried anyway, too worn out to care.

Chapter 5
Torture
★ ★ ★ ★ ★

Xavier must have fallen asleep because suddenly he found himself dreaming of the stone corridor. Small lanterns gave the passage a haunting, ghostly aura, and he shivered. Although he heard whispers and murmurs droning indiscriminately all around him, Xavier knew he was alone. Feeling a sense of purpose, of destiny, he shuffled stiffly toward the red door at the end of the passage. The murmurs rose like a storm, and as he reached for the rusted doorknob the sounds became deafening.

Xavier woke up disoriented and confused. Where was he? He sat up and looked around. Several seconds passed before Xavier remembered; he was a prisoner at the Institute.

A plate of bread, cheese, and mixed fruit sat invitingly on the table. His jacket and bag were gone from the floor, and gray sweat suits were folded neatly on the dresser with several pairs of bright white underclothes. A brisk knock drew his attention to the door just as it opened. A guard walked into the room followed by a female dressed in a white overcoat. The guard stepped to the side to allow the woman to enter, closed the door behind them, and leaned against its frame, watching Xavier.

"Well, hello there," the woman said sweetly.

Xavier dragged his eyes from the unyielding guard to the woman who stopped at the foot of his bed. She wasn't a young woman, yet she wasn't old, either. She was tall and quite muscular. Her tawny blonde hair was pulled back into a tight bun. Her lips were pursed together in a thin line on her pinched face as she considered him with disdain.

"When an adult speaks to you, boy, it's rude and disrespectful not to answer," she growled, glaring at him with small hazel eyes. "Now, shall we try again? Hello, there," she repeated in a falsely sweet tone.

Xavier cleared his throat, "Hello."

"Hello, ma'am," she corrected rigidly.

"Hello, ma'am," he parroted back.

"There, that wasn't too hard, now was it?" she began as she walked around his bed and placed a black medical bag on the small table. Xavier eyed the bag anxiously. "My name is Dr. Angelo. I'm the resident physician here. I give physical examinations to all the children brought to the Institute for assessment. So, if you'll..."

"There are other children here?" Xavier interrupted.

"You know, it's rude to interrupt a person when they're speaking," she replied, showing no indication that she even heard his question. She glared at him haughtily. "Now, as I was saying. If you'll undress, I can exam you properly." She stood with her hands on her hips, looking down at him expectantly.

"What? You aren't serious," Xavier blurted out.

"Of course I am. How else will I be able to examine you properly? Now, strip off those filthy clothes," she snapped impatiently. Then, she turned and began pulling instruments out of her medical bag.

"No," Xavier said quietly.

Doctor Angelo looked over her shoulder and regarded him with mild surprise. "Excuse me? What did you say?"

"I..." Xavier stammered, "I said, no."

55

"You will do what you are told, boy. Undress, now!" she demanded shrilly.

"No!" he replied.

Her eyes bulged, and she glared at him menacingly. When Xavier made no movement toward compliance, she nodded to the guard standing by the door. The guard straightened and strode across the room toward Xavier.

"Come on, kid. Do as the doctor says," he grumbled.

Xavier jumped to his feet, standing on top of the bed and balling his hands into fists. "Not on your life! She's not touching me!" he spat.

"Now, now. This will only take a few minutes, kid," the guard said heavily as he approached him.

"No! Stay back! Don't come any closer. I swear, I'll... I'll..."

"Do what kid? Don't you see there's no way we're leaving until Dr. Angelo examines you? And, if I have to strip you down myself to get it done, then that's what I'll do," he drawled.

"Forget..." Xavier's berating was cut short as the guard lunged at him and knocked him back onto the bed. In one swift movement, he had Xavier pinned to the bed with his arms wound painfully behind him.

"Get off! Get off me you great oaf!" Xavier yelled.

"Remove his pants and shirt so I can examine him thoroughly," the doctor demanded.

With the heat of embarrassment burning on his cheeks, Xavier felt the guard reach to the front of his jeans, unfasten them, and raked them down in one quick movement. Then, the guard flipped him onto his back. Before Xavier had time to register that he was no longer lying on his stomach, the guard yanked his shirt over his head. Within seconds, he had been stripped down to his under shorts.

The guard reached for him again.

"Stay away from me!" Xavier yelled, twisting free and jumping from the bed. He raced across the room to the door and pulled frantically. The guard cornered him there. "I mean it, stay away," Xavier growled.

The guard showed absolutely no signs of doing that, as he reached out and grabbed Xavier's arm.

Xavier wriggled and squirmed in the man's grasp. "Let go of me! Let go of me!" he growled.

The guard smiled down at him. "Now, let's not make this worse than it has to be, kid."

Anger burned over every inch of Xavier's body, and he kicked the man in the groin. The guard released him and stooped forward, gasping for breath. Xavier took advantage of the man's vulnerable state and punched him squarely on the nose, sending him staggering to the floor. The guard swore and wiped the blood trickling from his nose with the back of his sleeve. Unfortunately, Xavier hadn't done any real damage; he had only managed to royally tick the guard off. The guard climbed to his feet, glaring at the boy standing triumphantly before him. Suddenly, he backhanded Xavier, sending him to the floor.

Without a moment's hesitation, the guard grabbed an ankle, dragged him across the room, and tossed him onto the bed. The doctor turned with a syringe and a small bottle of clear liquid.

"Hold him still. This should calm him down a bit," she said undaunted.

"NO! Please, no. I'll do it. I swear! Please don't give me that shot. Please," he begged on the verge of tears and struggled in vain against the guard's paralyzing grip.

The doctor surveyed him curiously. "I think it's a bit too late for that young man. If anything, you'll remember this next week when you have your next physical." She inserted the needle into the bottle and began to extract a measured amount of the fluid.

"God, no. Please! I promise, I'll never give you trouble again. Please, God, please! Don't do it!" Xavier was crying now.

However, before the doctor had finished filling the

syringe, a yellow ball of light flashed above the bed. The three stared in wonder at the force as it swarmed above them. Then, it barreled toward the doctor, knocking her off her feet and shattering the syringe and bottle.

"Doctor? Doctor? Are you okay?" the guard asked, alarmed.

Dr. Angelo slowly got to her feet, glaring at Xavier. "You little beast!" she bellowed, rubbing her backside. She stomped to the bed, brushed the guard aside, and grabbed Xavier by the hair, whipping his head back so their eyes met. "You will be punished for that," she huffed heavily and paused. Strangely, the doctor's eyes calmed and her breathing slowly returned to normal.

"You know, I haven't told you my ability, have I? I always found it ironic that I entered a profession that heals and eases pain, when my ability is to cause it."

She smiled sadistically down at Xavier. Then, she released his hair, placed the palms of her hands onto his bare chest, and pressed lightly. Xavier's entire body exploded in pain. It felt as if every bone in his body was being splintered into pieces. He arched from the intensity of it and screamed. When she finally removed her hands from him, he fell back onto the bed, soaked in his own sweat.

"Now," she began sweetly, "we will perform this physical without anymore difficulty from you."

The door to the room bang opened. "What is going on in here?" Loren's voice was livid. "I could hear the boy in the next wing! If you cannot perform a physical without ... what did you do to the boy? What the hell did you do, you sick ..." That was all Xavier heard before he passed out.

* * * * *

Xavier opened his eyes several hours later to find the room absolutely dark and quiet except for the whooshing sound from the ventilation system. He tried to sit up but found that his feet and hands had been bound to the bed. With a frustrated groan, he pulled and kicked against the bindings when a light next to the bed flicked on. He blinked rapidly against the sudden brightness, trying to focus. The man sitting next to the bed gave him a brief smile, but his chiseled features held no kindness. His eyes were so dark that his pupils weren't visible. He wore a black suit and a blood red tie knotted neatly at the neck. Xavier could feel power oozing from every pore of the man, and a sense of foreboding crept through his body. This man was simply evil, pure evil. For several minutes, the man considered him thoughtfully without a word.

"Why are you afraid?" he asked quietly in a grating voice that sent goose bumps over Xavier's body. "There's no need to fear."

'Yeah, right! Then, why am I tied up? And, who're you?' Xavier's thoughts raced. But, before he could speak the questions aloud, the man was answering him.

"You," he began sternly, "caused quite a bit of ruckus during your physical. A guard had to restrain you so the exam could be completed." He paused, eyeing him astringently. "And, to answer your second question, my name is William LeMasters, but you may simply call me Master. I run this facility. I would be the reason you were brought here."

Xavier felt a surge of bitterness and glared belligerently at the man before him. *'Master?'* He thought with a bitter snicker. *'Who does this guy think he is? He obviously has a superiority complex.'*

"I do not find the thoughts of an insolent twelve-year-old boy all that informative or intriguing. But, you will need to learn your place, boy." LeMasters stood, peering down at Xavier with disdain. "Dr. Angelo seems to believe you're a bit too cheeky, and I'm afraid that your thoughts only confirm this. We here at the Institute do not shy away from physical punishments as a means of teaching children discipline and manners." He wandered to the foot of the bed and paused, never taking his eyes off Xavier. He seemed to be awaiting Xavier's response.

Frowning, Xavier considered what the man had said.

Was he telling him that they'd whip him or... did he... was he telling him they would torture him? He looked at the man smirking at him from the foot of the bed.

"Yes, to both of your questions, but torture is such an ugly word." They stared at one another for several minutes in silence. "Well," Master began conversationally, "I think the binds have long since served their purpose." With a wave of his hand, the bindings loosened and fell to the floor.

For a moment, Xavier stared in awe at LeMasters's lazy, almost arrogant display of powers, but finally, he sat up, wincing in pain.

"Yes," LeMasters sang, "I imagine you're quite sore after Veronica's punishment. A hot shower should help. There are clean clothes on the dresser. Go on and get that shower, and we'll talk when you're through."

Xavier slowly stood, grabbed the clean clothes, and entered the bathroom, clicking the door shut behind him. He stripped off his underwear and stepped into the steaming spray of water. LeMasters had been right. The shower felt heavenly on his cool skin and eased his aching body. After standing several minutes under the hot shower, he turned off the water and toweled dry. Then, he pulled on the bright white underclothes, gray sweatpants, and matching hooded jacket. Finally, after combing his fingers through the wisps of white curls on his head and taking a deep breath, he exited the restroom.

LeMasters was seated at the table with a dinner plate before him. He gestured toward the food, "Your dinner's arrived. You must be famished."

Xavier walked cautiously toward the table and was greeted by a whiff of chicken and dumplings. His stomach gave a great rumble.

"Please, sit. We can talk while you eat," LeMasters replied invitingly as he pulled out the other chair for Xavier.

Xavier sat down and inhaled the delicious aroma but hesitated. *Would they try to poison me?'* he wondered, toying with the food.

"No. We would not poison you. We are very interested in keeping you alive," LeMasters responded, leering down at him.

Xavier looked at the man wondering whether or not to trust his word, but his dark eyes were impossible to read; it was like peering into a bottomless abyss. He hastily looked away and tentatively took a bite of a dumpling.

"Why am I here?" Xavier asked, without looking up at the man across from him.

"Ah, well, that is an interesting question. But, I think there're more important questions that need to be answered first," he replied quietly.

At this, Xavier quickly looked up. The man was studying him. Calculatingly, Xavier laid his silverware down and grasped the edges of the circular table, bracing for the battle that he was sure was about to begin. He quickly began clearing his mind of any troubling thoughts. He thought about playing football for the school's team, hiking in the woods, and riding his mother's stallion.

"My brother informed me that you had tried this technique with him, and he wasn't certain that he got accurate information from you," he smiled without humor. "But, I informed Danson that you're just a boy and that he overestimated your capabilities. So, I told him I'd assess you myself," he said, watching Xavier closely. "Now, do you possess any other abilities other than electro forces?"

"No," he responded, not meeting LeMasters's eyes.

"Ah," he replied forcibly, "I see why Danson believed that you were less than truthful. So, let's try a simpler question. What is your name, boy?"

"Chad, Chad Pennington," he replied.

There was a moment of silence, and Xavier could feel the man's eyes boring into him.

"No," Master responded coolly, "I want your true name."

"Chad is my…"

"YOUR TRUE NAME!" he thundered, slamming his

fist down on the table and causing the silverware to hop and clatter.

Xavier jumped and stammered, "I...I...told you, it's Chad."

Xavier ventured a glance at LeMasters's face and found a look of pure Cynicism. A shiver slivered down Xavier's spine, and he had to look away.

"You will tell me the truth," William LeMasters whispered with eerie calmness, "one way or another. I can find out the truth the easy way or... well, let's just say the more *uncomfortable* way."

Xavier felt a lump of dread churn in his gut, and he immediately regretted eating. "My name is Chad Pennington. That's the truth!" he responded steadily, meeting LeMasters's eyes unwaveringly.

"No," he hissed. "That's not the truth, but the truth will be uncovered. The truth shall set thee free."

With morbid anticipation, Xavier watched as the man raised his left arm and a light, the size of a golf ball, swirled into a sphere in the palm of his hand. Then, with a flick from LeMasters's forefinger, the energy pelted at Xavier and struck him squarely in the chest. Xavier was knocked clean out of his chair and slammed against the opposite wall. He slid to the floor, his back feeling as if it had been snapped into two.

"The truth?" LeMasters asked lightly, standing to tower over the disheveled boy.

Xavier gasped for breath. "Chad Penning...ton," he muttered.

William LeMasters's eyes seemed darker, if that was even possible. "You will regret your insubordination, boy." In one fluid movement, LeMasters lifted his hand, raising Xavier into the air. "When I'm through with you, I will have my answers. I guarantee it," he told him with a treacherous smile. Then, with a flick of his hand, he tossed the boy across the room.

Xavier crashed to the floor in a heap. His arm

snapped, and he cried out in pain. LeMasters crossed the room in four long strides and knelt beside Xavier. "Now. What is your name, boy?" he asked.

Xavier whimpered. A sudden feeling of nausea wafted through him, and he felt LeMasters's cool hands on his face, forcing him to look at him.

"Well?" William LeMasters asked.

"Go to hell," Xavier groaned hoarsely.

Complete and utter fury contorted the man's face. "So be it," he muttered.

Then, LeMasters slammed his hands on Xavier's chest and pain exploded throughout every part of him. The torturous force continued to course through his body for several seconds, but to Xavier, it felt like an eternity. His entire body felt like it was on fire, and he screamed himself hoarse.

"Please," Xavier cried out.

LeMasters finally removed his hands. "Yes?"

But, Xavier couldn't respond. The pain still pulsated through his body, and another wave of nausea overwhelmed him. He turned his head and threw up.

LeMasters stood, looking down at Xavier with shock and disbelief. "It can't be true," he whispered.

Xavier was' drenched with sweat, and his hair was plastered to his head. He looked up at LeMasters puzzled.

Recognition shone menacingly in LeMasters's eyes. "Xavier. Xavier Wells. Jeremiah Wells's son." A sadistic laugh permeated the room. "My God! How could I have been so blind! The white hair and the eyes, the hypnotic eyes!" He paced the room manically, laughing. He turned and faced Xavier again. "Xavier. It's such a pleasure to meet your acquaintance. What other abilities does the son of Jeremiah have?" he asked.

Xavier didn't speak, but Master found out without needing him to.

"Electro force, telepathy, and anima lingua," he listed off gleefully.

There was a quick knock as the door swung open, and Loren walked into the room. "Oh, sorry sir. I didn't realize you were still interrogating the boy."

"Loren! Do you realize who this is? *This* is Jeremiah Wells's, King Wells IV's, son," he announced crazed.

"You're kidding!" Loren gasped, looking down at the nearly unconscious boy. "*He's* the King's son? What's wrong with him?"

"Oh," he began, looking down at the boy with indifference, "he had to be persuaded into answering my questions. I'll send Dr. Angelo in to check his vitals. Lord knows I want to keep the son of King Wells alive! Jeremiah would do anything for his son's safe return." Master chuckled. "The boy needs some mending up, Loren. I believe I broke his arm. Mend the boy and clean up this mess. I'll finish my questioning tomorrow when he's more conscious."

With those final instructions, LeMasters turned on his heel and strode out of the room, still laughing.

Loren knelt by the boy and began the task of rejuvenating his injuries, his mind reeling for an escape plan for the Prince of Warwood.

Chapter 6
The Rescue
★★★★★

Xavier was kept in seclusion for the next couple of weeks at the Institute with daily visits from LeMasters. Most of these visits turned out to be quite painful for Xavier, and by the end of his second week at the Institute, Xavier had become quite anxious and obsessively aware of any noise in the room. The whooshing of the ventilation system seemed as loud as an industrial steam engine, and the pinging of the water pipes were like an orchestra of jackhammers, each a cause for cold sweat and tears.

'I'm going insane,' Xavier thought miserably after a bout of tears over a loud creak from the bathroom door.

Suffering from severe depression, Xavier began to contemplate death as a blessing. Many mornings he awoke feeling a sharp disappointment that he woke up at all. He stopped eating. Not that he thought he could starve himself to death, but his nerves wouldn't allow his food to stay down. The few times he did manage to eat, a fit of nerves would twist his stomach into a knot until he threw up its contents.

Not to mention, Xavier was exhausted. He couldn't sleep because he always seemed to be listening for the creak of the door and another visit from LeMasters.

However, the few short periods of sleep he did succumb to were filled with horrific dreams that his abilities were being used to kill masses of people. Then, there were the dreams of his father, Jeremiah. The stories William LeMasters told him about his father were full of shady and monstrous deeds. Jeremiah seemed to be an equally horrible man.

"You've never met your father, have you?" LeMasters had sneered one afternoon.

Xavier had not answered for he was sprawled out on the cool linoleum floor, trying to ease his burning, painful body after another bout of 'questioning' for which he had no answers.

LeMasters paced nonchalantly as he continued, "Your father is an outcast of our kind. Did you even know that your father is a king? Do you even know what you are boy?"

Xavier moaned in response.

"I didn't think so. You're a member of an elite class of humans. Have you ever heard that humans only use ten to twenty percent of their brains?" He didn't even pause for an answer but continued his monologue, "For many years, our scientists believed that this explained our abilities. They believed that those with powers had simply inherited the ability to access the rest of their brains. However, all of this was a fallacy, a myth. Humans don't just use ten percent of their brains; they use all of it. It wasn't until modern technology that empowered scientists were able to determine what made us unique. We are simply neurologically different from everyone else. The Corpus Collosum, the tissue that connects the two hemispheres of the brain, is ten times larger in an empowered person than it is in a common person. This makes it possible for several simultaneous interactions between the hemispheres to occur. In addition, due to its enlarged size, the Corpus Collosum has taken on other functions as well. It acts as the brain for the empowered human's supernatural abilities. As far as we could gather through scientific investigation, this is an inherited trait." He paused and looked down at Xavier.

"But, we were talking about your father, weren't we? You've never met him? You should be thankful you haven't. He's a tyrant. He is a ruthless man and rules his kingdom with an iron hand. His citizens fear and loathe him, but they do not dare speak ill of him because if they do, they are arrested and put to death. Then, their families are banished from the kingdom, and their homes are burnt to the ground. But, even worse than all of that was how your father treated you and your mother. Your father abandoned you and your mother. I guess that was really a blessing in disguise because even when he was around, he was cruel and harsh toward your mother. He abused her when she was pregnant with you. He never wanted an heir, and he tried to induce a miscarriage by beating your mother unconscious. That is why you had to live with your grandparents. Your father doesn't want anything to with you, boy. He doesn't love you. He doesn't want you. I'm your father now."

* * * * *

The month passed with much of the same routine: numerous torturous visits from Master and brief solitude in between. Xavier became neurotic and jumped at the slightest noise or movement. His body was one enormous bruise; it even hurt to breathe. If given the opportunity, Xavier would have ended his own life rather than be subjected to another day of LeMasters's torture, but the opportunity never came.

"Master!" Loren burst into the room where he was once again punishing Xavier for his inability to provide answers to questions regarding his father's kingdom. "There's been a breach in security! They look like Royal Guards, sir."

For the first time, Xavier saw a flicker of fear in LeMasters's eyes. "Guard the boy. They've come for him," he hissed and exited the room in a run.

Xavier struggled to sit up, his muscles aching when a pair of hands lifted him to his feet. Xavier looked up into Loren's gentle eyes.

"Do you think you could walk?" he asked urgently.

Xavier nodded. "I... I think so," he replied unsteadily.

"Boy, you'll have to if you ever want to get out of here alive," Loren stated.

Loren dragged Xavier across the room toward the door. He slid his key into the lock and opened the door slowly. "Come, on. Stay close and keep your thoughts quiet!"

They slipped into the hallway and cantered toward a set of double doors. Loren approached it cautiously, drawing out his sword from the sheath attached to his side. As he peered through the small box-shaped window, he brushed Xavier behind him.

Xavier fought hard at keeping his mind clear and blank, but it wasn't easy with his heart racing the way it was. Then, what happened next blew his concentration completely, and he had little control over the thoughts that sprang into his mind.

Loren suddenly launched himself backwards, nearly knocking Xavier to the floor, as several men charged through the door dressed in long, ink blue silk cloaks trimmed with silver thread and clasps. The men were not armed, but an aura of pride and strength encompassed them all the same. They continued down the hall not realizing that Loren and Xavier stood behind the door. However, after a couple strides, the man leading the group through the corridor turned and pinned Xavier with an intense gaze. Then, without a word, the other men followed suit. One by one, the men separated and cleared a path for their leader, and Xavier glared up at the man, his chin tilted defiantly. The man wore a hood that shrouded much of his face from vision. Only his slate eyes encircled by dark, thick eyelashes could be seen clearly. He was taller than the other men and beneath the cloak a golden sash sprawled across his broad chest. He was obviously a man of status.

Xavier stared at the man beyond his entourage and felt a strange coolness sweep through him. He closed his

68

eyes to it and allowed it to overtake him.

"Xavier?" a voice questioned, and instantly Xavier recognized it as the voice of caution in the woods.

Xavier did not answer the voice but simply waited for it to continue. When it didn't, he opened his eyes. The man had stepped forward and now was kneeling before him. Xavier backed away apprehensively. The man reached up to the hood of his cloak and slid it down onto his back, exposing his face.

"Fear not, Son. I'm your father, and I'm here to free you," he reassured smoothly.

Xavier was astounded. He recognized the man at once from his nightmares. His eyes grew wide with fear, and he flattened himself against the wall with a groan.

The man kneeling before him was the spitting image of himself only about twenty-five years older. His white hair was shoulder length, and he wore a white goatee beard. His dark gray eyes looked tired and cumbersome, but his face was gentle and handsome.

"Xavier," the man replied as he lifted his hand to touch Xavier.

Xavier winced and cowered to the floor.

The man looked pointedly at Loren who gave him a grave expression. He looked back to the whimpering boy on the floor. "I promise you, the pain is over. I've come to take you home," he soothed as he stroked the boy's head.

The moment the man touched him, Xavier felt a great, comforting warmth seep throughout his body. He looked up at the man of whom he had numerous nightmares, but suddenly he was overcome with relief. He clamped his eyes shut, fighting the tears that were threatening to overflow but failed miserably. The man's large hands cupped his face gently, and his thumbs stroked the tears from his cheeks.

"Come, Son. It's time to go home," the man said, standing and looking at Loren once more. "Thank you, Loren. I appreciate you informing us of Xavier's existence here."

Loren straightened and looked at the man with admiration. "It was my duty, Sire. I only wished it could have been accomplished long before now," he paused, glancing at Xavier. "Jeremiah, the boy's been through quite a horrific ordeal. He may not be strong enough to make the journey tonight. In fact, I'm not sure if he has the strength to make it out of this building. I had planned to escape with him tonight even if your forces hadn't come. He hasn't eaten in days, I'm not sure if he's slept more than an hour at a time, and the punishments William exposed him to were..." Loren faltered and looked up at the King. "Jer, William tortured him. He knew the boy knew nothing of you, your whereabouts, or the castle's security. I think once he realized his identity, he got some sort of sick, twisted pleasure out of brutalizing the boy." Both men looked down at a teetering Xavier, who looked as though he was about keel over from exhaustion.

Jeremiah bent and scooped Xavier into his arms. "He'll make it. Even if I have to carry him the entire way," he said, his voice thick with emotion. He turned and walked back through the doors he and his guards had entered, and Loren and the guards followed. They made it as far as the third corridor when a barrier of the Institute's guards blocked their exit, swords drawn.

Loren stepped forward. "It's okay, men. I have everything under control. I'm taking our new prisoners to the west wing for evaluation," he said convincingly.

"I don't think so," a cold calculating voice came from behind them. The guards spun immediately, positioning themselves between Jeremiah and William LeMasters.

"Hold the boy," Jeremiah murmured to Loren, handing the now unconscious Xavier to him. He weaved his way through his men and faced LeMasters with cold, vengeful eyes.

"Jeremiah! Well, well, well. It's been a long time, hasn't it?" LeMasters asked wispily.

"Not nearly long enough, William. However, I'm

70

curious about something," Jeremiah began almost lightly. "Why would you stick around, let alone try and stop me, when you know I'd be hunting you down for how you treated my son. You'd have to have known that I would kill you for it," he finished forcefully.

Jeremiah raised an arm in front of him with a ball of energy forming brightly in his cupped hand. The sphere of energy pelted toward LeMasters with amazing speed, hitting him squarely on the chest. William was thrown several yards backwards and landed hard on the concrete floor. Pandemonium erupted as the facility's security came charging toward the group with their weapons raised. Jeremiah spun toward the guards, and with a flick of his hand, the swords flew out of the men's hands. Then, the Premier Royal Guard turned, threw back their cloaks, and attacked. Gold spheres spiraled toward the security men like a shower of fire. As the forces struck LeMasters's men, many were launched across the room; some fell to the floor in agony, whereas others simply slumped to their knees with blank stares on their faces. Loren, watching the confrontation, crept along the wall of the corridor, making his way with Xavier toward the exit.

Jeremiah and LeMasters were dueling at the opposite end of the hallway. Jeremiah propelled one of the Institute's guards at him, but LeMasters was prepared and blocked the attack. Then, LeMasters countered with a sphere of light of his own and lunged it at Jeremiah, who deflected it easily with a simple wave of his hand. Jeremiah surveyed the fighting behind him and spotted Loren. Loren met the unwavering, somber gray eyes.

'Get Xavier out! Now, Loren! Please, get my son to safety. You'll find the SUV's hidden in the forest just beyond the creek. Timmins, Henrick, and Ephraim should be standing guard. Send them here as backup to give you time to flee with the boy. Go. We'll meet you at the scheduled rendezvous point. GO! Now!' the Premier's voice echoed loudly in Loren's thoughts.

71

Loren nodded and slipped through the doors undetected by the guards fighting around him. He hurried through the woods, crashing through the thick brush. Before he could reach the convoy of vehicles, Timmins, Henrick, and Ephraim were thundering toward him in an outright sprint. Loren opened his mouth, but Ephraim, bringing up the rear, replied, "We know. We're on our way. Get the lad out of here!"

Loren splashed across a shallow creek and barreled to the first vehicle. He yanked open the passenger door, placed Xavier in the seat, and buckled him in. Then, he raced to the other side of the vehicle, sank into the driver's seat, turned the key in the ignition, and slammed the gear into drive, spinning out of the clearing.

He drove frantically for several minutes and did not slow down until he pulled onto the highway traveling north. He looked down at the boy beside him. The boy's face was thinner than it had been when he was first admitted into the Institute. His eyes were sunken with dark circles around them, and he had patches of hair missing. Guilt fell like lead to the pit of Loren's stomach. He should have found a way to break the boy out sooner. He jerked his gaze away from the unconscious boy and looked back to the road. The rendezvous point was a good three-hour drive from his current position. The sooner the boy was there, the safer he'd be. A quarter of a mile down the road, Loren pulled off the interstate and began a more obscured path north.

Three and half hours later, Xavier was still unconscious as Loren pulled into a gravel drive to a quaint little cottage overlooking the Atlantic Ocean. Loren exited the vehicle and crossed over to the passenger side door. When the door to the cottage opened, he swung around, pulling out his sword.

Alexandria Meagan, the King's legal secretary, stepped out of the cabin.

With a curse, Loren relaxed and tucked his sword back into its sheath.

"Is the boy with you?" she asked.

"Yes," he replied dryly, opening the door and lifting the boy into his arms. He surveyed the woman. "Jeremiah and the rest of the Guard are on their way here. I imagine they're about twenty minutes or so behind us." He carried Xavier toward the cottage.

Alexandria stepped aside to allow him to enter and gasped at the sight of the boy. "Dear, God!" she groaned. "What did they do to the poor boy? What did they do?"

"They nearly crucified him," Loren growled as he brushed past her and entered the bungalow. "Where can I lay the boy so he can be examined and rest undisturbed?"

"In here," she said and opened a door to a small bedroom that faced the sea. Alexandria stripped back the sheets and crossed the room to a closet. She turned with a quilt in her hands and watched as Loren gently laid the boy onto the small bed and tucked the sheet around him.

"Do you have a first aid kit?" he asked her, taking the quilt from her arms.

Alexandria nodded and left the room. A few moments later, she returned carrying a white box and placed it into Loren's outstretched hand. He laid the box on the floor next to him and removed Xavier's fleece jacket and t-shirt baring his bruised and lacerated chest. The woman gasped in horror.

Without a word, Loren cleaned and bandaged the boy's wounds thoroughly. Then, closing his eyes in concentration, he pressed his hands together and rubbed them back and forth vigorously before he placed them on Xavier's bare chest.

Alexandria watched as Loren's hands emitted a white light that crept throughout the child's body. Within moments, both the boy and Loren were a fantastic white light that was nearly blinding to look at. Then, as suddenly as it began, the light vanished, and Loren opened his eyes.

"Well," Loren sighed, covering the boy and then looking back at Alexandria, "I think we better fix up some soup. I imagine he's going to be mighty hungry when he awakens."

Alexandria nodded solemnly, and they exited the room, leaving the door slightly open.

The remaining men did not arrive until the chowder was bubbling in the pot. Loren and Alexandria were dishing up bowls of it when Jeremiah and the Premier Royal Guard barged loudly through the door.

"Where is he? I want to see my son," Jeremiah said at once.

Loren moved quickly to him. "Jeremiah! Yes, sir. This way, Sire. He's still out." He led Jeremiah into the bedroom.

Jeremiah looked down at the boy, who in his eyes looked extremely small and frail. Anger gnawed at his gut; William had escaped. The moment Jeremiah had turned and given instructions to Loren, William had disappeared. The boy moaned and whimpered feebly.

"Shhh," he soothed, stroking the white ringlets on Xavier's head. "Shhh, Son. It's all right. You're safe."

Jeremiah placed his hand on the boy's forehead and closed his eyes in concentration. The image of Xavier strapped to a bed with Dr. Angelo and William standing over him appeared in the darkness of his mind. With a swipe of his hand, the images disappeared, and the boy looked up at him wide-eyed.

'Xavier, you are safe. Do not fret over that man. He cannot harm you again. I will not allow it. I'm here waiting to talk to you. But, first, you must sleep.' With another slight movement of his hand, Xavier was unbound and standing in a flowering meadow with a soothing breeze. *'You have much healing to do. I'll see you when you awaken. Now, rest my son. Sleep peacefully.'* He stroked the boy's cheek gently and withdrew himself from the dream.

Xavier felt himself slipping into a deep serene sleep with dreams of horse rides in a meadow and swimming in a shimmering clear lake.

Chapter 7
Healing
★ ★ ★ ★ ★

Xavier woke some time later in a dark unfamiliar room. The full moon spilt light onto the small bed, and outside the window, he could hear the roar of crashing waves. He sat up and looked around. To his right, a door was slightly ajar, and light slivered into the room. Just beyond the door, he could hear murmurs of low conversations. Weakly, he untangled himself from the blankets and stood on wobbly legs. A sudden dizziness caused the room to spin, and Xavier clung to the bed, waiting for it to pass. When it did, he gingerly crept to the door and listened.

"So, how're Lucy and my girls?" Loren's voice filtered into the room.

"They're fine, mate," a deep voice responded. "Jer's been keeping very close tabs on them. Believe me; Lucy isn't in need of a single thing."

"Oh?" Loren's voice grinned. "And, just what needs have you been fulfilling, Jer?"

"Absolutely every need a woman can have," Jeremiah jeered playfully, and a group of male voices erupted in laughter and banters.

Carefully, Xavier swung the door open wide enough so that he had a clear view of the men sitting around the table. Loren was standing and playfully boxing with Jeremiah.

"Her every need, huh! You had better keep your hands off my woman, Jer. You may be my king, but I can still kick your butt!"

"Okay, Okay!" the deep voice called above the ruckus as a russet-haired man stood, raising his hands and trying to settle down the boisterous group. "Gentleman, the meeting is still in session, and we still have a few things to discuss."

"You know, Ephraim, that's always been your problem. You're always too serious. It's a good thing young Courtney doesn't take after his old man," Loren jested.

"And, obviously your problem has always been that you're never serious enough! So, I guess that's why the Premier inducted me into the Premier Royal Guard, to offset your childish behavior!" Ephraim replied unscathed.

The group groaned and chuckled.

"Now! Can we focus on the task at hand? The Clavis de Rex must be moved and placed under constant surveillance," Ephraim continued.

"Yes, that must be done. Let's consider the possibilities and meet again upon returning home," Jeremiah agreed, sitting down. The other men's playfulness died away as they sat down around the table with their king. "Now, is there anything else to be discussed?"

"Sir," Loren began, "have you heard anything from platoon eagle and the whereabouts of William LeMasters?"

"No," he responded smoothly. "I haven't heard a thing. However, I'm sure it's just a matter of time until we find him, and when we do," he stopped abruptly and turned toward Xavier. Xavier quickly sank back into the darkness of the room, but within moments, the door was yanked open and light flooded over his face.

"Xavier? How long have you been up?" Loren asked.

"Only for a few moments. Isn't that right, Son?" the

man standing in the doorway remarked.

Xavier blinked and looked up at the man in front of him. It was the man who had called himself his father, Jeremiah. Xavier wavered and started to collapse, but Jeremiah had been expecting it and caught him easily.

"Whoa, Son. You're too weak to be out of bed." He lifted him into his arms and carried him back into the room. "Are you hungry?" he asked, settling the boy onto the bed.

Xavier nodded.

The man nodded with a mild smile. Loren appeared at the door as though he had been beckoned, but then, Xavier thought, he probably had been. "Yes, Sire?"

"Some chowder and milk for the boy, please," he ordered aloud.

"Yes, sir," Loren said. He returned a few moments later, carrying a serving tray with a large bowl of steaming corn chowder and a large glass of milk. "Here you are Xavier. Eat up. You need your strength back." He placed the serving tray on Xavier's lap and left the room.

Xavier attacked the tray wolfishly and began devouring the food. His stomach rumbled painfully as he continuously shoveled spoonful after spoonful of soup into his mouth.

Tenderly, Jeremiah placed a hand on his arm. Xavier looked into his father's intense eyes, and a chill passed through him. His father's voice resonated inside his thoughts, *'Slow down, Boy. You'll make yourself sick.'* Xavier nodded and forced himself to chew and swallow each spoonful before stuffing more into his mouth.

Jeremiah smiled down at him. "That's better," he said aloud.

After a fourth helping of stew and his third glass of milk, Xavier was so full he felt as if he'd burst. He lay back in the bed with a sigh and looked at the man who had sat silently, watching him eat.

"Feel better?" he asked with a grin.

"Yeah," Xavier nodded.

"Yes, sir," he corrected gently with a smile. "You will answer adults as sir or ma'am, Son. Do you understand?"

"Yes...sir."

Then, an uncomfortable silence followed. "You're really my father?" Xavier asked finally.

"Yes, I am," he said seriously. "Do you want to talk about that?"

Xavier shrugged, not meeting his father's stare.

After a brief silence, Jeremiah spoke quietly, "I met your mother on holiday. I was staying at a cottage not far from your grandparents' home. I was walking on the beach when I sensed someone in distress. Your mother had fallen from her horse, and I found her a half a mile down the beach. She was injured quite seriously, and by the time I arrived, she was unconscious. I brought her back to my cottage and mended her. You see, among my abilities, I have the ability to rejuvenate, to heal. It takes time to complete, and the person being healed is extremely weak for a couple of days afterwards. I didn't know who she was or where she lived so she stayed at my cottage all that time. She was so beautiful!" he paused as he stared out the window, losing himself in the memory. After a moment, he looked at Xavier who was watching him intently. Jeremiah cleared his throat and continued, "Anyway, she stayed with me until she was better. Afterwards, she came to see me everyday during my stay there. We fell in love, and we were married in a little over a month. But, I made the mistake of not telling her the truth about me, the entire truth. I didn't tell her that I had these abilities, nor did I tell her that I was the absolute ruler of a society of people that the common person knows nothing about. That was my mistake, and I paid dearly for it. Your mother had a hard time with it when I finally did tell her. She didn't deal too well with the extent of my abilities, especially my ability to read her thoughts. Boy, did that infuriate her!" Jeremiah smiled, but the smile did not reach his eyes. There was something sad in his smile. He looked at Xavier. "I blame myself. Maybe if I'd been truthful from the start, she would have come back and stayed."

"No," Xavier answered dryly, shaking his head. "She wouldn't. My grandparents wouldn't have let her. Besides, Mom is afraid of stuff like that. Grandmother and Grandfather have always said that magic was the work of the devil. She probably believes them, at least a little bit."

He looked at his father, and caught the pain in his eyes. Instantly, Xavier felt guilty for hurting him. But, the feeling of guilt only made him angry, and the anger begin to consume him. What right did his father have to feel hurt? It was he, Xavier, who grew up in that vindictive household with grandparents who despised him. It was he, Xavier, who was tormented and taunted by the kids in his middle school because he looked so different. Suddenly, it occurred to Xavier that it wasn't his existence his grandparents disliked so much. It was because this man was his father. This man, his father, was different and so he was different. It was the difference that his grandparents hated so much.

"But, why didn't you try to visit me?" Xavier asked sounding wounded. "All my life, I didn't even know I had a father. Mother wouldn't tell me anything about you, and my grandparents would only tell me that you were a monster. Why? Why weren't you there?" Xavier felt himself losing control of his emotions. Suddenly his anger overtook him, and he wanted to lash out at his man who called himself his father. 'Father?' he thought bitterly. 'How can he be my father? He was never there!' Xavier felt a familiar coolness seep into his body. "Stop it! Stop it!" he yelled, jumping to his feet and standing on the bed. "I know what you're doing! Just stop it!"

"Xavier, calm down. Let me explain," his father began firmly.

"Don't tell me that! Don't you tell me to calm down! I won't! You don't know what I had to put up with! You don't understand what it was like! You were never there! I needed you, and you weren't there! Do you hear me? You were never there, and I needed you, *Father*." Tears streamed down his cheeks.

Jeremiah stood helplessly, watching his son unravel. He reached out to sooth him, but Xavier jerked away.

"Don't touch me! Don't you ever touch me! I hate you! You hear me? I hate you! It was because of you my own grandparents despised me. I reminded them of you. I wish I didn't have these abilities. I never asked to have them! I didn't ask to be different! I didn't ask to have you as a father!"

Jeremiah reached out for him again and again Xavier jerked away from him.

"NOOO!" Xavier wailed. However, weak and blinded by his tears, he stumbled and fell into Jeremiah.

Jeremiah caught his son who was now sobbing and lacked the strength or the will to be evasive. He pulled the child against his chest and held him tightly. "I'm sorry, Son. I'm sorry," he murmured into his ear.

He cradled Xavier for a quite while. Until, finally, hiccupping and exhausted, Xavier fell into a deep slumber in his father's arms. Gently Jeremiah tucked the boy back into the covers. He sat back in the chair next to the bed and looked at his son. Guilt and grief swelled inside him, and he buried his face in his hands.

"Hurts like hell doesn't it?" Loren said soberly from the doorway. "To find out that you've unintentionally hurt those you love most."

Jeremiah looked up at his best friend since childhood. "I messed up, Loren. I really messed things up, didn't I?"

Loren entered the room and stood at the foot of the bed. He looked at the tear stained face of the sleeping boy and then back to his friend. "Jeremiah, you did what was best for the boy at the time, just as it is now best for the boy to remain with you and his people. Don't feel guilty for that. The boy will understand. He's just overly emotional right now. Lord, with what he's been through, he has every right to be!"

Jeremiah stared at his son and nodded. He stroked

the boy's hair from his face.

"Come on, Jeremiah. Let the boy rest. There's plenty of time to work this out," Loren said, patting his friend's shoulder.

"I'll be out in a moment," the King said thickly.

Loren left the room, closing the door behind him. Jeremiah continued to stroke Xavier's hair, studying him. Guilt and despair continued to eat away at him; his son hated him!

Xavier lay quietly and peacefully, his breathing even. For a moment, Jeremiah considered entering the boy's dreams and telling him the complete story. But, in the end, Jeremiah sighed and shook his head. No, Loren was right; there would be plenty of time for explanations. The boy needed rest. He stroked the boy's cheek one last time and exited the room.

* * * * *

For the next couple of days, Xavier did very little but sleep and eat. Most of the Premier Royal Guard had returned home. Only Jeremiah, Loren, and five of Jeremiah's most trusted bodyguards, remained at the cottage. Xavier slowly regained his stamina and strength. He took to exploring the woods and the beaches and hunting for crabs under rocks and in estuaries. He was beginning to feel like his old self again. The nightmare from the Institute no longer plagued him during the waking hours, but during the night, he often woke screaming. His father would come to his aid every time, soothe him, and fill his dreams with pleasant images. By the week's end, Xavier's nightmares were subsiding, and he was feeling better but found it difficult to control his emotions at times.

"Yo, X," Loren called as he jogged toward him on the beach.

Xavier looked up from the starfish he was examining.

"Heads up!" Loren said, tossing him an oval shaped ball.

Xavier caught the ball just before it hit him squarely

on the chin. The oddly shaped ball resembled a football.
"What's this?" he asked, squinting up at Loren.

"It's a rugby ball. It's a popular sport in our society.
Have you ever played?" he asked.

"No. I've played football. Is it anything like that?"
Xavier asked.

"Well, somewhat. What do you say we get your dad
and the Royal Guard out here and play a game?" Loren
suggested.

Xavier's face dropped, and he handed the ball back
to Loren with a shrug. Without a word, he turned and
directed his attention back to the starfish.

"Xavier," Loren began, "you've got to let it go about
your father. He did what he thought was best for you at the
time. Your time at the Institute should've made you realize
that."

Xavier didn't look at Loren. This seemed to agitate
him, and he walked around to face the boy.

"Xavier, it wasn't your father's fault! I've known
Jeremiah all my life. If there had been a way to keep you
and your mother with him, he would have found it. And, for
the record, I would have done the same thing," he stooped
down to eye level with Xavier. "Xavier, you need…"

"Don't tell me what I need!" Xavier spat angrily. "I
know what I need and needed. I *needed* a father! But, he
wasn't there; was he?" He stood, glaring up at Loren. "So,
butt out, Loren. I didn't ask for nor do I need any advice
from you!"

"Xavier!" the warning came from behind him. Xavier
turned and found Jeremiah looking very stern, very large,
and very hard. He crossed the short distance between
them, his eyes never wavering from the boy.

Xavier felt a lump of dread lodge itself in his throat,
and he swallowed hard. He turned his gaze away from his
father, unable to look at his formidable, dominating stare.

But, Jeremiah cupped his chin in his hand and forced
his gaze back to him. "Xavier, you are not permitted to

speak to adults in the way you just spoke to Loren. You owe him an apology," he said very quietly.

Xavier opened his mouth in protest, but the words caught in his throat as Jeremiah's steely eyes bore into him.

"Now," Jeremiah whispered irrevocably.

Xavier stood defiantly, glaring up at his father, but finally, he turned to Loren and muttered, "I'm sorry, Loren. I didn't mean to be disrespectful."

"Thank you, Xavier," Loren said before looking at Jeremiah. "I'll leave you two alone." Then, without hesitation, Loren walked back to the cottage, leaving Xavier with an angry father.

"Son?" Jeremiah's stern voice came again, and reluctantly, Xavier faced him. "Your behavior with Loren was inexcusable and wrong. You will never speak to Loren or any other adult in that way again. If you choose to do so, I will punish you."

Xavier looked away, wondering what type of punishment he meant.

Jeremiah cupped Xavier's face in his hand once again and drew his eyes toward him. "Disrespect and blatant rudeness is something I will not tolerate. There is nothing that would infuriate me more than for my own son to embarrass me in such a way. So, if you do choose to misbehave in this manner again, I will take you over my knee and spank you." He paused, allowing the boy to assimilate his words. "Do you understand me, Son?"

Xavier's stomach did a flip-flop, and heat tingled across his face. He had never been spanked in his life, and the prospect of this man spanking him was unsettling to say the least. His grandmother had smacked him across the face exactly once, but most of the time, when he got out of line he had been locked up in his room and ignored. Ignoring him had seemed to be his grandparents' preferred method of punishment.

"Do you understand me?" Jeremiah repeated.

"Y...Yes, sir," he muttered, meeting his father's

unflinching stare.

"Good," Jeremiah straightened, and all the tension left his face. "Now, how about a game of rugby? I saw Loren carrying around his old secondary school ball. He was an excellent forward, but I must say I was a better back." He smiled.

Xavier nodded.

"Good, let's find Loren and con Ephraim, Henrick, and Timmins into playing." He wrapped his arm around Xavier and led him toward the cottage.

Minutes later, all the men became boys again as they taught Xavier how to play rugby. Xavier found it similar to football but with several exceptions.

In rugby, each team has fifteen players on the field at a time: eight forwards and seven backs. Although the point system is similar to American football, the methods of scoring have unique differences. A try, worth five points, is earned when a back runs the ball across the goal line and sets the ball on the ground. Like football, the scoring team can earn extra points through a conversion play. However, when a player or team is charged with a foul, their opponent is awarded a penalty dropkick worth three points. Another significant difference is that, in rugby, the ball cannot be passed forward and the play is continuous until someone scores.

After Xavier understood the basic principles of the game, they were romping and wrestling in a game of rugby, if you could call it that. They were wrestling and playing around more than they were obeying the rules of the game. During one scrum, Jeremiah got the ball and began racing forward. Loren lunged at him, but Jeremiah jab stepped, reversed direction, and spun out of his grasp, chuckling.

"You never could out maneuver me," Jeremiah boasted. At that moment, Xavier dove at his father's legs tripping him and sending him heavily to the ground. Loren laughed aloud and openly at the expression on Jeremiah's face as the boy tackled him.

"You know, Jeremiah, your cockiness was always your downfall. And, it looks as though your own son has put you in your place!" All the men hooted and laughed.

Jeremiah looked down at his son who was tangled amongst his legs, shaking with laughter. The sight of his son laughing so uncontrollably, lifted his heart, and he couldn't help but laugh along with him.

* * * * *

By the end of the month, Xavier was feeling very comfortable with his new life with a father at his side. He felt more confident and self-assured. It was as if an enormous puzzle piece in his life had suddenly been filled and fitted. Jeremiah was a kind, playful father who didn't hesitate to slug through swampy sand and estuaries helping Xavier hunt for crabs and sea turtle eggs. A fragile bond had begun to develop between Father and Son.

The men spoke openly about Warwood, and Xavier found himself listening eagerly to the seemingly endless stories and descriptions of his homeland on an island fifty miles South of Newfoundland.

"Have you heard of the Warwood Castle?" his father asked him.

"Well, I did a research paper on North American castles last year as my fifth grade project. It was one of the castles that I studied. Though, there weren't any pictures of it. Robbie suggested it as a topic," he answered.

"Robbie? Roberta Minnows?" Jeremiah asked, raising an eyebrow in amusement. "You and Robbie are best friends, right? How did you meet? At school?"

Xavier shook his head. "No, sir. Her father came over to my grandparents' one day to borrow a cup of milk. Anyways, Robbie and I just connected. She dragged me up the stairs, asking me to show her my room, and we've been friends ever since."

Jeremiah looked at Loren and grinned broadly. "Good ole Dublin! Can you see now why I chose him?"

"Chose him?" Xavier frowned with bewilderment.

85

"I had a trusted friend keeping watch on you and your mother while you stayed with your grandparents."

"Mr. Minnows? Mr. Minnows kept watch on me?" Xavier concluded.

"Yes, Son. Dublin had a young wife and was expecting his first child. He was an ideal choice. To the commons, he'd look like an ordinary family man. Plus he had abilities to do the work covertly without being invasive."

"The commons?" he was puzzled by his father's choice of words.

"The commons are people who do not possess abilities," Loren answered.

Xavier nodded. He recalled how Mr. Minnows had already been on his way when he had talked to Robbie that day when he had been followed in the woods and came home to an empty house for the first time in his life. "He can read minds, can't he?"

"Yes and no. He has the ability to read emotions. He would know if you were feeling fear or anxiety. That's why he knew you needed help that day," Jeremiah answered.

"Sir? Was it you that gave me the warning about the man in the woods?" Xavier asked, remembering.

Jeremiah smiled slightly. "Yes. I have always kept tabs on you telepathically. However, until recently when your abilities began to develop, it had always been one sided."

This news made Xavier feel better. All those times growing up when he had wished his father could be with him, and he had been, in a sense.

Jeremiah stroked Xavier's cheek and smiled, "Yes, Son. I was always with you, always."

Chapter 8
Missing
★ ★ ★ ★ ★

At the month's end, Jeremiah announced at the breakfast table that it was time to begin the journey home.

"We need to visit my in-laws, first. There are a few unfinished details that need to be sorted out," Jeremiah stated stonily.

All the men looked at their leader soberly. Xavier not only saw but also felt the change of atmosphere in the room. Just moments ago, the men had been jovial and carefree. They had been close friends with memories and stories about each other's lives. Now, it was profoundly different. Now, there was an air of hierarchy and levels of command— the vacation was over.

The trip to his grandparents' was long, and Xavier slept throughout most of the journey. He rode in the first of the two SUV's with his father, Loren, and Ephraim. Jeremiah grew increasingly anxious and ill tempered throughout the journey. There was very little talking among the men. It was as if the subordinates knew their leader was in a dark mood so they kept their idle talk to a minimum.

Xavier felt a sense of foreboding grow the closer they

drew toward his grandparents' home, and a few hours later when the convoy pulled up the Menes's drive, the foreboding grew into an unexplainable alarm. Xavier looked suspiciously at the house where he had lived all his life. It seemed different to him somehow as if it were no longer his, as if he no longer belonged. The house was a stranger to him.

Jeremiah turned to Loren and muttered quietly, "Stay here with the boy. I need to speak to them alone first to see if what I've been sensing is true." Loren did not question him but simply nodded.

"To see if *what* is true, Father?" Xavier questioned quickly. He didn't like the tone his father used, and the hair on the back of his neck prickled and rose.

Jeremiah turned. "Xavier, you must stay with Loren until I come for you. Do you understand?" He pinned the boy with such a penetrating stare that Xavier could only nod in agreement.

Jeremiah and Ephraim exited the vehicle. After stopping and speaking briefly to the men in the second vehicle, they approached the house. Xavier noted that his father never bothered to knock but entered the house directly, without hesitation. Something must have happened! He didn't need abilities to see that. His abilities! Why didn't he think of it? Xavier immediately closed his eyes and concentrated on his father. He felt his mind drift across the lawn and into the house until he connected with Jeremiah, but suddenly his entire body went cold as if he had been doused by a pail of ice water, and his father's voice rang in his mind.

"No, Son. Do not attempt to infiltrate my mind. You will not be successful. I have the ability to impede intruders. Now, stay where you are. I'll be out in a few minutes."

Moments later, Jeremiah and Ephraim sprinted from the house. Not strolled, not jogged, but sprinted! Jeremiah's face was unmasked with alarm. Then, Loren voiced Xavier's worse fears. "Oh, Lord! They took her!"

Instead of returning to his seat in the vehicle, Jeremiah raced around the SUV and yanked Xavier's door open.

"What's wrong, Father? Who took who?" he blurted out anxiously, though he was sure he already knew.

"Get out of the car, Son. You must stay here with your grand..."

Xavier interrupted, "Father! What's happened?"

Jeremiah stopped and looked at his son with anguish. "It's your mother. They've taken her!"

"What!" Xavier screeched.

"Boy, I can't talk about this now. We need to go after her, and you need to stay here with your grandparents until we return. Now, please get out of the car and go inside," he ordered, and Xavier scrambled out of the backseat. Jeremiah slammed the door shut and raced to the driver's seat. "And, don't wander off your grandparents' property. Dublin will be over any minute to keep you company. You hear me? Don't leave this property!"

The truck roared to life and spit gravel as Jeremiah tore out of the drive. Xavier watched as the vehicles disappeared over the ridge.

"Xavier!" Robbie squealed from behind him.

Xavier turned just as Robbie leaped at him, wrapping her arms around him and knocking him to the ground in a bear hug. She pecked his cheek with a light moist kiss.

"I missed you! Are you okay? I heard all about what happened from my dad! Are you okay?" she rambled off, looking down at him.

"Hey," Xavier managed to utter. "I'm okay, I guess. There's been a lot to deal with..." his voice faded into thought and worry over his mother.

"Robbie! Control yourself girl! Give Sire Wells some breathing room," her father's voice called from behind her.

The title shocked Xavier. Sire Wells? Lord, was he really a prince? It wasn't just the title that surprised him; it was that Mr. Minnows had said it with such revere and awe.

"Come on, you two. Let's get inside," Mr. Minnows

ordered softly, peering around the yard and to the edge of the woods.

Robbie stood and helped Xavier to his feet. "Sorry," she said ruefully. "I just, well, I really missed you. I was really worried that if, Le...Mas..." she shuddered, "well, if *he* found out who you truly were that he'd kill you."

"He very nearly did," he muttered much too quietly for Robbie to hear him.

If Xavier had expected a warm welcome, hugs, and kisses from his grandparents, he would have been sorely mistaken. The welcome he received was one of contemptuous glares and negation. However, this didn't bother Xavier. If they chose to ignore him, he wouldn't have to listen to their endless tirades.

Mr. Minnows helped himself to the gas stove and began preparing a light meal of celery soup. Grandmother opened her mouth ready to protest the nerve of this man coming into her house and using her food as if it were his own. Instead, she huffed and stormed out of the room, down the hall, and into the den, slamming the door behind her. Grandfather did not say a word either; he sat staring blankly at the table, his eyes red and puffy.

"Grandfather?" Xavier whispered. "Are you all right?"

His grandfather looked up blankly, not really seeing him at first. Then, recognition lit up his eyes. "Xavier?" Xavier thought he heard relief in his grandfather's voice. "I thought you had run away. Julia was so furious with us for allowing you to leave that she contacted *him*," he said vacantly.

Xavier concluded that his mother must've called his father when she discovered he was gone. "She came back? I thought grandmother said she ran away because of what happened at the school that day."

"No," Grandfather smiled apathetically. "She really did have a week seminar in Boston. Your grandmother said differently to Mr. Minnows because she was upset and afraid of the abilities you were demonstrating." He paused with a frown, and his gaze began to drift again.

"Grandfather? What happened to mother?" Xavier asked.

The old man looked at him despairingly. "I don't know," he said feebly. "I never saw them. Your mother said that the Premier Guard General had contacted her. It didn't make sense to me then, and it still doesn't. But, she said it had something to do with you, and that you had been kidnapped. So, when she said that she was meeting someone in the woods, I thought she meant *him*, but...then, she never came back." His gaze began to wander again, and he repeated disconnectedly, "She never came back. She never...she never came back." He burst into racking sobs. Then, staggering, Grandfather stood and stumbled down the hall to join his wife in the den.

Mr. Minnows and Robbie stood at the kitchen counter, staring at Xavier anxiously. If for nothing else than to escape their stares, Xavier quietly left the kitchen and climbed the steps to his bedroom. His room was just how he had left it three months before. His dirty laundry was scattered about and posters of the New York Jets still hung on the walls. There were even a dirty glass and dish from a midnight snack. Although nothing had changed, Xavier felt odd in the room. It was as if another boy had lived there. He felt like he had outgrown it, and that it was no longer his room. Even the memories of his life here felt disconnected and dreamlike. He sighed heavily with the realization that nothing would ever be the same for him again. That made him a little sad. Though, he couldn't understand why. His life here had been controversial and hard. He had been neglected and mistreated by his grandparents, and his mother never stood up for him even when she knew her parents were in the wrong. His mother! Guilt clawed at his gut. They had kidnapped her because of him, and here he was belittling her on something she had no say in. After all, they were her parents, and if they had thrown her out onto the streets, she and Xavier would have had no other place to

91

go. He walked to the window and peered out onto the lawn with an array of emotions wheeling through him.

"Are you all right?" Robbie's voice asked timidly from behind him.

He nodded without turning. "Yeah," he said unconvincingly even to himself. Lord, he wished she'd just leave him alone. He didn't want to talk about it. He didn't want to talk about anything.

Robbie walked over to him. "Are you sure? No one would think differently of you if you weren't, you know. With everything you've been through, you have the right to be upset." She placed a hand on his shoulder.

Xavier's head slumped at her touch, and he felt despair surging through him. He fought it the only way he knew how. He became angry, and the anger erupted in a low groan from deep in his throat. Unfortunately, the only person to unleash on was Robbie.

Suddenly, he spun on her, sending her stumbling backwards. "What do you know about it? You know nothing, Robbie! You have no idea what I've been through! No idea!" he spat dangerously quiet. The shock and hurt on her face only fueled his anger more.

"You're right," she said quietly. She didn't recognize this mood, and it scared her. "I don't have any idea what they did to you in that place. I don't have any idea what it'd be like to worry about your mother because some madman has kidnapped her. I have no idea what it would be like to suddenly discover what and who you truly are. I have no idea what it'd be like to finally meet a father who you have no memory of. I have no idea what it's like to be the heir to a throne. I don't know any of it! So, tell me, X. Please, I'm your best friend; we've always told each other everything. Tell me. Please!"

"We tell each other everything?" he bellowed sarcastically. "No, Robbie! *We* don't! We don't tell each other everything!" He was yelling like a madman, and he didn't care. "At least, YOU never did! If you'd told me what

92

was happening with me, maybe I wouldn't have been out in the woods that day. Maybe if you had told me, WILLIAM wouldn't have taken me!" Robbie gasped at the name, and her eyes widened with fear. Xavier ignored her response. "Maybe if you had told me, I wouldn't have been held captive and tortured for nearly TWO MONTHS because THAT'S what he did, Robbie! Every single day, William," another gasp from Robbie, "tortured me. He'd come into my cell, ask me strange questions that he knew I had no answers for, lay his hands on me, and my entire body would burn like it was on fire!" With slow calculating aggressiveness, Xavier stalked toward to the speechless girl. "And, sometimes for a bit of variety, he'd break a bone and then, send Loren in to heal it. Have you ever had bones repeatedly broken, Robbie? Have you ever been healed by rejuvenation powers?" Xavier was inches from her, and he dropped his voice to a murmur. "Well, with no anesthetic, the healing was as torturous as the abuse! I can tell you that! Do you know what day in day out torture can do to someone? Do you? It can make you crazy, and I thought I very nearly was! It got to the point where I'd jump at my own breathing! I would shake at the sound of his voice. I would ball my eyes out at the sight of him! I began to wish I were dead. Every night before I'd go to bed, I'd pray to God to let me die in my sleep. But, death never came, and everyday I'd wake up and face more torture!" He was panting feverishly with emotions he fought to hold back. "Is that what you wanted to know, Robbie?" He grabbed her roughly by arms and shook her. "Is it? Tell me, Robbie, is that what you wanted to know?"

Robbie's face was flushed with shock and tears were streaming down her face. She shook her head unable to speak.

"Xavier," Mr. Minnows's voice growled from the door. He stood tensely, filling the doorway with his arms folded across his chest. "Son, you'll need to release my daughter, now."

All anger deflated in an instant. He looked from Mr. Minnows to Robbie, who stood crying before him. He released her arms, stunned by how out of control he had become.

"Robbie, I..." he stammered apologetically but fell silent. How could he apologize for what he did? There was no apology that could make up for it. He bowed his head with shame.

"Robbie? Why don't you go on down to the kitchen. The soup's ready," her father said gently.

Robbie exited the room without a glance back.

Mr. Minnows studied Xavier for a moment. Then, sighing heavily he approached the boy. "Xavier," he began, "I know Robbie can be meddlesome, but you were completely out of line."

"I know, sir," he replied, without looking up.

"You know, she only wants to help you. She's always been a good friend to you. She didn't deserve that," he continued.

"I," he swallowed the large painful lump forming in his throat, "I know, sir." He felt tears threatening to overflow.

"What would your father think about your behavior tonight? What would he do if he caught you behaving like that? Would he approve?" he asked quietly.

Heavy tears spilled over Xavier's eyelids and down his cheeks. He turned his back to Mr. Minnows, ashamed. He felt coolness engulfing him as Mr. Minnows attempted to breach his emotions.

"I know what you're trying to do Mr. Minnows. Don't." He turned to face the man. Consumed with guilt, he gave a low groan and more tears ran over onto his cheeks. "You don't need to read my emotions! It wouldn't help. Even I can't make sense of them. There," his voice choked on a sob, "are...too... many of ...them! There's something wrong with me." Xavier broke down completely, falling to his knees sobbing.

Mr. Minnows knelt beside Xavier and stroked his back

until the outburst had subsided. "Xavier, there's nothing wrong with you. You've been through hell," he said frankly, and Xavier respected him for it. "You've had a horrific ordeal, and the disappearance of your mother has only compounded it. It's perfectly understandable for your emotions to be a little haywire." He paused and stroked the boy's cheek gently. "You know, your father will find her! I've known your father since we were kids. He's as stubborn as they come. If he wants something, there's nothing that can stop him. He will find her!"

Xavier looked up at him and smiled weakly. "Thanks, Mr. Minnows."

They sat in silence until Mr. Minnows patted his head affectionately and said, "Now, what do you say about going downstairs and apologizing to Robbie?"

"Yes, sir," he replied, wiping the tears from his cheeks.

* * * * *

For the next several days, Xavier stayed at his grandparents' home with Mr. Minnows and Robbie. Robbie never mentioned the outburst or asked him about his time at the Institute again. And, as the days passed, Xavier began to feel more and more relaxed.

One particularly dreary day turned out to be the most fun, and Xavier was beginning to enjoy himself for the first time since his return. The children had spent most of the afternoon in the barn playing in the loft and orchestrating hay battles. By late afternoon, the rain intensified into a torrential downpour, and when Mr. Minnows called the children in for supper, they raced out from the security of the barn and into the heavy rain. Xavier struggled up the muddy, slippery incline at the back of the house; when suddenly, Robbie grabbed his left ankle and yanked his feet out from under him. He fell face first into the muddy hill and slid to the bottom. He was covered with mud and muck, and he even had mud in his ears.

"Yuk, why did you do that?" he growled as Robbie

howled with laughter. He smeared the mud out of his eyes and glowered up at her. She was doubled over in hysteria and was dangerously close to falling over. "Okay, have it your way then," Xavier whispered with an ornery grin and ran at her.

Robbie's eyes widened, and she squealed as she tried to escape him. In just three strides, Xavier caught her by the waist, and the two tumbled down the hill landing in a tangled, giggling heap.

"Xavier! Look at me! I'm a mess!" she yelled through her giggles.

"Well? Let that be a lesson to you! Don't start something if you're not prepared to take the consequences!" he laughed heartily.

"Yes, Sire," she scoffed as she smashed a fist full of mud in his face.

This ignited an all out mud battle, and by the time the children reached the house, there wasn't one inch of their bodies free of mud. Mr. Minnows could hardly stand as he laughed at the sight of them.

Xavier did well to keep his mind off his mother's disappearance during the day, but at night as he lay in his bed waiting for sleep to come, he found himself dwelling on the torture she was undoubtedly enduring at the hands of William LeMasters. When sleep did finally overtake him, the onslaught of nightmares was of no help. One dream, in particular, haunted him.

The dream always began in a field. Daisies and Black-eyed Susans peppered the landscape like a checkerboard of color, and a narrow brook meandered along the eastern edge of the clearing. It was evening and the falling sun washed over Xavier's face in a golden hue. Long fingering shadows reached out from the trees that bordered the west side, casting half the field into darkness. His mother stood beside him, loosely holding Brewster's reins.

"Well?" Julia asked softly. "Are you coming?" She gestured toward the horse.

Xavier grinned and climbed onto Brewster's saddle. They rode Brewster around the field, Xavier controlling the reins. With a bump from his heel, Brewster began to gallop. He wielded the horse toward the gurgling creek and plunged through the water, spraying his mother on the back of the horse.

Julia squealed in his ear, "Jeremiah Xavier! I'm going to beat you, boy!"

Her laughter continued to echo in his ears as suddenly the field vanished. He found himself in a cell similar to the one at the Institute; only here, he was an observer, not the subject of torture. His mother lay on the table with her arms and legs strapped down. He tried calling to her, but she couldn't seem to hear him. He tried going to her, but he was rooted to the spot and couldn't move. All he could do was watch what was about to occur. Then, LeMasters entered the room, cocky and sneering. His mother cried and struggled against the binds at the sight of the ominous man towering over her. As he reached out to touch her, she cowered away from him, begging. Without questions or even speaking, he subjected her to the same torturous powers that Xavier had endured.

Then, one night this dream took an unexpected twist. When the cell materialized in Xavier's mind, his mother was bound to a table as she always had been in the dream. However, this time, LeMasters was not alone; Danson and Dr. Angelo were with him. They surrounded the table, looking down at his crying mother.

And, for the first time, LeMasters spoke. "Jeremiah is close. It's time to move on to the next phase of my plan. Oh, Jeremiah will suffer. He may have been able to save his son, but he will arrive too late to save his love," he smiled gleefully down at the sobbing woman. "It's nothing personal, but you've outlived your use. Goodbye, Mrs. Wells." They raised their arms in unison, and a great crimson light blinded Xavier.

"NO!" Xavier screamed, sitting up in his bed. "NO!

MOTHER!"

Mr. Minnows burst into the room and flicked on the light. "Xavier?" He was at his side in an instant.

"It's mom! They've killed her! They've killed her! Father was too late. They've killed her!" Xavier jumped from the bed and raced out of the room.

"Xavier! Xavier, calm down. It was only a dream," Dublin Minnows called as he ran after him.

"I've got to find Father! I have to find Father and tell him. I have to find Mother. I've got find her," Xavier rambled as he ran through the kitchen toward the back door.

"Xavier!" Mr. Minnows grabbed him by the shoulders and shook him. "It was just a dream!"

Xavier blinked slowly and tried to focus on Mr. Minnows. "What?" He shook his head. "A dream?" He frowned thoughtfully. Finally, he dragged his gaze back to Mr. Minnows with clear alert eyes. "Mr. Minnows?" He glanced around the room. "Why am I in the kitchen? What's going on?"

"You were sleep walking, I think. Do you remember the dream?" he asked.

The puzzlement on the boy's face contorted into wide-eyed terror, and he nodded. "They were torturing her, but William LeMasters sensed Father was near...and...they ...they killed her," he stammered with a shiver.

"What's going on? Is Xavier okay? I heard him screaming," Robbie asked from the doorway.

"He's all right, sweetie. Just a bad dream," Mr. Minnows replied, turning to his daughter.

"Do you think Father has found her yet? Do you think she'll be okay, Mr. Minnows?" Xavier asked.

"I *know* your father will find her. He'll bring her back. I have no doubt of that!" he said earnestly, patting the Xavier's head. This seemed to satisfy the boy, and he was able to get both children back to bed after a small snack and a mug of warm milk.

Dublin reclined on the bed, staring at the ceiling

unable to sleep. He looked down at the sleeping children on the floor next to him and smiled. The children had long since fallen asleep and were snuggled next to one another in sleeping bags. Robbie had refused to leave Xavier after his nightmare and had insisted they camp out in the boy's room. The two children were sleeping peacefully now, but Dublin was wide-awake. The boy's dream concerned him. He feared that it might not have been a dream at all but a premonition. He had heard that a prophet's ability to foresee the future sometimes occurred in their dreams when their minds were most relaxed. Lord, he hoped he was wrong! He knew Jeremiah would find Julia, but if he was right about the boy's dream, he could only pray that Jeremiah would find her in time.

* * * * *

The following week, however, Jeremiah returned alone. Robbie and Xavier were in the barn, taking turns performing acrobats off the loft ladder into an enormous pile of hay.

"Wahoo!" Xavier exclaimed as he did a flip and flopped easily into the hay.

"That was awesome, X. Watch this!" Robbie dove off the ladder in a graceful swan dive and at the last moment tucked her head and landed gracefully on her back.

"Terrific! Hey, watch this!" he said as he climbed the ladder once again. Xavier threw himself off the ladder, did a twist and two flips, before landing on his backside.

"Whoa, that was…"

"Xavier?" Jeremiah called from the barn door.

"Father!" he gasped, jumping to his feet and racing to him. Jeremiah embraced his son with a grievous sigh.

"Hello, King Wells," Robbie chirped behind them.

"Hello, Robbie," he smiled weakly down at her. "How've you been?"

"Good, Sire. I'm going up to the house and help Dad with lunch," she told Xavier and skipped out of the barn.

"Father? How long have you been here? Where's

mother? Did you find her? Is she okay?" he blurted out in one long breath.

Jeremiah looked at his son, looking up at him so trustingly, so assured that he had fixed everything and brought his mother home to him. How could he tell him? He had rehearsed several scenarios, but now, none of them seemed right. How could he tell him?

"Father?" Xavier questioned.

"Son," he began hoarsely, "your mother... Julia..." he stopped and tears swelled in his eyes. "Your mother is... She's dead, Xavier."

"What?" he whispered, staring up at his father, willing for his ears to take back what he had just heard. "No, she can't be," he muttered, shaking his head. The nightmare of his mother's torturous death lingered in his memory like a horrible ghost. "No! No, no, no!" His eyes flashed accusingly at his father. "You said you were going to help her. Mr. Minnows said you would bring her back!"

"I tried, Son. I tried," he moaned, running a shaking hand through his hair.

"NO! YOU SAID YOU WOULD! I WANT MY MOTHER!" Xavier threw his fists against his father's chest, and began punching him with all his strength. "NO! SHE CAN'T BE DEAD! I WANT HER, FATHER. GOD, PLEASE, NO! NOOOOOO!" He burst into tears and sobbed uncontrollably, his anger dissolving into anguish. "Please, Father. Please, I want my mom. Please!"

Jeremiah hadn't tried to shield his son's blows. Instead, he pulled him close and cried with him. "I'm sorry, Son. I'm so, so sorry."

Chapter 9
Warwood Castle
★ ★ ★ ★ ★

For Xavier, the trip to Newfoundland the next morning was uneventful and unmemorable. To him, it seemed as if the world had moved on without him. He and his father traveled with the Minnows family to the airport where Loren, Ephraim, and the rest of the Premier Royal Guard met them. They continued the journey to the kingdom of Warwood by Leer Jet. Xavier did not speak at all throughout the entire journey. Robbie seemed to be keeping her distance from him. She stayed close to her parents and her younger sister, but occasionally she'd throw a worried look in his direction. Xavier often found himself between Loren and his father. His father would not leave his side, which he began to find a bit smothering. All he really wanted was to be left alone. He wanted a place to hide.

By late that afternoon, the group arrived at a small airport on the island of Warwood. As they exited the aircraft, Xavier saw a cartel of limousines with blackened windows waiting like bodyguards along the side of the runway. Jeremiah and Loren led Xavier to the second limo.

Xavier had no idea what to expect in regards to his father's kingdom, but as the vehicles coasted toward the towering gatehouse jutting upward from a glistening white wall that stretched in either direction before curving out of sight, he was simply in awe. As the caravan rolled across the drawbridge and through the archway of the gatehouse, Xavier couldn't help but crane out his open window to get a glimpse at its dwarfing size. Loren pulled him back into the vehicle, chuckling.

"Pretty magnificent, isn't it?" he said, pressing a button on the console and rolling up Xavier's window.

Xavier could only nod his response and turned to take in the sights of his new home like a thirsty nomad spotting an oasis. Five guards stood at post just inside the entrance, dressed in navy and silver uniforms. Their ink blue capes swayed in the light breeze, and they knelt as the caravan passed. As the cars pulled slowly into an enormous courtyard within the castle's walls, an eager crowd converged toward the limos.

"Who are all these people? Why are they waving at us?" Xavier asked.

Loren smiled. "They are your loyal subjects, Your Highness. They are citizens of your kingdom. They're eager to see their king's son. They're waving to you, Xavier."

'My kingdom?' Xavier thought with an awkward shudder. 'This is my kingdom? I must be dreaming.'

Loren chuckled at the boy's expression of dismay. "Don't worry. Jeremiah won't throw you to the wolves until you've had some time to settle in and adjust."

Xavier looked at his father in the mid-cabin of the limousine. He looked quite comfortable and quite at home waving out the window to the people who came out to greet the vehicles. Xavier looked beyond the mob to a bustling open market. People meandered among the numerous stands, selling anything from fruit, to cloaks and robes, to jewelry.

"This is Center Square. Peddlers and craftsmen bring their goods here to sell," Loren told him, peering out at the enormous cluttered market.

Finally, the vehicle crept to a gentle stop in front of the small portable shops at Center Square, and his father's door opened.

"What's going on?" Xavier questioned.

"Ah, well, your father has been on holiday for over a month. I imagine he's going to make a public statement now so that you'll be left alone until the time is right for your Induction into society," Loren said in a hush.

"My what?" Xavier frowned.

"Your introduction, your acceptance," Loren clarified.

Outside the car, Jeremiah's voice rang out authoritatively over the chime of voices chanting his name. "My friends. My colleagues, my brethren!" All the voices stopped at once. "I appreciate this warm welcome and happy returns you present here for us today as does my son. Unfortunately, the boy has been through quite an ordeal as I am sure you are all aware, and he needs his rest. However, I would like to invite all citizens to come to your prince's Induction next Saturday. We shall have a wonderful celebration for his return home. Thank you for honoring my wishes. Good evening to you all." Jeremiah returned to the limo, and the vehicle continued its short journey to the palace, leaving the market behind them.

Several moments later, the car rolled to a stop, and Xavier peered out the window. An enormous marbled palace rose before him with ivy climbing its walls in a web of green. Four turrets soared into the sky from the four corners of the building with a guard in each tower's flue. And, along the roofline, looming at each nook and cranny, hideous gargoyles leered down at him in smiles that looked more like snarls. The creatures appeared so life like that Xavier expected them to swoop down on him at any moment. He shifted uneasily as he continued to study the watchful beasts. But, upon closer inspection, Xavier realized that the gargoyles' mouths served as drainage pipes for the storm gutters from the roof. He smiled at the thought of water gushing out of their gaping mouths, and suddenly the creatures didn't seem so menacing.

Xavier's gaze drifted down the smooth pale walls and the string of stained-glass windows until his eyes settled on the arched entrance. Engraved angels, that looked more like chubby babies, played peek-a-boo among the vines and leaves there. At the summit of the archway, an etched seal comprised of two crossed swords and four animals loomed importantly. Xavier's eyes swept over the massive building once more before whispering, "Wow!"

Jeremiah got out and opened Xavier's door. "Come on, Son. Let's get settled. It's been a very long day," he said as he held his hand out to the boy.

Xavier placed his hand into his father's, suddenly feeling very tired. Jeremiah led him into the building with several guards following them. Jeremiah guided him through an atrium and down a long hallway. They entered a grand vestibule where a broad sweeping staircase ascended up to a landing. Jeremiah shepherded him up the stairs and over to a large gold door. With a wave of Jeremiah's hand, the door sprang open, and they entered a spacious room. At the far side of the room, a string of beautifully stained glass windows towered toward the ceiling. On its adjacent wall, a spectacular stone hearth illuminated the room in a soft, wavering light. To his left, Xavier found a foyer that opened up into dinning room and a large curving stairwell. He stepped away from his father, spinning around with fascination.

"Welcome home," Jeremiah replied.

"Home? I live here?" he responded, unable to sound anything but amazed.

Jeremiah chuckled. "Yes, Son. This is our home."

A plump woman tottered into the room, rosy cheeked and all smiles. "Sire! It's so good to have you home! May I take your cloak, sir?"

"Ah, Mrs. Sommers! Yes, thank you. Xavier, this is Mrs. Sommers, the residence assistant and your governess," he said, waving Xavier to him.

Xavier turned and approached the bubbly woman.

"My word. Oh, my goodness," tears filled the woman's eyes, puzzling Xavier. She pulled him into a warm bear hug and squeezed the breath out of him. When she finally released him, Xavier couldn't help but smile at her genuine affection. "Prince Wells, it's so wonderful to see you again. I haven't seen you since you were an infant. You've grown to be such a handsome boy. You look so much like your father when he was your age."

"You knew my father when he was a boy?" Xavier asked, his curiosity sparked.

"Of course! I've been the residence assistant and governess here since your father was a toddler. I could tell you some stories..."

"Ah, Emma. Let's save the stories for another time, shall we?" Jeremiah interrupted. "Besides, I'm not so certain I want my son to know some of those stories."

"Yes, Sire," she answered dutifully but winked secretively at Xavier.

"Would you please show the boy to his room and get him a bath? We'll have dinner in the dining hall this evening," Jeremiah ordered, and Mrs. Sommers nodded. Then, he turned to Xavier and placed a hand on his shoulder, regarding him softly. "Go on, Son. Get cleaned up, and I'll see you in an hour for dinner. I have a couple of loose ends I need to take care of."

"Come, Xavier," Mrs. Sommer's gentle voice called from behind him. Xavier turned and followed the woman up the granite staircase. As she led him the short distance down the loft walkway, Xavier peered over the banister and watched his father on the floor below speaking softly to a tall man in a black suit. Jeremiah clapped the older man on the back and chuckled before exiting the room.

"This is your room," Mrs. Sommers announced, drawing his attention to the first door. "And, your father's room is next door," she told him, pointing to the last door at the end of the walkway. Mrs. Sommers opened the door to the room and flicked on the light. Xavier's mouth dropped in amazement; his room was fit for a... well, a prince! In addition to the blue marbled hearth where a lazy fire licked the aspen logs, the room's entire far wall was a patchwork of windows that overlooked a luscious patio garden. Aside from the permanent fixtures in the room, it was elaborately furnished with a beautiful oak sleigh bed and matching bureau, four large oak bookcases filled with a variety of children's books and reference books, a desk with a state of the art computer, and lastly, but most importantly, toys! There were toys and games cluttering the large window seat, there were games stacked on two additional bookcases, and there were toys spilling out of a large oak chest.

"Wow," he said simply.

She smiled. "Your father did it," she confessed. "He did it all by himself. The day he got notice that your abilities were manifesting, he spent the day preparing your room."

"He did?" he questioned quietly.

"Yes, dear. He did," she said earnestly.

Xavier peered around the room again with a renewed appreciation.

"Well, sweetie. Let's get that bath," she announced and ushered him through a door at the right of the room.

The bathroom was bigger than his bedroom at his grandparents', and the bathtub resembled a small swimming pool. There was even a separate shower stall enclosed in frosted glass. Every piece, every tile, every bit of chrome shined like new.

"Okay, off with those clothes, young man," Mrs. Sommers ordered, tugging at his sweatshirt.

"No!" he blurted as he jumped back. "I...I'll do it myself," he replied anxiously.

Mrs. Sommers stepped back uneasily. "All right, Young Sire. Calm down; you're safe here." She looked down compassionately at the boy. "Okay, you undress yourself, and I'll start your bath and lay out your dinner clothes."

Xavier nodded solemnly and watched as Mrs. Sommers turned, started his bath, and then left the room. Once alone, he stripped off his clothes and sank into the tub, relaxing in its warmth. When Mrs. Sommers returned, her eyes widened with dismay. The ugly welts on Xavier's chest and back had faded considerably but were still very noticeable. Xavier tensed and covered himself.

"Here...here are your... dinner clothes and some fresh under clothes," she stumbled, trying to mask her distress. "You'll find your loafers in the closet. If you need anything at all, just call. Okay?" She smiled sweetly at him before she left the room.

* * * * *

An hour later, Mrs. Sommers led Xavier into the dining hall. His father sat at the far end of the table and smiled when he entered the room. Mrs. Sommers escorted him quickly to the seat on Jeremiah's right.

"Hello, Son. Did you find your room satisfactory?" Jeremiah inquired.

"Yes, sir. Thank you, it's great," he replied with mild fervor.

Jeremiah beamed at his son.

The thin, older man dressed in the black suit he had seen his father with earlier entered the room carrying a large pot. "Soup, Sire?" the man inquired.

"Yes, Milton. Thank you," Jeremiah answered and motioned toward the table. "Xavier, this is Milton, my personal assistant. Milton this is my son, Xavier."

"How do you do, Young Sire?" Milton drawled in a low smooth voice.

"Hello, sir. Nice to meet you," Xavier responded, extending his hand to the servant.

Milton shook his hand and nodded a greeting before ladling out soup into their bowls. Then, he left the room as quietly as he had entered.

Father and Son sat in silence, both toying with their food. Jeremiah watched his son and after a moment cleared his throat.

"Xavier?" he began. "We should discuss what happened to your mom. We really haven't discussed any of it."

"No." Xavier interrupted almost harshly. He glared up at his father. "No, sir. I don't want to talk about it."

Jeremiah considered him a moment. "We really should, Son. Bottling it up won't help ..."

"Neither will talking about it, *Father*," he blurted, his voice raising an octave.

"Xavier?" Jeremiah warned. "Please keep a respectful tone."

Xavier lowered his eyes submissively and dropped his spoon with a clang. He slouched defiantly in his seat with a heavy sigh. *'Fine,'* he thought bitterly. *'He can talk all he wants, but I don't have to listen to him. He can't make me listen or talk about anything.'* He folded his arms across his chest and pouted.

"Son, you're going to have to remember that I CAN read minds. And, your thoughts and anger are so strong you might as well be shouting them. So, you may not need to talk for me to communicate with you."

"Stop it!" Xavier stood up, livid. "Stop it! I don't want to talk or *communicate* about any of it! It won't bring her back so why bother? I - don't – want – to – talk – about - it! Got it? So, just leave me alone!" he yelled, throwing his napkin across the table.

"Sit down, Xavier," Jeremiah said evenly, though anger was edging into his voice.

"NO! I won't!" he shouted. "You've been my father for, what, barely a month! You can't tell me what to do and order me around. I don't have to listen to *you!*"

Jeremiah straightened noticeably and his eyes thundered. "Yes, you do because I AM your father," Jeremiah's voice rose. "And, you better get a hold of that temper of yours before you say or do something you'll regret. Now, sit down."

"Make me!" the boy growled, glaring challengingly at Jeremiah.

Jeremiah's chair squealed in protest as he jumped to his feet, his eyes burrowing into Xavier. "If you don't watch that tone you choose to use with me, you'll find your backside very sore, young man," he cautioned quietly.

"Go to hell, *Father*," he hissed and stomped out of the room, sending his chair clattering to the floor.

"Xavier!" Jeremiah's voice thundered after him.

Xavier raced through the foyer and up the stairs. He could hear his father's heavy footsteps just paces behind him.

"Sire, there's a call from..." Milton's voice trailed away at the sight of Father and Son. The Premier looked positively livid.

"Not now, Milton!" the King growled as he passed the servant and bounded up the steps three at a time. "Xavier! Stop right there, Son!" Jeremiah warned.

But, Xavier did not stop. He ran to his room, slammed the door shut, and locked it quickly behind him. He barely took a step toward his bed when he heard the door handle rattle.

"Xavier! Open this door at once!" his father growled.

"No! Go away!" he spat, backing farther into the room.

In the next instant, the door flew open with an ear splitting bang. Jeremiah stood on the other side of the door with one hand raised, and his eyes flashing with anger. In three long strides, he had the boy's arms pinned in his hands.

"What do you think you're doing? What did I say would happen if you disrespected an adult again?" he grumbled.

Xavier looked up at his father with wide eyes, but did not answer.

"What did I say?" Jeremiah growled, shaking him.

Tears spilled over Xavier's cheeks. "I don't want to

talk about her, Father!" he sobbed. "It hurts too much. Please! God, please, don't make me! Oh, God!" The boy wailed and dropped to his knees, his entire body shaking.

Jeremiah's anger evaporated instantly. He knelt beside the boy and scooped him into his arms, holding him close to his chest like an infant. When the sobs began to subside, Jeremiah carried the boy to the bed and sat next to him, rubbing his back soothingly. For several minutes, not a word was said.

Finally, very quietly, Jeremiah spoke, "Okay, Son. We won't discuss this tonight, but Xavier, we will talk about this. In order to begin the healing process, we must face what happened to your mother. Do you understand?"

Xavier responded hoarsely, "But I don't want to heal. I don't want to forget her."

"Son, moving on and healing doesn't mean you'll forget her! Your mother would not want you to die with her."

Xavier nodded but said nothing more. He closed his eyes, relaxing under his father's gentle touch, and soon he was drifting off to sleep.

Jeremiah stayed with Xavier even after he had fallen asleep. He watched the boy sleep peacefully before him. Then, carefully so as not to wake him, he removed Xavier's shoes, undressed him, and pulled the plush quilt up around him. With a gentle stroke to the boy's soft jaw, Jeremiah stood and quietly left the room.

Chapter 10
Discipline
★ ★ ★ ★ ★

That night, Xavier dreamt of the long stone corridor again. He stumbled down the passage with unexplainable fear. A breath of cool air tickled the back of his neck, and somewhere he could hear a chorus of dripping water. The roughly cut stone was damp and cold, and along the walls, oil lanterns dangled recklessly with their flames flickering from the draft that haunted the passage. The low hum that vibrated and echoed all around him intensified the closer he drew toward the red door at the end of the corridor. Something of great power lay just beyond it. The brass knob rattled as if the power, lying in wait like a predator, fought to escape. Ever so slowly, Xavier reached for the knob and turned it. The door was locked. Suddenly, the corridor and the humming power faded and the exhilaration of the unknown was lost.

As the dream shifted, Xavier found himself, once again, in the clinical white room of his mother's prison. She was tied to a table, wearing a simple hospital gown. Her eyes were sunken and dark, and she was sobbing quietly.

The moment the door to the cell opened, his mother's sobs intensified. She pleaded and begged, and for the first time, Xavier was able to hear her words.

"Where is my son? What have you done to him?" she demanded weakly.

Of course, William LeMasters did not answer. He glared hungrily down at her with wild, beastly eyes. Julia looked up at him. Slowly, her face paled, and her eyes grew wide with quiet realization.

"No," she moaned, shaking her head. "Please, no! Please don't!" She struggled frantically against her binds, crying uncontrollably. LeMasters reached out to stroke her cheek, but she savagely jerked her head away. "NO!" she screeched.

He glowered down at her for several seconds, his face stone-like and angry. Then, he smirked heinously down at her as he raised his arms and delivered torturous blow after blow into her until she went limp with exhaustion and no longer had the strength to fight against him. Xavier watched as his mother endured every punishment LeMasters could fathom. He witnessed as LeMasters inflicted abuse on his mother that was outside the use of empowerments, abuse that was as old and as barbaric as ancient nobility rights. Abuse that he wished he could close his mind to but couldn't. Abuse that no twelve year old should ever witness. His mother's cries resounded in his memories long after he awoke.

* * * * *

The next morning, Jeremiah, true to his word, entered Xavier's room. Xavier had just finished showering and had a towel wrapped around his waist. His small, bared chest displayed the apparent torture he had endured at the hands of William LeMasters. Anger surged through Jeremiah as he surveyed the vivid, pink scars screaming on the boy's skin. Then, Xavier turned.

"Good morning," Jeremiah replied, quickly masking his feelings with a smile.

"Morning, Father," he replied, not quite meeting his eyes.

112

"Get dressed, Son. I've invited Dublin and his family over for breakfast, and we need to have a little talk before we face our guests."

"Mr. Minnows?" he said blankly. Then, the boy's face lit up. "Robbie's coming?"

Jeremiah nodded. Immediately, Xavier scurried to collect the clothes on top his bureau that Mrs. Sommers had laid out for him while he showered. Quickly, he pulled on his clothes and sat on the edge of his bed, pulling on his socks and shoes. He looked at his father expectantly who was ambling about the room, looking at the toys and books. Jeremiah was a very large yet trim man. Even through the ink blue cloak, Xavier was left with little doubt that his father's bulk was all muscle. A surge of pride, admiration, and respect wafted through him. Finally, Jeremiah turned and caught Xavier studying him, and a great coolness engulfed Xavier's entire body.

"Father," he began, sighing dejectedly, "I'll talk. There's no need to invade my thoughts."

His father smiled briefly and nodded. "Okay, Son. You know, you're the only person I know in our kingdom that can do that."

"Do what, sir?" he questioned, puzzled.

"Know when I'm breaching your thoughts," he said simply. "Now," he began as he crossed the room and sat on the bed next to Xavier, "let's discuss a few things. First, Son, your behavior last night at the dinner table was handled very poorly. You were rude and insolent. If you choose to behave like that again, your temper won't be the only thing hot. Do you understand me?"

"Yes," Xavier muttered.

"Yes, sir," his father corrected.

"Yes, sir," he repeated.

"Good." Jeremiah nodded with satisfaction. He studied Xavier's downcast head a moment, his face softening. "Xavier," he began, "I know it hurts to talk about what happened to your..." he stopped abruptly, a muscle

113

quivering in his jaw. As he continued, his voice dropped in volume, "I know it's hard to talk about your mother. It's not easy for me either, Son. No matter what you may think, I loved your mother. I would have done anything for her. In fact, I did. It was by her request that I didn't visit or write you. She felt your grandparents would have been tougher with you if I had." He sighed and rubbed his jaw, peering down at Xavier. He stroked the boy's cheek with the back of his hand before continuing. "Dublin told me that you dreamt of your mother's death. What did you see?"

Xavier squirmed on the edge of his bed. Lord! He didn't want to relive that! "Please, Father," he pleaded, "I can't." His thoughts drifted to the dream.

"Xavier, I wouldn't ask if I didn't think it was important. Come on, Son," he coaxed, turning the boy to face him. "Tell me about the dream."

Xavier closed his eyes and released a raspy moan. "They had mom tied down to a table," he spoke in a quiet rush.

"Who do you mean by they?" Jeremiah asked softly.

"William, Danson, and Dr. Angelo. They had her strapped to a table and they... they were torturing her," his voice quavered. "Then, they got word that you were near, that you had come to rescue her, and they ki... killed her. They joined their abilities and killed her. They killed her, Father!" he sobbed. "Oh, God! It should have been me! They kidnapped her because of me! She was looking for me when they took her. It should have been me! I should have died, not her!" A great despairing howl erupted from his throat. He clamped his eyes shut and covered his face with his hands, trying to hide from the guilt that consumed him. He felt weak and unworthy to be the Prince of Warwood.

"Don't think that!" Jeremiah hissed and grabbed Xavier's arms roughly.

Xavier opened his eyes and was greeted by a fierce stare of resolution.

"It is not your fault, Son. Dear, God! Have you been

114

hording these thoughts all this time?" he gasped. "It's not your fault! There's only one person that carries that blame, and that's William. Not you. Not me. Not anyone but William. Okay?"

Xavier's eyes brimmed with tears, and he nodded briskly. "I just," he fought back tears. "I just, I miss her, Father. I really miss her."

Jeremiah softened and pulled the boy into his arms. "I know. I miss her too."

* * * * *

At breakfast, the Minnows family was jovial and lively. They joked, laughed, and told stories. Father and Son welcomed the change, and Xavier found himself lost in the enjoyment of it.

"Oh, come off of it Jer! You know that Loren was the catalyst of all the mischief we got ourselves into. Don't blame me for that little indiscretion!" Dublin laughed.

"Yeah, yeah. Loren was the mastermind; I'll give you that. However, if I remember correctly, Dub, it was you that placed the bursting bubbles in the commode! Poor Mr. Peel!"

"Oh," Dublin choked out through his laughter. "That's right! Mr. Peel was on the commode when it blew up." Dublin could barely utter the last of the words for his wild laughter had rendered him helpless.

"He thought that I had tried to kill him and refused to come into work the next day. My father was furious! I couldn't sit properly for a week thanks to you," Jeremiah smiled sheepishly.

Dublin Minnows laughed loudly and heartily. His wife, Tamarah, elbowed him and gave him a reproving look, which only increased his laughter.

Mrs. Minnows was a pretty petite woman with short blond hair and electric blue eyes that were like peering into tropical pools of water. Their youngest daughter, Brittany, was the spitting image of her.

"In case you haven't noticed, your dad and my dad

and Loren and Ephraim were all buddies growing up," Robbie told him. "I've heard some wild stories about all the trouble they got into. Dad's right, though. Loren always seemed to be the engineer." She smiled.

"It appears so," Xavier laughed.

As the adults moved on to less jovial conversations, Robbie turned to Xavier and asked, "Are you nervous?"

"Nervous? About what?" he asked, looking at her.

"Are you nervous about your Induction?" she repeated.

"Oh, I guess. Are you?" he shrugged.

"Why would I be nervous? Only royalty have Inductions, X. It's sort of your right of passage to the throne."

"Oh," he said thickly, and his stomach fluttered. He lowered his spoon, suddenly not hungry. He turned to Jeremiah who was now giving directions to Milton.

"Father?" he muttered, tugging on Jeremiah's sleeve.

"What is it, Son?" Jeremiah asked, turning to him.

"It's about my Induction. It's this Saturday?" he asked.

His father nodded, "Yes, what about it?"

"What exactly happens at an Induction?" he asked, his brow furrowed.

Jeremiah chortled. "You're anxious about the ceremony?"

Xavier nodded.

"There's nothing to be concerned about. You'll do just fine. Basically, it's a banquet. I must make a speech and recite lines from The Chronicles," he began.

"The Chronicles?" Xavier inquired.

"The Chronicles is a book. It contains our laws, customs, and history. I will be performing the Royal Oath Ceremony from the Chronicles," he answered. Xavier nodded. "And," he continued, "let's see. There's dancing and a formal dinner. Your duties as the guest of honor will be greeting your guests, dancing with delegates' daughters,

116

and adjourning the Induction Ceremony," Jeremiah explained.

"I have to dance? I have to dance with strange girls?" Xavier asked, horrified.

Dublin snickered loudly and coughed in his apple juice.

Jeremiah kept a straight face. "Yes, Son. It's your duty."

"Sire, I'd be careful calling officials' daughters strange, even if it's true," Dublin joked.

"Dublin!" Mrs. Minnows gasped, smacking his arm. "What a horrible thing to say!"

"But, I don't know how to dance!" Xavier blurted out, becoming more anxious by the minute.

The table grew instantly quiet, and all eyes fell on Xavier. He felt heat in his cheeks and bowed his head.

"Oh." Jeremiah looked down at his son frowning. "Ah, well, I guess, ah…"

"Goodness, Jeremiah!" Mrs. Minnows said exasperated. "Xavier, honey. I can teach you to dance. Don't worry, sweetie, you'll be ready for your Induction." She reassured him with a smile. Xavier relaxed and smiled back at her.

"Thank you, Tamarah," Jeremiah replied.

By the end of breakfast, the group made their way into the reception room, where they sat sipping tea next to the crackling fire. The adults began to discuss upcoming political proposals from work.

Robbie rolled her eyes in boredom. "Xavier, show me your room," She prompted. "Let's leave these old fuddy duddies to talk about boring stuff."

"I heard that!" her father growled jokingly.

Robbie stuck her tongue out at her father and bounced toward the stairs. Xavier, however, paused, remembering the crash course in manners Mrs. Sommers had taught him.

"Father? May I be excused?"

117

"Yes, Son. You may," he nodded.

"Mr. and Mrs. Minnows, thank you for coming to breakfast. We greatly appreciated your company. Please excuse me?" he curtsied toward the Minnows. Brittany snickered at her mother's side.

Mr. Minnows rose and nodded to Xavier. "Thank you, Sire. It was a privilege."

As Xavier led Robbie up the staircase, she hissed in disgust, "What was that all about?"

He shrugged uneasily.

"Well, don't expect me to do all that bowing and *"yes, Sire"* stuff!" she told him.

"Please, don't. You're the only normal thing in my suddenly very weird life," he muttered.

The children climbed the stairs and entered Xavier's room.

"Wow!" Robbie exclaimed. "Look at all the toys!"

Xavier grinned. "Yeah, I know. Mrs. Sommers said that Father did it all himself."

"He's got great taste in toys! Look at this Xavier! A Game Cube!" She wandered around his room, aimlessly looking over his toys before finally sitting next to him on the bed. "Boy, it's a far cry from your room at the Meneses'."

Xavier nodded without a word.

"Oh, Jeez! I'm sorry, X! I didn't mean to make you feel bad and think of your mom." Robbie guessed. "I just didn't..."

"Robbie, it's okay. I'm okay with it. I mean, I miss her," he paused. "I miss her a lot, but Father and I talked it all out this morning. I'm doing better." He smiled feebly at her.

She gave him a funny look.

"What?" he questioned his brow furrowing.

"Well," she began hesitantly, "when my family came this morning, Milton led us into the receiving room to wait for you and your dad. And, well, a couple of maids were talking about a...fight that...you and your dad had," she said not meeting his eyes.

Xavier blushed. "Oh, they were, were they?" he said quietly. He stood and crossed the room. "What did they say?"

"Well," she continued uneasily, "They said that they heard you shouting at him. They said that you acted like a spoiled little prince and that King Wells should have taken a strap to your backside." At the look on Xavier's face, Robbie pressed on quickly, "My father told them to keep their mouths shut. He told them that they had no right to discuss such personal matters about the Premier and his son, and such talk could get them fired." She watched him, fidgeting absentmindedly with the books on the shelves. "Xavier?"

He didn't look at her.

"Is what they said true? Did you really yell at your father, the *King*, like that?" she asked, almost whispering.

He still wouldn't look at her.

She guessed the truth. "What were you thinking? Jeez! Look, I know you're not used to having a dad around, so here's some advice. Fathers are a lot of fun, but if you spark their anger, you'd better watch out."

"Oh, thanks a lot!" he chastised. "All I need is one more person's advice!"

"I'm only trying to help! I mean your mom ignored your occasional sassiness, but believe me, X, your father won't."

"Okay, okay. Enough lectures. Don't you think my father's already told me all this? Let's just drop it, okay? Can we change the subject?"

Robbie shrugged and fidgeted with a model of a B-52 aircraft on his nightstand. "So, did your father say when you'd begin school?" she asked finally.

"School?" he said blankly. "No, we haven't really talked about that."

"Well, maybe you should ask him. I start after the Induction, and it would be nice if we could start together."

"Yeah," he groaned.

"What's the matter?" she asked.

"Well, my last school experience wasn't all that pleasant, now, was it?" he grumbled.

"Oh, I guess not. But, Xavier, you're the Prince of Warwood! You're bound to be popular! Don't worry about it," she consoled.

He nodded, hoping she was right when Brittany skipped into the room, humming.

"Hi, ya!" she chirped. "What cha' ya doing?"

"Nothing, just talking, Brit," Robbie told her. "What do you want?"

"Nothing. I just came up to play with you guys!" she told them.

Brittany was an annoying, precocious 8-year-old who often tattled on Robbie for the littlest things. Xavier had sat through many of Robbie's tyrants about Brit's nosiness. There had been several moments in Xavier's life when he had wished he had a brother or sister. However, a couple of minutes in Brit's company, he became very thankful that he didn't.

"OH, NEAT!" she ran to his toy chest and began pulling out toys. Within minutes, Brit had all his toys strung all over his room. This didn't bother Xavier or Robbie because as long as she was playing with toys, she wasn't pestering them.

"Did you know the most popular sport here is rugby? Wells Academy has five intramural teams..."

"*Wells* Academy?" Xavier asked, snickering. "You've got to be kidding!"

"Xavier, you're royalty! Of course, they'd name things like schools after your family! Now, as I was saying, the school has five teams: the Knights, the Chameleons, the Owls, the Stallions, and the Eels. I was thinking about trying out for the Knights. Are you going to try out for a team?" she asked.

"I don't know. I haven't really thought about it. I think I would like to," he said.

120

"I heard the Chameleons were horrible last year. Even the Eels kicked their butts, and they're normally the weakest team in the kingdom," she groaned.

"Why did you yell at your daddy?" Brit interrupted, approaching them carrying a figurine of a stallion. They had forgotten she was there. Xavier felt his face grow hot.

"Shut up, Brit!" Robbie yelled.

"Well," she whinnied, "he did! The maids heard him!"

"I said, shut up!" Robbie hissed, pushing her little sister.

"Ow!" she cried. "I'm telling Mommy!" She stomped out of the room.

"Uh, oh," Robbie groaned. "We've got trouble."

"We?" Xavier smirked.

"Oh, be quiet! Come on," she growled, grabbing his hand and pulling him from the room.

From the top of the stairs, they could hear Brit melodramatically retelling the incident.

"And, then, she...she pushed me," Brit wailed.

Mrs. Minnows glared up at Robbie. "Roberta Ann Minnows! March yourself down those steps at once, young lady!"

With a groan, Robbie descended the stairs with Xavier following her.

Mr. Minnows stood and joined his wife, looking reprovingly at Robbie. Jeremiah was leaning casually against the mantle, watching the exchange with mild interest.

"Do you mind explaining what happened?" Mrs. Minnows reprimanded.

"Well, it was Brit's fault. She's always so nosey and..."

"Roberta," her father interrupted with quiet sternness, "that is not what your mother asked."

Robbie stiffened and sighed. "She was taunting Xavier. She was teasing him about what the maids had said." She glared at her sister.

Her parents rounded on Brit. "Brittany Marie! That is none of your business. How dare you bring that up to the Prince!" Mrs. Minnows scolded.

Jeremiah straightened and looked at Dublin questioningly.

Dublin Minnows sighed, "Your maids were gossiping about an argument you and Xavier had last night."

A shadow of anger flickered in the Premier's eyes. He nodded and a long drawn out silence followed.

"Well," Dublin cleared his throat in the awkward silence. "The new school term started last Monday. Tamarah and I are enrolling Robbie at the academy after the Induction. I thought maybe the kids would feel better starting a new school if they could do it together."

"Xavier will not be starting the academy until after the first term. I've arranged for Sir Lafayette to tutor him," Jeremiah announced.

"Oh?" Tamarah raised an eyebrow and looked questioningly at Jeremiah.

"What!" Xavier rebuked, stepping forward. "But, Father, I want to attend the academy with Robbie and all the other kids!"

Jeremiah looked at him solemnly. "I'm sorry, Son, but I wish to have you home schooled until you've had time to adjust to your new life."

"I'd adjust a lot quicker if I could be around other kids and go to school like everyone else. Father, please!" he begged.

"Xavier, I said no. I will not change my mind about this," his father warned.

"This is bull! You don't want a son! You want a prized prince that you can keep locked up like some kind of jewel!" Xavier yelled disdainfully.

Jeremiah's body went rigid. "Son! You better curb that attitude, now!" he growled with quiet finality.

"Why? Because it's true? Because you know I'm right?" Xavier spat, glaring up at his father.

"Xavier, your father is only looking out for you..."

"Oh, shut up, Dublin! No one asked you!" The words tumbled out of his mouth before he could stop them.

"Xavier!" Jeremiah boomed so dominantly that even Mr. Minnows flinched. Seizing Xavier roughly by the arm, Jeremiah muttered with barely controlled fury, "Please, excuse us." Then, he dragged Xavier past the Minnows family and toward the stairwell.

"Father," Xavier pleaded. "I...I'm sorry." He stumbled and fell to the floor.

Jeremiah's hard-set face did not waver and did not soften. He lifted the boy and carried him up the steps.

Xavier squirmed in Jeremiah's grasp. "Father, I said I was sorry, please."

"Sometimes sorry isn't enough," he clipped.

Jeremiah tightened his hold on the boy as he continued up the stairs to Xavier's room. He kicked the door open and stalked over to the bed. In one fluid motion, he sat and pulled Xavier across his lap.

"Father don't, please!" Xavier begged. For the first time in his life, Xavier was about to be spanked, and when the first blow came, Xavier yelped and tried to scramble from his father's grasp. But, Jeremiah did not relent and pinned him more firmly over his knee. His father spanked him, then. Boy, did he spank him, and Xavier couldn't suppress the cries that bellowed out of him each time his father smacked him. The spanking was hard and thorough, leaving Xavier with little doubt of his father's strength or resolve. Finally, Jeremiah lifted a sobbing Xavier and stood him in front of him.

"What did I say would happen if you ever disrespected an adult again?" he growled, anger swarming in his voice.

Xavier shifted uneasily, tears still rolling down his face. He rubbed his backside with a grimace, avoiding his father's eyes.

Jeremiah lifted his chin, forcing him to meet his

123

unwavering stare. "What did I say?" he repeated quietly.

"You," he cleared a sob from his throat, "you said that you'd spank me."

"Am I a man of my word, Xavier?" he asked.

"Yes, sir," Xavier muttered.

"Remember that, Son. Now, you will go down those steps and apologize..."

"Father, please. It'll be embarrass..."

"No, Son!" Jeremiah demanded. "You WILL go and apologize to the Minnows and especially to Mr. Minnows for your insolence. Then, you will excuse yourself and return to your room and wait for me. Is this understood?" Jeremiah asked evenly.

"Yes, sir," Xavier mumbled, hastily wiping his face with the back of his sleeve.

Jeremiah stood and gently cupped the back of the boy's head and directed him to the open door. He led Xavier out the door, down the stairs, and into the reception room where the Minnows stood looking apprehensive.

"Dublin," Jeremiah called as they entered the room. "My son has something he'd like to say to you and your family."

Xavier ventured a glance at Robbie who stood watching him anxiously. He realized then that she and her parents must have heard everything that occurred upstairs. He blushed and stared at the floor in front of his leather shoes.

"Son?" Jeremiah prompted.

"I'm sorry," he mumbled inaudibly.

"Xavier," Jeremiah said softly in his ear. "You'll need to speak loudly enough so that they can hear your apology."

Xavier sighed and cleared his throat. "I'm sorry, Mr. Minnows. I shouldn't have spoken so rudely to you. You didn't deserve that. And, Mrs. Minnows, Brit, Robbie, I'm sorry if I frightened you." His eyes fluttered briefly to Robbie, and she gave him a weak smile.

"Thank you, Xavier. We accept your apology. We,

better than anyone, know how tough you've had it lately. But, we also know that your father is a good man, and he'll do right by you," Mr. Minnows replied, patting his shoulder.

"Yes, sir," Xavier said quietly. "Now, if you'll excuse me, I have to go to my room. Goodbye, Mr. Minnows, Mrs. Minnows."

"We'll see you soon," Mr. Minnows smiled.

Xavier nodded and looked at his father.

"Go on up, Son. I'll be up as soon as I see to our guests," Jeremiah told him.

Xavier nodded and, glancing at Robbie, he muttered, "See ya."

"See, ya," she replied.

Xavier turned and climbed the stairs to his room.

"Jeremiah," Tamarah began, "don't be too rough on the boy."

"I don't believe I have been. The boy needs to learn discipline and self-control before he does something dangerous to himself or others," Jeremiah said calmly.

"Ah, Jer," Dublin cleared his throat nervously. "Something happened at the Meneses' after Julia's disappearance that you should be aware of. I didn't tell you right away because... Well, the boy had just lost his mother, and he was going through a lot at the time..." He looked grievously at his daughter.

"Daddy, no!" she gasped.

"Honey, Xavier's his son. His behavior that day may have been a warning sign of what is to come. He must know," Dublin reassured.

"What is it? What happened at the Meneses'?" Jeremiah asked, his piercing stare darting between Father and Daughter.

Dublin told Jeremiah of Xavier's rage and violent reaction to Robbie's questioning, and how he attacked her.

"Robbie, do you know what provoked the outburst?" Jeremiah asked.

"No, not really. I'm not sure. But, Sire, they really

125

tortured him at the Institute. Please, don't punish him. He didn't hurt me, not really," Robbie pleaded.

Jeremiah raised a brow and regarded Dublin for verification.

Dublin frowned. "He bruised her arms where he grabbed her."

Jeremiah nodded. "Thank you. I'm sorry our visit turned out to be an unpleasant experience."

"Not at all, old friend," Dublin said and patted Jeremiah on the back. "Thanks for having us. Take care of that boy. He's a good boy; he just needs a father's love and guidance."

"Thanks, Dub. I'll be in the office late tomorrow morning."

"Jeremiah, if you'd like. I can begin Xavier's dance lessons tomorrow evening," Tamarah told him.

"That sounds fine. I'm sure he'll appreciate that. Thank you," Jeremiah said.

He walked them to the door and watched the family descend the stairs before closing the door with a soft click. Jeremiah turned and looked at the stairs with dread. The boy was bottling up so much anger! Where did it all come from? Would he be able to reach him? He didn't have a choice; he had to get through to the boy.

Xavier sat stiffly on the edge of the bed, waiting for Jeremiah. What would happen now? He sat not moving for several minutes until he heard his father's footsteps on the stairs, and his gut lurched with anxiety.

Moments later, Jeremiah filled the doorway. Slowly, he entered the room with his hands stuffed in his pockets, his eyes set to the floor. After a couple of strides, he stopped and looked at Xavier with dark, angry eyes. His jaw was set and a muscle rolled across his cheek.

'Uh, oh! Something's happened,' Xavier realized with trepidation.

"Son, Dublin just informed me that you attacked Robbie while you were at your grandparents."

Xavier's stomach dropped with dread, and he struggled to swallow through his painfully constricting throat.

"He told me that you bruised her!" his voice grew stronger.

Xavier's eyes dropped from his father's harsh glare.

"What the hell were you thinking?" he growled.

"I wasn't," Xavier answered quietly. "I wasn't thinking; I was feeling. I just got so angry."

"Why?" Jeremiah asked, the edge gone from his voice.

Xavier looked at him with tears swelling in his eyes. "I don't know! Father, what's wrong with me?" The imminent tears fell silently.

"Come here, Son," Jeremiah ordered softly.

Xavier went to him, and Jeremiah enclosed him in his arms. His father's warmth radiated into his body, and he felt safe. He felt loved. For the first time in his life, Xavier felt truly loved, and this only made his anger grow.

Chapter 11
The Nightmare
★ ★ ★ ★ ★

The truth was Xavier kept having nightmares. He dreamt of his mother's death again that night, only this time the dream took a horrifying twist. Xavier found himself watching the entire event, every detail, through William LeMasters's eyes. He heard LeMasters's every thought, felt his every feeling, and watched every excruciation LeMasters inflicted on his mother. The images of his mother's agony flickered repeatedly in the dream, as did LeMasters's demonic glee and excitement of watching her die.

An overwhelming sense of guilt washed over Xavier, nauseating him. He watched as every muscle in his mother's body contracted and slammed her violently against the table as an electro force coursed through her body. Still, all he could feel was a sickening fascination. His mother's eyes were two glistening pearls as they rolled into the back of her head. Her tongue lolled to one side, and she gagged on the fermented saliva oozing from her mouth like a rabid animal. Her hands clawed at the table. Her fingers scraped the table's surface with a hair-raising, teeth aching squeal, and Xavier's stomach reeled as her fingernails snapped one by one and tore away from her hands. A low throaty scream vibrated from her and grew louder and louder until she was shrieking hysterically.

Her screams chorused with his as he bolted upright in his bed drenched in sweat and... Oh, God! He had wet the bed! He felt the burn of embarrassment steal across his face as he threw back the covers with a curse and stood. Suddenly, light spilled over him as the door to his room opened, and a shadow stood poised in the doorway. Xavier threw the covers over the darkened spot on the sheets and stooped onto the bed to hide the front of his pajama bottoms.

"Xavier? Are you all right, Son?" Jeremiah's voice questioned as he stepped into the room.

"Yes!" Xavier barked. "I'm fine!"

Jeremiah stood silently just inside the doorway, peering down at him.

"I said, I'm fine," Xavier repeated. "It was just a dream."

"By the way you screamed, I'd say it was more than just a dream. Maybe we should talk about it. It might help," Jeremiah suggested.

"No! I'm fine! It was only a dream. God! Why do we always have to talk about everything? Just leave me alone!" Xavier shouted.

"Xavier? What's going on?" Jeremiah questioned, flicking on the light and crossing the room. "You're behaving very defensively. Is there something..."

Xavier abruptly threw a blanket over himself, "It's nothing!"

Jeremiah stopped awkwardly as he registered the boy's flushed face, and his eyes dropped to the blanket in his lap. Xavier squirmed and did not meet his eyes. Then, without a word, Jeremiah moved toward him and lifted the blanket.

Xavier's blush deepened. "You must think that I'm a big baby. A baby who wets the bed whenever he has a bad dream," he muttered.

"No," Jeremiah said simply. "I don't. What I think is

129

that my son has experienced terror and evil that would make most grown men crumble. I think most men would have gone insane if they had to endure what you did at the hands of that psychopath."

His words helped. Xavier looked up at him, his eyes brimming with pain.

Jeremiah smiled encouragingly. "Well, what do you say to changing these sheets and getting on some dry pajamas?"

While Jeremiah stripped the bed and removed the wet sheets, Xavier changed into dry pajamas. Then, together they made up the bed with fresh, clean linens.

"In you go," Jeremiah said, tossing Xavier playfully onto the bed. Jeremiah pulled the covers over him and sat on the edge of the bed. He stroked a stray milky curl from the boy's brow, and Xavier felt himself relaxing under his father's gentle hand.

"It must have been a terrible nightmare. Do you want to talk about it?"

Xavier shook his head briskly, his eyes widening with horror.

"I really think we should. You *need* to talk about it," Jeremiah told him.

"No! I don't. I'm fine Father!" he implored.

"Xavier," Jeremiah began.

"No! Please," a whimper trembled out of Xavier, and his entire body shook. "I... I can't. I just...can't."

His father nodded. "All right, Son. We won't talk about it tonight. Relax and go back to sleep," he soothed and continued to gently stroke him.

* * * * *

The next morning Father and Son sat quietly, eating breakfast. Xavier was exhausted and looked as though he'd fall asleep in his breakfast.

"Son?" Jeremiah began, "I know you don't want to, but we really should discuss your dream."

"It was nothing," Xavier lied.

"Well, you and I both know that's not true," Jeremiah said. "Tell me."

Xavier sank back into his chair and stared at the bowl of fruit in front of him.

Jeremiah waited. Finally, he lowered his cup of tea, his frown deepening. "Xavier," he said quietly, "if you won't talk to me about it, I'll be forced to invade your thoughts to find out..."

"No!" he blurted. "Father, don't!"

Jeremiah reclined back in his chair, stretching his arms and interlocking his fingers behind his head as he studied the boy. "Okay, then, talk. I will find out one way or another."

Xavier sighed indignantly. "It's the same as before. Mom's death keeps replaying over and over like a broken record. Only this time, I dreamed that I'm William LeMasters. I'm the one punishing her," his voice broke. "Father, I felt happy watching her die! How sick is that? I mean, what kind of person enjoys watching their own mother suffer and die screaming in pain?"

Jeremiah straightened and slid his chair back. "Come here," he whispered.

Xavier went to him, wiping his eyes almost angrily.

Jeremiah pulled him onto his knee. "Son, it was a dream! And, those feelings weren't your own; they were William's. There's nothing to feel ashamed or guilty about. You had nothing to do with your mother's death. It wasn't your fault, and I'll say that as often as it takes for you to believe it. It wasn't your fault." Xavier nodded, and Jeremiah held him closely for a moment. "Sometimes," Jeremiah continued softly in his ear, "our dreams have a way of telling us something important. We often can learn from them. And, sometimes dreams have a way of forcing us to face issues that we're unwilling to face when we're awake. For instance," Jeremiah paused and inhaled deeply, "we've never discussed what happened to you at the Institute." He felt the boy's body tense.

131

"What does that have to do with anything?" Xavier asked quietly, pulling away from his father.

Jeremiah's brow rose, "You tell me."

"I don't know! How should I know? You brought it up!" he blurted, standing up.

"Yes, I brought it up," Jeremiah agreed. "Why haven't you? Why haven't you talked about it?"

"I don't want to! I want to forget it ever happened!" he said feverishly.

Jeremiah straightened in his chair and looked solemnly at the boy. "Can you hear yourself?" he asked kindly. "Listen to yourself, Xavier. You're agitated, and you don't want to face what happened to you at the Institute. Maybe if we talked about it..."

"NO!" Xavier spat. "No!"

Jeremiah stood, exhaling slowly. "I'm sorry, Son, but you will discuss it."

"Please! Don't make me, please," he begged. Xavier felt his body grow cool as Jeremiah's darkened eyes penetrated into him.

"No! Stop it!" Xavier screamed and ran from the room.

It was futile to run; he knew. Even as he climbed the steps two at a time, he felt his father's presence following him and penetrating into his thoughts. He slammed his bedroom door shut as if it alone would block Jeremiah's advances. Then, his bedroom door opened, and Jeremiah stood before him. He looked down at Xavier with an eyebrow raised in a mild reprimand.

"Son, you know I will learn of it. There's only one choice you have to make here. Do you tell me, or do I find out by extracting those memories?"

Xavier huffed and paced the room like a caged tiger. He felt desperate and trapped. There had to be some way to avoid all of this. He stopped and glared up at the infuriatingly calm man.

"Why? Why do you need to hear this from me? I'm

sure Loren could tell you everything that happened! Why don't you ask him?" Xavier implored harshly.

"I have, but Loren's perspective on what you endured is irrelevant here. You're the one having the nightmares, not Loren. It's you who needs to come to terms with it," he said calmly as he entered the room, carefully stepping over the toys strung across the floor.

"What do you know? You don't know a damn thing, Father! Just leave me alone!"

Jeremiah pinned him with a dark glare. "Son, I realize this is very hard for you, but I do not appreciate the attitude."

Xavier hissed a curse, stomped to the far wall of windows, and sank to the floor burying his face in his arms.

"Enough of this, Xavier. Stop stonewalling," Jeremiah crossed the room and stopped in front of him. "Start talking or I start infiltrating."

Xavier raised his head, his eyes flashing with anger. "You want to know what happened? You want to know? Fine! I'll tell you." Xavier stood, overwhelmed with his raging fury. His voice grew louder, harsher. "I was tortured because of *you*, Father! He kept asking me question after question about you. Of course, I knew nothing about you. He knew that too, but it didn't stop him from asking and punishing me for not having the answers! A month passed and the questions never changed, but the punishments did. He began snapping bones: a leg, an arm, a wrist. I couldn't tell you how many times LeMasters broke my arm. Of course, Loren was sent in to heal it, which in itself was torture, and Dr. Angelo refused to give me any pain relief. Do you know what it feels like to have a bone rejuvenated, Father? I'll tell you! It felt as if the bone had been replaced by a hot branding iron. I screamed for nearly an hour as the rejuvenation ran its course. I guess, I should be thankful that William allowed me some time to recover before he would return and do it all again. Besides all of that, he would tell me awful things about you! He told me that you never wanted a child and left mom and me. He told me that you struck and abused mother when she was pregnant with me. I feared you. I despised you. I blamed you for everything that was wrong in my life! Is that what you wanted to hear?"

"Xavier," Jeremiah groaned, pulling the boy into his arms.

But, Xavier fought against him. "No! I hate you! I hate you! I hate you! I hate you!" he wailed, pelting his father with punch after punch.

Jeremiah didn't move. He watched as Xavier's anger unraveled into anguish, and finally, Xavier sank to the floor howling.

"I'm so tired," he hiccupped between sobs. "I'm so tired, Father. I'm tired of feeling..." he hiccupped, "so damn bad!"

Jeremiah dropped to his knees beside him. "I know Son. I know," he whispered, stroking Xavier's wet jaw. "But, I promise you this, it will get better, now. The pain will weaken over time."

Xavier nodded and the two sat in silence for several minutes. Finally, Xavier looked up at him with red swollen eyes. "I didn't mean it, Father. I don't hate you."

"I know, Son. I know."

Chapter 12
Kingship
★ ★ ★ ★ ★

Late that morning, Jeremiah strode into Xavier's room dressed elegantly in charcoal slacks, a crisp white shirt, and a burgundy tie knotted neatly at the collar. His ink blue cloak sailed behind him as he moved past Xavier to the closet.

"Son, I have a lot of work to catch up on today. After a long vacation, there are many things to be done."

Xavier felt a stab of disappointment. Was this how it would always be? His father running a kingdom and having little time left for him? Xavier frowned.

"Anyways," his father was continuing, "would you like to come with me today and shadow me around? It can be a sort of bring-your-son-to-work kind of day?"

Xavier's face brightened. "Can I? Yes, sir! I'd really like that!"

Jeremiah smiled broadly and turned back to the closet. He looked over his shoulder at the grinning boy. "Well? Go and brush your teeth and wash your face."

Xavier obediently dashed into the bathroom. He returned to the room just as his father pulled a sweeping, fluid cloak from the closet. It was identical to the cloak his father wore, ink blue with silver clasps and trim.

Jeremiah turned to him. "Now, a prince can't shadow his father without his robe, can he?"

"Wow! It's fantastic," Xavier whispered, running his hand over the fabric.

Jeremiah smiled. "Now you go ahead and get dressed. I'll meet you in the reception room in 10 minutes," Jeremiah announced, striding to the door.

Xavier nodded, already busily peeling off his clothes.

Moments later, Xavier, dressed in gray slacks, a white shirt, and the satin cloak, descended the steps. He stopped suddenly at the sound of his father's angry voice.

"I do not care to hear your excuses!" he boomed. "How dare you discuss my personal matters? My relationship with my son, our conflicts, and how I choose to discipline him are of no consequence to you! How dare you?"

"Please, Sire! Forgive me," a high squeaky voiced pleaded.

Xavier leaned over the banister and peered down at the conflict below him. His father stood very dominantly over a young blonde woman bowing before him and grasping desperately at his legs. A stockier older woman stood next to them with her head tucked submissively. Jeremiah stepped back out of the younger woman's clutches.

"Collect your things, Gloria. You're fired. I don't ever want to see you inside the palace walls again," he said vindictively.

"No! Sire, I beg you," she wailed.

"Gloria, go!" he said in disgust.

"Sire!" she pleaded.

"NOW!" he yelled, pointing toward the door. Gloria stumbled to her feet and left the palace, sobbing.

Jeremiah turned to the older woman. "Edith," his demeanor changed, and his stance relaxed considerably. "I'm very disappointed to see that you were involved in this!"

"I am so sorry, Sire! I acted inexcusable! I shouldn't

have encouraged her gossip," Edith muttered. "Please, Sire. I know nothing else. My family has been servants for the royal family for generations. I don't know what got into me, sir. Please, forgive me. I will gladly volunteer my services for Master Wells's Induction, without pay of course. Please," she pleaded.

"All right, Edith. You will work the Induction Ceremony, and you will not receive a Christmas bonus. But, Edith, let me make this perfectly clear, if you ever do something like this again, you will regret it. Do we understand one another?"

"Yes, Sire. You have my word," she bowed.

"You may go," Jeremiah said, waving her away. He watched the maid leave the room.

Then, he turned to Xavier and sighed heavily. "Well, Son. I'm afraid the events in this house the last couple of days may be all over the kingdom by now. Gloria is a talker and makes no attempt to keep information to herself."

"Great! Just great!" Xavier mumbled.

"Well, we best be going. I have a meeting with Judge Calhoun this morning," he said, waving Xavier down to him.

Jeremiah led him through the residence doors, and out onto the foyer where the Premier Royal Guard stood waiting. Loren was among them.

"Loren!" Xavier beamed.

"Hey, Little Sire. How're things going?" he asked, patting him playfully on top his head. Then, he directed his attention to Jeremiah. "Sire? There seems to have been a disturbance last evening on the lower floor. Your *groupies* were attempting to breach your residence to get a look at your son," he taunted, smirking at Jeremiah.

"My groupies, huh?" Jeremiah challenged as he wrestled Loren into a headlock. Loren struggled free, laughing and giving Jeremiah a playful shove.

"Temper, temper, Sire!" he bedeviled.

"You know something, Loren? I don't have the foggiest idea why I keep you around. All you are is a huge pain in the..." he looked down at Xavier who was listening intently, "ah...backside. You need to take a lesson from Ephraim and learn your place in this relationship. *I* am the king; *you* are the servant," Jeremiah teased with a wide grin.

"Yeah, yeah, yeah," Loren laughed and stooped to eye level with Xavier. "Your father! He thinks he's sooo important!" He rolled his eyes. "But, he forgets, I knew him when he was a snot nosed brat. I could tell you some wild stories about the trouble he caused."

"The trouble *I* caused! If I remember right, Loren, you could always be found at my side when there was mayhem, and in most cases, you caused it," Jeremiah chuckled.

Loren stood. "You know, Sire, the mark of a good king is a man who knows how to take responsibility for his own actions. I think maybe you should work on that."

The other guards chuckled. Jeremiah shook his head mildly exasperated and humored.

"Okay, okay," Jeremiah announced, allowing the laughter to die down. "Xavier will be accompanying me to the Governing Hall today. Loren you're assigned to prince detail. Everyone else fill in at our flank. I do not want Xavier to be made a spectacle of by curious citizens or reporters."

"Yes sir," the men said in unison.

As the group made their way down the wide sweeping staircase, Xavier found himself sandwiched between his father and Loren. The remaining Premier Royal Guard surrounded them like a shield.

"Is the Clavis de Rex secure?" Jeremiah asked Loren quietly as they walked down the long hall to the exiting vestibule.

"Yes, sir. I...the Keeper of the Key is guarding it until the Induction Ceremony. Afterwards, it will be tucked safely away in the vault, and three guards will be on duty at all times."

Jeremiah nodded, "Good. Have we heard anything from platoon eagle?"

"Two, maybe three days ago. They stuck pretty close

to LeMasters for the first few days, but he sensed their presence and slipped away from them."

"Weren't they trained in blocking techniques?"

"Yes, Sire. But, LeMasters's telepathic abilities were too strong, and he was able to break through their meager defenses," Loren admitted.

Jeremiah muttered a string of curses and sighed exasperatedly. "Loren, we're vulnerable to his attacks if we're unprepared."

"Father?" Xavier interrupted. Both men looked down at him in surprise; they had forgotten he was there. "What's the Cavus Recks?"

"The Clavis de Rex," he pronounced clearly, "or King's Key, is an important key."

Xavier opened his mouth to ask more, but his father raised his hand, stopping him. "Not now, Son," he hushed as the palace door opened.

There were several women standing idly in the drive, but the moment the door opened, they came charging toward the entourage. "Sire! Sire!" the women screeched.

"Your father, the heartthrob. I told you he had groupies," Loren murmured into Xavier's ear, and Xavier snickered.

The Premier Guard fought to keep the women at bay. "Ladies, Ladies," his father soothed. "I do wish I could stay and visit, but I have a lot of work to do today. Please do not plague my son with your affections. He still needs time to adjust to his life here. However, both my son and I look forward to seeing you at his Induction. So, until then, please, excuse us."

The ladies squealed excitedly but moved to the side and allowed them to pass.

"Suave, Jer. Very suave," Loren murmured so only Jeremiah could hear him.

"I aim to please," he muttered back, grinning.

They walked across the horseshoe shaped drive inscribing a beautiful, floral garden. The smell of sweet marsh orchids and crocuses wafted into their faces as they approached a cylindrical building across from the palace. It was a very unusual looking building. It reminded Xavier of a cylinder box set his mother had once owned where each box fitted inside the slightly larger one. Then, after the boxes were full of knickknacks, they could be stacked one on top the other, narrowing to the top. This building was constructed in a similar fashion with four tapering circular levels. Another unique aspect of the building, aside from its architecture, was the overall appearance of the building. It was pitch black! Its dark slate walls and dark tinted windows made the building appear threatening and ominous, and as they drew closer to the massive structure, a chill shivered through Xavier.

But, whatever feelings and impressions the exterior gave, the interior was an all-together different story. The moment the group entered the huge black doors Xavier froze. The bright white walls, stained-glass skylights, and the oases of small gardens and fountains gave the building a cheerful almost festive atmosphere. The area was bustling with activity as men and women in business attire, a few wearing long judicial robes, went about their daily business.

Jeremiah clapped Xavier's shoulder affectionately. "The first floor is the judicial department. It handles all legal matters from small disagreements between citizens to first-degree criminal cases. Come, my office is on the second floor legislative department. We need to get going, or I'll be late for my appointment with Judge Calhoun," Jeremiah said. He took Xavier's hand and led him through the crowded commons.

As they made their way across the elongated common room, Xavier was acutely aware of the numerous stares and whispers following them so he pretended to be engrossed in the room's décor. His head spun around, determinedly taking in the beautiful surroundings. Colorful fragments of light waltzed playfully on the floor and walls from the skylights above them. Along the walls, delicately pieced mosaic murals depicted the floor's function. Life-sized tiled images of judges and arguers assembled in bright, vivid colors were magnificent works of art.

"What does that say?" Xavier whispered to his father, pointing to the tiled lettering above one of the murals.

"It's Latin. It means truth, justice, and integrity," he told him.

Finally, they came to a pair of enormous oak doors at the end of the judicial commons. The guards opened the door and allowed Jeremiah to enter first with Xavier at his side. They entered a wide marbled stairwell that spiraled upward. Following his father's lead, Xavier climbed the steps to the second level.

The second floor corridor also served as a commons area for the floor's workers. Although this area was not as large as the lower floor, it was still quite grand. Like the first floor, it also had intricate stained-glass skylights, fountains, gardens, and beautifully arranged collages along the walls. However, the collage scenes here were quite different. These mosaic pictures were of men and women writing, debating, legislating, and voting, and in the center of each mural was the image of Jeremiah wearing a long ink blue cloak.

"Come, my office is at the other end of the hall," Jeremiah said, tugging Xavier's hand.

Men and women skirted around them as they made their way down the hall, nodding briefly to his father but looking intensely at Xavier. Jeremiah led him through the commons to the door at its end. Once inside, Jeremiah settled himself behind his desk and waved Xavier to him.

"Son, come and sit with me, and I'll tell you what I do while I am here."

Xavier walked to his father, and Jeremiah pulled him onto his knee and motioned to the heap of papers in front him.

"Do you see all these papers? Each represents a bill or proposition that has come before me for reviewing. Now,

141

after I read these, I meet with the delegation who wrote it and critique it." Seeing Xavier's confusion, he explained. "I make a judgment on whether it's a good proposition or not, and I give suggestions for its improvement. No bill can be passed into law without my approval. However, I usually go by what the delegates vote through because they're elected officials and represent my citizens. Do you understand?"

"I think so," he said. "You read other people's ideas and decide whether they're good enough. Right?"

"Exactly," he smiled. "But, this is only part of my job. Like I told you, first floor is the judicial department. That's where all disputes and law suits turn up. If there is a major violation in the law, such as someone killing another person, or treason, I reside as a part of the Elite Court. I have a more powerful vote than the other judges, and only I can decide a split vote."

Xavier nodded thoughtfully. A buzzer rang from Jeremiah's desktop and a feminine voice sang, "Sire?"

"Just a minute, Son," Jeremiah leaned forward and pressed a green button on the intercom box sitting on his desk. "Yes, Alexandria?"

"The delegates would like to meet this morning concerning issue 167 and bill 133," she announced.

"They would? I thought we already worked out the complications with those. They were supposed to go up for vote while I was away," Jeremiah said with uncertainty.

"Yes, Sire. That's what they *said*, but personally, I think they were hoping to meet your son a couple of days earlier than the Induction," Alexandria chuckled. "And, Sire, your decision on case number c47-3 is needed by this evening."

"Oh," his father answered with understanding, "I see. Please inform Cecil Calhoun I'd like to meet with him at 10:45 this morning to discuss the case. Oh, and Alexandria? Tell the delegates, I will meet with them 11:40, and I will bring my son."

"Yes, Sire," she replied.

"Why would they be so keen on meeting me?" Xavier asked.

"Well, Son, you are their future leader," Jeremiah responded.

The day went on in much the same way. In between meetings, Jeremiah would explain facets of his job as king when another group hoping to meet Xavier would interrupt them. By late afternoon, Xavier believed that he had shaken hands with just about everyone in the building. After the final wave of people, a group from the third floor common wealth and tax department, Jeremiah looked at his son.

"I guess today was good practice for your Induction on Saturday. You'll have less people to greet now," Jeremiah said, smiling. "Well, I've finished what I needed to for today; what do you say we head home?"

Xavier nodded eager to leave.

Loren and the detail of guardsmen ushered them back to the palace, and as they climbed the royal stairway, a voice pulled Xavier's attention to the foyer below them.

"I know Pop! I'll clean it when I get back! The guys are meeting in the Coliseum to do a bit of practicing before rugby try outs in a few weeks!" A boy with dark, untamed, auburn hair appeared from a doorway in the antechamber below. He was tossing a small ball from hand to hand peering through the doorway when the ball changed form and molded itself into a minuscule figure of a cat. It was then that Xavier realized that the object was not a ball at all, but an entity of light. The cat climbed over the boy's shoulders rubbing against his neck affectionately. The boy absentmindedly brushed at the figure.

Ephraim appeared in the doorway. "Court, you said you'd clean out that chamber last week! If you had done it then, I wouldn't be asking you to do it now. Would I?" Ephraim's deep voice said matter-of-factly.

"Jeez, Dad! Come on, I've got to practice if I'm going to make the Knights this year!" the boy whined.

"Yo, Hardcastle! You great oaf! Let the boy go!

You're only young once!" Loren bellowed from beside Xavier.

Father and Son looked up at the group. Ephraim's eyes scanned the group and saw Jeremiah. "Your Highness." He bowed his head respectfully as did his son. "Sire, I must say, I do not admire who you keep in your company."

"Yes," Jeremiah chuckled. "They seemed to have lowered the standards for the Royal Guard, haven't they?"

"Now, now. Play nicely," Loren mocked.

"Jefferson, I'd appreciate it if you kindly butt out of my affairs with my son!" Ephraim chided playfully.

However, the boy seemed to know he had won his argument because he grinned ear to ear at Loren, "Loren! My man! Tell my old man that a man has to practice rugby if he's to kick butt in try-outs."

Loren produced a serious expression and called down to Ephraim, "Hey, old man! A man has to practice if he's to kick butt in try-outs!"

"Cute, real cute, Jefferson! Watch who you call old man, old man! I'm a year younger than you!" he laughed up at him. Still grinning, he looked at Xavier. "Xavier? How're things with you?"

"Fine, sir," he responded.

"I'm glad to hear that. I'd like you to meet my son, Courtney," he motioned to the boy beside him.

"Hi," the boy nodded up at him.

"Hi," Xavier greeted back.

The boy turned back to his father, "So?"

With a heavy sigh, Ephraim nodded.

"Yes!" the boy celebrated, jumping up in the air, and as he did so, the little figure on his shoulder jumped with jubilation as well before turning back into a ball and disappearing. "Hey," he called up to Xavier, "you want to come?"

Xavier looked at his father who shook his head. "I don't think it's a good idea, Son." Xavier visibly deflated.

"Jer," Loren whispered, "let the boy go. How's he going to fit in if you seclude him from normal kid activities? Come on, Jeremiah. He needs a bit of normalcy right about now. Court'll look out for him."

Jeremiah seemed to be contemplating the idea, and Xavier looked up hopefully. He really had no choice with his son looking at him so wishfully.

"All right. But, I want you back at the palace by 5:00. You'll need to get cleaned up before dinner, and you have dance lessons at the Minnows at 6:30."

Xavier nodded eagerly.

"Okay then, go on. Go change your clothes into something more suitable."

It was Xavier's turn to whoop.

Chapter 13
Fitting In
★ ★ ★ ★ ★

Xavier followed Courtney Hardcastle down the hall, out of the palace, and into the sunshine. A group of women lingered next to the gardens in the center of the U shaped drive. They paid Court and Xavier little attention as they continued to take turns staring through binoculars at the second level of the palace.

"What are they doing?" Xavier asked in a hush.

"Probably trying to get a glimpse of your daddy in his underwear," Court snickered. "If you haven't figured it out yet, your dad is the most eligible bachelor in the kingdom." Court smirked playfully. "Wait a minute! Come to think of it," Court said, stopping and looking at him intently, "maybe they're trying to get a good look at you. After all, you're a bit of a mystery. No one's really seen you, and your father won't let anyone either. In fact, I'm surprised he even allowed you to come with me."

"He wasn't going to," Xavier responded, "until Loren talked him into it."

Courtney's infectious grin was back. "Good ole Loren! He can always talk Jeremiah and my dad into stuff. From what I've heard, he always could. When they were kids, I guess they got into loads of stuff. Maybe our fathers are afraid he'd blackmail them with their past deeds or something."

Xavier looked back at the ladies. "Well, if they're hoping to see Father, they're looking on the wrong side of the palace."

With a snicker, the boys continued around the building and toward the rear of the palace. A wall of giant evergreens completely enclosed the back lawn, hiding whatever lay beyond them from view.

"It's a garden," Court said, catching Xavier's stare.

Xavier looked ahead of him and saw a large roughly finished stonewall extending in either direction and standing nearly fifteen feet high. "Are we going to have to walk around that?" Xavier asked wearily.

"Nope. Not if you know where to go, you don't," Court said as he led Xavier to the intersection of the wall of green and the wall of stone. "Come on," Court whispered as he hugged against the stonewall and squeezed inside the cluster of evergreen trees. Xavier followed him, feeling the needles rake against his face, but after a few feet, the sharp branches were no longer jabbing him in the back. The enormous tree had been pruned in the center, and Xavier was able to stand freely. Court knelt, his hands exploring the surface of the stonewall.

"Your Highness," he waved Xavier down to him. "If you feel along these stones, you'll find one stone that feels quite a bit different than the others. That's because it is. It's a fabrication, a fake." He paused, feeling around. "Ah, here it is! Feel the difference?"

Xavier ran his hands over the stones and indeed did feel a difference. The fake stone felt smoother, less granular. "Yeah," Xavier nodded.

"This stone pulls out and reveals a lever for a secret doorway. This is a great secret to know when you're running late for school or rugby practice." As he spoke, Court lifted the false stone and pulled a lever. Instantly a stone door, which by all accounts was invisible to the naked eye, popped open allowing a light breeze to waft across their faces.

The boys walked through the door, and Xavier found himself inside another tall evergreen. They fought their way through the sappy, scratchy branches and out onto a clearing. Then, Xavier saw it! Out before them, across an immense field of yellowing grass, stood an enormous stadium that looked like a relic from the medieval days of gladiators.

"Wow!" was all he could say.

Court beamed. "I know. Awesome sight; isn't it?" he said as he gazed admirably at the stadium before them. "Come on," he said and marched purposefully across the open yard toward the stadium's entrance several hundred yards away.

Xavier had to run to catch up with him. "Ah, Court? Could you do me a favor and not call me Your Highness or Sire or any term of power. Just call me X. I don't want them to know. I just want to be one of the guys, okay?"

Court looked at him thoughtfully. "Sure, X. Whatever you want is fine by me."

By the antique impression of the stadium's exterior, Xavier was surprised to find that the interior was quite the opposite. Inside, enormous state of the art scoreboards towered at each end of the stadium, and the field was the best all-weather turf money could buy. The stands were equipped with benches and backrests, and concessions could be found on a medium on either side of the stadium.

"Yo! It's about time, Hardcastle! Jeez, we had to let Mac's little brother play just so we'd have even teams!" called a boy with sleek dirt brown hair and freckles.

"Perfection can't be rushed Calhoun! Besides, I grabbed us another player, so little Sean gets to play after all," Court called cheekily.

A small mousy boy with blond hair whooped.

"A new kid?" Calhoun asked as his eyes settled on Xavier.

"Hi! I'm X," he told the boy.

"X? What kind of a name is that?" jeered another boy with straw blond hair.

"It's not a name. It's an initial," Xavier answered matter-of-factly.

"An initial huh?" replied Calhoun. "Well, I'm Ken Calhoun, and this is Mac Clarke."

The blond boy nodded, surveying him haughtily.

"Are we going to stand around talking all day, or are we going to play?" another boy whined.

"What do you think?" Court asked sarcastically. "I was just waiting for you all to shut your yaps."

"Funny, Hardcastle! You're an absolute riot; you know that?" Calhoun responded dryly before turning to the rest of the boys. "All right, then, let's get it started!"

The boys quickly chose teams, and with Xavier placed on Court's team, the game began. It became obvious to Xavier that these boys had been playing the sport since they could walk and talk, and suddenly he was glad that Loren and his father had taught him the basic rules of the game. At least he could pretend that he knew what he was doing. But, to Xavier's amazement, he actually played pretty well, and he even prevented the opposing team's key play from resulting in a score. By the time the game was over, even though Xavier's team had lost, he was feeling pretty good about himself.

"X?" Ken Calhoun called. "You're not bad. Have you ever played on a rugby team before?"

"No," he answered.

"I haven't seen you at school. How come?" Mac commented.

"I just moved here," Xavier responded.

"What's your ability?" Mac asked him.

"Electro forces, anima lingua, and telepathy," he told him.

"Telepathy! You're such a liar! No one's telepathic but the King," Mac accused.

Ignoring Mac, Ken gave Xavier a strange look and asked, "You have three abilities?"

Xavier nodded.

"How old are you?" he asked, his eyes narrowing.

"Twelve," Xavier answered slowly, looking at each boy's face and seeing a mixture of shock and skepticism.

"He's lying! He can't have three abilities, and there's no way he's telepathic. Only the royal family inherits that ability! I bet he's a lowly merchant. It'd be like a merchant to try something like this!" Mac responded snidely.

"A merchant? What's a..." Xavier began, but Court was tugging on him.

"Well, cheerio, mates. I've gotta get home and clean out the storage chamber before my old man has my hide. See you at school tomorrow," Court chirped and pulled Xavier off the field and away from the group of boys. "Come on, Your Highness," he hissed under his breath to Xavier.

"Hey, wait a minute! Hardcastle! X!" Ken called after them.

Court pulled Xavier out of the stadium and back across the field. "For someone who wanted to keep a low profile, you sure gave them a lot to chew on," Court sighed as they slid behind the blue spruce to the hidden door.

Xavier frowned. "I don't understand."

"You told them you have three abilities!" Seeing Xavier's puzzlement once again, Court explained, "Most kids our age usually have just one ability, but no twelve year old has ever had three! And, you told them you could read minds! It's like Mac said, only royalty inherits that ability!"

"Oh," Xavier mumbled. "I didn't know. I guess I really don't know much about this...this place."

Court opened the secret passage, and they climbed through to the other side. "Don't worry about it, mate. It doesn't matter anyway. If they haven't figured out who you really are by now, they'll find out soon enough at your Induction."

The boys fought their way out of the pines in silence.

Finally, Xavier asked, "Ah, Court? How many abilities do you have?"

He eyed Xavier before answering, "Two. I can conjure electro forces, of course, and I can transport."

"Transport?" Xavier questioned.

"I can move from one place to another instantly," Court explained. "Though, I just developed the ability this summer so I'm not that good at it yet. The first time I tried to transport to the Coliseum, I ended up at Heinz Stadium in Pittsburgh. I had to call Dad to come and get me."

"Whoa, really?" Xavier gasped with a snicker.

Court grinned. "Yeah, it was embarrassing. My brother, Drew, teased me relentlessly for a solid week, but I figured he was just jealous. Not many people can transport, not even the King! But, your father has loads of abilities that the average citizen doesn't."

"Really? How many empowerments does Father have?" Xavier asked as they retraced their steps back around the palace.

"I think the last count was twelve, but no one knows for sure, other than the King himself. You'll have to ask him," Court responded.

"How many abilities does your father have?" Xavier asked.

"Well, Dad's pretty secretive about his powers. He doesn't like to talk about them so I'm not sure even I know all of his abilities. But, like me, he can transport. He's also an inclementor, which means he can change weather patterns. He's telekinetic and can make things move by just thinking about it. And, oh, yeah, he's an augur. He can see people who are transfigured, camouflaged, or invisible."

Xavier bit back the questions bubbling inside him, and as they rounded the corner to the front of the palace, they saw Robbie. "Hey! Robbie!" Xavier blurted.

The women patrolling the palace's front lawn looked at Xavier disdainfully as if he had interrupted something important. Then, with an indignant huff, the women turned back toward the palace and resumed their gawking.

"Hi," Robbie greeted as her eyes traveled up and down his disheveled appearance. "What have you been doing, Xavier?"

Instantly, upon hearing Xavier's name, the women jerked their heads toward the children and became very still. As their gazes shifted from Robbie to Court and finally settling on Xavier, their eyes grew enormous with awed recognition, and one woman cried out in delight. The Prince was standing before them, and for a moment, they stood mesmerized!

However, the children did not witness the women's reaction and continued to talk playfully. "Playing rugby! Court took me to the Coliseum to play with some of his friends."

"Ah, well acquaintances, really. They're not really my friends," Court mumbled.

"Jeez, whiz! I wish you had called me, Court. I would've liked to have gone!" Robbie whined.

Court rolled his eyes and shrugged, "Sorry Rob, maybe next time!"

"Don't roll your eyes at me, Courtney Aaron Hardcastle! Don't tell me you share your father's idea that women shouldn't play rugby!" Robbie growled, punching his arm.

"Ouch! Of course not! If my father knew you like I do, neither would he!" Court laughed, throwing his hands up in surrender.

Robbie grinned at these words and looked at Xavier with smug satisfaction.

"I assume you two already know one another, then," Xavier stated the obvious.

"Ah, yeah! Actually, we're cousins." Robbie made a face at Court. "His mother and my mother are sisters."

Xavier nodded suddenly realizing that he had never really known Robbie all that well. They had never talked about her family beyond her parents and Brit. He felt guilty for that; he should have asked! Wait a minute! He had! He had asked her if her grandparents were still living. She didn't seem to want to talk about it and had changed the subject. She probably had been told not to talk about them or Warwood. Why had everyone lied and kept the truth from him?

Robbie's eyes grew wide. "Xavier! What are you doing running around outside the palace? I can't believe that the King would allow you to go out *before* your Induction! It's supposed to be bad luck for citizens to see the Prince the week before the Induction."

"Well, obviously the King doesn't believe in that old fashioned superstition!" Court remarked.

"It's not superstition! I heard that's why his father's cursed!" she said.

"Cursed?" Xavier questioned. "What do you mean?"

"Your Majesty!" shrieked a voice to Xavier's right.

Xavier didn't have time to even turn his head before three sets of hands seized him, and Courtney and Robbie were knocked aside. The women began, rubbing their hands in his hair and over his body.

"Oh, Young Sire! What a pleasure to meet you," a raspy female voice whispered in his ear.

"Oh, what a cutie!" another female voice squealed. "He looks just like his father."

Xavier felt himself being lifted off the ground, and panic rose within him. What did these women want? Would they hurt him?

"Stop! Stop! Let go of me! Let go of me! Let go!" he yelled, panic spiking into his voice.

"LADIES!" Jeremiah thundered, and instantly the women stilled.

The King stood a few yards from the palace's entrance with the Premier Royal Guard standing like angry statues behind him. Just beyond the men stood a very frightened Robbie and a very anxious Courtney.

"Please, release my son," his father continued without

153

compromise.

The women immediately obeyed him, and Xavier felt his feet touch the ground. He stumbled past the women over to his father.

"Go inside, Xavier," Jeremiah said quietly, his steel eyes never leaving the ladies.

Xavier looked up at Loren. Loren was not dressed in his usual Royal Guard attire. He wore jeans, a t-shirt, and sneakers. But, Loren, like the other guardsmen, looked unwavering at the women.

"Sire," he heard one woman squeak. "We meant no harm. We only wished to worship him, to touch your son." She scuttled over to Jeremiah, embracing him as she slid to the ground bowing at his feet.

"Inside, Son." Jeremiah repeated firmly, looking down at the woman clinging to his legs.

Xavier watched as Loren and Ephraim quickly grabbed the woman and lifted her to her feet. Then, he weaved through the Royal Guard and went inside the palace with Court and Robbie following him.

"Are you okay?" Robbie hissed with awe.

Xavier nodded silently.

"Crickey, I've never seen anyone act like that before!" Court groaned as they made their way down the long hall toward the antechamber and stairwell.

"Great!" Xavier moaned grievously. "Do you think Father will forbid me to go out at all since three nut heads attacked me my first day out?" Xavier turned and looked at Robbie and Court.

The pair looked at one another apprehensively and did not answer him, but their expressions had been answer enough.

"Great! Just Great!" Xavier growled.

They entered the antechamber and began to ascend the stairs to the royal residence when a voice called out, "Courtney? Is everything all right? We were just starting dinner when Loren got the call that the Premier's son had been attacked."

Xavier turned and saw a very pretty brunette standing in yet another doorway opposite to where he had first seen Courtney and his father.

"Yes, Mrs. Jefferson. All is well. This is Xavier," Court said, nodding in Xavier's direction.

Mrs. Jefferson walked toward the children and stopped at the foot of the stairs. "My word!" she began wistfully. "You look just like your father did at your age. It's so nice to meet you, Xavier. Loren has told me a lot about you." She extended her hand up toward him. "I'm Lucy Jefferson, Loren's wife."

Xavier dreamily descended the stairs to shake her hand, grinning like a fool the entire time. She was gorgeous! He shook her hand, and when she smiled warmly up at him, his stomach did somersaults. Finally, remembering his manners, Xavier cleared his throat, "Ni...Nice to me...meet you, Ma'am."

"Mom! Erica put itching powder in my makeup again! Now I can't wear it, and I look hideous without it!" a tall, slender, teenage girl whined from the doorway.

"Sarah, get your sister. I would like you both to meet our prince, Xavier Wells," Mrs. Jefferson told her.

"I can't meet the Prince without make-up on! What will he think?" she bellowed unhappily. Then, her eyes settled on the children and finally on Xavier. "Oh," she gasped.

"Sarah, it's not the end of the world! Besides, I'm sure the Prince would rather see you in your natural beauty. Wouldn't you, Sire?" Mrs. Jefferson asked, her eyes pleading with him.

"Oh, yes, ma'am," Xavier smiled at the girl who was simply a younger version of her mother.

Complete jubilation unfurled on the girl's face, and she smiled. "Thank you, Sire. If you'll excuse me, I'll go and get Erica." She disappeared and returned with a smaller girl with hair the color of sunshine. Watching the younger girl approach him, Xavier was instantly reminded of Loren.

"Girls, I'd like you to meet, Xavier, the Premier's son," she announced. "Sire, I'd like you to meet Loren's daughters, Sarah and Erica."

"Hello," Sarah said dutifully and curtsied.

But, Erica simply stared at him. "If you're King Wells's son, where have you been all this time?" she asked matter-of-factly.

"I was living with my, my mom," he said defensively, feeling a fresh wave of pain surge through him.

"Erica! I really don't think that's any of your concern!" Loren's voice warned.

Jeremiah, Loren, Ephraim, and the rest of the Premier Royal Guard stood just inside the entryway. Loren crossed the foyer to his wife and daughters. Putting his arm around his wife, he said, "Well, Xavier, I see you've met my family."

"Yes, sir," Xavier responded.

"Well," Loren began, looking at his family, "girls, why don't we go and finish preparing dinner." He looked back to Jeremiah and bowed his head slightly. "Good evening, Sire."

Jeremiah straightened. "Good night, Loren."

"Well, Court. I imagine you better get inside before your mother has your hide," Ephraim announced, waving Courtney down to him.

"See ya, X, and good luck," Court murmured as he passed Xavier.

Xavier nodded his appreciation, and Court went inside the Hardcastle residence.

"Robbie?" Jeremiah called.

"Yes, Sire?"

"Would you please go on home and ask your mother if she could find time to come to the palace for dance lessons. After the incident today, I think it's best if Xavier stays indoors."

Xavier felt his heart sink. So, his father would confine

156

him to the palace now.

"Yes, Sire," she responded with a courtesy and obediently trotted off.

"Father, why can't I go to the Minnows' for dance lessons? It was a freakish incident! It'll probably never happen again!" Xavier bleated.

"I do not wish to discuss this out on the foyer, Son. Let's go inside," his father said, walking past him and up the stairs with Ephraim and several guards following.

"Father," Xavier whined impatiently.

"Xavier," Jeremiah turned and pinned him with a severe glare, "we'll talk inside."

"But..."

"I will not repeat myself again, boy," Jeremiah growled quietly.

Xavier, muttering bereavements under his breath, stomped up the steps past his father and threw open the door, slamming it loudly against the adjoining wall.

Jeremiah was behind him in an instant. "Xavier!" he spat. The boy turned and glared up at him. "You better cool that temper of yours before you ignite mine and find yourself with undesirable consequences," he said quietly, looking pointedly down at his son.

With his mouth clamped shut, Xavier marched himself up the stairs and into his bedroom, slamming the door behind him.

Jeremiah shook his head with dry amusement.

"He seems to have inherited his father's temper," Ephraim spoke from behind him.

Jeremiah stared up at the boy's bedroom door and muttered, "Regrettably, yes."

Chapter 14
The Emblem
★ ★ ★ ★ ★

Xavier paced the length of his room, his anger still very raw and consuming. Lord! He had exchanged a life of freedom to be a prince locked in his own castle! It was all so stupid! He released a frustrated growl and kicked the bedpost, but immediately regretted doing so as he hopped around his room in pain. He rubbed his foot vigorously until the pain lessened.

Then, Xavier wandered to the windows and peered out at the garden flourishing on the patio. His father's room opened out onto the lush garden. It was an odd sight, a garden on a third floor balcony. Irises and orchards of various color and variety neatly edged a small basin of water at the base of a pale marble fountain. A rich emerald moss shingled over the granite stones set into the earth along a narrow path. The patio door to his father's room stood slightly ajar, and curtains swayed in the light breeze, giving Xavier a peek-a-boo view of his father's room.

Xavier had managed to explore just about every room in the palace except this one, and he found it impossible not to explore it now. He quickly slipped out onto the walkway and tiptoed to his father's room. The door opened with a soft moan as if protesting his entry into the King's bedroom. The entrance into the room was a small hall with a walk-in closet to the right. He crept forward and was amazed at what unfolded before him. Like his room, his father's room had a hearth. However, this fireplace was much bigger and had a beautifully carved onyx mantle. Above the mantle, a portrait of a man with pale hair and hypnotic eyes stared down at him. On its frame, the name, Jeremiah Xavier Wells III, was engraved with large, looping lettering. Across the room on the interior wall was a massive king-size four-poster bed covered by an ink blue satin comforter that had an embroidered emblem stitched in gold, red, and silver thread in the center. Xavier moved to bed and studied the stitching. A border of grape leaves circumscribed two swords crossing in the center, and amidst the blades were four intricately stitched figures: an owl, a lizard, a snake-like creature, and a stallion. Xavier ran his fingers lightly over the figures when his attention was drawn to the nightstand, more particularly, the photograph on the nightstand. Stunned, Xavier turned and picked it up. It was a picture of his mother and him taken last Christmas. How had his father gotten it? Had his mother sent it to him? Why hadn't she ever told him about his father?

"She was beautiful," his father's voice came from doorway.

Xavier jumped and quickly replaced the picture frame on the stand. "Father, I..." Xavier began, feeling like a cat caught eating a canary.

Jeremiah grinned. "Son, do not fret. This is your home. No room is off limits to you. Although, I would appreciate the common courtesy of knocking before you enter my bedroom. Agreed?"

"Yes, sir." Xavier smiled back. He looked back at the emblem on the spread. "What's this?"

Jeremiah crossed the room and sat on the bed next to him. He studied the emblem in silence before answering. "This," he began as he traced the emblem with his fingers, "is the royal seal. This is the emblem of our society. Each animal represents the core abilities of the empowered. The owl represents flight and divination, but not a soul has inherited the ability of flight in centuries. The chameleon represents the ability to hide, camouflage, and transfigure. That too is a rare gift. There are only five other people in the kingdom that have the ability to transfigure aside from me."

"I'm sorry. I don't understand; what ability?" Xavier interrupted.

"The ability to change form. Transfigurers can change form into any living thing."

"Anything?" Xavier questioned, amazed. "Can you change into a wolf?"

"Yes, Son, anything," he smiled feebly.

"You can change into other people, too? I mean, can you change into someone else and pretend to be them and no one would know it was you?"

"Yes. However, there are a few people, four to be exact, that have the ability to see the chameleon's true identity. They're called Augurs. So, if I were to masquerade as another person, I would have to be careful to avoid them." Jeremiah smiled. "Now," he pointed back to the quilt, "the eel represents the ability to conjure electro forces, obviously. As for the stallion, he represents the superior grace and agility of our people."

"But, aren't there a lot of other abilities than those four? Court says he's a transporter," he frowned, trying to assimilate the information.

"Yes, there are many different abilities. However, all abilities are derived from these basic four. Transportation developed from the aeronautic ability, the ability to fly. And, of course, transfiguration comes from the chameleon, metamorphic ability. Understand?"

Xavier nodded slowly, "I think so. Father? Court said that only royalty have telepathy. How is it that Mast... William had telepathy."

160

With a sigh, Jeremiah stood and crossed the room. He stared out the patio doors a moment before answering, "Because he is royalty. His grandfather once ruled the kingdom, Coasta in England, but he was a cruel and vicious man. Many of his citizens fled his kingdom and came here. Finally, militia forces grew tired of his tyranny and overthrew him. He and his family were banished from the kingdom forever. Can you imagine how horrible he must have been to have his entire kingdom turn on him?" Jeremiah turned and faced him.

Xavier nodded.

"Now, we need to talk," he began, crossing the room and leaning against the mantle.

"Yes, sir," Xavier tucked his head submissively.

"You will not be taking dance lessons out of the palace, Son. I'm sorry, but I will not alter my decision. In a few weeks, after your Induction, things will calm down and you should be able to do nearly anything you'd like. But, right now you're a rare and intriguing enigma, and everyone is very curious. And, that can be dangerous at times."

"Please don't lock me up in this palace! I need to be out and about. I only know a handful of people here, and most of them are adults. I want friends, father," Xavier pleaded.

"Son, you'll make friends, *after* your Induction," he said kindly.

"No, sir. I won't. I'll make a fan club. No one will want to be my friend just because they want to be with *me*. It'll be the throne or you they'll be interested in! And, even if they weren't, how could I ever be sure?"

"Xavier, I understand how you feel, but your safety is my first priority. Now, those women didn't intend to scare you, but they were in frenzy. It's difficult to say whether or not they would have harmed you," Jeremiah said evenly. "I'm sorry, Son, but you must remain in the palace until after your Induction."

Xavier huffed indignantly.

161

"Since we're on the topic of safety, on Monday Sir Lafayette will be coming to the palace for your lessons. You will have studies from eight to noon, Monday through Friday."

"Studies? You mean, I'm still going to be home schooled? Father, I want to go to school like all the other kids in the kingdom!" Xavier argued.

"No, you will have a tutor for the first couple of months. Today's event only confirmed my concerns. For the time being, it's necessary for your safety," Jeremiah said with finality.

"Please! Don't do this to me!" Xavier begged.

"I'm not *doing* anything to you, Son. I'm attempting to protect you," he said calmly.

"I don't want to be protected! I want a normal life!"

"You're a prince. A normal life isn't always possible."

"Yeah, but you don't have to go out of your way to make it less normal!" Xavier couldn't mask the contempt in his voice.

His father frowned at him warningly, but Xavier didn't care. He knew that his father was wrong about this, and he wasn't going to allow him to lock him up in the palace for two months without a fight.

"What if I refuse? What if I refuse to do my studies unless I go to school?" Xavier challenged.

"You will do your studies, Xavier," Jeremiah said, his temper wedging into his voice.

"How can you make me, Father? I'll make the teacher's life miserable here! I'll, I'll..."

"STOP! Stop right there, Son," Jeremiah growled, storming across the room and towering over Xavier with pure dominance. "You've entertained those thoughts far enough! You WILL do your studies, and you WILL NOT interfere with the professor's ability to do his job," he ordered.

Xavier rolled his eyes dismissively.

"DO I MAKE MYSELF CLEAR?" he added vehemently.

Xavier stared back at his father defiantly. But, after a moment, Xavier ceded to his father's will and tore his eyes away from his father's in a silent submission.

"Sire?" Milton stood awkwardly in the doorway. "Mr. Yaman and Mr. Bracus are waiting for you in your study, and dinner will be ready in thirty minutes."

"Thank you, Milton," he nodded to the subordinate. After a moment, Jeremiah looked back at Xavier. "Well, Son, I think it's time you take that shower and get cleaned up for dinner. Go on. Mrs. Sommers has already set out your dinner clothes. I'll see you at dinner."

Xavier nodded and left his father's room.

* * * * *

When Xavier entered the dining room, his father had not yet arrived.

"Your father will be here shortly. He's finishing up a conference with the governors," Milton told him as he led him to his seat next to the head of the table.

"Governors? We have governors?" he asked Milton.

"Oh, yes Young Sire. We have two, one for each region of the kingdom. There's a governor for Wellington and a governor for Merchant District."

"Which area does the palace reside in?" Xavier asked.

"Neither, Sire. The palace is a division all to itself. The nickname people have given to those who live inside the palace walls is Royals. Your friend Robbie lives just inside the palace walls so people would refer to her and her family as Royals. Royals are usually seen with much respect but contempt at the same time," Milton explained.

"Contempt? Why?" he asked.

"Isn't it obvious, Young Master? People are jealous of what others have that they want for themselves," Milton said simply.

"So people don't like Royals?" he asked, still confused.

"No, it's not that. They envy them," Milton told him.

Xavier frowned in thought. "If the people inside the palace's walls are called Royals, what are the other people in the kingdom called?" he asked.

"Well, the rest of the kingdom are separated into two groups: Merchants and Wellings. The Merchants, who live in the Merchant District, are typically a hard working group of people comprised of farmers, store clerks, and others with similar service jobs, but they have little money. Those who live in Wellington are known simply as Wellings. Wellings are usually diplomats, judges, guards, and people of that sort. They're well off and live comfortably but desperately want to live within the palace walls."

"How did the Royals come to live within the palace walls?" Xavier questioned.

"Your father. People with jobs closest to the Premier live within the walls. Loren and Ephraim are both generals for the Premier Royal Guard. If you hadn't noticed, your father has always placed you under the guard of Loren, and if he was off or not available, then Ephraim got that privilege."

Xavier nodded, trying to take it all in. "Will people envy me, too, since I'm a Royal?"

"But, Sire, you're more than that. You're *Royalty*; you're our prince! People will love and respect you. They'll worship you," Milton told him.

Xavier thought for a moment. "So everyone will think I'm some sort of hierarch? They'll treat me like a...a celebrity and look up to me?"

"But, Your Highness, you *are* a hierarch! So, yes, they'll look up to you," he smiled kindly.

Xavier slumped, suddenly feeling as if a heavy burden had been placed upon his shoulders. "I never asked to be one," he mumbled.

"Neither had your father," Milton said quietly.

A moment later, Jeremiah appeared through a door at the end of the dinning room followed by two aged men. The first was a squat, plump man with thinning white hair. His face was smooth and youthful even though he had to be in his sixties. The second was leaner and taller. He had gray hair, and a thick bushy mustache the same color. The small round spectacles on his face made his eyes look twice their normal size.

"Thank you both for meeting me on such short notice. I'd appreciate anything you could do to alleviate the tension around here," his father was saying and paused to shake both men's hands heartily.

"Ah, is this he? Is this your son, Sire?" the squat man asked in a nasal voice.

"Yes, Robert. This is Xavier." Jeremiah's shoulders straightened with pride. "Xavier?" he said, waving the boy toward the men.

Xavier stood, and after placing his napkin on the table, he joined his father and the two men. "Yes, sir?" he responded as he reached them.

"I'd like to introduce you to the governors of the kingdom. This is Governor Robert Yaman," he introduced as he gestured to the shorter of the two. "And, this is Governor Simon Bracus." He waved to the thinner man.

"Oh, so very nice to meet you both," Xavier said, shaking each man's hand.

"That's a firm handshake you've got there, Prince Xavier. That's a mark of a good honest man," Governor Bracus said, jovially patting Xavier on the back.

"Which governor are you?" Xavier asked.

Governor Bracus stood a bit taller, "I'm the governor of the Merchant District, young Sire."

"So that would mean," Xavier's gaze traveled to Mr. Yaman, "that you are the governor of Wellington?"

Governor Yaman nodded and said briskly, "Quite right, Sire. Now, if you don't mind, I must be on my way. It's been a pleasure meeting you." He nodded to Xavier before looking back to Jeremiah. "Sire, my wife and I will see you at the Induction this Saturday. Until then, good evening to you, Your Highness." The plump man bowed and exited the room. Then, Governor Bracus shook Jeremiah's hand heartily and followed.

* * * * *

After dinner, Mrs. Sommers insisted Xavier change into a suit before his dance lesson. Xavier was not happy. "Why? Why do I have to wear that thing?" Xavier whined, wrinkling up his nose at the sight of the black suit she was pulling from his closet.

"Because it's appropriate, young sire," she said sweetly.

"Appropriate? It's just a dance lesson! I'll look ridiculous! I'm not wearing it," Xavier announced cheekily and turned for the door.

"Now, wait a minute, Jeremiah Xavier," Mrs. Sommers ordered. She hadn't yelled at him; in fact, her voice was still quite soft, but it was how she said it. Mrs. Sommers, although soft, gentle, and grandmother-like, was not a force to be reckoned with. "You will wear the suit without any further whining, young man," she said, looking down at him with gentle eyes.

In the end, Xavier wore the black suit, and when Robbie and her mother arrived, Robbie doubled over in hysterical laughter at the sight of him.

"Whoa! Xavier, you look like... a... funeral director!" she managed to choke out between giggles.

Xavier noted with disdain that Robbie was comfortably dressed in faded jeans and a sweatshirt, and he groaned inwardly.

"Now, Roberta! I think he looks absolutely handsome!" her mother chided. "Besides, he probably should get used to dancing in formal clothes anyway. Come Saturday, he'll be wearing a tuxedo."

"A tux?" Xavier blurted. "I have to wear a tux?"

She smiled kindly at him.

Robbie was making gagging and choking faces at Xavier as they entered the ballroom, but this did not escape Mrs. Minnows's attention. "That's enough out of you, young

166

lady. Do you honestly think that with Xavier dressed in a tuxedo that I'd allow you to wear any old thing? No, ma'am. I bought you a gown for the occasion."

"A dress?" Robbie said aghast. "Do I have to?" she whined.

"Yes, you do, and there will be no argument about it, young lady," she responded sternly.

Now, it was Robbie's turn to sulk and pout, and Xavier couldn't help but grin at her.

"Now," Mrs. Minnows began, looking back to Xavier, "Your Highness, we only have four days before the Induction. So, I thought we should go over three basic dances: the polka, the three-step, and the waltz. You'll need to know the waltz for the dances with the politicians' daughters, so we'll start with it."

A surge of butterflies fluttered inside Xavier at the thought of dancing with girls, but he nodded in agreement. "Yes, Ma'am," he muttered.

After nodding to Robbie, who turned on a CD player to a slow rolling tune, Mrs. Minnows dropped him a curtsy, but Xavier stared back dumbfounded and didn't move.

Robbie laughed, "Hey, Casanova! You're supposed to bow back! It's common courtesy, you idiot!"

"Robbie!" Mrs. Minnows said sharply. "How rude! You should talk to Xavier with more respect than that; after all he is our prince." She turned back to Xavier. "It's okay, dear. When a lady bows to you before a dance, you should always bow back as a sign that you're ready to begin the dance. Like this." Mrs. Minnows demonstrated.

Xavier nodded.

Throughout the lesson, Xavier made numerous mistakes and pretended he couldn't hear Robbie's snickers or snide comments. However, by the end of the lesson, he could dance an entire tune without stepping on Mrs. Minnows's toes.

She grinned broadly at him. "Bravo, Young Prince! Bravo! Now, if you'll practice those steps three or four times before I come back tomorrow evening, you should do just splendidly at your Induction! Tomorrow, we'll go over the Polka and the three-step." She looked at Robbie. "Let's go dear! It's nearly 8 o'clock. Your father will be wondering about us."

Xavier walked them out of the ballroom to the front door.

"See ya tomorrow," Robbie called as they walked through the door and past Ephraim and another guard standing at their posts on the landing.

"Goodnight," Xavier called after them. "And, thank you, Mrs. Minnows."

"My pleasure, Sire," she smiled at him.

Chapter 15
Escape
★ ★ ★ ★ ★

The day of the Induction was finally upon Xavier, and he felt as if he had eaten a can of inchworms the night before. Thanks to Mrs. Minnows, Xavier's dancing abilities were no longer the problem, which made him feel somewhat at ease. However, it was the idea of everyone in the kingdom looking at him that gave him the lurching feeling in his stomach and made him want to throw up. He continued to lie in bed and stare at the ceiling, contemplating his day. If people had told him three months ago that he'd be rich and famous, he would have told them that they were raving mad. But, here he was on the morning before everyone in the entire kingdom would know him on sight. Not that it mattered much, since his father would be hording him away in the palace like a secret treasure. Anger surged through Xavier, and he sighed heavily.

"I don't care," he said aloud, "I'll run the professor off. If Father can't keep a teacher, then he'll have to send me to the academy." He nodded to himself adamantly and hopped out of bed.

The sun poured into his room from the patio windows. The sky was an electric blue with several low cotton ball clouds. It was a perfect day—a perfect day of which he'd be seeing very little!

"Who's to say I have to remain in the palace until after the Induction," he muttered as he pulled on jeans and a sweater. "I've got to get out of here for a while, or I'll go crazy."

Xavier hopped toward the door as he pulled on his sneakers, slowly opened it, and peered around. There was only one way out of the palace undetected. He'd have to sneak through his father's room, out onto the patio, and then, climb down the lattice along the wall there. Lord, it would be so much easier if he could just transport! He crept down the hall, praying his father was already up and out of his room.

When Xavier entered his father's room, his father was nowhere in sight. The bed's sheets were askew, and he could hear the shower running. Steam looped out of the door in great white waves as he hurried past the bathroom and out onto the patio. Without another thought, Xavier swung his leg over the edge of the patio and felt for a foothold. He quickly clambered down the lattice, hopped to the ground, and turned only to run straight into Loren.

"Strange way to leave your own home, X. Don't you think?" he asked, smirking.

Xavier exhaled loudly and pleaded, "Loren, please! I need a couple hours of being normal before the Induction. Please! I've been cooped up in that palace for nearly a week."

Loren regarded him seriously. Sighing he said, "Okay. You know I'll catch hell for this when your father finds out. And, he will find out, Xavier."

"I don't care! I need this, Loren."

Loren studied Xavier a moment his features sober and serious. Finally, he smiled. "All right, get out of here before I change my mind." He dismissed him with a wave of his hand.

Grinning, Xavier took off toward the back of the

170

palace and slipped through the secret passage. When he finally entered the stadium, he found a group of boys playing rugby when an argument broke out.

"You cheat! You know it was a foul!" Ken Calhoun yelled, standing toe to toe with a redheaded boy.

"Bloody hell ...it was completely clean, and you know it, Calhoun!" the redheaded boy bellowed, bumping Ken deliberately with his shoulder. "All you Wellings are alike, ya know that! A bunch of cry-babies!"

Suddenly, Ken punched the boy and chaos followed with every boy taking a side. By the time it was all over, Ken and a group of boys stormed out of the stadium chased by the other group's taunts.

"Man!" a smaller boy groaned, looking down at his torn, blood smeared shirt. "Ma is going to kill me!"

The second group began to make their way off the field complaining loudly. As they approached Xavier, the red haired boy looked up. "Hey, mate! Did you see that last play? Was it or wasn't it a foul?"

"Sorry. I didn't see it," Xavier told them.

"Man! They're a bunch of cheats!" the smaller boy said.

"Are you new around here?" the redheaded boy asked. "I've never seen you at the academy."

"Yeah, I just moved here," he told them.

"Well, welcome to the neighborhood. My name is Beck, and this is Harry, Garrett, and Frankie," he said as he nodded to the boys behind him.

"Hey," Xavier greeted. "My friends just call me X."

"Well, we're going to the wood to go swimming. You want to come?" the smaller boy, Garrett, asked.

"Sure, but isn't it a bit cold for swimming? I mean it's barely sixty degrees!" Xavier said.

"Naw, that's nearly a heat wave around here! Just view it as a challenge, X. Anyone can swim when it's ninety degrees out, but only a select few can swim when conditions are less favorable!" said Beck proudly.

The boys marched out of the stadium and across the field, chatting loudly and making crude noises. They continued along the palace wall to the far side of the property where the wall disappeared into a thick forest. The boys weaved through the wood staggering and joking. Xavier felt instantly at ease with these boys. They didn't question him about his abilities. It was as if abilities didn't matter; they just enjoyed being together and hanging out. Two minutes into the hike, a small lake emerged out of the thick vegetation. The boys immediately stripped down to their underwear and plunged into the water.

"Jeez! What happened to your back?" Garrett hissed.

Xavier had forgotten about the still healing marks that LeMasters had left behind. He shrugged nonchalantly. "It looks worse than it is."

The boys seemed to sense his unwillingness to discuss it, and, to Xavier's relief, they did not press him on the issue. The troupe's attention was drawn away by Beck who stood upon a rock formation at the far end of the small lake.

"Hey, girls! Check it out!" he sang and then flung himself off the rock, twisting into a graceful swan dive. A competition had begun.

"Yo, Beck. Watch this you sissy!" Garrett called as he raced off the edge of the rock, did a double flip, and dove into the water.

"Bracus, you show off!" Beck laughed as he pushed Garrett under the churning surface.

One by one, the boys took turns performing various acrobatic feats and showing off. One boy cannon balled into the water and was taunted relentlessly over its simplicity.

"Jeez, Frankie!" Garrett ribbed. "That's something my five-year-old sister would do!" The other boys howled.

Finally, it was Xavier's turn. He climbed the rock and stood proudly at its summit, looking down at the riotous splashing below.

"Hey! X is up!" Beck called, and all the boys looked

172

up at him expectantly.

"Give it your best shot, little girl," shouted Garrett.

"Don't chicken out," Harry taunted teasingly up at him.

"Yeah, no pansy stunts," called Frankie.

Xavier grinned flippantly. "You mean like your cannon ball, Frankie?" There was a loud, unified groan and heckling following this comment, and Xavier's challenger blushed.

Laughing, Xavier raced across the rock and threw himself over the edge with great force. He was able to complete two twists and two flips before turning his body into a dive just before he hit the water. When he emerged from the water, a deafening cheer surrounded him. He smiled broadly, but as a sudden coolness shivered through him, his smile fell. At first, Xavier hoped it was the water causing the chill, but he knew better. It was Jeremiah. Xavier groaned inwardly and closed his eyes to concentrate on rejecting his father's advances. However, Jeremiah's abilities were too strong to be denied, and Xavier knew it was a matter of time before his father or the Premier Royal Guard appeared at the lake to drag him back to the palace. He had to leave.

"Yo, X. Where're ya going?" Garrett called from the water.

"I've got to go," he told him, grabbing his jeans.

"Ah, come on, X!" Beck began.

"No, really! I've got to go," he said, looking at them begrudgingly. "Man, I'd like to stay, but I can't. I really wish..." Xavier's words fell short as each boy's gaze shifted to look beyond him, and he knew instantly that someone had emerged from the wood. By the boys' expressions, he knew without a doubt who that someone was. Xavier closed his eyes with exasperation.

"Sorry, boys. He cannot stay." Jeremiah's voice came from behind him. "Son? Get your clothes on and let's go," he said with barely controlled calmness.

Xavier turned. His father and the Premier Royal

173

Guard stood at the edge of the forest. Loren stood behind Jeremiah with a grimace. Xavier sighed and shook his head.

"Son? Whoa! Wait a minute! Crikey...you're Xavier Wells!" Beck said incredulously.

Xavier nodded as he pulled on his clothes. "Thanks, guys. It was fun," he said before leaving with his father and the guards.

"What were you thinking?" Jeremiah spat, no longer able to contain his anger. He cupped the back of Xavier's head with his hand and directed him to follow Loren through the wood.

"I was thinking that I needed to get out of that prison you call a palace!" Xavier responded cheekily, stomping ahead of him.

Jeremiah grabbed him by the arm and spun him around. The Premier Royal Guard immediately stopped. "I suggest that you not arouse my anger further by talking insolently toward me, young man."

"What are you going to do, Father? Ground me?" Xavier blurted, knowing exactly what his father would do, but he seemed incapable of stopping himself.

"So help me, Xavier!" Jeremiah's voice boomed.

"Sire," Loren interrupted, "not here."

"Stay out of this, Loren!" He looked at Loren menacingly. "You aided and abetted this little escapade with no thoughts to his safety."

"Oh, come on, Jer! You can't lock the boy up! That's not a solution!" Loren remarked.

"Stay out of it, Loren!" Jeremiah released Xavier and stepped threateningly toward his friend.

The other guards watched the situation tensely.

"No, Sire. I can't do that," Loren said quietly.

Jeremiah stomped toward Loren and challenged, "What did you say?"

"Look, Jer. As my king, I am and always will be your humble servant," he said calmly. "But, I'm not addressing you as your subordinate. I'm telling you as your friend that you're completely out of line," Loren finished boldly.

Jeremiah and Loren stood toe-to-toe, glaring at one another.

"This," Jeremiah growled, "has absolutely nothing to do with you!"

"That's enough!" Ephraim shouted, wedging himself between the two men. "Sire! Loren! I said THAT'S ENOUGH!"

The situation felt heavy and thick, and Xavier found himself holding his breath. His hands were clenched so tightly that his fingernails had embedded crescent shaped crevices into the palms of his hands.

"Gentlemen, please leave us. We'll meet you back at the palace," Ephraim told the remaining guards.

Jeremiah and Loren stood like statues and continued to glare challengingly at one another as the other men left.

"Jer, it's just us now. We're your best friends. You can't avoid this any longer! Loren and the boy are right! You've turned the palace into a prison!" Ephraim said.

Jeremiah abruptly turned away from them, and with a loud sigh, he looked heavenward for several seconds. Finally, his head and his shoulders slumped as though an invisible puppeteer had released his strings.

Ephraim studied his friend. "It's because of Julia, isn't it?" he said quietly.

Xavier's head snapped up at the sound of his mother's name.

"You can't bring her back," Ephraim continued.

"I know that!" Jeremiah spat, turning to face him.

"Do you?" Loren asked quietly. "You've been after the boy to grieve and to talk about her death, but have you?"

"What's that got to do with it? That's different," Jeremiah growled, backing away from the two men.

"No, it's not," Ephraim whispered. "She's gone, mate."

"I know that!" He began pacing like a caged lion, and Xavier watched his father warily. Jeremiah turned and spat

175

savagely at them, "Jesus! Don't you think I know that? I live with that every day!" His voice cracked, drowning in aguish. "Don't you think *he* lives with it every day? Don't you think I'm reminded of it every time I look at him?" He pointed almost accusingly at Xavier. "I couldn't save the one person he needed the most, and now I have to live with that for the rest of my life!" Jeremiah continued to pace, fighting for control of the emotions swelling inside him. Finally, losing the battle for control, he sank to his knees and cradled his face in his hands with a moan of despair. His entire body shook. "Oh God! I loved that woman! The things she had to endure...She didn't deserve that! I should have seen it coming... I should have known he'd go after her."

Dumbfounded, Xavier stared down at his father. He had no idea that his father still loved his mother. Cautiously, he approached him and touched him lightly on the shoulder. Jeremiah looked at him, startled. Then, he pulled the boy into his arms and held him tightly.

"Father?" Xavier mumbled into his shoulder. "It's not your fault, remember? Remember what you told me? It's not mine, and it's not yours! Remember?"

Jeremiah inhaled deeply, reigning in his grief, "Yes, Son. I remember." He smiled feebly down at Xavier, and whispered, "I'm sorry, Xavier. I shouldn't have lost my temper." He grasped Xavier's chin and lifted it until the boy met his eyes. "But, when I walked into your room and found your bed empty and you were no where to be found, it scared the hell out of me!"

"I'm sorry, Father," Xavier said. "I didn't want to scare you. I never wanted that. I just wanted to get out and be normal before everything came crashing down on me. I'm sorry for back talking you." Xavier tucked his head shamefully. "I should be punished for talking to you the way I did and embarrassing you in front of your men. I'm really sorry."

Jeremiah smiled. "I think we both deserve a good spanking. But, I'll tell you what; I'll let you off the hook if you'll do the same for me. What do you say?"

Xavier looked up at him and grinned, "Sure, but only this one time."

Jeremiah laughed and hugged him tightly once again. "I love you, Son," he whispered. "You're worth more to me than my own life. You are my life. I would never recover if something were to happen to you."

"But, Father," Xavier said quietly. "I can't survive another day cooped up in that palace! I couldn't stand it if I had to stay there for two solid months. Please! Let me go to the academy this Monday with Robbie. Please! I'm begging you!"

Jeremiah regarded him thoughtfully.

"PLEASE!" he pleaded.

"I'll consider it," Jeremiah said finally. "Let's see how the Induction goes tonight."

Chapter 16
The Induction
★ ★ ★ ★ ★

By dinnertime that evening, Xavier stood in front of the full-length mirror in his room, struggling with a black bow tie. Groaning with frustration, he cursed under his breath and threw the tie to the floor.

"Need some help with that, Son?" Jeremiah asked, his eyes twinkling with humor.

His father strode elegantly toward him, wearing an identical tuxedo with the same blue satin vest. The only difference between his father's appearance and his own was the golden sash his father wore under the tuxedo jacket with the initials JXW IV and the kingdom's emblem embroidered in navy.

Jeremiah picked up the tie and spun the boy around to face the mirror. "Watch," he said simply, and he slowly demonstrated how to tie a bow tie. "Are you nervous?" he asked, straightening the tie at Xavier's neck.

"Yes, sir," Xavier said and began to fidget with the collar of his jacket.

Jeremiah placed a hand on his son's constantly moving hands. "Calm down. You'll be fine. When you feel anxious or especially nervous just take a few slow, deep breaths, and remember that I'll be there with you." He smiled reassuringly, and Xavier meekly returned the smile. "Come. We should get going," he said softly as he patted Xavier's shoulder.

Father and Son exited the palace with the Premier Royal Guard and their families in tow. The moment they exited the building, Jeremiah reached for Xavier's hand and held it tightly as they walked up the drive toward a glowing crystal building. The building appeared to be constructed completely of glass. A vandal could have a field day throwing rocks at its walls and never grow bored.

As if reading his thoughts, Jeremiah said, "Magnificent, isn't it? Though it looks fragile, it's actually quite durable. The glass is bullet proof." Xavier looked at the building with renewed appreciation.

A crowd was beginning to gather at the Reception Hall's entrance. Jeremiah tightened his grip on Xavier's hand and muttered, "Looks as though we have a welcoming committee."

As they approached, the crowd grew steadily quieter. Xavier felt vulnerable and naked without the Royal Guard surrounding and shielding him from the numerous staring eyes. Each citizen bowed as Jeremiah and Xavier walked past. Xavier's heart thumped strongly in his chest; he was sure the crowd could hear it.

Then, Jeremiah leaned down to him and whispered, "Smile and wave, Son. They're here to meet you."

His heart leaped at the realization, but he managed to plaster a smile on his face and wave at the crowd. A group of schoolgirls dressed in frilly gowns strained eagerly to get a glance of him. When he finally drew near, the girls began to giggle and whisper.

Loren stepped up from behind Xavier and nodded toward the girls. "Well, Young Sire, it looks as though you've got some groupies of your own!"

When Xavier looked back at the girls, they giggled more excitedly. Maybe it was because of Loren's comment or maybe it was because he was feeling a bit more comfortable, but whatever the reason, Xavier smiled and winked playfully at the girls. The girls squealed loudly, drawing Jeremiah's and the entire Premier Guard's attention; Xavier simply shrugged and smiled ruefully at his father's silent, questioning eyes.

Ephraim leaned in toward Jeremiah, chuckling. "It looks as though he's inherited his father's flirtatious charm as well."

Jeremiah smiled, "It appears so."

They entered the hall, laughing and found Mr. and Mrs. Minnows waiting in the entrance foyer with their daughters at their sides.

Xavier had to look twice at Robbie. He hardly recognized her! The navy velvet dress she wore gave her a very feminine curve and made her look much older. She even wore make-up, Xavier noted. She looked beautiful. It was a huge change from the tomboyish, blue jeans and t-shirt Robbie he had grown accustomed to, and he didn't know what to say. So, Xavier simply stared at her with a gaping mouth.

"Robbie?" Court blurted from behind him. "Is that you? What happened to you?"

Court's mother smacked the back of his head warningly. "Courtney Aaron! Be a gentleman!"

Robbie self-consciously looked over her own appearance with a frown and looked at Xavier questioningly.

Xavier smiled and breathed, "Robbie, you look fantastic."

She positively beamed at him. "Thanks," she said, smoothing out the folds of her dress.

"Come, we better take our positions before they open the doors to the guests," Jeremiah said, leading the way through the double doors and into an elaborately decorated ballroom.

There was row upon row of tables and chairs nearly filling the Hall, and off to the right, an elevated dance floor

180

was clear and freshly polished. At the front of the room, a grand table with two golden chairs in the center stood apart from the other tables. Jeremiah led them to this table, where he and Xavier took the seats in the center while the others filed in on either side of them. Moments later, people began to enter the ballroom, eagerly looking toward the grand table. One by one, guests approached the table and introduced themselves to Xavier. Xavier thought the line of introductions would never end, but forty-five minutes later, the line dwindled and the servants began serving the meal.

"How you holding up, Son?" Jeremiah asked him.

"Okay," he shrugged, stabbing an asparagus shoot with his fork.

"It hasn't been too bad; has it?"

"No, sir," he muttered, trying to swallow his food past the knot of nerves twisting in his throat and stomach.

Jeremiah chuckled lightly and patted Xavier's leg reassuringly, "You'll make it."

After the dinner dishes were collected and the symphony began to play a slow, lolling tune, Jeremiah rose from his chair and clapped Xavier on the shoulder. "Excuse me, Son. Someone's got to get this party started," he said, giving him a wink and approaching Mrs. Jefferson. "Lucy? Will you honor me with a dance?" he asked, holding out his hand toward her.

"It would be my pleasure, Sire," she smiled as she placed her hand in his and rose from her seat.

All eyes turned toward the King and Mrs. Jefferson as he led her to the dance floor, turned, and took her into his arms. Xavier watched as his father gracefully swept across the floor in a mesmerizing waltz. He was a beautiful dancer and seemed completely relaxed even though every person in the room followed his every move.

"Sire?" a light voice came from behind him. He turned to see Robbie. "May I have this dance?"

Xavier smiled. "Sure," he said, getting to his feet. He took her hand awkwardly and allowed her to lead him to the floor next to his father. She turned into his arms, and they danced across the floor. Xavier's legs felt wobbly, and he stepped on Robbie's foot. Robbie winced, and he smiled apologetically at her. When she smiled back, calmness seeped into him like a warm hug. Robbie could always relax him with a simple smile.

"Do you really think that I look great?" Robbie asked, looking vulnerable.

"Yes, Robbie. You look terrific," he responded with a smile.

"Thanks," she said, blushing and kissed him lightly on the cheek.

Now, it was Xavier's turn to blush.

"Robbie, may I cut in? If it's all right with you Sire, I'd like to dance with you?" Lucy Jefferson asked. His father looked down at him and winked. Xavier smiled broadly up at him.

"Yes, ma'am. It would be an honor."

Jeremiah took Robbie's hand and twirled her over to him. "May I have a dance?" he asked.

Robbie's blush deepened, and she giggled. "Of course, Your Highness."

"How are you doing, Xavier? Still nervous?" Lucy asked.

"Yes, ma'am. A little," he muttered.

"Don't be, you're doing wonderfully." She smiled down at him, and Xavier felt his stomach somersault and his entire body grow tingly warm.

All too soon for Xavier's preference, the overture ended, and Lucy and Robbie left them. Father and Son remained on the dance floor for two lines of females had formed to dance with them. Xavier danced with girl after girl until his legs grew tired and sore. His face hurt from the fixed smile plastered on his face for each new dance.

An hour and half later, the symphony ended their performance, and the crowd on the dance floor returned to their seats. However, Jeremiah did not sit; instead, he walked in front of the head table and faced the crowd of people, settling back in their seats.

"Ladies and Gentlemen!" he called above the chatter and instantly there was silence. "As many of you know, a significant aspect to the Induction Ceremony is a prince's rite of passage and induction into his royal position. So, without further delay, I, King and Rightful Heir of Warwood, invoke the Rite of Passage and Royalty Induction for Jeremiah Xavier Wells V." Jeremiah turned to Xavier. "Son, would you please come forward and stand before me."

With butterflies twittering in his gut, Xavier stood on wobbly, gimpy legs and went to his father.

Jeremiah smiled encouragingly down at Xavier and squatted in front of him. "Are you all right, Son?" he asked quietly.

Xavier nodded briskly.

"Just follow my instructions and listen carefully to your oath. This is an important ceremony. Not only does it introduce and legitimize your position as the Prince of Warwood, but it also marks your entrance into manhood." As Jeremiah spoke, he unbuttoned Xavier's jacket, slipped it off his shoulders, and handed it to Milton who had appeared silently at his side. Milton returned to his post behind the grand table with Xavier's jacket folded over his forearm. "Ready?" Jeremiah questioned.

"Yes, sir," Xavier sighed.

Jeremiah stood and announced, "I call on the Keeper of the Chronicles to come forward."

Lucy Jefferson stood and moved to a gold podium at the end of the head table. With great care, Lucy extracted a very fragile, ancient leather bound book from a gleaming golden box. She carried it to Jeremiah who gently lifted it from her hands. Jeremiah watched as Lucy returned to her seat next to Loren. Then, he opened the book and turned to Xavier and the silently awaiting crowd.

Straightening to stand tall and proud, he began, "Jeremiah Xavier Wells V, we, your family, your friends, mentors, and humble servants, have gathered to officially recognize and sire the honor of the Prince of Warwood upon you. This is a sacred time and a symbol of your entry into manhood. Do you solemnly pledge to uphold the integrity, the protection, and the humble sovereignty of the Commonwealth of Warwood? And, do you vow to be intolerant of all that blasphemes and treasons your throne and your nation? Do you pledge to hold true to all that is holy and sacred, and to teach your children such? And do you intend to do so, even at the cost of all that you have, all that you are, even your very mortal life? If so, say, by the grace of God, I do."

"By the grace of God, I do," Xavier announced.

"Are you ready to assume the responsibilities of royalty, by letting go of your childish ways and preparing yourself toward becoming a noble and humble lord of Warwood? Will you discipline yourself toward steadfastness, patience, self-control, financial stewardness, time management, and fearless conviction? Will you accept your position in the community by faithfully upholding the burden of power through such disciplines? If so, say, I will by the grace of God."

"I will by the grace of God," Xavier repeated.

Jeremiah grinned down at him before looking up and commanding. "Would the Keeper of the King's Key and the Premier Royal Guard please approach your future king?"

Loren, Ephraim, and the Premier Royal Guard stood and approached them. While the guards formed a circle around the king and the boy, Loren carried a small, weathered, oak chest to Jeremiah and opened its lid. Jeremiah pulled a white satin glove out of the box and slid it on his right hand. Then, as he lifted the Key from the chest with his gloved hand, a sound of awe filled the room. A little over a foot long and resembling a small staff, the Key was a spectacular object. It was made of gold, and its handle was encrusted with diamonds, rubies, and emeralds.

Xavier barely noticed his father giving Loren a quick

184

nod, and Loren filing in with the rest of the Premier Royal Guard encircling them. He continued to stare at the Key in his father's hand with great fascination. Something clicked deep in the recesses of his mind. It was like a deeply suppressed memory fighting to be known. Somehow, Xavier knew the Key. *'Or it knows you.'* The thought came without warning, and Xavier was startled by it. How could a *key* know someone? He shook the insistent thought from his mind. No, he didn't know the Key; he had never seen it before in his life. But, still, he couldn't shake the feeling that the Key...belonged to him somehow. There was simply no other way to describe it. The Key was beckoning him; it belonged to him. When Xavier finally dragged his gaze from the Key to his father's face, he found Jeremiah looking down at him in bafflement and, although later Xavier would question whether or not he really saw it, fear.

Whatever Xavier had seen in his father's face was gone as Jeremiah cleared his throat and continued with the ceremony. "Son, please kneel before me and these witnesses."

Xavier dropped to one knee at his father's feet. Jeremiah stepped forward and placed his left hand upon Xavier's head. "I, the King of Warwood, encumber upon you this day, the 10th of August in the year of our Lord, to show yourself a Prince of Warwood." Jeremiah removed his hand and tapped Xavier's shoulders with the Key as he proclaimed, "I dub you Jeremiah Xavier Wells V the Prince of the Commonwealth of Warwood, in the name of the Father, the Son, and of the Holy Spirit. May these blows remind you of the duel you have entered, and though your fight may not be a fleshy one, nor are your weapons made of earthy material, you are in a contest with a very real enemy. May your weapons, your empowerments, be mighty and pull down the strongholds of the enemy in the name of your God and kingdom." Jeremiah paused, inhaled deeply, and winked down at Xavier.

After he replaced the King's Key in the wooden case,

he turned back to Xavier. "Prince of Warwood, please rise." Jeremiah reached inside his cloak and withdrew a royal blue sash with the kingdom's emblem and the initials JXW V stitched in gold. "I, your father and rightful heir of this throne, crest you with the family emblem of our kingdom, to be worn over your left breast as a symbol of your dominion, your faith, and your virtue over our great kingdom." Jeremiah slid the sash into place across Xavier's chest. "God save you, Prince of Warwood." Then, he kissed Xavier's forehead and turned him by the shoulders to face the crowd of guests. "Please kneel before your prince and state your citizenship oath."

Chairs squealed and moaned as the guests and the Premier Royal Guard knelt before the Xavier. The entire Hall chanted, "May the Lord bless you and forever keep you; May the Lord cause His face to shine upon you, and be gracious unto you; May the Lord lift up His countenance upon you, and give you peace. We, your humble servants of Warwood, solemnly oath to honor, obey, respect, and keep you as our just and deserving Lord and commander. So say us all."

"Please rise and welcome, Prince Jeremiah Xavier Wells V," Jeremiah bellowed.

Instantly, there was a thunderous applause, and Xavier stared around the hall, speechless.

As the ceremony came to an end, Xavier and his father stood at the door with Loren, Ephraim, the Minnows, and few high political figures, shaking hands and saying farewell to the guests. The group of giggling girls, to whom Xavier had winked at earlier, approached Xavier shyly. The other girls nudged a brunette with enormous pale gray eyes toward him. This was the only girl out of the group who had danced with him. However, throughout the dance, they hadn't uttered a word to one another. He didn't even know her first name! Xavier bowed slightly to the girl and grasped her outstretched hand, bringing it lightly to his lips as he had seen his father do. The girl turned scarlet.

"Thank you for coming, Miss," Xavier said softly.

"Applegate. Maggie Applegate. Thank you, Sire," she dipped a curtsy with a coy smile. "Hope to see you at the academy, Your Highness."

"Me too. I mean...I... hope to see you..." he stammered, blushing.

The girl nodded and skipped over to her friends. As Xavier watched the girls form a giggling huddle, a voice whispered into his ear, "I'm telling you, you're a rival for your father's heartthrob status." He turned and met Loren's grinning green eyes.

Xavier chuckled, shook his head, and turned back to the line of guests. His mouth dropped open in marvel. The remainder of the giggling girls had joined the adjournment line, each with her hand stretched out eagerly toward him. He looked back to Loren who diverted his eyes and stifled a laugh with the back of his hand.

Nearly thirty minutes later, the group finally made their way back to the palace.

"Did you see Ken and Mac at the Induction?" Court asked, moving into step next to Xavier.

"No. Were they there? I wish they would have come up to me and said hello," Xavier said.

"No," Court responded, rolling his eyes, "you don't. Look, I just play rugby with the guys occasionally. They're not my friends, and they're certainly not yours, X. You should have seen them when all those girls lined up to dance with you. Man, talk about jealous! I'm telling you, I've known those guys all my life, and if they think someone else is getting more action than them...Well, they'll make your life miserable. You best stay far away from them, X."

"They can't be that bad," Xavier said.

"They are," Robbie added. "I overheard them at the punch and tidbits table. They said that they knew you had been hiding something at the field the other day. They said that," Robbie hesitated, looking between both boys, "They were making fun of you, Xavier. They made the usual stupid comments about your appearance. Nothing you haven't heard before."

Xavier frowned and looked at the adults ahead of them. They had long since reached the palace, and Jeremiah stood talking to Mr. and Mrs. Minnows by the front doors.

"I'm sorry, Xavier, but it's the truth," Robbie whispered.

"Naw, it's okay. It's like Beck says, Wellings are a bunch of crybabies anyways," Xavier muttered.

"Beck? Beck Wilcox? How did you meet him?" Court questioned.

Xavier told them about his morning escapade.

"That was a stupid thing to do! Your father must have been really worried! I mean, to walk in your room and find it empty and you nowhere in sight. Xavier, that's how he lost your mom! THEY kidnapped her in the woods near her home! Didn't you stop to think how that would remind him of your mom's death?" Robbie said.

"Don't you think I know how my mother died?" he snapped at her. The group fell silent, avoiding eye contact with one another.

But, Robbie was right, and Xavier knew it. He hadn't put any consideration in to how his little escapade may have reminded his father of his mother's death. He had only thought of his own wants and needs. Suddenly, he felt ashamed. He looked at his father who was laughing heartily at a joke Loren was acting out. Xavier didn't deserve to be a prince. A prince was supposed to be thoughtful and self-sacrificing. His behavior the last week had been quite the contrary. Guilt squirmed in his gut and ate away at him.

Moments later, Jeremiah said his goodbyes to Mr. and Mrs. Minnows. Robbie mumbled, "Bye," before trotting off with her parents.

"Let's go, boys. Get a move on," Ephraim called from the door.

Xavier weightily stumbled to the door with Court at his

side, throwing him fretful glances. Without a word, Xavier made his way down the hall to the anteroom at the foot of the royal staircase. Finally, with his goodnights announced and taking Xavier by the hand, Jeremiah led him up the stairs and into the royal chambers.

"Are you feeling all right?" his father asked him softly as they climbed the stairs to their bedrooms.

Xavier nodded, tears stinging the edges of his eyes. He blinked furiously, fighting them back, but Jeremiah wasn't buying it. He stopped and peered down at him. "What is it, Son?"

Xavier looked away miserably. "Robbie helped me to realize how selfish I've been lately. I didn't give any thought to how you would feel to find me missing this morning, and how that might remind you of Mom's disappearance. I only thought about how I needed space and how I wanted to get out and make new friends."

"Son," Jeremiah cooed, "I think you're being too hard on yourself."

"Am I? I don't think I've been hard enough on myself, Father. I mean, what kind of king will I make?"

"A terrific one," his father reassured, placing his hands on Xavier's shoulders. Xavier looked away doubtful. "You will make an excellent king, Son. I know it."

Xavier looked at his father's earnest face and then nodded. "I'm really sorry, Father. I'm sorry I scared you this morning. And, if you don't want me attending the academy, I'll understand."

"Well, I've been doing some thinking about that, and like you, I had some help in seeing how unreasonable I've been. So, I've decided to enroll you at Well's Academy this Monday. You were right. I can't hide you away in the palace forever, and I don't want to. Come Monday morning, you and I will go to the academy and enroll you."

Xavier couldn't contain his smile. "Really? I can go?"

Jeremiah smiled down at him. "Yes, Son. You can go. Tomorrow morning, we'll visit the Merchant District to get your school uniforms and supplies."

"Thanks, Father. Thank you," Xavier gushed and, for the first time, hugged Jeremiah, rendering him speechless.

Chapter 17
Rivals
★ ★ ★ ★ ★

That night Xavier dreamt of the hallway with the red door again. It started much the same way, but this time Xavier found the door opened easily in his hand. He stepped into a white pentagonal room with a door on each wall. In the center of the room, the King's Key hovered at eye level. He warily stepped toward it and pulled it from the air. Xavier stared in awe at the Key in his hand. It vibrated with unseen power and was warm to the touch. As the warmth began to seep into his body, Xavier felt overwhelmingly content and peaceful. He smiled down at the Key, which seemed to be telling him that it belonged in his hands.

"Give it to me, boy," a voice snarled from behind him.

Xavier whirled toward the familiar chilling voice and felt his heart stop when he came face to face with William LeMasters.

"Give me the Key!" LeMasters snapped, grabbing at him.

"No!" Xavier hissed, dancing out of reach. "Never!"

Just as LeMasters's hand clamped down on Xavier's arm, he dissolved away with his surroundings, and Xavier found himself in another chamber, alone. This chamber was very different than the first. The kingdom's emblem encompassed the entire far wall and appeared to be a mosaic of precious jewels that sent dancing shards of light around the room. A long cherry altar stood against the wall, supporting three unique vessels: a small black opal vial, a gold case, and a decrepit wooden chest. Xavier immediately recognized two of the vessels. He crossed the room and ran a hand lightly along the altar. A soft humming drew his attention to the wooden case of the King's Key. As he drew closer, the humming amplified into a knocking that rattled the box, but the instant his hand touched the aged wood, it stilled.

"Son?" a muffled voice called. "Son? Wake up, Son." Jeremiah's voice pulled him from his dream.

He opened his eyes to find his father seated on the edge of his bed, gently shaking him. "Ah," Jeremiah smiled, "Good morning, Young Prince."

Xavier stretched and yawned noisily. "Morning," he mumbled.

"Get a move on, kiddo. We're leaving in forty-five minutes for Nottingham's," Jeremiah announced as he patted Xavier's leg and stood.

"Nottingham's?" Xavier questioned, sitting up.

"It's a tailor shop," he told him. "We'll get you sized for your school uniforms there. Then, we'll need to visit Wellington Bookstore for your school supplies and books. Then, I thought we'd round up some people, and play a Sunday game of rugby, and have a picnic lunch in the Coliseum. What do you say?"

"I say what are we waiting for? Let's get going," Xavier replied, hopping out of bed and racing into the bathroom to get his shower.

When Father and Son exited the palace, they found Loren and the chauffeur waiting by the limo. Loren beamed at the sight of them. "Sire! Little Sire! Good morning! Are we ready to do a bit of shopping?"

"Yep," Xavier grinned. "Are you ready to have your butt kicked in rugby this afternoon?"

"Whoa! I sure hope you have the moves to back up that hefty challenge little boy!" Loren teased, boxing playfully with him. When Xavier made contact with Loren's jaw, Loren melodramatically threw himself against the vehicle with a grunt. "Crikey! Where did you get that wicked left hook?" he asked, grinning and rubbing his jaw.

"All right, Son. Save it for the rugby pitch. If you hurt Loren, he won't be able to do his duty this morning," Jeremiah said with a grin.

Laughing, the group piled into the limo and traveled the short distance to Nottingham's. The moment Jeremiah and Xavier entered the shop, several faces turned toward them in shock, and the clerk behind a counter stared at them with his jaw dropped open.

"Good morning!" Jeremiah boomed happily. "My son needs to be fitted for his school uniform."

The man behind the counter jerked out of his state of revere and stammered, "Oh. Ah, y...yes, Sire." He looked down at Xavier and then back to the Premier. "What will he need, Sire?"

"Everything: seven sets of brushed twill slacks, five long sleeved shirts and five short sleeved shirts, seven vests, seven sweaters, seven blazers..."

As Jeremiah rattled off the list of clothing items Xavier would need for school, Xavier began to peer about the room. The shoppers had resumed their browsing but kept throwing awed looks toward Jeremiah and Xavier. One woman in particular, continued to inch closer and closer to Jeremiah.

"Son?" Jeremiah stroked his cheek to gain his attention.

"Yes, sir?" he whispered, pulling his gaze back to his father.

"The gentleman needs you to stand on the stool so he can take the measurements he needs," his father said, nodding to the stool that the man had placed before him.

Xavier nodded and stepped onto the stool. The man immediately set himself to work, measuring every inch of Xavier's body as the woman finally made her way over to Jeremiah.

"Sire?" she asked tentatively. "My name is Catherine Stokes. Governor Yaman is my uncle." She batted her eyes at him coyly.

"Oh, yes," Jeremiah smiled at the young woman. "It's so very nice to meet you Catherine." He extended his hand to her, and she took it with a blush.

"This is your son," she said, nodding to Xavier, but her eyes never left Jeremiah. "I saw him at the ball. He dances beautifully like his father."

"Thank you," Father and Son said in unison. Xavier continued to watch the woman closely. There was something in the way she looked at his father that he didn't like.

"Well, Sire," the clerk announced, returning from the back room. "We have everything in stock. However, the blazers will need to be taken in a bit, but they should be ready by Wednesday." He handed several packages to Xavier and Jeremiah.

"Thank you, Jon," he replied with a nod before turning to Catherine. "It was so very nice to meet you, Miss Stokes. We must get going." He shook her hand one last time, turned, and led Xavier from the building.

At Wellington Bookstore, people were more forceful, Xavier noticed. They all seemed eager to speak to his father and discuss politics and policies. Jeremiah showed great patience with their constant interruptions.

"Which lessons will he be taking this term, Sire?" asked an elderly woman behind a long counter wearing a scarlet Wellington Bookstore smock.

"He will be taking the basic core, anima lingua, and telepathy control," Jeremiah said just before a short thin man with wiry hair nudged him. "Oh, hello Richard. How's the family?"

"Oh, fine, fine, fine," the man muttered neurotically. "Sire? I w...was wondering if...if...if the personal protection bill m...made it to your desk yet."

Jeremiah sighed inwardly. "Yes, Rich, it did."

"Have y...you had a ch...ch...chance to review it?" he asked eagerly.

"Yes, I have, but I must say, I do not support the idea of allowing citizens to use more powerful abilities against their common man. A mild electro force should be sufficient in stunning a burglar or intruder until the proper authorities arrive. I do not think death is a fitting punishment for robbery or breaking and entering."

"Sire?" the clerk interrupted the conversation. "Does the Prince need parchment, mathematical tools, or pens and pencils?"

"Yes, ma'am. He will need all materials," his father answered before Rich drew his attention back to the protection bill discussion.

"Young Sire?" the woman looked to Xavier. "Would you like a black bag with gold and red trim, a gold bag with black and red trim, or a red one with gold and black trim?" She held up each bag as she described it.

"The black, please," he answered.

"Hey, X!" a voice called from behind him. Xavier turned and found Ken Calhoun and Mac Clarke browsing through rugby books.

"Or should we say, Your Highness?" Mac said with smugness.

"Just X is fine. What are you guys up to?" Xavier asked, trying to sound friendly.

"Not, much. Just wasting some time before lunch," Ken Calhoun said, holding up a book titled *Famous Rugby Players of the Warwood Kingdom*.

Xavier stepped away from his father to join the two boys.

"See you're getting your school supplies. I heard that

195

you were having a tutor for the first couple of months. Well, at least that's what my dad said," Mac said with a smirk.

"Who's your dad?" Xavier asked.

"He's a member of the Premier Royal Guard. He's Ephraim's right hand man. His name is Timmins Clarke," Mac said, jutting his chest out with pride.

"Oh, yeah! Timmins," Xavier nodded. "He's your dad?"

"Yep, Calhoun's father is a judge, Judge Cecil Calhoun," Mac continued.

"Yeah, I've met him," Xavier nodded to Ken. "Well, Father changed his mind, about school I mean. He's enrolling me at the academy Monday."

"Yeah, I bet you have Loren to thank for that. I heard all about your little adventure yesterday morning and how your father went berserk," Mac jeered, nudging Ken.

Xavier narrowed his eyes at the sneering boys. "He didn't go berserk!"

"That's not what Dad said. He told me that your father nearly tore Loren's head off," Mac said viciously. "I always thought King Wells was a bit unstable."

"Shut up! That's a lie!" Xavier blurted, stepping toward the boy.

"Are you calling my father a liar?" Mac challenged, bumping his chest into Xavier.

"If he told you all that, I am!" Xavier growled.

With his face twisting in fury, Mac shoved Xavier and sent him sprawling onto the floor. In an instant, Xavier recoiled and lunged at Mac, knocking a rack of books noisily to the floor. He managed to get in several punches before Loren got to him.

"Xavier!" Loren growled, lifting his struggling body off the other boy.

"Let me go Loren! I'm going to rip his head off!" Xavier shouted, struggling in vain against Loren's paralyzing embrace.

"What's going on here?" Jeremiah asked firmly and

196

with a wave of his hand, lifted the shelf and books back to their proper place.

Instantly, Xavier stilled but did not answer.

"It seems that we've had a little dispute. I'm not sure what it was all about though," Loren answered, lowering Xavier to the floor.

"Boys?" Jeremiah inquired.

"We didn't do a thing!" Mac responded meekly, getting to his feet and wiping his bloody nose with the back of his sleeve. "He just went berserk and attacked me!"

"You're a liar just like your old man!" Xavier yelled, lunging at Mac again, but Jeremiah intercepted him.

"Xavier! That's enough!" Jeremiah said forcefully.

Xavier froze in his father's arms and glared menacingly at Mac. "It's true! His father has been gossiping about what happened in the wood yesterday. He made it sound as if you went crazy and attacked Loren!"

Jeremiah released Xavier and surveyed Mac's and Ken's shuffling feet and downcast eyes. "Is this true, Mackenzie Clarke? Has your father been sharing Royalty matters with you?"

Mac slumped visibly. "No, Sire. He hasn't. Ken and I eavesdropped on a Premier Royal Guard meeting. We overheard what happened in the wood."

"What would your fathers say about this?" Loren scolded.

Mac shrugged uncomfortably, the smirk long gone from his face.

Jeremiah stepped forward. "Since you seem unsure, boys, let me help you with that," Jeremiah said with smooth dominance. "I know Cecil is an old fashioned kind of man, Kenneth. He would be furious that his son was engaging in idle gossip and disrespect toward the King. I believe your father would spank you within an inch of your life. Isn't that right?" Ken nodded briskly, not meeting Jeremiah's eyes. "And, your father," Jeremiah continued, looking down at Mac, "is a respected Premier Royal Guard. He would be

197

furious if he discovered you've been eavesdropping on confidential Royal Guard meetings. Most likely, he'd give me the task of choosing and enforcing your punishment. Isn't that about right, Mackenzie?" Jeremiah questioned.

Mac nodded. "Yes," he choked on a sob, "yes, Sire."

Xavier smirked at the boys haughtily but not before Jeremiah caught it. "Xavier, I'd suggest that you not appear too smug. You're behavior here was less than admirable."

"What? But, I didn't start this Father!" Xavier griped indignantly.

"That may be true, Xavier, but you handled it very poorly," Loren reprimanded.

"You've got to be kidding me! They start the fight, but it's me who gets in trouble!" Xavier blurted.

"We do not resort to fist fights to solve petty arguments and differences of opinion, Son," Jeremiah grumbled. "You owe these boys an apology."

"What?"

"Now," Jeremiah said quietly.

Xavier opened his mouth to protest, but shut it quickly at his father's glare. He looked at the boys in front of him, and finally muttered, "Sorry."

The boys nodded, but didn't look at him.

"Okay, I think we've had enough shopping today. Loren would you gather the packages? Xavier and I will be waiting in the car," Jeremiah ordered.

"Yes, Sire," Loren said and walked toward the counter.

"Let's go," Jeremiah commanded softly. "Goodbye, boys," he nodded to Mac and Ken. "Your fathers will be informed about this little incident."

Jeremiah guided Xavier out of the shop and into the limo. He sighed heavily and looked at his son. "Xavier, you need to get that temper under control. The academy will not tolerate a moody little prince running their school."

"I don't plan to run anything, Father! I was just standing up for..."

"There are more appropriate ways of doing that, Son!" Jeremiah muttered angrily.

Xavier huffed as Loren opened the door and climbed inside. "What the hell do you think you were doing in there, X? Did you even think? Well, obviously you didn't. What kind of image does this give you as future king?"

"I don't care," Xavier mumbled.

"I think you do," Loren continued severely. "What about how your behavior reflects on your father? Did you think of that? You had better do a better job of controlling your anger, boy. It'll get you in some major jams if you continue to let it control you."

Xavier looked back and forth between his father and Loren. Both men glared down at him. *'Great! I might as well have two fathers! I wonder if they'll take turns thrashing on me next,'* he thought moodily as the men looked away.

Suddenly, Jeremiah turned back to Xavier with a jerk and stared omnisciently down at him. Xavier swallowed hard. *'Had he heard his thoughts?'*

"Yes, I did. And, yes we would," his father remarked aloud, drawing Loren's attention.

"What?" Loren questioned, looking from Father to Son.

"Xavier's not particularly happy about receiving reprimands from the both of us. He's concerned that we'll both punish him in the future, and I informed him that we most certainly would," Jeremiah told him.

"You can bet your little behind *we* would!" Loren told Xavier, pointing menacingly at him. "If you ever pull another stunt like that again on my watch, I can guarantee I'll be there to put some heat to your backside." The car pulled away from the bookshop, and Xavier slumped into the seat between Loren and Jeremiah.

As the car pulled through the palace gates, Xavier muttered, "I'm sorry. I'm sorry if I embarrassed you, Father. I'll try to do better at controlling my anger. I...I'm sorry."

Jeremiah looked down at the boy and then, looked at

you'd get a handle on that temper of yours."

"Yes, sir. But, they were putting you down, and I didn't feel like I had a choice."

"Son, people who are envious of you will find any means to make you forget yourself and do something you'll regret. There's always a choice on how to handle it. You could have just walked away," Jeremiah told him.

"Would you?" Xavier challenged. "If it had been someone talking about me or Mother, would you've been able to walk away?"

Loren watched his friend with sparked curiosity. The boy had asked a tough question. He knew Jeremiah well enough to know that he would clobber anyone who spoke poorly about the boy or Julia.

Jeremiah glanced at Loren with dread. "I don't know, Son. I hope that I wouldn't."

The car pulled up in front of the palace where the picnic entourage had already begun to gather. Tamarah and Dublin Minnows approached the car with Robbie and Brit trotting behind them.

"How was the shopping trip?" Tamarah asked as Jeremiah and Xavier climbed from the car.

"Fine," Jeremiah said, looking at Xavier. "We got everything we needed, right, Son?"

"Yea...Yes, sir," he answered.

The group mingled for a moment until Loren announced, hugging his wife close to his side, " Well, it looks as though everyone's here! Let's get this party started!"

The group gave a loud cheer of affirmation and began the trek to the Coliseum in one loud boisterous group. The men walked in front of the children, joking and teasing one another like boys. The children placidly followed their rambunctious fathers, watching and listening.

"You'll never guess who I ran into in the Razorbill Cove yesterday morning, Mitch Crumford," Ephraim announced.

"Mitch Crumford?" Loren guffawed. "Jer, didn't you

and Mitch have a little rival thing going when we were kids?"

"You should know, Jefferson! You started it!" Jeremiah laughed.

"What? What on earth are you talking about, Sire?" he asked, looking wide-eyed and innocent.

"Jefferson, you're thick! You were always the instigator of all the jams we got into as kids!" Ephraim challenged playfully.

"Now, now, fellas," Loren shook his head, "I think maybe you're confused and not remembering properly. Who put the itching powder in Mitchie's jockey shorts? My memory may not be that great, but I believe that was you, Jer." Loren snickered. "He wriggled in his seat all through Latin! That poor boy's backside itched for a week!"

"Yeah, I remember. And, my backside was red for a week! My father was furious!" Jeremiah snickered.

"Okay, boys," Tamarah announced playfully, "enough bickering, or I'll start freezing mouths shut."

"I always knew you were a cold, cold woman, Tamarah. I never understood what Dub saw in you! But, of course, he always was a bit of a "stiff." Just think! If we hadn't loosened him up with our adventures, he would've squeaked when he walked," Loren laughed.

Dublin charged at Loren and seized him in a headlock, which was a hilarious sight for Loren was a good half-foot taller. "Boys, boys!" Rebecca Hardcastle chastised. "Save it for the game. There are innocent ears listening. So unless you'd like to see your shenanigans relived through your children, I suggest you keep your stories to yourselves."

Dublin released Loren and gave him a light shove.

"Rebecca, you've obviously never met my daughter, Erica. She manages mischief all on her very own." Loren nodded in Erica's direction in the line of children following them.

Court looked at Erica indignantly. "Imagine that! Your own father ratting you out like that!"

Your own father ratting you out like that!"

"I know! Who needs an enemy when you have a father like that!" Erica laughed.

"No doubt, she's her father's daughter," Ephraim snickered. "But, I have to admit, Courtney can manage a bit of mayhem as well. Just last week after an argument with Andrew, he coated his brother's bed with sneezing powder. He used so much of the stuff that I couldn't even walk pass the room without a ten-minute sneeze fest. It was three days before I could get close enough to neutralize it. The mattress was ruined, though. I had to toss it."

The men chuckled.

"It seems that I'm the only father here who has a perfectly well behaved son," Jeremiah gloated playfully.

"Excuse me, Your Highness," Dublin blurted. "I wouldn't be so sure about that if I were you! I happen to know of an incident where *your* son super glued his grandparents' mouths shut."

"He what!" Jeremiah coughed.

"Did you really do that, X?" Erica asked, looking at him in awe.

"Well, yeah, but it was an accident! It used to scare me when they'd take out their dentures at night. So, I thought if they'd glue them on permanently..." Xavier shrugged. "I guess I used too much." The children and men around him burst into uncontrolled laughter.

"Can someone tell me, then," Dublin continued after recovering from his bout of hysteria, "why would we, in our right minds, allow our children to become such good friends? Imagine the trouble they could conjure up with all those deviant minds working together!"

"Dad!" Robbie yelled, laughing.

"I know. We must be absolutely nuts!" Jeremiah added.

"I don't know about you guys, but I've had enough of this," Xavier whispered to the troupe of children around him. "It's time to retaliate. On the count of three, we attack.

202

The children charged toward their fathers. Ephraim had it the worst. His four boys tackled him to the ground with a loud grunt and piled on top of him. However, when Xavier jumped onto his father's back, he barely even stumbled. Chuckling, Jeremiah grabbed Xavier, flipped him over his shoulder, and lowered him to the ground. He pinned the boy there with one massive hand and began tickling him with the other.

"Just-what-do-you-think-you're-doing, Son," Jeremiah chortled between Xavier's infectious laughs.

"Help!" Xavier cried out between giggles. Court, Robbie, and Erica immediately abandoned their own fathers and charged at Jeremiah. The four children were able to struggle the King to the ground and pile on top of him.

"That's enough, kids," Lucy said lightly. "Let the Premier up. Now, kids, do you think we can make it to the stadium before nightfall?"

The children piled off the Premier, and Jeremiah stood and brushed himself off, laughing lightly.

"Yeah! You kids better just behave yourselves before the "Moms" get involved!" Loren scolded, grinning and shaking a finger at them.

"I meant *big* kids, Loren," Lucy said, eying her husband mirthfully which was followed by a collective laughter.

When the group finally arrived at the stadium, they found that it was already occupied. A group of boys were playing rugby and taunting one another playfully. Suddenly, the boys howled in primitive, bloodthirsty whoops and shouts before piling on top of the poor soul with the ball. Then, Xavier recognized the scarlet head.

"Father? Can we invite those boys to stay and play with us?" Xavier asked.

"Sure, Son. The more the merrier," he smiled.

Xavier approached the boys with Court at his side. "Yo, Beck!" Xavier yelled. The boys froze and looked at him. "Can we join in your game?"

The red headed boy grinned from ear to ear, "Hey, X! How's it going?" He jogged over to him with the rest of the boys following.

Xavier nodded at the other boys.

"Hey, X," Garrett said sheepishly, his eyes drifting past him to Jeremiah.

"Well? What do you guys say? Want to play a bit of rugby with us?" Xavier asked again. "We've got food too. I'm sure there'll be enough!"

The boys didn't respond but continued to stare past Xavier toward the King. Xavier followed the boys' stares and looked at his father in a silent plea.

Jeremiah understood and stepped forward. "Boys, we'd really appreciate it if you would stay. It would make for a better game, and like my son said, we do have more than enough food to feed you afterwards. What do you say?"

Beck returned from his state of awe with a jerk. "Yes, Sire. We'd be happy to play a game with you and Xavier."

Within minutes, the teams were chosen, with the four men, and Ephraim's two oldest boys, Drew and Dennis, on one team and all the other children on the other. They out numbered the Premier's team two to one and received the ball first. The kick-off went straight to Xavier, and he raced forward, making his way toward the sideline. But, he didn't get far before Drew plowed into him, knocking him out of bounds and slamming him onto the ground.

"You're playing with the big boys, now, Prince," Drew hissed into Xavier's ear, shoving his face into the soppy turf as he stood. Gasping for breath, Xavier slowly got to his feet and dried his face on his shirt tale.

"Andrew Ephraim Hardcastle!" his mother snapped from across the field. "Not so rough! You're not playing with boys your own size!"

Embarrassed Xavier waved at Mrs. Hardcastle and called, "I'm okay, Mrs. Hardcastle. It didn't even hurt." He grinned challengingly at Drew, and Court snorted a laugh from behind him.

from behind him.

"Do that again, brother, and you'll find that little brother can play just as dirty if you know what I mean," he growled softly to Drew as they walked to the center of field.

Even with Drew's intentional fouls, the game remained light and enjoyable.

During another possession of the ball, Xavier ran into trouble and threw the ball back to Erica who seemed to have a clearer path. Erica ran several yards until Loren caught up with her, lifted her from the ground, and dizzily swung her in circles.

"Caught you, little girl," he laughed, setting her on her feet and watching her stumble off balance.

After a brief scrum with Court as half back, the ball was back in motion. Court advanced the ball several more meters when once again, Loren appeared, but Court was ready and tossed the ball back to Xavier. Xavier tucked the ball and raced along the sideline toward the goal line. He dodged a lunge from Drew and was just steps away from scoring. Then, coming out of nowhere, Jeremiah scooped him off his feet, and Father and Son tumbled to the moist ground. Xavier released the ball to Beck, who snatched it up and scored. Jeremiah stood, his shirt soaked from the wet turf, clinging to him like a second skin. He helped Xavier to his feet.

"Not bad, Son. You showed some really good moves there. Not bad at all."

Xavier beamed.

On a kick return, Jeremiah received the ball and easily maneuvered through the children, but Xavier wasn't fooled by his father's fancy footwork. The moment Jeremiah jabbed to his left, Xavier went right and drove his shoulder into Jeremiah's stomach and wrapped his arms around his torso. Xavier's hit only paused Jeremiah, and he continued down the field with Xavier in tow flapping behind like a towel on a clothesline. However, this hesitation was all that was need for Beck, Court, Robbie, and Garrett to leach onto the

"Man, X!" Garrett laughed barely able to breathe. "You... looked... hilarious."

"Yeah," Robbie giggled. "You looked like a rag doll hanging on your dad like that!"

"Oh man!" Garrett's laughter increased, though Xavier couldn't see how it was possible. "She just called you a *doll*!"

The other boys jested and hooted.

"Robbie thinks Xavier's a *doll*? Why didn't you say something sooner, Rob? I think X has a right to know when someone's sweet on him," Court teased.

"Oh, really," Robbie huffed, getting to her feet. "Boys are such idiots!" She stomped away, leaving the boys hooting louder than before.

Garrett was laughing so hard that he was completely useless the next scrum, and Drew easily maneuvered by him and scored.

"Children!" Lucy called from the sideline. "Lunch is ready! Big kids, too," she added, smiling at Jeremiah and Loren.

The group charged toward the women and greedily began filling their plates with sandwiches and tidbits. They mingled briefly before they naturally segregated themselves. The women remained together near the food, talking lightly of women's matters. The men migrated into the stands and sat talking and teasing one another like boys. Occasionally, their taunts grew so loud and obnoxious that it wasn't until one of the women glared at them that they'd calm down again.

The children sat in the middle of the field, reliving moments of the game and laughing at each other's attempts in tackling one of the men. Xavier sat with his friends not really listening to their stories. Instead, he watched his father with his childhood friends, laughing and heckling Dublin. When Jeremiah turned and caught Xavier watching him, he looked questioningly at him. Then, his face relaxed, and he grinned. Xavier couldn't remember a time when he felt so at home, so comfortable, so happy in his entire life, and he grinned back.

Chapter 18
Wells Academy
★ ★ ★ ★ ★

"The Key," William LeMasters demanded, "I need that Key!"

"But, the Key is useless without the boy!" Danson muttered. "There's no way the boy will be left unguarded now!"

"Let me worry about the boy!" William barked. "You just get me that Key! The plan is still workable even with the unforeseen hiccups. In fact, it turned out much better than I could ever imagine! The woman wasn't part of the plan, and look how wonderful that turned out! I've never seen Jeremiah in such agony before. It was priceless," Master gloated.

Xavier jerked awake, shaking and saturated in his own sweat. Slowly he sank back into his bed, kicking the twisted blankets off his body. He lay fitfully for some time until he was finally able to fall asleep again.

★ ★ ★ ★ ★

The next morning, Mrs. Sommers entered Xavier's room, humming. She marched over to the windows and yanked back the curtains. The room exploded in light, waking the boy instantly.

"Good morning, sweetheart," she sang. "Time to get up."

"Morning, Mrs. Sommers," he yawned grumpily.

"I had your school clothes laundered last night," she rattled on as she bustled over to his closet, pulling out the school uniform. "It's going to be pleasant today, so the summer weight slacks and a short-sleeved top should be appropriate." She flung the clothing on the foot of his bed and looked down at him. "Well? Get a move on. You better get washed up and dressed. Your father is already having his breakfast."

Once he washed the sleep from his face and dressed, Xavier wandered into the dining hall and found his father leaning back in his chair with a newspaper and a cup of tea in hand.

"Hello, Son. Ready for your first day of school?"

"Yes, sir." Xavier sat at the table as Milton ladled oatmeal into his bowl.

"Good. The Minnows will be riding along with us this morning. I thought you'd feel more comfortable facing your first day with an ally."

Xavier grinned at his father, "Yes, sir!"

Jeremiah stood. "Okay, then. The car pulls out in thirty minutes. So, after you finish your breakfast you better go and pack your school things, and I'll meet you in the reception room."

Xavier nodded, scooping a large spoonful of oatmeal into his mouth.

Jeremiah patted him on the shoulder and left the room.

* * * * *

The limousine pulled up in front of the Minnows residence just before eight o'clock. No sooner had the vehicle come to a halt than Robbie came bouncing out the front door, grinning with a very tired looking Dublin following her.

"Hey, X," Robbie chirped as she slid to sit next to him.

209

"Dad says we'll probably have most of our classes together! Except for our empowerment courses since you have two other abilities than me. I'm really excited. It'll be different going to a school with other people who are empowered. Won't it? Court says the electro force course is a good time. The professor is really cool, he says. Did you know Court already has a second ability? He can transport. I wish I could transport. I hear it's unusual for kids our age to have multiple abilities. Well, except for you of course. " Robbie continued to rattle on and on.

Dublin smirked at Jeremiah and shook his head. "Yes, her mother and I are very worried about the long term effects that excessive talking and oxygen deprivation might have on her health."

Robbie paused and shot her father a scowl before returning to her chatter. Both men chuckled.

When the car finally pulled up in front of the school, Loren opened the back door, and Jeremiah climbed out of the car followed by Xavier. The school was an enormous gothic influenced stone building. Several children in identical uniforms stopped to stare at Jeremiah and Xavier, and he was thankful when Dublin and Robbie joined them.

"Come on, X," Robbie said, grabbing his arm and yanking him up the stone steps toward the arched entrance.

"You best do what she wants, Xavier! If she doesn't get her way, she might yank your arm out!" Dublin teased. Both men laughed and followed the children up the steps.

Just inside the shadows of the entrance, a pinched woman loomed, watching the group climb the stairs. The children stopped abruptly in the entranceway and peered up at the woman who stared down at Xavier with curiosity. Xavier returned the woman's stare with unbridled boldness, and he thought he saw something darker spark in her eyes before she turned to greet the approaching men.

"Ah, Madam Bowerman, it's good to see you again," Dublin said, shaking her hand heartily.

"Dublin, it's good to have you back in the kingdom,"

she beamed, but the smile didn't reach her eyes, Xavier noticed. She turned to Jeremiah. "Sire, as always, it's a pleasure." She curtsied and extended her hand to him.

Jeremiah took her hand and brushed it against his lips. "Hello, again, Madam Bowerman. I appreciate you allowing the children to enroll late for the term."

"Oh, not at all! Of course we'd make special allowances for the Prince!" she said, looking down at Xavier. "Well, if you'll follow me, we'll get the children registered."

She led the group through the door and into the building. As they continued down the crowded corridor, Bowerman smiled at Jeremiah. "This hall is never this congested. It seems the word is out that the Prince has arrived for his first day of school."

Jeremiah nodded with a small grin as Madam Bowerman turned to the crowd of students, watching them. "All right, all right! You've seen him, now kindly get yourselves to class," she chided. Slowly, the students began to disperse, and she led the group into the office.

A dumpy, older woman sitting behind the counter looked up as they entered, and her eyes grew enormous at the sight of Jeremiah. She jumped to her feet with her mouth flapping humorously as she tried to find the words to speak.

Finally she managed to squeak, "Sire! Ah...ah...it's a...an honor, sir!" She bowed vigorously again and again and sent the rolls of fat around her abdomen rippling and jiggling like water disturbed by a rock.

Jeremiah approached the woman and took her hand into his, kissing it as he had Madam Bowerman's. "Nice to see you, Jeanette," he told her.

"Jeanette, would you provide Mr. Minnows with enrollment papers and work up a class schedule for his daughter, Roberta, as well as one for the Prince." She nodded toward Xavier.

Jeanette's eyes nearly bulged out of her head as her gaze settled on Xavier. "Oh, my! Hello, Young Sire! It's so nice to see you. Oh, my, you're a spitting image of your father."

"Thank you, Ma'am," Xavier remarked with a smile.

"Premier Wells? If you'd follow me, I'll start the admissions interview with you and your son," Madam Bowerman stated.

Jeremiah and Xavier followed her into her office, and she closed the door behind them with a light click. She gestured toward the seats and said, "Please, have a seat."

Father and Son sat across from Madam Bowerman who settled herself behind a large walnut finished desk. She smiled briefly at Xavier and then directed her attention to Jeremiah. "I assume you were able to obtain the boy's records from his previous school?"

"Yes, Ma'am," Jeremiah responded, digging into a pocket inside his cloak. He withdrew a thick envelope, extracted and unfolded the papers inside, and handed them to Madam Bowerman. "As you can see, the boy received excellent marks at his old school."

Bowerman studied the papers a moment. "Hmm, yes. I see that, but the curriculum at his old school seems," she looked up and flashed another smile, "well, less than challenging." She looked back at the transcript in front of her. "He may need to be placed in remedial math for the first semester, maybe even a remedial language arts course as well. We do not want the Young Prince to get in over his head; do we?"

"What!" Xavier blared, straightening in his seat. "I don't need remedial anything. I want to be in the same classes as everyone else!" He looked beseechingly at his father. "I can do the work! I know I can!"

Jeremiah studied his son's determined face and turned back to the headmistress. "Madam Bowerman, I think my son's up to the challenge. I appreciate your concern, but I'd like him placed in the standard curriculum, please."

"As you wish, Sire," Bowerman sighed. "I was just looking out for the boy's best interest."

"And I appreciate that, Madam Bowerman," he told her.

Bowerman scribbled something in her notes and then looked up. "I see the boy has his uniform, but where is his royalty sash?"

"Sash?" Xavier questioned.

"I have it here," Jeremiah answered, pulling the blue sash that had been presented to Xavier at his Induction from his pocket. "I wasn't sure if you'd honor that tradition."

"Oh, yes, Sire!" Madam Bowerman said. "I guess I'm just old fashioned that way."

Xavier looked at the sash and then back and forth between his father and the headmistress. "I don't have to wear that thing, do I?"

"Yes, Young Sire. You will wear the sash at all times. I think it's important for the other students to know your position in our society and demonstrate the proper respect they should toward you."

"No!" Xavier strained to maintain his temper but was quickly failing. "I don't want to stand out from anyone! I don't want to be any different than anyone else!"

"But," Madam Bowerman began calmly, "you are different. You are the heir to the throne. I'm sorry, Sire, but it's been a tradition in this school for hundreds of years for the heir or heirs of the king to be clearly identified with the royalty sash. That tradition will continue as long as I am headmistress here."

Xavier huffed and flung himself back into the seat. Jeremiah looked down at him warningly before returning to the interview with Madam Bowerman.

* * * * *

Thirty minutes later, when Xavier and Robbie entered their first class, every pair of eyes trailed to them and, eventually, settled just on Xavier and the sash. One by one, whispers began to fill the room and attracted the professor's attention. A thin wiry man with wild honey hair turned toward them.

"Ah, new students!" he exclaimed. "Welcome, please come..." his eyes drifted to the sash, and he faltered. "Ah, welcome." Shaking his head, the professor regained his composure and continued, "Come on in and find a seat. I'm Sir Underwood. Welcome to Beginning Abstract Mathematics. Leave your enrollment cards on my desk so that I can include your name in my class roster."

Doing as they were told, both children laid their cards on the desk and found seats next to one another near the rear of the room. Quickly, Xavier busied himself with digging out his mathematics text and leafing through its pages. However, he could still feel every eye on him.

Sir Underwood cleared his throat, "Now, ladies and gents. Where were we?"

"The Distributive Property of Multiplication, Sir," called a student.

"Ah, yes. As you can see by the example..." he continued.

Feeling the class's attention leaving him, Xavier ventured a glance around the room at the other students. Erica Jefferson sat in the back of the room next to Xavier. She didn't seem too interested in the professor's discussion. A sphere of light hovered an inch above her desk, and she was entertaining the boy next to her by manipulating the light into interesting shapes. Then, it took the form of Sir Underwood's head, and with a flick of her finger, the minute head began moving its lips and a soft "Blah, Blah, Blah" emitted from it. The boy next to her snorted, attracting Sir Underwood's attention, but Erica was deep in concentration and didn't see his approach.

"Miss Jefferson?" he questioned, stopping next to her. "I must say, that is a fond likeness of me, but don't you think that if you made more of an effort to pay attention in my class, you could earn an exemplary mark on your end of term report?"

The light dissolved. "Yes, sir," Erica answered quietly.

"Good," the professor commented with finality. "Just think of the impression you're making in front of the Prince!" He nodded toward Xavier.

Xavier blushed as every eye fell on him once again. Once Sir Underwood resumed the lesson and the class's attention was drawn to the front of the room again, Xavier continued his inspection of the room. Ken and Mac sat along the wall, whispering intently, and from their frequent glances in his direction, Xavier was left with little doubt that he was their topic of conversation. At the opposite side of the room, Beck and Garrett sat watching Sir Underwood closely and taking notes. Harry, sitting behind them, looked dangerously close to nodding off and kept jerking his head upright whenever his nose would loll downward and touch his desk.

Then, Xavier met a pair of pale silver eyes, staring unwaveringly back at him. Instantly, he was enchanted. After several long seconds, the girl finally blinked, breaking the hypnotic state between them, and Xavier was able to study the girl properly, recognizing her at once. She had been in the swarm of giggling girls who approached him outside the Reception Hall the night of his Induction Ceremony. It was Maggie Applegate. Xavier smiled at her, and she quickly looked away, her face becoming flushed and pink. Courtney, who was sitting behind Xavier, snickered, "A new groupie?"

The rest of the morning went quickly. After attending his core courses, Xavier felt fairly confident he'd do well in mathematics and literature, but he was equally confident that Latin was going to be a nightmare. However, he found history to be his favorite subject. The class focused on the history of the empowered society and the weaving of that history into the world's most commonly accepted events. For example, El Nino did not cause the great blizzard of 1994 in the eastern United States like many people believed. Actually, it had been started by a teenage glaciator—one who has the ability to create very cold conditions and turn objects into ice—who got overly excited that a girl he'd asked out had said yes. Thankfully, no one had been hurt, but the kingdom's civil workers had to work overtime to thaw the kingdom and the affected areas!

Another more serious event was the great Chicago fire of 1871. The story of a cow kicking over a lantern and starting the fire in a barn had been nothing more than folklore. Actually, the fire had been started by a pyrotector—one who has the ability to create fire or flame. In addition to the fires in Chicago, he set fire to nearly two-dozen buildings and homes throughout the kingdom. As a result of his blatant endangerment of lives, his powers were stripped, and he was banished from the kingdom.

"How can powers be *taken* from someone?" one student asked Madam Peel, their history teacher.

"There's only one way an empowered can be stripped of his or her abilities, the Clavis de Rex," Madam Peel told them.

"The what?" blurted another student.

"The King's Key you idiot!" Beck snapped.

"Okay, okay. That's enough Mr. Wilcox," Madam Peel chastised.

"So, anyone who touches the Key will lose their powers?" Robbie questioned.

"Oh, no, honey. Normally it's quite harmless. Only the king or his heir can control it, so only the king or his heir can take powers away from an individual."

The entire class glanced uneasily at Xavier.

"How many of you attended Sire Wells's Induction Ceremony?" Madam Peel asked. Nearly every hand shot into the air, and Madam Peel nodded. "The object that King Wells used to christen young Xavier with his birthright as prince was the Clavis de Rex. Whether you realize it or not, you were a witness to a very rare sight. The Key is rarely removed from its casing. It's safe to predict that many of you will not see the Key again until Xavier becomes king or inducts his own heir one day."

216

Again, Xavier felt every eye on him, and he sank deeper into his seat.

Chapter 19
Dragon Lady
★ ★ ★ ★ ★

Xavier was starving as he and Robbie made their way through the lunch line. But, when he reached the counter, he did not receive the bowl of vegetable chowder, turkey sandwich, and fruit cup that the other students were given. Instead, the cooks beamed at him as they handed him a plate filled with sweet mashed potatoes, mixed salad greens, and a prime rib steak.

"Welcome to Wells Academy, Sire," a cook chirped happily.

Xavier simply nodded at a lost of what to say. Ducking from the numerous prying stares around him, Xavier quickly led Robbie to a table at the back of the cafeteria and sank into the seat next to Court, his face hot with embarrassment.

"Hey, X," Court greeted.

"Hey," he muttered back.

"What's up?" Court asked, studying his sulky face.

But, before Xavier could answer him, a familiar voice drawled loudly above him, "Well, it seems that the cooks are taking good care of Prince Wells."

Xavier looked up to find Madam Bowerman sneering

down at him, and every student in the cafeteria was looking at him and his plate of food. There was a sudden outburst of whispers, and Xavier looked around the room, seeing the unmistakable envy on some faces.

"Lord, knows, the normal slop isn't fit for a prince to eat," she continued.

Xavier felt his stomach jerk with anger. "Really?" he challenged as he met her eyes. "I thought the chowder looked mighty good to me. In fact, I was just preparing to trade for it."

Xavier stood and spotted Beck two tables away. "Excuse me, Headmistress," he muttered smugly as he walked around her and across the cafeteria very aware of every pair of eyes, every head turning and following him. "Hey," Xavier greeted with a nod as he stopped next to Beck's table.

"Hey, X," Beck said, nodding back.

"Would you like to trade lunches?" Xavier asked.

"What? Come on, mate! You don't want to do that!" Beck argued.

"Yes, I do. What do you say? My prime rib for your chowder and sandwich?"

Beck's gaze traveled past Xavier toward the headmistress. Xavier stepped into his line of vision. "Well?"

"Ah, sure," Beck answered and grinned.

The cafeteria burst into fevered whispers as Xavier took Beck's tray back to his table. He walked around Headmistress Bowerman and sank into his chair.

"Sire? I'd like to see you in my office after lunch," she announced tightly, and the whispers took on a heightened energy as the headmistress left the hall.

"Jeez, X," Robbie hissed, "Why did you do that? You made her angry! Didn't you see her face?"

Xavier shrugged, "What was I supposed to do? She was making me stand out as something special!"

"But, you are! You're the Prince of Warwood for God's sake!"

"Yeah, well, I never asked to be treated special!" he muttered.

Following lunch, Xavier entered the Headmistress's office. The secretary sat behind the desk typing furiously and looked up as he entered. "Oh! Yes, Sire? What can I do for you?" she asked, jumping to her feet.

"Madam Bowerman wanted to see me after lunch," he told her.

"Oh? Well, have a seat. The headmistress is making her lunch time rounds." She nodded toward a row of chairs and resumed her typing.

Xavier sat listening to the hum of the lights above him and the constant clicking from the secretary's word processor. Moments later, the door swung open drawing a draft of air across his face.

Madam Bowerman swept into the office and ordered, "Jeanette, please get me King Wells's daytime number."

'That doesn't sound promising,' Xavier thought as the headmistress turned a glare onto him. He gulped with trepidation but glared back determinedly.

"Sire?" she motioned toward the door to her office. "After you."

Xavier stood and entered the headmistress's office. "Sit down," she snapped, closing the door behind them.

Xavier stared at her stunned by the sudden change in her tone. She bore down on him like a hawk swooping in on its prey.

"I said sit down!" she screeched.

Xavier sunk into a chair as Madam Bowerman soared to the other side of the desk and perched herself on the edge of her seat, peering down at him. Jeanette waddled into the room with an index card. She handed it to the headmistress, cast a glance at Xavier, and quickly left the room, closing the door with a soft thud.

"Now," Madam Bowerman began, "I realize that you are new to this academy, and you're unfamiliar with how things work in this kingdom, but that is no excuse for you to

220

undermine my authority here as headmistress! Your behavior in the cafeteria was garish and pompous."

"Pompous!" Xavier exclaimed. "It was not! I just..."

"Let me finish!" she bellowed. "Yes, it was pompous. You made a mockery of me, young man! You were completely out of line! What would the King say? How would he react knowing his son was misbehaving toward an adult?"

Xavier shrugged, not meeting her eyes.

"Well," the headmistress began almost gleefully, "allow me to tell you. I've known your father for a number of years, and I think I can safely predict his reaction. I believe he'd be furious, to say the least. I dare to say, he wouldn't hesitate to march into this school and set you on the straight and narrow. Does that sound about right, Young Sire?"

Xavier did not respond.

"Okay then, let's just see." Xavier watched with distress as she picked up the receiver and began dialing.

Xavier sat fuming, not trusting himself to speak. *'Father will understand,'* he thought. But, even as he thought it, he began to panic, knowing full well that his father would not understand, and there'd be hell to pay.

"Yes, Alexandria, this is Headmistress Bowerman calling. I need to speak to King Wells, please." She smirked at Xavier as she waited to be connected to his father, which faded the moment Jeremiah came on the line. "Hello, Sire! I'm so sorry to interrupt your busy day, but we're having a bit of trouble here with young Xavier," she told him, sounding truly concerned and baffled. "He's having difficulty displaying the proper respect toward those in authority." She paused and listened, and Xavier could hear his father's voice resonating through the receiver. "Yes, Sire. Yes, Sire. He's right here." The smirk was back, and she extended the receiver toward Xavier. "He wishes to speak to you."

Xavier took the phone with morbid anticipation. "Yes, sir?" he mumbled into the phone.

"Son, would you explain to me what happened the

221

last time you were disrespectful toward an adult?" Jeremiah said stonily.

"Father! She didn't tell you the whole story! She was..."

"Answer my question, Son. Excuses will not help!" he snapped.

"But, Father! She was embarr..."

"Xavier!" Jeremiah warned.

Xavier huffed. He felt his cheeks burning. "Father, please! She's sitting right here."

"Don't make me ask again; now answer my question."

"Yes, sir," he responded, shifting in his seat. "You spanked me," he gushed quietly.

"Yes and let me make this perfectly clear to you. If you disrespect the headmistress or any adult at school, I will not hesitate to march over there and take you over my knee again. Understood?" his father growled.

"Yes, sir," Xavier said meekly.

"Good, we'll discuss this more at home. The car will pick you up out front at 4 o'clock sharp. Now, let me talk to Madam Bowerman again."

"Yes, sir." Xavier handed the phone back to the sneering headmistress. "He wants to speak to you," he mumbled, not meeting her eyes.

She took the phone from him and said, "Thank you, Xavier. Are we fully aware of the consequences that will ensue if you choose to continue this juvenile behavior?"

Xavier gave a curt nod.

"Good. Now, you may go on to your next class."

Xavier stood and exited the room, without looking back.

* * * * *

The day didn't seem to improve for Xavier, and in Xavier's opinion, the end of the day couldn't come soon enough. His telepathy professor was a harsh and unforgiving man.

"Stop fidgeting boy and concentrate!" Sir Spencer

222

snapped, his stormy gray eyes burrowing into him.

"I'm trying," Xavier grumbled after thirty minutes of attempting to impede the professor's intrusion into his mind and thoughts. "Can't I start with a simpler task? Blocking is too difficult. Maybe I can work my way up to impediment."

Sir Spencer glared at him. "No, Sire, you can't. You are, after all, the heir to the throne. Therefore, the ability to block is the most dire skill for you."

Xavier sighed. "Great! That should make my life easier," he grumbled.

Sir Spencer heard his comment and thundered over to him, grabbing him roughly by the chin. "It's not my job to make things easier for you!" he spat. "It's my job to mold you into an honorable, powerful king! Now, do it again!"

Xavier prepared himself to block Sir Spencer's next mental assault when a thought occurred to him. "Sir? If only heirs to the throne inherit the skill of telepathy, why is it that you have the ability?"

"Maybe you should ask your father that question," he said stiffly.

"But, I asked you, sir," Xavier said, not wavering.

Spencer regarded him a moment. "Your father is my brother," he said simply.

"Brother?" Xavier immediately scanned the professor's appearance. Aside from Spencer's eyes, he and Jeremiah held little resemblance. Spencer's dark brown hair was a sharp contrast to his father's pale hair. The men were comparable in height, but Spencer did not carry the same bulk of muscle as the King, though he was by no means skinny. However, it was his dark gray eyes that confirmed his claim, and Xavier believed him.

"Yes, now can we get back to work?" Spencer snapped.

So, another twenty grueling minutes of unsuccessful attempts at impediment ensued, leaving Xavier with a pounding headache.

As bad as the telepathy lesson was for Xavier, the

anima lingua lesson was worse. As Xavier entered the room and approached the professor, fifteen sets of eyes followed him. The other students in the class were much older, all in their mid to late teens. Drew Hardcastle muttered something to the boy sitting next to him, and they both snickered at Xavier.

"All right," the professor began harshly, "your performance during Friday's assessment was dismal! So today we will…" The professor's eyes settled on Xavier. "Yes?"

"Sir, I think I'm supposed to report here for anima lingua. I'm Xavier Wells," he said softly.

The professor looked down at him in irritation. "It's quite obvious who you are, Sire Wells. Now, find a seat so we can move on with this lesson!" He waved impatiently at the rows of tables each with a caged animal in the center.

Xavier quickly found a seat at an empty table with a caged albino gerbil.

"As I was saying, we can not move on until you've mastered the task of bonding and directing an animal around a simple barrier. Now, take a moment to bond with the animal on your table. Connect with it, make it feel at ease, and gain its trust. An animal will not follow your requests unless it trusts you. You have fifteen minutes to do this so don't waste your time. Well? What are you waiting for? Get started!" he barked at the class.

Xavier lowered his head and rested his chin on the table so that he was eye level with the gerbil. It stood on its hind legs, its whiskers twitching as it sniffed the air timidly. Xavier inhaled deeply, trying to relax and concentrate on reaching out to the animal.

A loud snort jerked him from his concentration. It was Drew. "Twins?" he laughed again. "Yeah, I can see the resemblance." He looked toward Xavier. "They're both short, puny, and have white hair." A second snort of laughter drew the professor's harsh glare.

"Hardcastle!" he snapped. "Since you seem to have

time to joke around, could I assume that you're ready for the demonstration?"

"No, sir. I'm sorry Sir Blaire," Drew mumbled meekly.

However, Xavier found he couldn't concentrate after that and never developed the essential bond with his animal. When Sir Blaire called on him for his demonstration, his gerbil kept running head first into the wooden barrier, again and again.

"Wells! The assignment was to guide the animal around the wooden block, not have it commit an excruciatingly slow suicide!" Sir Blaire bellowed, and the class snickered. "Now, rescue that poor animal and practice this technique at home!"

Xavier retrieved the gerbil and returned it to its cage. He sank back into the group and watched, with disgust, Drew Hardcastle's perfect demonstration.

Needless to say, at the end of the day when Xavier and Robbie exited the building, Xavier was completely wiped. Robbie, on the other hand, was chattering nonstop.

"Electro force is really fun; isn't it? I've always wondered how Erica and Court could change the shape of their electro force. I guess having an older sibling helps you learn things like that. And, history was absolutely enthralling! I mean, who would have guessed all those events had actually occurred because an empowered citizen had caused it! So," she turned to him as they descended the steps toward the awaiting limo, "how were your empowerment courses?"

"Fine," he muttered.

Loren stepped from the vehicle. "Let's go kids! Have you seen my girls or any of the Hardcastle boys?"

"No," Xavier mumbled, climbing into the limo.

"I saw Erica. She said she was going to walk home. I don't know about Court or his brothers," Robbie answered, climbing into the car and Loren followed.

"How was your day?" he asked as the car pulled away from the school.

225

"Great!" Robbie smiled.

Xavier sat staring out the car window and did not answer.

Loren looked sympathetically at Xavier. "Xavier, I know it must be difficult trying to fit in when everyone wants to treat you differently, but they do so not only to show respect toward you but toward Jeremiah as well."

Xavier looked at Loren anxiously. "Is he very angry?"

Loren sighed. "He was at first, but I think I managed to help him see how difficult it's been for you. He'll be more in a talking mood than a punishing mood, I think." He smiled at Xavier who smiled feebly back.

"She called your father!" Robbie sputtered. "Boy, that was a bit extreme! Loren, she embarrassed him in front of the entire school and drew attention to the special treatment he was getting—as if he had asked for it! All Xavier did was exchange the special meal the cooks gave him for one like everyone else's."

"Robbie, could you tell my father that? Maybe he'd believe that she over reacted if we both tell him what happened," Xavier pleaded.

"Sure, X," she reassured him with a smile.

"Well, it looks as if you won't need to wait to do that," Loren told them, looking at the palace as they rounded the horseshoe shaped drive. Jeremiah stood outside the palace with Ephraim Hardcastle, Dublin Minnows, and Governor Bracus. He and Ephraim were laughing at something that Bracus had told them. The four men turned and watched the car pull up in front of the palace. "Okay, let's go," Loren said with a sigh as he climbed out ahead of the children.

Xavier climbed out of the car behind Loren and Robbie. He kept his eyes fixed to the ground, not wanting to meet his father's eyes.

"Have a good day at school, kids?" Dublin Minnows asked.

"Great, Pop!" Robbie chirped, pecking him on the cheek.

"How about you Xavier? Did you have a good day?" Dublin asked him.

Xavier shrugged. "Some parts of it were okay," he muttered.

"Sire, it wasn't all Xavier's fault!" Robbie pleaded. "Madam Bowerman singled him out and embarrassed him in front of everybody! All he did was trade the special meal the cooks made him for an ordinary one."

"Really? Is this true, Son?" Pride crept into Jeremiah's voice.

Xavier finally looked up at his father. "Yes, sir."

"Whom, may I ask, did you give your food to?" Governor Bracus asked.

"Beck, Beck... I'm afraid I don't know his last name," Xavier frowned.

"Beckley Wilcox? The boy who played rugby with us yesterday?" Jeremiah questioned.

"Yes, sir."

Governor Bracus stood noticeably taller and regarded Xavier with renewed respect. "A merchant? You gave your royal meal to a poor boy?"

"Well, I didn't know he was poor. I just know he was nice to me, and he seems like a good person," Xavier said.

Bracus looked at Jeremiah with a broad grin. "I don't think we need to worry about the future of this kingdom one iota. Integrity cannot be taught, and this boy has it through and through. You're a lucky man, Sire. A very lucky man."

What happened next, astounded Xavier.

"Sire, it is an honor to serve you," Governor Bracus announced, kneeling before him and bowing his head.

Xavier looked to his father unsure of what to do.

"Place your hand on his head," he mouthed silently.

Xavier looked back to Governor Bracus who remained stooped before him, waiting. Slowly, Xavier extended his hand and placed it lightly on the man's balding crown.

Bracus raised his head, took Xavier's hand in his, and kissed it lightly. "May God bless you and keep you, Young

Sire," he muttered, blessing him with the sign of the cross before standing and wiping his moist eyes. "Excuse me, Sire," he told Jeremiah who simply nodded. He got into a silver Volvo and drove away from the palace.

* * * * *

Later that evening, Xavier had just finished his bath and was working on his homework when Jeremiah walked into his room.

"Your door was open," he said.

"I know." Xavier continued working, without looking up. "I figured you'd be up sooner or later."

Jeremiah raised a brow and regarded his son in silence. Xavier looked at him then.

"Father, what Robbie and I told you is the truth," Xavier implored.

"I know, Son. But, answer this: Did you challenge Madam Bowerman in front of other students; did you do it for the sole reason to publicly defy her?"

Xavier thought a moment. He knew the truth and, it seemed, so did his father. He looked back to him. "Yes, sir. I guess that was part of it. But, Father, she really did embarrass me, and most of the adults kept treating me as if I were the Holy Grail! It's bad enough that I have to wear the sash all the time; does the school have to make it more difficult for me to fit in? Please, can you tell them to treat me like any other student? Please!"

Jeremiah sat on the edge of the bed. "Okay, Xavier. I'll make you this deal. The special treatment will end, but you're going to have to do better with controlling your temper. I do not want another phone call like I received today. Understood?" he demanded.

"Yes, sir."

"Good," he stood and stepped toward him. "What's the assignment?"

"Mathematical Properties. We studied it at my old school; it's no big deal," he shrugged.

Jeremiah patted his son's shoulder. "Don't stay up

too late. I want you in bed by 10 o'clock."

"Yes, sir."

Jeremiah turned to leave.

"Father?" Xavier called.

Jeremiah turned. "Yes, Son?"

"Is Sir Spencer my uncle?"

A dark emotion shadowed over his father's face, and his body stiffened. At first, Xavier wasn't sure if he'd answer. But, finally, he said roughly, "Yes, Michael Spencer is my half brother."

"Half brother?"

"Yes, we had the same father, but different mothers. Look, Son, I'm not comfortable discussing this right now." Jeremiah paused and looked away. "I'm sorry, Son. Some other time, okay?" he said quietly.

"Yes, sir. Goodnight, Father."

"Goodnight, Xavier."

Chapter 20
Revenge
★ ★ ★ ★ ★

For the most part, the days that followed were better for Xavier. Although he was still required to wear the royalty sash, the staff did their best to treat him as they would treat any other student. As the third week of school came to an end, rugby tryouts were about to begin.

"Yo, Xavier!" Court called from a bulletin board next to the headmistress's office. "Check it out! Rugby tryouts begin next Thursday for the Knights. You game?"

"You bet!" Xavier responded, studying the notice.

"There's a rugby assembly tomorrow. We can sign up with the team's sponsor then," Court said.

"Hey, what're you guys up to?" Robbie called as she and Erica approached the boys.

"You'll be late for lunch," said Erica. "Believe me, you don't want to be late on Salisbury steak day. They get really crusty and chewy." She made a face.

"Rugby tryouts for the Knights are next Thursday." Court told the girls, pointing to the poster.

"Really?" Robbie exclaimed, pushing the boys aside. "Are you going to tryout, Xavier?"

Before he could answer, Ken and Mac advanced

toward the group. "Ah, look Mac, it's the ghost fan club," Ken chided. Mac chortled melodramatically.

"Bugger off, Calhoun," Court growled.

"What's the matter, Courtney? Am I hurting Little Prince's feelings?" he taunted. "Lord knows, he has enough people kissing his butt! His head is as big as the Goodyear Blimp!"

"Now, Kenneth," Xavier began calmly, "I understand you have deep-seeded insecurities and feel a need to prove yourself as a jackass, but must everyone suffer?" The group beside him burst into a howling laughter.

Ken charged at Xavier with a growl, but Erica and Court stepped between them.

"What's going on out here?" Headmistress Bowerman bellowed from the office doorway.

"Nothing, Madam. We're just playing around," Erica lied.

She surveyed the group with suspicion, but when her eyes settled on Xavier, an even darker emotion flashed to the surface.

"Sire Wells? I'd like to see you in my office," she hissed.

"Why?" Xavier blurted.

"Madam, X wasn't doing anything, really. We were just playing around," Court said, stepping toward the unyielding force of nature barring their escape.

"I said," she snapped, glaring at Xavier, "in my office, now!"

Xavier looked at the others and grumbled, "You better go ahead. I'll catch you all later." He glowered at Bowerman, before crossing to the office door.

"Now, the rest of you, get to lunch and quit loitering in the halls," Bowerman snapped. The group started down the hall in silence when Madam Bowerman's voice stopped them. "And, Mr. Hardcastle? I don't ever want to hear you or any other student refer to Prince Wells as X again. It's inappropriate considering the position he will obtain

231

someday. You must always remember your place."

Court scowled silently at Bowerman, before turning with the others and continuing toward the cafeteria.

"His place is being my friend!" Xavier hissed from the door. "You had no right to talk to them like that!"

"Shut your mouth, *boy* and march yourself into my office this instant!" she blared.

"No, I'm going to the cafeteria with my friends!" he grumbled, trying to step past her.

"No you will not!" She bellowed and grabbed him by the arm. "Not unless you would like to see *Daddy* marching into this school."

Xavier froze and glowered up at a very smug headmistress. After a moment, Xavier turned, stomped through the door and into her office without another word.

"Jeanette, get the King Wells's number ready. I'll call if I need it," the headmistress said lightly following Xavier.

Xavier slumped dejectedly into a chair across from the headmistress's desk.

Bowerman sat down and cleared her throat. "Young man, aside from the cheekiness you displayed in the office doorway, you must've known that fighting is strictly forbidden."

"I wasn't fighting!" Xavier roared.

"Sire, please keep your voice down and maintain a respectful tone!" she hissed.

Xavier huffed, crossing his arms and glaring at the floor.

"Now," she began falsely sweet, "as I was saying, fighting is forbidden. Students caught fighting are usually suspended for three days and their parents are called in."

Xavier's head snapped up, and he stared at her in alarm.

She smiled wickedly. "However, I think we can resolve this without hassling your father. After all, he's a very busy man."

Xavier expelled a breath he hadn't realize he was

holding.

"So," she stood and began to pace behind her desk. "I think that a week's worth of detention should suffice. Tomorrow you will report to the cafeteria for pots and pans duty immediately following lunch during your break. Is that understood?" She stopped and looked down at him.

"Yes, ma'am," Xavier muttered.

"All right then, you're dismissed. Get yourself to lunch."

When Xavier entered the cafeteria, Court, Robbie, and Erica were huddled in deep conversation at the back of the room. Xavier got his tray of food—chewy, crusty steak—and made his way over to them.

"Bunch up guys," he said, sinking down next to Erica.

"X!" Robbie gasped. "We thought Dragon Lady had you imprisoned. How did you get away this quickly?"

"Lucky, I guess. I have detention for a week, pots and pans duty," Xavier grumbled as he stuffed a spoonful of mashed potatoes in his mouth.

"What! Why?" Court blurted.

"How am I to know? You all heard her! She's mad!" he spluttered.

"What a witch!" Court muttered.

"For some reason, she's determined to make my life miserable." He studied each face at the table. "So, I think it's time to equal up the score."

"Hear, hear!" Erica cheered, slamming her fists onto the table. "Now, that's my kind of king. I'm with ya, X. Consider me your humble servant of vengeance!"

Xavier beamed and then looked at Court and Robbie. "What do you say guys?" Seeing their hesitant faces, he pressed on. "Come on! Think of how wonderful it would be to get one up on Dragon Lady!"

Slowly a grin spread across Court's face until he was beaming. "I'm in, X! I wouldn't miss that for anything in the world!"

"Robbie? Please! You've always been there for me;

don't back out now!" Xavier pleaded.

Slowly, Robbie nodded. "Okay, I'm in."

They erupted into a thunderous cheer, attracting curious glances from the tables around them. Then, the children began to set up a plan for the total and utter humiliation of Headmistress Bowerman. They considered placing a bucket full of some disgusting liquid on top of the door jam to her office so that when she opened the door, it would tumble over, but Erica said that the idea was too cliché. Then, Erica came up with a brilliant plan!

"We'll use invisibility lotion!" she blurted. "Dragon lady always has afternoon tea following lunch! I know. I've seen the cooks taking it to her office! Since you have pots and pans duty, X, you can pour invisibility lotion in her tea!" She paused in thought. "Oh, man!" she hissed with an enormous grin. "Oh, man! Guys! What event did Dragon Lady arrange for tomorrow afternoon?"

Slowly Erica's grin spread onto every child's face at the table.

"The Rugby Opening Assembly!" Court laughed. "Blimey, Erica! Remind me never to tic you off. You're positively wicked!"

* * * * *

The next day after lunch, Xavier found himself elbows deep in pots and pans. Erica had given him the invisibility lotion during lunch, which was tucked safely in his blazer pocket.

"Prince Wells?" one of the cooks said, patting his arm and snapping him from his thoughts. "I think you've done enough for one day. Why don't I finish those?" Xavier stepped back and allowed the woman to continue the washing.

He eyed the silver platter with a cup of tea steaming in the center. "Is that the headmistress's tea?"

The woman nodded, "Yes it is. I'd planned to take it to her after the pots and pans are finished."

"Well, why don't I take it for you? I mean, it's the

least I can do since you're finishing up for me." He smiled sweetly at the woman.

"Well, isn't that nice of you! Thank you, Young Sire. I'd appreciate that!"

"Not a problem," he told her, picking up the tray and carrying it out of the kitchen.

Once outside the door, Xavier lowered the tray to the floor and withdrew the bottle of invisibility lotion from his pocket. He carefully dripped five drops into the cup. After replacing the bottle in his blazer pocket, Xavier lifted the tray and walked toward the headmistress's office, humming.

Jeanette was not at her usual spot behind the reception desk. So, Xavier continued toward Madam Bowerman's open office door.

"Madam Bowerman?" he called into the room.

"Come in," she snapped impatiently.

Xavier stepped into the room, and as Bowerman's eyes settled on him, a smirk stretched across her pasty face. "Ah, Prince Wells. How was your first day of detention?"

"Just fine, Ma'am. I've brought your tea from the kitchen," he replied charmingly as he laid the tray on her desk.

"Thank you," she told him as she brought the cup to her lips and sipped. "You better get a move on. You don't want to be late for the rugby assembly."

"No, ma'am," he responded, backing out of the room. He raced down the hall and out into the courtyard where Court, Robbie, and Erica were enjoying the mild day, lounging around the large oak in the center of the courtyard.

"Well?" Erica asked, jumping to her feet. "Did she drink it?"

"Yeah," he huffed out of breath. "But, I mustn't have used enough. It didn't work."

Erica shook her head, smiling. "It doesn't happened immediately, but believe me, by assembly time, Dragon Lady will have body parts missing."

* * * * *

235

As the entire school made its way toward the gymnasium for the assembly, many were horsing around, laughing, and obviously enjoying the break from the usual routine. Once students were seated in the stands, Madam Bowerman—with no invisible parts—approached the PA system on a portable platform and faced the students with her hand raised. Quickly the crowd of children became quiet and watched the headmistress expectantly—four students in particular.

"Thank you," she called. "As you all know, rugby season is upon us. Most teams begin their tryouts next week. So, I believe..." She paused and rubbed her face.

Xavier noticed a twitch in the headmistress's left cheek.

"I believe a discussion on sportsmanship is in order," she continued. "So let's..." She paused again as another spasm rippled across her cheek.

"Here we go," Erica whispered.

"So," she said forcefully, "let's discuss what would constitute proper sportsmanlike behavior."

Suddenly, Madam Bowerman's entire lower jaw disappeared followed promptly by her throat. The crowd of children released a collective "Eww!" and several students in the crowd screamed.

Madam Bowerman seemed confused by the outburst. "Please, Please. Silence, please," she ordered, which was an interesting and perversely hilarious sight without a jaw. "That is enough!" she yelled over the speakers.

Madam Bowerman tried to continue her speech on sportsmanship, but the crowd of children made it impossible. Then, the bewilderment on Bowerman's face suddenly vanished as the majority of her head disappeared. All that remained was her top jaw, scalp, and eyeballs. The entire gym erupted in disgusted shock. However, Court, Xavier, Erica, and, reluctantly, Robbie shook with uncontrollable laughter.

"Children! Children! I really don't understand what

has gotten into you!" she griped.

The children watched as the secretary, Jeanette, floundered onto the stage and tried to explain. She danced around the very flustered Headmistress flailing her arms. She seemed to be just as taken aback by Bowerman's appearance as the children were and didn't seem to want to get too close to her. Finally, she ended up screeching, "Headmistress, your face is...is gone!"

Xavier didn't think he could possibly laugh any harder, but he was wrong. Tears streamed down his face as he doubled over in a fresh wave of hysterical laughter. His stomach screamed in agony from it, and his lungs protested for air.

"Oh, God! Look at her go!" Court blurted between his own fits of laughter.

They watched as the headmistress raced from the gymnasium, trying to cover her face with her hands with Jeanette following and flapping her arms like a frantic chicken.

"Children?" a stern voice called from behind them. "Something tells me you had a hand in all this." Sir Spencer stood towering angrily above them.

Erica wiped the tears from her face and asked, "Why is that, sir?"

"Oh, I don't know. It could be that it just sounds like something your deviant mind would conjure up, Miss Jefferson. Or, it could be the fact that I know Sire Wells hand delivered the headmistress's tea this afternoon. Or, it could be that you're the only ones laughing while the other students seem shocked and surprised." Sir Spencer paused and looked around at the other children in the gymnasium before glaring back down at them. "Or," he began more forcefully, "it could be that I possess telepathy, Miss Jefferson, and I know for certain that the four of you orchestrated this mess!"

The grins fell from their faces.

"So," he began stonily. "The four of you march

yourselves to my classroom this instant while I see to Headmistress Bowerman and call your fathers!"

Silently the children stood and left the gymnasium. They made no sound as they sauntered to Sir Spencer's classroom. The four children sat for some time in the room without a word to one another. Finally, Court jumped to his feet with a whoop.

"I don't care what happens! Man, that was excellent! Did you see her run from the gymnasium? You were right X! Getting even with Dragon Lady was worth any trouble we might face. It was great!" Court bellowed as he gleefully danced around the room.

"That's good to know because, believe me, trouble is what you've got, Son!" Ephraim snarled.

All four heads swung to the room's entrance and found their fathers standing just inside the doorway with Sir Spencer. Court deflated visibly and sank into the nearest chair.

Loren stepped forward. "Erica Paige Jefferson! I smell your handy work all over this catastrophe!" he snarled. Xavier hadn't seen Loren this angry since the bookshop.

"I'm sorry that the headmistress couldn't meet with us, but I think you all understand," Spencer said, a smile teasing at the corners of his mouth. "Funny, I thought invisibility lotion lasted for only a few minutes."

"It does," Loren told him, "unless it's taking internally. In that case, the effects can last for a couple of days."

The children snickered, but after a glare from their fathers, they bowed their heads meekly.

Sir Spencer nodded with a grin. "I'll inform her of that. You may take your children home. Obviously, Madam Bowerman wishes to deal out their punishments at a later time."

"Thank you," Jeremiah said roughly.

Xavier recognized the edge in his father's voice. His stomach gave a great twist, and his eyes blurred with dread.

"Gentleman, I'm not sure about you, but I don't think

any punishment Madam Bowerman chooses for these little heathens would ever be enough. Although my son doesn't seem to regret his actions yet, his backside will soon enough," Ephraim's deep voice announced as he strode over to Court and pulled the boy to his feet.

"Wait!" Xavier began. "It wasn't their fault. The whole idea was mine. I put the lotion in her tea. I gave her the tea. It was me, not them. They shouldn't be punished."

"Really, now?" his father questioned, stepping toward him. "And, you're willing to take on the punishments for each of your friends?"

Xavier gulped. "Yes, sir. I am," he answered, lifting his chin with determination.

"NO!" Court blurted. "X, I can't let you do that! We all played our part; we can't let you take the fall, no matter what!" Court turned to his father. "I'm ready to go home, Dad." With a quick glance at Xavier, Court exited the room with his father.

"Roberta Ann. Let's go. Your mother and sister are waiting in the car," Dublin said quietly. Robbie smiled weakly at Xavier and left.

Loren and Erica rode with Jeremiah and Xavier back to the palace. When they reached the royal stairs, Loren turned to his daughter.

"Well, young lady, you better go on in," he said soberly, motioning toward their door. "Your mother is waiting. You and I will talk when my duty ends in an hour." Erica nodded and sulked through the door.

"Son," Jeremiah spoke quietly, "Go up to your room. I'll be there shortly."

Xavier climbed the stairs and entered the receiving room.

Mrs. Sommers came bustling over to him. "Hello, Young Sire. There's an after school snack for you in the dining room. Did you have a good day at school?"

"I can't; I have to go to my room," Xavier muttered. He walked past Mrs. Sommers and trudged up the stairs to

239

his room.

Jeremiah entered the residence, closing the door behind him. "Ah, good afternoon, Mrs. Sommers."

"You're home early. Did the boy have some trouble at school, Sire?" she asked.

"Trouble would be an understatement, Emma," Jeremiah could no longer hide his grin. "He and a few of his friends placed invisibility lotion in the headmistress's tea. She was giving a speech on sportsmanship in front of the entire school when it took effect." He chuckled lightly and shook his head. "They started quite a pandemonium from what Spencer could tell me when he wasn't laughing."

Xavier was quite certain of what was in store for him, and the moment he entered his bedroom, he couldn't seem to stand still. Full of nervous energy, Xavier moved about the room picking up dirty laundry and toys strung across the room. He had begun unpacking his schoolbooks onto his desk when Jeremiah entered the room.

"Well, well, well," he began, peering approvingly around the room. "It seems that if I ever want you to clean up your room all I need to do is wait for you cause a bit of mischief at school and then, just send you to your room. I can come back later and give you more time. I'm sure there's a load of dirty laundry under that bed you can clear out."

"Father," Xavier gripped, "I just want to get it over with."

"What exactly is it that you want to get over with?" he asked.

"Aren't you going to spank me?" Xavier asked, suddenly feeling hopeful.

"Oh," Jeremiah said with a sigh, "well, I think that's a foregone conclusion, Son. Don't you think you deserve it for the humiliation you put Madam Bowerman through?"

Xavier nodded, but for the life of him, he couldn't feel sorry for having done it. In fact, he still found the image of Bowerman fleeing the gymnasium with Jeanette on her heels very amusing. He fought to hide his smile as he looked at his father, but Jeremiah had already seen it and glared imposingly down at him.

"That's what I thought. Ephraim's right! You may not regret your actions, but I can guarantee your backside will." Jeremiah's face grew ominous, and Xavier gulped.

Chapter 21
Midnight Meeting
★ ★ ★ ★ ★

The children found Madam Bowerman's punishment much more devastating than what they had endured at the hands of their fathers. All four children were barred from participating in any extracurricular activities for the remainder of the first term—which was for another five weeks— and had to serve detention duties for two weeks. The detention wasn't a big deal, but the suspension from extracurricular activities meant they wouldn't be able to play on a fall rugby team because they were banned from participating in tryouts.

"Jeez! Can you believe it?" Court exclaimed indignantly. "No rugby! That's not fair! I mean, the invisibility lotion only lasted two days! Why should we be punished the entire term?"

"Really, she's such a witch!" Erica grumbled as they stomped down the hall, following their meeting with Madam Bowerman to discuss their punishments.

"Well, you guys. We did embarrass her in front of the entire school," Robbie told them. She was met by three daggering stares. "Well," she said feebly, "it's true."

"I say we make her misery last as long as ours," Erica

242

hissed, and she abruptly spun and faced the other children. Court and Xavier very nearly ran into her. "What do you say—a chain of practical jokes and pranks to drive Dragon Lady nuts? Mission casus de draco?"

"What the heck is she talking about?" Court asked Xavier.

"I don't know, but I heard this can happen. Sometimes, people possessed by evil talk in tongue," Xavier teased.

"You idiots! Don't you study your Latin at all?" Erica snapped, smacking them.

"Mission downfall of the dragon," Robbie said.

Erica grinned, "Exactly. What do you say?"

"Ah, Erica? How did your father punish you?" Court questioned.

"What's that got to do with anything?" she asked.

"Well, it's obvious whatever he did didn't work because if it had you wouldn't be so keen on starting more trouble with the headmistress!" he told her.

"Babies!" she hissed.

"Babies?" Xavier barked. "Court's right. See if you think we're still babies after your father…"

"How our fathers punished us doesn't matter!" she raged.

Court and Xavier rolled their eyes.

"We'll do it smarter this time," she whispered. "Are we just going to let her get away with this without a fight?"

Xavier and Court looked at one another fully aware they had just lost the argument.

Apparently, Erica was also aware of this fact for she grinned and continued, "Okay. We'll meet later and create our battle plan."

"I can't! I'm grounded for three weeks," Court announced.

"So am I," Erica sang. "I meant, we'd sneak out tonight after our parents go to bed so they won't notice our absence." She flashed the boys a smile, turned, and strode down the hall.

Court and Xavier watched the girls as they walked into the gymnasium. "You realize that we're never going to be upstanding citizens with Erica in our mists," Court groaned.

Xavier nodded. "Yeah. We're doomed."

The boys went their separate ways, each to his own empowerment class.

* * * * *

That evening, Jeremiah came into Xavier's room to tuck him in. "Ready for bed, Son?" he asked as he strolled into the room.

"Yes, sir." Xavier was already in bed with the covers pulled up to his chin.

His father sat on the edge of his bed and smoothed out the covers. "Did you finish your homework?"

"Yes, sir."

"Good boy. Goodnight, Son. I love you." Jeremiah kissed him on the forehead. "Sleep tight."

"Goodnight, Father."

The moment Jeremiah shut the door behind him, Xavier threw back his covers and jumped from his bed fully clothed. He glanced at the clock. He had two hours before he was to meet the other children at the secret door in the palace wall. He threw corn chips and sodas that he had snuck up from the kitchen into his backpack. Then, he arranged his pillows on the bed so that his absence would be concealed, turned off the lights, and waited.

An hour later, Xavier heard his father's heavy footsteps approach and stopped outside his door. Xavier stiffened at the subtle coolness seeping into him and quickly, almost panicking, emptied his thoughts. After what seemed like hours, Jeremiah finally withdrew from Xavier's consciousness and continued down the hall to his room.

Finally, the clock read midnight, and Xavier got to his feet and slipped on the backpack. Slowly, he opened the door. The walkway was dark except for a golden wavering light, drifting up from the receiving room's hearth. Closing the door softly, Xavier crept down the hall and into his father's room. Moonlight spilled into the room through the patio doors and fluttered on the bed like white doves. Jeremiah was sprawled across the bed with the sheet twisted around his waist. Xavier tip toed to the bed and studied the sleeping King. His bare chest rose and fell in time with his breathing, and his white hair was tousled and messy. It wasn't often that he could really look at his father without his knowing. He looked peaceful and gentle.

A feeling Xavier could not describe swelled inside him. Recklessly, he brushed his fingertips across Jeremiah's jaw and felt its rough sandpaper surface. The moment he touched his father's skin however, Xavier's body went cold, and he found himself spiraling into Jeremiah's sub consciousness.

Suddenly, Xavier found himself on a beach. Behind him, a quaint beach bungalow stood creaking in the stiff sea breeze. A squeal drew his attention to a couple playing on the shore. A young woman ran into the surf and squealed again as the rolling water lapped against her legs like an eager pet.

"Jeremiah! It's too cold," Xavier immediately recognized his mother's voice and stepped forward.

"Ahh, it's not cold," Jeremiah told her, grabbing her around the waist and lifting her into his arms.

"Don't you dare!" his mother laughed.

"What?" Jeremiah chuckled, carrying her deeper into the surf.

"Jeremiah! Don't you dare!" she shrieked through her laughter. "NO!"

Jeremiah tossed her into a large breaking wave. She emerged from the seawater, shrieking and laughing hysterically.

"You're dead, mister!" she hissed and charged at him.

Jeremiah was so consumed with laughter that he didn't even try to escape her advance. She plowed into him, and they tumbled into the water. When they resurfaced their laughter was gone, and they were clinging to one another, kissing.

Xavier was torn between embarrassment of witnessing such an obviously intimate moment between his parents and a desire to see more. He wanted to stay in that dream forever and watch his parents who were so obviously in love. He never got to see them like this. He wondered if this was a dream or a memory. He hoped it was the latter and that he was witnessing something concrete, something real, something tangible that had occurred between his parents.

Reluctantly, Xavier withdrew from the image and found himself swaying unsteadily next to his father's bed. He jerked his hand away from his father's face and stared. A smile toyed at the corners of Jeremiah's mouth. After one last look at his father's sleeping image, Xavier turned and stole across the floor toward the patio door.

"Julia," his father moaned hoarsely and sighed.

Xavier froze and looked back at the still sleeping King who hadn't moved. Then, quietly, he walked out onto the patio and felt a sudden chill. Ignoring the fact that the chill was not coming from the night air, Xavier climbed down the side of the building and raced to the back of the property and into the pine trees.

"Is that you, X?" came Court's voice.

"Yeah," he hissed as he strained through the thick foliage. "Is everybody here?" he asked, looking around.

"They are now," Erica commented.

"All right, then, let's go," Court announced, opening the passage.

The children slid through the secret passage and raced along the outer side of the palace wall toward the wood. One by one, they disappeared into the dense, nebulous vegetation. For several minutes, the group traveled in silence. The persistent chill came again, shuddering through Xavier, and he fought to ignore it.

246

"Erica? Where are we going?" Court called.

"The lake. Our camp fire and talking won't draw attention there," she told them.

But, Erica was wrong. A man enfolded in a black cloak had been watching the castle when the Young Prince escaped. He followed the boy behind the castle where he met his little entourage of schoolmates. He followed the children as they circled the palace and entered the wood. The man knew that if there were any chance of losing the children it would be in the wood. However, the little vagabonds were thrashing through the leafage so noisily, a blind little old lady could have followed them. He sat in the darkness, watching the children as the campfire licked playfully on their faces. He found the fire very helpful as he weighed the risks and formulated a plan.

* * * * *

"Xavier!" Jeremiah yelled blearily and bolted upright in bed.

Sweating and panting, he slid his feet onto the floor and stood. Trying to shake the ominous feeling the dream had left behind, Jeremiah rubbed his face vigorously. He had been having a very pleasant dream about Julia and the time they spent on the coast during their honeymoon. But the serene image of Julia's smile was rudely replaced by a tremendous storm, bearing down on his son who was huddling around a small fire. The storm crashed down on the boy, and then, it simply disappeared, leaving a more terrifying image in its wake—William LeMasters.

With a groan, Jeremiah shook his head as he padded across the room and into the bathroom. He frowned at the strained and worrisome image staring back at him in the mirror. Almost irritably, he splashed water on his face as if it alone would wash away the anxiety mounting in him, but he knew he'd never be able to fall asleep again unless he checked on the boy and convinced himself that his son was safe and sound in bed. Irritated by his own over-protectiveness, Jeremiah closed his eyes and allowed his mind to soar into the room next to his and.... He couldn't connect! Terror spiked and rippled through his body as every hair stood on end. With a start, Jeremiah tore out of the bathroom, down the hall to the boy's room, and hurled the door open with a slam. Without pausing, he flicked on the light, strode over to the bed, and ripped back the blankets.

"Oh, God!" he sobbed as the implications of his dream slammed into his thoughts. "EPHRAIM!" he yelled, running from the room. "EPHRAIM!"

* * * * *

The children sat, laughing and roasting marshmallows by the fire, quite unaware of the man watching them or the danger they were in.

"That has to be the stupidest idea I've ever heard!" Court bellowed.

"Oh, come on! It's not that bad," Robbie whined, looking to the others for confirmation but received snickers instead. Finally, she smiled and laughed along with them. "Okay, you're right. It's horrible." The laughing continued heartily until Erica's face grew wide with alarm.

"Shh!" Erica hissed, holding her hand up. "Stop! Did you guys hear that?"

The group got very quiet and listened.

"Is this some kind of joke, Erica?" Court snorted.

"No! Now, shut it, you idiot!" Erica growled.

A twig snapped a few yards into the leafage. Every child went rigid.

A sudden chill engulfed Xavier, and his father's voice rang in his mind. *'Xavier? Where are you?'*

He closed his eyes in concentration. "The lake," Xavier responded a loud.

"What?" Court asked, fear shivering into his voice.

"Someone's here. We're afraid," Xavier continued.

Court opened his mouth to speak again when Robbie elbowed him hard in the gut. "DON'T! He's speaking to the Premier! You'll break his concentration!"

248

'We're on our way, Xavier,' Jeremiah consoled.

Xavier opened his eyes. "Father and the Royal Guard are coming."

"Not soon enough, I'm afraid," hissed a voice just beyond their vision. Thunder rumbled from somewhere in the distance, and a sudden icy gust swept over them extinguishing their fire with a loud sigh.

The children huddled, clinging to one another and listened. A soft rustling came from their left followed by a sneering chuckle.

"Oh, children," the voice taunted, "Children, children, children." A flash of white light sliced through the darkened sky followed by a resounding crack. All four children jumped.

"Run!" screamed Erica, bolting. The rest of the group followed, crashing blindly through the vegetation.

Xavier struggled to keep up with the other children, but soon found himself losing sight of Court's white sweater in the blanket of night. Then, he tripped and went sprawling onto the ground. He struggled to get to his feet when a quick blow to his head knocked him unconscious.

* * * * *

As soon as Ephraim exited the palace, he teleported to the lake, but the children were nowhere in sight. Suddenly, he heard one of the children scream to his left followed by a rustling of leaves and a thump as something, or someone, fell to the forest floor. With his heart in his throat, Ephraim stumbled through the wood toward the sounds. He no sooner entered the wood than a large limb swung across his path, striking him across the torso and knocking him to the ground. Gasping to catch his breath, he looked up to the figure looming above him.

"Y...You!" he choked.

* * * * *

Xavier staggered through the foliage, bleeding profusely from a gash on his forehead. Another clap of thunder announced the arrival of a torrential downpour.

249

Within minutes, he was soaked down to the skin. He hardly noticed the movement in front of him just moments a beam of light settled onto his face.

"Xavier?" It was Loren. He raced to Xavier and caught the boy just as he tumbled.

"Jeremiah! He's here! I've found him!"

Loren carried the boy through the forest until Jeremiah appeared. His pajama bottoms were drenched and muddy, and the thick shrubs had lacerated his bare chest in several places. Jeremiah hadn't even bothered to put on shoes, and his feet looked like bloody stubs. Jeremiah took the boy into his arms and carried him the remaining distance to the palace.

Chapter 22
Changed
★ ★ ★ ★ ★

Xavier opened his eyes and found himself in his own bed. Sunlight stabbed into the room through a gap in the curtains. His father lounged in an armchair next to his bed, his head resting against the back of the chair and his eyes closed. Xavier sat up too quickly. His throbbing head reminded him of his injuries, and he gasped, falling back into the pillows, his hands clutching his head.

"Head hurt?" Jeremiah whispered.

Xavier jerked his eyes toward his father. "What do you think?" Xavier hissed, rubbing his head.

"Everyone has been very worried about you. You've been unconscious for two days," he told him.

"Really?" Xavier muttered.

Jeremiah sat up in the armchair and contemplated the boy before him. "Do you mind telling me what the hell you were doing sneaking out in the middle of the night? What was going through that head of yours?"

"I guess I thought it would be fun to get out and play with my friends," he shrugged, rubbing his temples.

"Was it fun?" his father spat.

"Well, yeah, if you don't include the head contusion,"

Xavier said matter-of-factly.

"You had me worried out of my mind! William was in the wood! I could feel his repulsive presence, and Ephraim said that he actually saw him! Do you really want a repeat performance of your time at the Institute? If Loren hadn't found you when he did..."

"Jeez, Jer!" Xavier rumbled. "It wasn't as bad as all that. I'm not afraid of Master William."

"You should be!" Jeremiah spat. "William is a madman with a God complex who wants to dominate the world."

"Shut up!" Xavier screamed.

His father jumped to his feet. "What did you say to me boy?"

"I said, shut up Mr. High-All-Mighty!" Xavier challenged. "I don't want to talk about it!"

Jeremiah moved toward him when the door opened.

"What's going on? We can hear you two yelling downstairs!" Loren said.

Father and Son glared at one another before finally calling a silent truce and looking toward Loren.

Jeremiah cleared his throat. "What is it, Loren?"

Loren looked at Father and then Son. "Well," he began. "Xavier has quite a crowd of visitors downstairs waiting to..."

Loren was interrupted by a loud group of children, shoving their way into the room.

"X, my man!" Court bellowed. "How's the head?"

"How do you think it is?" he grumbled.

"Son?" Jeremiah called from the door. "We'll finish our conversation later."

"Whatever," Xavier sighed.

Anger flashed into Jeremiah's eyes as he started toward the boy again, but Loren grabbed him and pulled him from the room.

"Xavier! I'm so glad you're okay! I was really scared," Robbie cried, throwing her arms around him.

"Were you, now?" he asked flatly.

She pulled away and looked at him bewildered. "Of course, you're my best friend!"

"Some best friend! You deserted me! All of you!" he called over the chattering happy faces. "When things got too scary, too rough, you deserted me to Master William! You left me! Me! Your future king! If I were already king, I would have you banished from the castle for the lack of allegiance you exhibited in the wood."

"X," Court laughed, "you're not serious, are you?"

"Damn right, I'm serious! You left me Hardcastle! Why would I want friends like that?" he bellowed at their shocked faces. "I never asked you to come here, and I don't want you. So, get out!"

"Xavier," Robbie whispered, "I'm sorry if you feel that we abandoned you. It was..."

"I don't want to hear it! Your apology is not accepted. I'll never forgive you!"

"But, it wasn't our fault! It was so dark! I couldn't have seen my hand even if it had been two inches from my face!" Robbie cried.

"I don't want to hear your excuses! Just get out!" Xavier yelled.

Not knowing what else to do, the children left the room in silence.

* * * * *

The next school day, rumors were rampant over what had happened in the wood. One rumor was that Xavier had snuck out with some friends to the lake. Then, to show off for a couple of girls, he roused his powers and nearly burnt half the wood down.

Another rumor was that Xavier had lured a group of children into the forest where they were held captive and tortured. When others would ask the gossipers why Prince Xavier would do such a thing, the answer was simple: "Well, he was held captive at the Institute for two months and tortured. It had to have messed with his mind. He's probably insane." The buzzing and the rumors regarding the wood incident floated through the halls, but Xavier seemed immune to it all.

Court, Erica, and Robbie kept their distance from Xavier who still seemed very bitter and stormy. Xavier refused to speak to them. As the week pressed on, Xavier's mood never waned.

"Maybe if we apologize again, he'll snap out of it," Robbie said imploringly to Court and Erica.

"I'm not apologizing again!" Erica contended. "I mean, holy cow! It was pitch black, and we were being stalked. What were we supposed to do? Sacrifice our lives for him?"

"Come on, Erica. I know Xavier! He's probably feeling horrible for what he said but he's too ashamed to make the first move," Robbie told them.

Erica wavered and looked toward Court for support, but he simply shrugged.

Finally, Erica sighed. "All right, fine. Here's the deal. Robbie, you go and talk to him. If all is well, we'll join in. Okay?"

"Okay," Robbie agreed. Then, she turned and strode down the hall toward Xavier.

Xavier stood leaning against the door jam of Sir Spencer's classroom and leafing through his Latin book, when he heard Robbie approach him, but he didn't look up. She cleared her throat to get his attention, but he still did not look at her.

"Xavier?" she finally whispered.

Xavier looked at her then with cold, turbulent eyes. It was like peering into the ocean during an arctic winter storm. "What do you want?" he snarled.

"Look, Xavier, the guys and I are really sorry if you felt like we abandoned you that night in the wood. We didn't intend to do that. Is there something we can do to make it up to you?"

"Yeah," he spat. "You can leave me alone!"

"Come on, Xavier! We've been best friends since kindergarten! You can't just let our friendship end like this!" Robbie cried.

Xavier stomped toward her with clenched teeth. "I don't care! I don't want anything to do with you or those morons! Got that? Just stay away and leave me alone!" He turned to walk into Sir Spencer's classroom.

"Xavier?" she begged, grasping his shoulder. "Please..."

The moment her hand touched him, he spun and struck her hard across the face. Robbie fell to the floor, her mouth beginning to bleed.

"I said, leave me alone!" His yell echoed down the hall, and every student stopped and stared.

Court and Erica ran to Robbie's side. Court affronted Xavier, pushing him away from Robbie as Erica helped her to her feet.

"Back off, mate," Court warned, giving Xavier another shove backwards.

"Shut it, Hardcastle!" Xavier growled, pushing him back. "Take your cousin and your little girl friend and get lost."

"Man," Court hissed, "you're such a git! Maybe everybody's right! God knows, with that evil lunatic, LeMasters, holding you captive all that time, maybe you have gone barmy."

Xavier punched Court, sending him to the floor with a grunt. Erica ran to Court's side.

"What are you doing, Xavier? Stop it! Just stop it!" she cried, glaring up at him. But, the moment her eyes rested on Xavier's face, they grew enormous, and she froze. Finally, awkwardly, she dragged her eyes away from him and helped Court to his feet.

"Come, on. Let's go. We don't want him for a friend anyway," Erica muttered.

Xavier turned and barged into Sir Spencer's room, slamming the door behind him. He stopped under Sir

Spencer's arresting scowl.

"What was all that about, Xavier?" he asked in a low voice.

"Nothing. Just a disagreement," he shrugged.

"It didn't sound like nothing. You hit those other chil..."

"What does it matter?" he interrupted spitefully. "It's my business! Anyways, why would I listen to a *Neo-mix* like you?"

Sir Spencer's eyes flashed dangerously. Xavier was suddenly reminded of Jeremiah. So, it appeared the brothers had the same short fuse.

"That's an ugly term that could easily be used to describe you, Your Highness. After all, your mother was also a common," although his voice was calm, his eyes were fiery. "I think the headmistress may need to be informed of your misdemeanor with your friends."

"I don't care! Tell her! And, they're not my friends!" he spat at the man boldly.

"Well, I see that there's no reasoning with you," Sir Spencer sighed impatiently. "Let's go. Madam Bowerman can decide how to handle you." He grabbed him by the elbow and threw open the door.

Xavier jerked his arm free from Spencer's grasp. "Get your impure hands off me! I'll walk on my own!" he yelled, his voice vibrating down the hall. Xavier marched past Court, Robbie, and Erica and stormed down the hall toward Bowerman's office.

Erica watched him with mingled anxiety and bewilderment. She could have sworn she had seen something peculiar after he struck Court. The Prince's face had been contorted and indistinct. She wasn't sure what she had seen, but coupled with his recent odd behavior, it didn't take a genius to figure out something was wrong!

* * * * *

That evening at dinner, Jeremiah and Xavier ate in silence, which suited Xavier perfectly. When Milton began serving the roasted duck, Mrs. Sommers burst into the room looking disturbed.

"Sire? Mrs. Hardcastle, Mr. Jefferson, and Mr. Minnows are here and wish to see you in private. They say it's urgent."

"Thank you, Emma. Show them into the library. I'll be there in a moment." After Mrs. Sommers waddled from the room, Jeremiah turned to Milton. "Milton, go ahead and serve the boy his meal. I'm not sure what this is all about or how long it will take."

"Fine, sir. I'll have your meal placed in the oven to keep it warm," he nodded as he placed Xavier's portions on his plate.

"Excuse me, Son." Jeremiah stood and left the room.

Xavier had lost his appetite. What did Dublin Minnows, Loren Jefferson, and Rebecca Hardcastle have to say to his father that was so important to interrupt their meal? He quickly wolfed down his food to Milton's disgust and raced from the table. He hurried past the stairs, through the reception room, and toward the library door at the far end of the room. Carefully he rested his head against the door and listened. Only murmurs could be heard through the door so, quietly, Xavier turned the knob, and voices spilled out.

"I'm telling you Jeremiah! He's acting very peculiar! I'm very worried!" Rebecca Hardcastle clamored.

"I've noticed it as well," Dublin Minnows agreed more calmly.

Xavier felt panic swell and rise within him. They were on to him! He must warn the others! But, Jeremiah's steady voice pulled him from his desperate thoughts.

"How do you mean peculiar? What has he done?" he questioned.

"He's never home! When he is home, he hardly says two words to the boys. Court's been neglecting his chores, and Ephraim hasn't said a word about it. And, then," she faltered, "then there're the times when we're alone together. He's cold and distant. He seems uncomfortable to be around me. He skirts around me like I'm the bearded lady! Jeremiah, he's taken to sleeping on the couch!"

So, the conversation was about Ephraim Hardcastle, not him! Damn him! The plan was compromised. Concern of a different sort filled him with urgent thoughts. They would have to move quickly for the plan to still be effective.

"That doesn't sound like Ephraim," Jeremiah was saying.

"That's not all, Jer," Dublin Minnows interrupted gravely. "He was supposed to be on duty last night! When I came to the palace to discuss an issue with Loren, Ephraim was not at his post."

"Well, Dublin, I don't think that's cause for alarm. Guards are allowed to take breaks occasionally," Jeremiah said.

"I know that, Sire, but he didn't get his relief to take his position at the door, and when I came out of the Jefferson residence an hour later, he still wasn't there. No one was!"

"That does sound a bit strange," Jeremiah admitted. "I'll speak to him when he comes on duty at ten." There was a long pause. Only the shuffling of Dublin's shoes could be heard. "What?" Jeremiah questioned at last. "Is there something else?"

"Well," Dublin drawled out, "yes, Sire. There is another matter we need to discuss... Xavier."

Xavier stiffened at the sound of his name. *'Oh boy! Here it comes,'* he thought dryly.

"Xavier? What about him?" Jeremiah's voice became strained.

"Did you know that your son and our children are at odds with one another?" Loren asked.

"Odds?" Jeremiah asked.

"Xavier and the children had an argument at school today. According to Robbie, she was trying to make amends with what occurred in the wood last week," Dublin added.

"What happened in the wood? But, those kids didn't have anything to do with it," Jeremiah said confused.

"Well, I guess Xavier thinks they abandoned him and left him to fend for himself against William," Loren told them.

"He blames them?" Jeremiah said incredulously.

"It appears so," Dublin Minnows stated bitterly. "He gave Robbie a fat lip, Jer."

"What?" he whispered. "He hit her? Robbie's his best friend..."

"Spencer witnessed it," Loren interrupted. "He spoke to the boy, but Xavier got very belligerent with him. He called him a Neo-mix!"

"A Neo-mix!" Jeremiah hissed. "Where in the hell did he hear that?"

"I don't know, Jer, but needless to say, Spencer took him before the headmistress and told her what had happened. But, he wasn't punished! Headmistress Bowerman seemed to think the other children had it coming!"

There was a very long pause. "I'm very sorry. He hasn't handled this latest episode well. Please, if you'll wait here, I'll go and retrieve him."

Xavier stumbled back from the door and turned into Milton. The servant grabbed him by the collar just as Jeremiah came out the door. Jeremiah's gaze fell from Milton to Xavier and then back to Milton.

"He was eavesdropping, Sire," Milton answered the silent question.

Jeremiah looked down at the boy. "Come here, Xavier. We all would like a word with you, as I'm sure you're well aware." He motioned toward the open door where the three other adults stood inside, peering out at him.

Xavier lifted his chin stubbornly and strode into the library.

"Have a seat, Son," Jeremiah's stern voice commanded.

"I think I'd rather stand," Xavier drawled.

"I said, sit!" his father barked.

Xavier sat, glaring haughtily at the four adults in front of him.

"Since you've already heard most of our conversation, I think I'll just save all of us some time and come to the point. Why did you hit Court and Robbie?" Jeremiah asked.

Xavier shrugged. "I felt like it, I guess."

"Not good enough! Try again," his father clipped.

"They were bugging me!" he mumbled.

"Bugging you? Bugging you!" Jeremiah spat. "So you punched them for bugging you?"

"Courtney's your friend. What you did irrevocably damage that friendship. He's very angry, Xavier," Rebecca told him.

"So?" Xavier yelled, jumping to his feet. "Why would I care if that peasant, that... that servant, is my friend or not? Court always did have trouble keeping his place, anyway. He liked to think that he was my equal, but he's not! I'm the Prince of Warwood. He's my servant. I don't have to listen to this!" Xavier snapped, stepping toward the door, but Jeremiah's voice stopped him.

"Sit, down!" he boomed.

Xavier glared up at his father, and when he made no moves toward compliance, Jeremiah charged toward him, lifted him from the floor, and forcibly placed him back in the chair.

"You will remain seated," Jeremiah said dangerously low as he stooped in front of the boy and fixed him with a prevailing glare. "You will listen to what Mrs. Hardcastle and Mr. Minnows has to say. And, you will accept whatever punishment we decide for you because, Son, you are so very wrong. You had no right to hit those children, nor are you superior to them." He observed Xavier's harsh glance at these words and continued, "Yes, you are the Prince of Warwood, but you are not king, yet. Nor is it a guarantee that you will be. Now, keep that bottom in that chair and that mouth shut. Don't you ever speak like that to them again. Do you understand me?"

The only response Jeremiah got from the boy was a passive cast of his eyes. Jeremiah stood and nodded to Dublin.

"Xavier," Dublin Minnows began quietly, "Robbie has been nothing but a friend to you. She stood by you when times were tough. She defended you, helped you, and loved you. Did she really deserve to be hit like that?"

"I never asked her to be my friend!" Xavier muttered. "I never asked her to do anything for me!"

"Never the less, she did, and not once did she ask for anything in return. And, now, the best excuse you can give me for hitting her is that she was bugging you. Do you realize how infuriating it is for me to hear that my daughter was physically assaulted for the sole reason that she was bugging you?" Mr. Minnows told him.

Xavier shrugged, but did not meet Mr. Minnows's cold eyes.

There was a long pause. Xavier could feel their eyes burrowing into him, but he didn't look up. It was Jeremiah who finally broke the silence.

"Dublin, Rebecca, I'd like to include your thoughts on the best course of action here." He turned to Mrs. Hardcastle. "What do you think would be a suitable punishment, Rebecca?"

Xavier looked at Mrs. Hardcastle who looked down at him with compassion.

"Oh, I'm sure Courtney would appreciate an apology for starters. Beyond that, I think the boys should work it out themselves. After all, he was the one hit; he should be the one to decide on how to deal with it."

Jeremiah nodded. "I understand, Rebecca, but I can not allow Xavier to face repercussion from Courtney only," Jeremiah said, looking down at Xavier. "I think a two week grounding and no rugby will be acceptable additions."

"So what?" Xavier said, shrugging indifferently.

261

Jeremiah glared at Xavier before looking to Dublin Minnows who appeared less forgiving. "Dub?"

"Well, I might be more generous and understanding like Rebecca if I truly believed the boy was sorry, but I have seen no indication of that here. I only see a very contemptuous, self-centered, pompous young man who has absolutely no remorse. My daughter cried herself sick. She doesn't understand what she said or did to cause Xavier to hurt her, but she swears she must have done something because she believes Xavier wouldn't have hit her if she hadn't done something to upset him."

Xavier shook his head in disgust. *'What an idiot!'* he thought with a smirk. He could have done anything to her, he realized, and she would have believed that it was her fault.

Dublin's head whipped in Xavier's direction the moment he heard the boy's snicker. His eyes grew wildly angry, and he lunged at Xavier. It was Loren, not Jeremiah, who stepped between them.

"Whoa! Dub," he urged. "I think you need to calm yourself."

"No," Jeremiah intervened. "Let him go Loren. He has every right to punish the boy how he sees fit. Xavier needs to learn that sometimes his actions have more than one consequence."

Loren released Dublin who had calmed considerably. Dub looked at the boy, sitting smugly in front of him. "What has gotten into you, Xavier?" he questioned. "This isn't like you. You were always such a good friend to Robbie. I don't understand it."

Xavier did not respond; he glared audaciously at Dublin Minnows not at all regretful.

Finally, Dublin turned to Jeremiah. "I think if I may, I would prefer to punish him myself, Sire." He turned back to Xavier and whispered irrevocably, "Over my knee."

Xavier snapped to attention and jumped to his feet. "What!" he blurted, but the men ignored his outburst.

Jeremiah nodded. "I'll leave you to it, then. We'll wait in the reception room."

Mrs. Hardcastle and Loren left without a word. Jeremiah spoke softy to Dublin and glanced at Xavier before exiting the room and shutting the door firmly behind him.

"Xavier?" Mr. Minnows began stonily as he moved toward him. "I've always thought of you as a son. With the amount of time you've spent at my house through the years, you might as well have been. So, the fact you've compelled me into spanking you for the first time is not easy for me. I do not enjoy this task," he sighed sadly, taking the boy by the arm and sinking into the chair with him.

Moments later, Xavier threw open the door and stormed, red-faced, out of the library. Dublin Minnows followed wearily and looked at his old friend. "It's not easy disciplining that boy; is it?"

Jeremiah shook his head as he watched the boy climb the stairs two at a time and slam his bedroom door shut. "No. I don't think parenting was ever easy."

Chapter 23
The Final Betrayal
★ ★ ★ ★ ★

Late that night, Xavier was awakened by the shuffle of feet outside his bedroom door, and Loren's urgent whispers.

"I'm not sure how it was breached, Sire," Loren muttered as two sets of footsteps scurried passed the door and down the stairs.

Xavier threw back his covers, followed the voices out onto the landing, and peered over the banister to the scene below. His father, dressed only in pajamas bottoms, stood at the residence door with Loren beside him. Several guards in uniforms and blue cloaks stood before them.

"What do you mean it's gone?" Jeremiah hissed.

One guard spoke up timidly, "Well, Sire, Ephraim came into the vault and said that the Key was needed. He's your second in command! Who was I to question him? So, I unlocked the vault, and he took the Key!"

Jeremiah looked to Loren. "Go get him."

"I've already tried. Rebecca says he hasn't been home all evening! He didn't even report for duty tonight, and Henrick had to cover his shift. No one has seen or heard from him. He's missing, Jeremiah," Loren said, shaking his head. "The Clavis de Rex has been stolen. Do you realize what this means?"

"Yes, Loren," Jeremiah barked. "I'm very aware of the implications of this catastrophe. The Key..." he sighed. "If it's who I think it is behind all of this, our society as we know it is in grave danger. Was the prophecy touched?" Loren shook his head. "No, sir."

Jeremiah's resolve strengthened. "Gentlemen!" he began, turning toward the guards. "We must get the Key back! I cannot tell you how important it is that the Key remains in our possession! Organize a search team. Do not rest until you have it."

"Yes, Sire!" the men saluted. Jeremiah dismissed the guards, and they turned and rushed from the palace.

"Jer?" Loren said quietly. "I don't mean to criticize, but why doesn't the Prophet have the boy's prophecy? Wouldn't it be safer with him?"

Jeremiah regarded his friend soberly. "You know I'm as clueless as your are, Loren. I can only repeat what he said twelve years ago: the prophecy must be stored with the King's Key."

"But, Jer, don't you ever wonder about it? Why did the Prophet order for the prophecy to be kept with the Clavis de Rex? What's so important about the boy's destiny that would warrant such unusual storage?"

"Yes, Loren, I do wonder about it, but that doesn't change anything. We will learn the answers to all our questions in a few months on the boy's thirteenth birthday. So, until then, I, like you, must be patient and protect him and the prophecy."

Loren nodded.

Xavier didn't understand. *'What were they talking about? What prophecy?'*

Jeremiah turned and fastened onto his son's wide questioning eyes. "Xavier?"

Loren whipped around his sober face finding Xavier. Xavier didn't like the way the men studied him. He felt exposed, vulnerable.

"Son, come here," his father called.

Xavier straightened and glided along the loft toward the stairs. As Xavier descended the steps, Loren whispered something to Jeremiah and left the royal residence.

"Xavier, I need you to return to your room and pack a few things. We'll be leaving the kingdom tomorrow," Jeremiah said, meeting him at the bottom of the stairs.

"Why? What's happened? What was stolen?" Xavier asked.

"Son, I need you to do what I tell you without asking questions that I can't answer right now. Please, trust as your father I'm doing what is best for you and do as I tell you! Go pack a bag!" Jeremiah insisted.

"No! I won't do anything until you tell me what's going on! Why must I go into hiding?"

If Xavier expected Jeremiah to be angry at his insolence, he was greatly surprised. His father smiled weakly at him and patted his shoulder.

"I will tell you everything once you're safe and secure out of the kingdom. But, for now, I need you to trust and obey me without question," Jeremiah said quietly.

Reluctantly, Xavier nodded and returned to his room.

* * * * *

When Xavier awoke the next morning, his father was not in the palace. Milton would only tell him that he'd be back later.

"Your father gave me strict orders that you are not to leave the residence. You're to stay put until he returns. Understand, Young Sire?" Milton told him during breakfast.

Xavier sank into his chair sulking, but he didn't argue.

By the time Xavier finished his breakfast and returned to his room, his pinned up anger was on the verge of exploding. He was a prisoner! He had to find a way to escape from the palace before the King returned. He had not packed a bag nor did he intend to; he was not going anywhere with Jeremiah. It was time to leave and continue with the next phase of the plan. But, how was he going to get out of the palace?

A sharp tap, tap interrupted his thoughts, and he was drawn toward the windows. Xavier peered through the glass beyond the patio garden and found Beck Wilcox and Garrett Bracus standing on the lawn below. They waved up at him and pointed to the rugby ball Garrett had tucked under his arm.

Xavier grinned and nodded. This was his chance to escape the palace and blatantly defy Jeremiah in the process. But, one problem still remained; how was he going to get out of a well-guarded palace? This thought churned in his mind as he descended the stairs and approached the main entrance. When he opened the door, he found it, as suspected, heavily guarded. Four guards stood rigidly outside the residence door, and half a dozen more lined the walls of the anteroom below.

"Yes, Sire?" one guard questioned.

"I," Xavier straightened his shoulders with determination. "I must meet my father at the Governing Hall."

"That's not what he told us. He gave us specific orders to guard the residence and not to allow you to leave until he returns," the guard answered.

"There's been a change in plans. I'm to meet him at the Governing Hall this instant!" he told the guard.

"I beg your pardon, Sire, but you and I both know that's not true. I think it's best if you'd just turn yourself around and wait for your father to come home." The guard smirked.

Xavier scowled and stomped back into the residence.

"And, Sire?" the guard called after him, chuckling. "If I were you, I wouldn't attempt to climb down the patio wall either; your father has it guarded as well."

Xavier shot the guard a contemptuous glare before slamming the door in the man's face. Well, if they weren't going to let him leave, he'd just have to distract them long enough so he could sneak out. But, what could he do? Xavier stared thoughtfully into the roaring fireplace. Slowly, an idea began to form in his mind, and a wicked grin slipped across his face.

Moments later the housemaid was screeching, "Fire! Fire! Fire!"

Milton rushed into the room, and the guards crashed through the front door. The draperies in the receiving room were ablaze and black smoke was beginning to fill the room. Milton yanked the enflamed curtains from their rods, flung them to the floor, and began stomping out the fire. As Milton and the guards extinguished the fire, Xavier slipped out the door and out of the palace.

Beck and Garrett were waiting just outside the door. "Yo, X! We're gathering some people to play a game. Interested?" Beck asked.

"Yeah, but let's get out of here. Technically, I'm grounded. So, if the old man finds me out here my game is over before it ever starts."

When the boys arrived at the stadium, there were close to two-dozen kids gathering in centerfield. Ken Calhoun and Mac Timmins stood to the side barking out orders to the other children who could care less.

"Come on! Come on! We can't play until you stop mucking about so we can choose teams!" Ken was whining.

"Hey, everyone!" Beck announced as they approached. Every head turned, and the crowd of children went silent. Court, Robbie, and Erica were among the group, and their eyes immediately fastened on Xavier.

"About time, Wilcox," Ken grumbled. "Can we choose teams and play now?"

"Sure, Calhoun. I'll even let you have first pick," Beck said with a smile, but it was obvious that he despised the other boy for his smile didn't wipe the contempt from his eyes.

"All right then," Ken scanned the crowd and stopped at Xavier. "I'll take the Prince."

Xavier moved to stand next to Ken.

"Don't let it go to your head, Sire," he added quietly.
"I knew it would drive Court batty. I understand you *girls* had
an argument. Wasn't it you who gave Minnows that fat lip?
I must say, I don't know what took you so long to do it.
Robbie is so irritating that I would have punched her ages
ago."

Xavier shrugged and looked at Robbie who had just
been selected by Beck and joined the team along with Court
and Erica.

As soon as the teams were chosen, the game began.
After a kick-off, Xavier's team gained the ball. Xavier played
a back position, and Ken, playing half back, kept passing
him the ball. Possession after possession, Xavier was
slammed to the ground, then punched, kicked, and kneed in
attempts to get the ball. If it had been an officiated game,
penalties for dangerous play would have been called. But,
as it was, Xavier was clobbered repeatedly, and his
teammates wouldn't come near him to help. They hung back
and watched as Xavier was pulverized and slaughtered. It
was becoming painfully apparent that Ken had only selected
Xavier to be on his team so that he could control the amount
of hits he received.

The tackles gradually grew more violent and painful.
During one particularly harsh scrum, Court drove Xavier out
of bounds and slammed him into the turf. Xavier's head
spun as he struggled to his feet and staggered unsteadily.

"Ow, that had to hurt," Ken laughed.

Xavier stumbled toward his team to restart the game
with a scrum, and once again, Ken tossed him the ball. He
no sooner caught the pass than several players from the
opposing team burrowed him into the ground, elbowing him
in the mouth and kneeing him in the groin. Xavier's
teammates stood cackling a few yards away as he coughed
and spat. Slowly, Xavier stood and wiped the blood from his
mouth.

Ken staggered toward him laughing freely. "Well,

Sire? How special do you feel now?" he sneered.

Xavier felt fury rocketing through his body and ebbing away his sanity as he glared around at the laughing faces. What did these little pompous brats know! They had no idea what he was capable of, and maybe it was time to give them a taste of his capabilities. Maybe it was time to reveal who he truly was! Slowly, a smile slid across his blood-smeared face. Yes, it was time to go!

"You want to know how special I am, do you?" he whispered.

It was almost comical how quickly the children's sneers dropped from their faces as Xavier raised his arm and displayed the electro force swirling in his hand. His grin grew enormous, and his eyes darkened. The children watched wide-eyed as Xavier hit Ken with an electro force so intense that it propelled him several feet into the air before he crashed to the ground with a loud grunt.

As reprimands and shouts erupted all around him, Xavier spun and sent several more children across the field. The shouts changed into screams of terror as the children ran for cover. With a manic laugh, Xavier continued to pelt force after force at the retreating children, knocking them to the ground.

"Go get King Wells!" Court hissed to Robbie and Erica before creeping up behind Xavier. Just as Xavier raised his hands to begin his assault on the group again, Court tackled him, drove him into the turf, and punched him across the temple. Pain exploded in Xavier's head.

"Grab his arms and legs!" Court yelled, and four other boys raced to help him.

Suddenly, Xavier's body went limp in the boys' grasps, and Court looked up nervously at the other boys' pale, terrified faces. The tension around them felt close and thick, like during the sudden calmness in the eye of a tornado just before the most devastating blow. Court's jaw quivered as he anticipated the backlash he was sure was about to come.

Then, it did. Xavier began to laugh. His entire body shook as a deep-throated laughter grew into a roar that seemed ill fit for such a small boy. As suddenly as the laughter began, it ended, and Xavier effortlessly repelled the boys away from him and stood.

"Children, children, children," Xavier chided in a deep masculine voice. It was not a voice of a boy but a voice of a man. The children anxiously watched the small pale-haired figure. "You have no idea who you're dealing with here," he growled and bombarded the boys with fury of electro forces, sending them several yards across the field.

Xavier glided toward Court who lay grimacing, rubbing his elbow.

"You always wondered; didn't you?" Xavier whispered, eerily calm.

"What?" he gasped.

"You always wondered what was done to him at the Institute. Didn't you?" Xavier smiled.

Court gave him a bewildered look but didn't answer.

"Well, young Hardcastle, you will wonder no more," Xavier said. Once again, his eyes grew large and dark as he raised his arms to attack.

* * * * *

Erica and Robbie stormed into the Governing Hall and raced up the steps to the legislative floor. They spotted Loren standing guard outside the King's office and raced toward him.

"Daddy!" Erica cried. "Daddy, it's Xavier! He's gone berserk! He's using his empowerments against the other boys in the stadium."

Every person in the commons froze and stared at the girls in horror.

"What?" Loren gasped. "Oh, God!" He turned and ran into the office. Seconds later, Jeremiah burst from the office with Loren on his heels.

"You girls stay here," Jeremiah told them as he and Loren stormed out of the Governing Hall.

271

Robbie and Erica considered one another for a moment. Then, without a word they raced after the men.

* * * * *

Court's entire body contracted in pain, and he screamed. Xavier continued the torturous force until he heard a loud splintering crack as the bone in Court's arm broke. A collective groan erupted from the other children, cowering behind Xavier.

"Stop, X! Stop! What's wrong with you?" Harry yelled. "You're acting crazy!"

"Crazy? Crazy!" Xavier bellowed, turning toward the tall lanky boy. "You dare to question your future king! You dare to call *me* crazy? I'd say it's you that's crazy."

Xavier raised his hands, preparing to attack, but Garrett and Beck had had enough. The boys charged at him and tackled him to the ground, punching him repeatedly. For a moment, the only thing Xavier could see were white pinpricks of light in a sea of black, but as soon as his vision cleared, he turned on Garrett and Beck with a great vengeance that ended with the boys twitching and sobbing in agony.

"XAVIER!" a voice thundered from across the field.

He spun around and found Jeremiah and Loren advancing on him. Xavier took a hesitating step backwards. Within several long strides, Jeremiah was towering over him.

"What do you think you're doing?" he bellowed, grabbing him violently.

Xavier narrowed his eyes with spite and jerked his arm from his father's grasp. "Whatever the hell I want, *Jer!*"

Jeremiah's hand came quickly, too quickly for Xavier to react. He struck him hard across the cheek, sending him to the ground. Jeremiah looked down at him with disgust. "At this moment, I'm ashamed to be your father!" he growled.

Xavier rubbed his burning cheek. "Like I care! I hate you! Having you as a father has been nothing but one long, embarrassing, terrible experience," he spat. He stood in front of Jeremiah, his hands clenched into fists at his side.

As he continued, his voice grew stronger and angrier. "I never asked to have you as a father! It's because of you that my entire life has been miserable! It's because of you that I was teased and abused so relentlessly. Even my own grandparents despise me! If my father had been anyone but you, they probably would have loved me. Instead, I got to hear everyday that I was a bastard child of a no good, abusing freak, and how much I was turning out to be just like him! And, what about Mother? It was because of you that she was kidnapped and murdered. William was trying to get to you. So, thanks to you, I no longer have a mother! Thanks to you she died. It's your fault she's dead! I wish it had been you! It should've been you who died! You like to think that you're so much better than William LeMasters, but you're not. You've caused me more pain throughout the twelve years of my life than LeMasters ever did! I've always gotten along fine without you. I don't need you, Father, and I never asked to be your son."

Xavier raised his hands and a ball of energy appeared immediately. The electro force gathered quickly in his palm and spiraled toward Jeremiah who was not expecting it. The force hit the King in the abdomen and sent him staggering backwards and to the ground.

Then, Xavier bolted from the stadium.

* * * * *

As Robbie and Erica emerged from the secret passage in the palace's wall, they saw Xavier exit the stadium and sprint toward the wood.

"Oh my God! Of course! Why didn't I see it before?" Erica gasped and marched after Xavier with Robbie on her heels.

"What is it?" Robbie asked.

"Didn't you find it a bit odd that your best friend since kindergarten suddenly did a one-eighty immediately after LeMasters stalked us in the wood?" Erica blurted.

"Erica, what are you getting at? Just spit it out!" Robbie pleaded.

"Xavier! Only, it's not Xavier!"

"What! Erica, have you lost your mind? Of course it's Xavier; look at him!"

"No, listen to me Robbie! I've been having trouble with my vision lately. I couldn't focus on faces very well," Erica told her.

"So? You may need glasses. What's the big deal?" Robbie shrugged.

"That's not it!" Erica turned to Robbie and looked at her wildly. "Robbie, my vision *only* blurred on faces! My Augur ability was manifesting itself!" She pointed violently at the receding white-headed boy. "That is not Xavier! He wears the face of William LeMasters! We've got to get Daddy and the Premier!" She turned to sprint toward the stadium.

"Wait!" Robbie called after her, watching Xavier's imposter slip into the wood. "We'll lose him! Someone has to follow! Go and get King Wells and your dad. I'll follow Xavier," she huffed impatiently, "or whoever he is. King Wells can track us through his telepathy ability. But, if you're right and that is William LeMasters, someone must follow him or we may never find Xavier until it's too late."

"But, Robbie..." Erica protested.

"Erica! We're going to lose him! Go get King Wells!" Robbie yelled, and not waiting for a discussion, she sprinted toward the wood.

Chapter 24
Disguises
★ ★ ★ ★ ★

The last memory Xavier had after the midnight meeting in the wood was Court's white sweater and a sudden, hot pain as something or someone struck him on the head. Afterwards, Xavier had awakened in a dark-marbled room. The room was bare aside from an open lavatory in one corner, a small table and chair, and the bed he was lying on. Xavier struggled against the binds that held him to the bed and released a frustrated growl. Then, the door opened and a familiar face waddled into the room. Lewis, the fat guard from the Institute, grinned fiendishly down at him.

"Hello again," he said in a high nasal tone as he approached Xavier. Then, without another word, he struck Xavier across the face. Xavier's cheek stung, and he could taste blood in his mouth.

"Stop it, Lewis," a child's voice ordered. A boy about Xavier's age entered the room. "You know Father doesn't want him damaged. He has plans for him."

"Father? Who are you?" Xavier sputtered, studying the boy's pale complexion, dark hair, and dark eyes.

The boy surveyed Xavier with mild interest before

answering. "My name is Fox Adrienne LeMasters. William LeMasters is my father."

"Poor you," Xavier grated.

The boy glared at him. "It doesn't really matter what you think. I have my orders to put you under sedation."

"Sedation?" Xavier questioned.

"It's one of my abilities, catalepsy. I can put people asleep. So, I guess you can say that I'm a kind of anesthetic," he said, smirking and raising his hand out in front of him. A violet light appeared in the boy's palm, and Xavier watched with apprehension as the light floated toward him. He could feel soothing warmth radiating from the force as it hovered briefly over his body. Then, it sank into Xavier, and the warmth seeped over every inch of him. Almost instantly, every muscle in his body went limp, and Xavier fell asleep.

* * * * *

When Robbie entered the wood, a faint rustling drew her attention westward. As quietly and carefully as she could, she meandered through the growth and vegetation. It was slow going, trying to follow LeMasters without attracting his attention, and, just when Robbie thought she had lost him, she heard a voice.

"There you are!" It was Madam Bowerman! "Everything has gone as planned. Danson arrived last night with the Key."

"Good," he said curtly.

Robbie crept closer and watched the odd pair from behind a shrub.

"But, William, what good is the Key if you can't control it, if you don't know how it works?" Bowerman questioned.

"I know how it works. The Prince must be coerced into operating it; only the King or his heir can wield the King's Key. But, don't fret; I have a plan."

Bowerman nodded and then smirked at the boy in front of her. "How are things at the palace, *Sire*? Did I hear correctly? Did you actually allow Dublin Minnows to spank

276

you, or was Danson just pulling my leg?" she taunted.

Xavier's imposter shrugged nonchalantly. "What was I to do? I couldn't very well blow my cover, now could I?" The woman giggled, and he glared moodily up at her. Finally, Bowerman was able to contain her laughter, and the boyish image grinned. "Aside from the fact that my idiot brother nearly blew the whole plan with his terrible impersonation of Ephraim Hardcastle, things are going along just beautifully! I think I've arranged it so that the only person who'll be upset when the boy dies is his old man. Can you imagine the guilt Jeremiah's going to feel when his son's body floats up in the lake after they had such a horrible argument?"

Xavier's laugh grew deep and masculine. Unable to look away, Robbie watched as the pale-haired boy melted away, and William LeMasters molted in his place. Then, Madam Bowerman followed with a transfiguration of her own into a woman Robbie didn't recognized.

Suddenly, William spun in Robbie's direction.

"William? What is it?" the woman next to him questioned.

"It seems that I've been followed, Dr. Angelo," he said untroubled before directing his attention back to the bush Robbie was hiding behind. "Come on out little one," he cooed. "I know you're there, Robbie. Come on out."

There was no use in continuing to hide so she stood.

The woman's face became pinched with dislike. "Oh, it's you."

"Come, child." Although his voice was gentle, LeMasters's dark glare burrowed into her with brutal coldness. His hypnotic eyes beckoned and allured her, and Robbie found herself stumbling toward the tall, dark man unable to tear her eyes from the two black orifices gleaming down at her. She inhaled laboriously, trying to regain her breath that fear had squeezed from her lungs.

"Please, do not fear me. I don't intend to hurt you," he told her.

"That's a lie," she said simply with more bravery than she felt. "If you can speak that lightly of killing Prince Wells, then, I imagine you'd kill me without a moment's hesitation."

William contemplated her with amusement. "Ah," he nodded, "I believe I've underestimated you, young Minnows. Maybe you're not the brainless sidekick I had first thought."

Robbie tightened her contemptuous glare on him, and William laughed heartily. "My, my! If looks could kill little girl..." He looked at the woman. "We'll take her with us, Veronica. There may be a need for her. Lewis told me that the boy is having difficulty keeping the Prince under sedation. If Prince Wells causes trouble in the next phase of the plan, we may need her to convince him to be more cooperative."

The severe woman nodded and grabbed Robbie roughly by the arm. "Just give me a reason, and I'll kill you slowly."

William, Dr. Angelo, and Robbie hiked deep into the forest and beyond the lake. Robbie had never been this far into the wood and wasn't sure if she'd ever be able to find her way out again. However, they seemed to be following some sort of old path. Although it was mostly overgrown with plants and moss, every so often, Robbie caught a glimpse of the polished, white-marbled stones under her feet. Finally, the wood thinned into a small clearing and out in front of them stood a decrepit lookout tower that had long since crumbled to half its intended size. Robbie knew without asking, exactly where they were—the ruins.

In earlier times, the ruins had served as a look out tower for the kingdom, but it also led to a fallout shelter, or more accurately, a fallout city, that was used in case of an all out invasion or a battle within the kingdom's walls. Underneath the entire area of the wood was an intricate, confusing system of passages and chambers.

Dr. Angelo shoved Robbie through the half-rotten oak door, and Robbie fell to the grimy floor. With an irritated sigh, the woman lifted her by the arm and shoved her after

William LeMasters. William led them down passage after confusing passage until Robbie was left with little doubt that she'd never be able to escape on her own. With each step deeper into the ruins, all hope of the Premier finding her and Xavier and saving them seemed more and more remote. Suddenly, William stopped and turned on Robbie, knocking her onto the damp floor. He glared down at her.

"Jeremiah is tracking you?" he spat. Not waiting for an answer, he seized her roughly and sent a sharp electro force through her body that rendered her unconscious. Then, he lifted the limp child onto his shoulder. Dr. Angelo looked at him questioningly.

"Jeremiah can't track her if she's not conscious," he told her simply. "Never the less, I imagine that we don't have much time."

* * * * *

Jeremiah stopped suddenly, and Loren nearly ran into him.

"What? What is it?" Loren asked in alarm.

"It's Robbie. I can't get a reading on her anymore. She...she's closed."

"What could cause..." Loren began. "Jer, she's not de...dead. Is she?"

"I don't know, Loren. She may just be inside a lead lined room, or she could be unconscious or too stressed. It's hard to say for sure." The King proceeded forward in a rush. "But, I do know he took her into the ruins."

"The ruins! He might've well taken her to the Syrian Desert! It'll be impossible to find her in that maze!"

* * * * *

Robbie woke some time later on the floor of a dark marbled room. She sat up and peered around. Xavier was strapped to a bed next to her.

"Xavier!" she blurted, rushing to his side. "Xavier?" She shook him, but he did not respond. "Xavier?"

"He can not hear you," said a boy with untidy jet-black hair. "He's under my empowerment."

279

"Your empowerment? Who are you?" she asked.

"Fox. Fox LeMasters," he said, strolling across the room toward her. Although he wasn't much taller than her, he was thinner, much thinner, maybe even a bit malnourished.

"LeMasters? You're that maniac's kid?" she accused.

The boy's black eyes flashed furiously. "You better watch what you say about Master!"

But, before Robbie could respond, the door to the chamber swung open, and William waltzed into the room and looked down at Robbie. "Fox, are you making our new guest feel at home? Would you like anything to eat or drink?"

"No," Robbie muttered.

Master nodded smirking and looked at Xavier. His smile fell and his brow wrinkled with apprehension. "Fox?"

"Yes, Master?" The boy stiffened.

"Why is the Prince waking?" he turned and glared accusingly at the boy.

"I tried to tell you. He's fighting it," the boy whispered timidly. "I can't seem to keep him under for as long as I could. I have to repeat the procedure every thirty minutes now."

The man stared down at the boy. "Are you telling me that you're a weaker empowered?"

"NO! I...I've kept him under this long didn't I?"

A slow smile spread across William's face. "Good. But, we won't need to subdue him any further. My plan is ready."

"You know how the Key works then?" the boy asked.

"Yes, unfortunately, only Jeremiah and that boy can wield it." He motioned to the still unconscious Xavier. "Now, I'm afraid I'm going to have to ask you and Miss Minnows to leave." He motioned both children toward him just as Julia Wells entered the room.

Robbie's jaw dropped. "Mrs. Wells? I...thought...we thought you were dead."

"Oh, she is," said Mrs. Wells in a harsh voice.

"This is not Julia Wells, child. This is my assistant, Dr. Angelo, but I believe, you knew her better as Madam Bowerman," William told her.

"What are you doing?" Robbie snarled.

"We're arranging a little reunion between mother and son," the woman cooed.

"What? That's cruel! Xavier has had a hard enough time accepting his mother's death and moving on with his life. This could crack him. How could you do that? He's just a little boy!"

"No! He's not just a little boy," William hissed. "He's the Prince of Warwood! He's Jeremiah Wells's heir! You see child, sometimes in war, the innocent must die to annihilate the enemy." He grinned fiendishly down at her and pulled her from the room, closing the door and leaving the imposter alone with Xavier.

*****

Xavier slowly opened his eyes. How long had he been out? The boy had put him under some kind of empowerment. He had known it even in the dream-like state he'd been placed under and had fought against it. Now, he was awake. He looked around blinking fiercely to clear his blurred, hazy vision. What he saw then made him question whether or not he was truly awake. His mother! Although her head was cradled in her hands and he couldn't see her face, he knew without question it was his mother. His eyes swelled with tears.

"Mom?" he croaked.

She looked up and smiled warmly. "Hi, sweetie." She leaned toward him and rested her hands over his.

"Mom?" he repeated, blinking incredulously. "Is it really you?"

"Yes, Xavier. I'm here," she patted his hand.

"MOM!" he choked out and flung himself into her arms. "You're alive! We thought you were dead. I thought you were dead." He pulled away and looked up at her with moistened cheeks.

"I know, Son. I know, but I'm here now. I'm not going anywhere."

"What happened? Where've you been?"

"Master William has kept me captive all this time, but he says he'll let us go if we do what he wants," she told him feebly.

"What does he want?" Xavier questioned.

"He wants us to help him. He has a key that he needs your help with," she told him.

"My help? How am I to help him? What would I know about a key?"

"Well, it's a special key," she told him, standing and retrieving a small decrepit oak chest from the table in the center of the room. Xavier immediately recognized it, and his breath caught in his throat. She turned and opened the chest. "This key."

Xavier approached his mother and peered inside the box at the Clavis de Rex. He ran his hand over the glittering handle. The moment his hand touched the curiously cold surface of the Key, he felt warmth tingling into his hand and up his arm. He yanked his hand back and stared.

"Wow," he whispered.

"It opens all the powers known and some unknown to the empowered society," she whispered. "It's called the King's Key, Clavis de Rex. Only a king of Warwood or his heir can control it. In ancient times, the king would use the Key to strip criminals of their powers, but it can also be used to give powers to those the king saw fit."

"Really?" Xavier looked at the Key with awe. This he had not known. "It can give powers?" He stroked the Key again, drawn to its power like an addict to his drug. "But, why would William want the Key if only a king can use it?"

"That's why he brought you here. He wants you to endow him with all the powers the Key provides," she said.

"What!" Xavier yelped, jumping backwards. "He must be nuts if he thinks that I'd even consider it! I won't do it! I won't! I'd sooner die first!" he spat.

"You won't need to Son. He says he'll kill me if you don't," she said, her voice trembling.

"What?" he gasped horrified. "He'll kill you? I won't let him, Mom. I won't let him! Don't worry, I'll protect you."

"How? You're just a boy. How are you going to protect me from a fully grown empowered man?" she implored.

"Well, I must have something he doesn't! Why else would he need me to work that Key?" he asked, jabbing a finger at the King's Key.

His mother fell silent and studied the boy before her. Then, she smiled. "That's right! I didn't think about that! That's what we'll do then, Son. We'll fight him together!" She paused in thought. "Xavier? Maybe you could use the Key to give me some powers so I could help you."

"I... I don't know, Mom," he stuttered.

Fury glistened in his mother's eyes, just briefly, before she blinked it away and smiled down at him. "I understand, but, Xavier, the only reason we did not stay at the palace with your father was that there were some citizens who thought I didn't belong because I was not an empowered and threats were made against my life. If I had powers, I could live in the kingdom with you and Jeremiah."

Xavier was tempted. Oh, how fantastic it would be to have both a mother and a father. He could almost envision his father's face when he returned to the kingdom with his mother. Gradually, he reached for the Key and stroked its length. The warmth danced up his fingertips, and he smiled at the aura of power he felt there.

"That's it," his mother coaxed. "We could all be together."

Xavier's smile fell, and he froze. He withdrew his hand and looked uncertainly up at the woman in front of him. "Wait a minute. Why didn't Father use it?"

His mother looked down at him puzzled, "What do you mean?"

"If the Key has been around for centuries, why didn't

Father use it to empower you so we could've stayed when I was a baby?" he asked.

Anger flashed to the surface of his mother's face, and she scowled at him. "Fine!" she blurted. "If you don't want my help, if you don't want me to be with you, don't use it to help me. I'll just return to your grandparents. I'm sure your father will let me visit occasionally. Of course, that's only if William doesn't kill me first." She burst into tears and dropped the wooden case. The Key spilled out with a clatter and slid across the floor.

Xavier watched his mother crumble into a hysterical mess.

His heart felt as if was being shredded with every sob she sputtered. "Mom?" He touched her shaking shoulders. "Okay, I'll do it. I'll do it. Please don't cry." He bent down, picked up the box, and crossed the room to retrieve the Key. The moment his fingers enclosed around the gleaming object, energy surged through his body with such intensity that it drove him to his knees. He gasped for breath. "M...Mom?" he stuttered. "I...I can't...it's too...powerful." He looked up to a very dry face, but it wasn't his mother's. Dr. Angelo stood before him, smiling.

"It's okay, Xavier. I have faith in you," his mother's voice said, but it was Dr. Angelo's mouth that moved to the words.

"What's going on?" he asked, shaking his head.

She seemed to think he meant with the Key. "It's the magnitude of all the abilities of the empowered," his mother's voice told him through Dr. Angelo's mouth.

Xavier threw the now cold Key across the room. "NO!" he shouted.

Even after the Key was out of his hands, the image of Dr. Angelo remained. She continued to talk to him as if she were Julia.

"Please, Xavier, I want to be with you and your father. Please," she pleaded.

Xavier began heaving in panic. He crossed the room

and fell against the wall. He clung desperately there, struggling to regain his breath.

"Honey? Are you okay?" his mother's voice came again. "Maybe if you sat down, you could handle its power."

"No," he growled, gaining courage and strength. He turned and faced the woman with an electro force spinning in the cup of his hand, but she was unaware of it and continued to coo at him as if she were his mother.

"Xavier, honey. Please! Don't you want me to be with you?"

"No, I don't want *you*. I want the woman you murdered, you evil witch!" he spat, raising his arm and hurling a ball of electricity toward her.

Dr. Angelo soared across the room and slammed against the wall. Slowly, she staggered to her feet. "So, my little disguise didn't work," she muttered, stumbling toward Xavier, with blood trickling from the corner of her mouth. However, the moment Xavier lowered his hand, Dr. Angelo retaliated with an electro force of her own, but Xavier had been expecting it and blocked it with a shielding force.

This infuriated Dr. Angelo into a tantrum, and she screeched as Xavier propelled another force in her direction. This time it struck her squarely in the chest, and Dr. Angelo crumpled to the floor like a rag doll. Guarded and cautious, Xavier approached the motionless woman and knelt next to her. She was unconscious but alive.

Chapter 25
The Premonition
★ ★ ★ ★ ★

Xavier crossed the room, grabbed the Key from the floor, and slipped it into his belt loop. Then, he raced to the door and pulled. It was locked. Now what? The Key! He could use the Key! Slowly, he withdrew the glimmering staff from his waistband and stared down at it, his stomach fluttering. Energy resounded through his hands with tremendous intensity. It almost scared him. He closed his eyes and wondered what power would help him most. He needed the door unlocked. Suddenly, the Key went deathly cold in his hands, and a loud click drew his attention back to the door. With bated breath, he inched toward it and pulled. The door opened! Xavier's studied the Key in his hands. Was that all there was to using the Key? He only needed to wish for something, and the Key provided the empowerment to achieve that wish? If it was so simple to use, why hadn't Father used it so that his mother could have stayed in the kingdom when he was a baby?

Shaking the persistent questions from his head to concentrate on his current task, Xavier stepped into a five-sided-room with four other doors. Something about this room seemed familiar though he didn't understand why. As far as he knew, he had never set foot inside this room before. So, why did he have the peculiar feeling that he had? The black walls and white tiled floor sent a violating shiver down his spine. Something wasn't right. The room was too quiet. It lacked the normal sounds of an empty room. The gushing of air from a ventilation system and the nearly inaudible hum of overhead lights were nonexistent. But, it wasn't just the lack of sound that trouble Xavier. It was that the empty room vibrated with a powerful, silent energy. Something was going to happen here, he realized. Something horrible! Xavier gulped back the mounting fear trying to consume him and looked around desperately for an exit.

He frowned. Which door? With nothing left to do, Xavier simply guessed. He yanked open a door at the far side of the room. This door led to short corridor lined with six more doors. Xavier ventured through the first door. It appeared to be a boy's bedroom, though no boy could be found, so he closed the door and continued to the next room. This door was locked. Closing his eyes in concentration, Xavier squeezed the Key in his hands. Almost instantaneously, he heard the familiar click of the door unlatching. He opened it and peered in. The room was completely blackened, but as the light from the hall spilled into the room, he saw a bulk lying on a rickety bed. The moment the light fell over the bed, the bulk sat up.

"Ephraim? Is that you?" Xavier gasped. He looked horrible. He had a couple weeks worth of growth on his face, and he was battered and bruised.

"Sire Wells? Dear Lord, did that madman get you too?" He jumped from the bed and strode over to him, grasping him by the shoulders. "Are you all right?"

"Yes, sir. I've escaped from my room..."

"What the..." Ephraim grabbed the Key from Xavier's hands and looked down at him fearfully. "How did you get this?"

"They were trying to trick me... Look, it doesn't

matter. We need to get out of here!" Xavier took the Key from Ephraim and tucked it back into his waistband.

Ephraim eyed the Key a moment before nodding and leading the way back down the hall. "Come on," he said. "I regained consciousness as they were bringing me down. I think I remember part of the way out of here."

He led the boy back out into pentagonal room. After studying the room a moment, Ephraim grabbed Xavier's hand and pulled him toward a door on the far right. Then, the door behind them sprung open, and William LeMasters entered the room not at all surprised to see them there.

"Well, well, well," he chided. "Sire Wells and his bodyguard, Ephraim Hardcastle."

Ephraim nudged Xavier behind him and turned to face the dark man. "Let's see if you can take me now when you can't hide in the shadows like a bloody coward," he spat.

Xavier had never seen Ephraim so confrontational. He had always been meek and submissive in the presence of Jeremiah, but the man who stood in front of him now was anything but meek. Ephraim faced William with contempt and utter defiance.

William smiled smugly. "Oh, I don't think I'll need to do that Mr. Hardcastle. You see, I believe the boy will do as I ask willingly."

"Never! You murdered my mother, you lunatic! I won't do anything you want!" Xavier spat.

"Oh, I think you will because if you don't, your little girl friend here will be punished," William sneered as Danson pulled a squirming Robbie into the room.

"Let me go!" she spat as her heel struck Danson's shin sharply.

Danson grimaced and hissed a string of curses. "You little vixen," he growled and slapped Robbie to the floor.

"Keep your filthy hands off of her!" Xavier yelled, fighting against Ephraim's arms.

William gave a throaty, bellowing laugh. "Well, he's certainly Jeremiah's boy! He has the same savior complex."

"Let the girl go, William. She has nothing to do with any of this," Ephraim snarled.

William shook his head. "Haven't you been listening, Hardcastle? She," he pointed at the weeping girl, "has *everything* to do with it! Without her, the boy won't do as I've requested. But, he will." He leered down at Xavier. "Won't you, boy?"

Xavier felt defeat drop over him like a heavy weight, enslaving him with helplessness. He lifted the Key from his waist and begrudgingly stepped toward LeMasters. What could he do? Lord, he wished his father was there! He would know what to do! He would fix everything!

Suddenly, the entire room shuddered and seemed to come to life as the air around them converged with a loud whoosh. A cloud of energy glowing in the center of the room began to swirl into a mighty whirlwind. Xavier could feel its heat kissing his face as Ephraim grabbed him and pulled him to the floor. Then, as suddenly as the tornado of energy had begun, it ended and a figure stood in its place. Xavier's eyes trailed up the well-defined, powerful legs to the broad chest and shoulders until he found himself looking into the dark slate eyes of his father.

"Father," he croaked, racing toward him.

Ephraim jumped to his feet and grabbed him. "No, Your Highness. Stay back."

Jeremiah turned slowly, methodically, toward the still cowering figures behind him. William stood, and for a moment, the men studied one another with quiet contempt.

"Stay here, Xavier," Ephraim told him and moved to stand next to the King.

"Release the girl," Jeremiah demanded.

The air around them was close and tense; a battle was about to begin. Xavier backed against the wall and prepared himself. Then, a thought occurred to him: only he and his father could wield the Key; that had to account for something. Maybe he could help. After all, these men had killed his mother. No, not just killed her but crucified her.

They had to pay for that! With his mind made up, Xavier stepped forward and stood next to his father the Key still clutched in his hand.

Jeremiah looked down at him in surprise. "No, Son," he muttered. "I can't do this if I have to worry about you. Back away."

"No," Xavier said, never taking his eyes off William. "I think I have a right to do what I can to fight my mother's murderers."

Jeremiah turned to him. "No, Son. I will not allow this." He grabbed Xavier by the arm and yanked him back. "This isn't a game; I may have to kill these men."

"I can help!" Xavier pleaded.

"No!" he barked. "My son will not be made into a murderer at 12 years old. Stay here, and don't interfere with my ability to fight. Now, put the Key away and do not use it again!"

Receding to his father's wishes, Xavier nodded and backed against the wall, sliding the Key into his waistband.

Jeremiah turned back to William and Danson. Ephraim had not moved; he stood unwavering, his hands spread out at his sides ready to fight. Jeremiah returned to his comrade's side. "I said, release the girl!"

"Or what?" William challenged.

"Release the girl, and I may allow you to live," Jeremiah hissed, throwing back his cape so that he had free use of his arms. "What will it be, William?"

William glared unfaltering at his nemesis. "I don't think so, Jer," he whispered.

"I was hoping you'd say that," Jeremiah growled. "There're so many things I'd like to collect retribution for."

Suddenly, Jeremiah's arm shot up and in the same instant a force shot across the room, hitting William and hurling him into the wall. William fell heavily to the floor and didn't even take the time to get to his feet as he sent a spiraling force at Jeremiah, hitting him in the shoulder. This knocked Jeremiah off balance, and he stumbled backwards,

290

which gave William enough time to get to his feet and conjure a more devastating force. This hit the King in the abdomen, and he fell to his knees, wincing.

Ephraim could not help Jeremiah for he was valiantly battling with Danson, and although he appeared to have the advantage, Danson was fighting back viciously.

"Father!" Xavier screamed and took several hurried steps toward him, but Jeremiah held up his hand and briskly shook his head, stopping Xavier. Then, he swung his open hand toward William and pelted him with another force. This time, William was thrown ten feet into the air, and he slammed against the ceiling before falling with a loud thud to the stone floor. Jeremiah got to his feet and stood over the man lying on the floor, wheezing and coughing.

Both Ephraim and Danson froze and stared at William's shaking body. Then, Danson fled from the room and abandoned his brother, but Ephraim made no attempts to stop him. He was watching Jeremiah with tremendous apprehension.

Robbie raced to Xavier and threw her arms around him. Xavier held her as he watched his father, towering over William, his hands clenched into tight fists.

"Jeremiah. Jeremiah, don't," Ephraim whispered, grasping the King's shoulder. Xavier had never heard Ephraim speak to his father with such force before.

Jeremiah shrugged the hand off of him and said without looking up, "Get the children out of here."

"Jeremiah!" Ephraim's voice became stern. "Don't do it." Ephraim grabbed his friend by the arm and tried to pull him away from LeMasters, but Jeremiah shoved Ephraim away from him.

"Hardcastle! I just gave you an order. Now, get those kids the hell out of here!" he boomed, his voice echoing around the room.

But, Ephraim did not obey the order. He charged at Jeremiah, drove him across the room, and pinned him against the wall. "No! This is not going to happen! It's not!"

Jeremiah released a frustrated growl and knocked Ephraim backwards. "Back off, Ephraim!"

Then, Ephraim punched the King and tackled him to the floor, pinning him there. Ephraim wasn't as big as Jeremiah, but his sudden attack had caught him off guard. "Damn it, Ephraim. Let go of me! You *know* what he did to Julia," Jeremiah's voice cracked with raw anguish. "You *know* what he put her through... how we found her! He deserves to suffer a long, painful death. Now, I'm ORDERING YOU, RELEASE ME!"

Ephraim, struggling to keep the King pinned to the floor, looked up at Xavier. "Xavier, get Robbie out of here. GO!"

Xavier darted through the door behind him, pushing a stunned Robbie out before him. They sprinted down a stone corridor with battered lanterns dangling from the walls, when suddenly Xavier froze.

"What?" Robbie stopped and looked back at him questioningly.

He spun around, staring: rough cut stone, oil lanterns, and the door! The door they had just exited was red. The dream! He had dreamt of this corridor. Icy tentacles of trepidation wrapped themselves around his chest squeezing the breath from him as the recognition sank in.

"What is it?" Robbie questioned.

"This hall," he muttered, "I've dreamt of it. I've been here in my dreams." Xavier stared back at the red door. As the horror crept from the recesses of his mind, he clutched the Key with instinctive protectiveness. Suddenly, everything around him clouded over in a sea of black as a vision of a great explosion and a wall of fire bellowing through the ruins' passages bombarded his mind. He blinked and the fiery image disappeared.

"Oh, God!" he gasped, looking at a wide-eyed Robbie. "Robbie! You have to get out of here! Now! Something horrible is going to happen! Go! I have to go back for

Ephraim and Father."

"Xavier?" she began, fear creeping into her voice.

"GO!" he shouted at her as he turned and race back toward the door.

Xavier crashed through the red door and found that Jeremiah had gained the advantage over Ephraim and stood towering over him. Both men had battered and bleeding faces.

"FATHER! We've got to get out of here!" he screamed.

Both men looked at Xavier, stunned. All anger seemed to drain from Jeremiah's face as he looked at his son. "Xavier?"

"Now! We have to go now! There's a bomb or something! This place is going to go up any second."

William choked and coughed, spluttering blood onto the white limestone floor. A sickly laugh seeped from him, and after another spasm of coughing, he cackled. They looked at the morbidly injured man who was laughing in uncontrollable hysteria.

Jeremiah's eyes widened. "God Almighty," he hissed.

Instantly, both men sprinted toward the door. Jeremiah swooped Xavier into his arms and raced out of the room and down the corridor with Ephraim following close behind. They turned a corner and found Robbie and Loren.

"Loren! Grab the girl! Run!" Jeremiah yelled.

Without question, Loren picked up Robbie and ran. They raced through the confusing maze of passages and corridors.

"There!" Ephraim yelled. "Take the passage on the right. No, no, the right! It's the way out!" A great rumble shook the earth around them and bits of the ceiling crumbled down on them. "GO!" Ephraim yelled.

They raced down the passage and burst through another door. They found a set of stairs spiraling upward toward a sliver of daylight. The men took the steps two or three at a time, racing against the growing fiery wall roaring after them.

"Father! It's coming!" Xavier screamed.

The group reached the platform, feeling the heat grazing at their backs. They had no more than stepped out of the ruins, when the invisible velocity of the explosion punched them twenty feet into the surrounding woods. Jeremiah swiftly rolled over his son, shielding him with his body as debris fell to the ground around them. Finally, when the shower of rock and earth ended, Jeremiah pushed himself up onto his elbows and looked around.

"Ephraim? Loren?" he called.

"We're fine," Loren called from their right.

"Yeah, just bloody fine," Ephraim croaked from their left.

Jeremiah looked down at Xavier, his eyes brimming with worry and tears. "Son?" he choked.

With a painful lump in his throat at the sight of his father crying, Xavier nodded.

"Thank God," he sighed, laying his forehead against Xavier's and pulling closer to the boy. "Oh, Jesus," he muttered, his voice breaking.

Jeremiah sat up and lifted Xavier into his lap hugging him close. Jeremiah buried his face in Xavier's shoulder and sobbed silently. The knot in Xavier's throat dislodged and tears streamed freely down his cheeks. He wrapped his arms around his father and wept with him.

Chapter 26
A New Beginning
★ ★ ★ ★ ★

In the week that followed, things did not return to normal for the King and Prince. Xavier gradually became more and more distant and refused to speak to anyone. By the third day, Xavier had barricaded himself in his room and wouldn't eat. Jeremiah grew increasingly worried about the boy and stopped going into work.

"Jer, he used the Key," Ephraim told him when Jeremiah questioned him about what had happened to Xavier in the ruins. "As you know sometimes those that have acquired powers by the Key can have a mental break..."

"I know all about the Key's folklore, Ephraim! I don't believe in it," Jeremiah barked, but the truth was he had already considered it. Although there was absolutely no scientific evidence to support the superstition, he feared that the curse of the Key was the cause of this depression that Xavier seem to be shrouded in.

"Well," Ephraim shook his head, "I was only with the boy moments before you arrived. You may want to ask Robbie. She may know something."

Jeremiah nodded. "I just may do that."

Ephraim stood at attention, "Will that be all, Sire?"

"No," Jeremiah said, smiling weakly and patting him on the shoulder. "Thank you, my friend."

Ephraim shrugged. "I just wish I knew more about what happened to the lad."

Jeremiah straightened and looked pointedly at the man in front of him. "That's not what I meant. I mean," he paused and rubbed his bruised jaw, "thanks for preventing me from doing something that I would have regretted."

Ephraim grinned mischievously. "I'm not so easy to ignore anymore, am I?" he asked, playfully boxing with Jeremiah.

Jeremiah couldn't help but chuckle. "No, you're not!"

Ephraim laughed and returned to his post outside the royal residence. Jeremiah shut the door behind him and entered the receiving room. He fixed himself a drink from the bar and sat next to the hearth, staring into the flickering flames. Lord, he hoped it wasn't the Key that kept his son in this trance. But, if it wasn't the Key, then, what was it?

Following the explosion in the wood, the realization of how close they all had come to death had hit Jeremiah hard. The boy had wept relentlessly in his arms and, at first, he had thought the boy was venting his own pinned up tension. But, Xavier had not been able to stop, and he had to be carried out of the forest! When Xavier finally did stop crying, a simple question or comment would send him into hysteria again. Finally, the boy withdrew to his room, stopped eating, and became uncommunicative.

Jeremiah sighed and gulped down the amber liquid in one swallow. The Key had not caused his son's depression; he was certain of that. Something else had happened, something horrendous!

* * * * *

The next morning, Jeremiah paid a visit to the Minnows.

"Jeremiah? Is everything all right? Robbie says Xavier hasn't been back to school," Tamarah asked, opening

296

the door wider.

"No, Xavier isn't well," Jeremiah told her. "That's why I've come. Tamarah, I need to speak to Robbie. I need to ask her about what went on down in the ruins."

"Go get her, dear," Dublin said, patting his wife's shoulder. "Come on in, Jeremiah."

Dublin led Jeremiah into the sitting room.

"Is he that bad, Jer?" Dublin asked quietly.

Jeremiah nodded, his throat constricting painfully. "Dub, he's awake, but yet he's not. He's put himself in some kind of a trance. I've been trying to break into his thoughts, but I haven't had much luck. I'm hoping that Robbie will be able to tell me something that'll help me to breach his sub consciousness."

"Okay, just go easy on her..." Dub was interrupted by Robbie's entrance.

She looked anxiously from King Wells to her father.

"Honey," Dublin motioned her over to him. "Sire Wells has some questions he needs to ask you." Robbie sat on her father's lap and looked at Jeremiah uneasily.

Jeremiah cleared his throat. "Robbie, Xavier is not well. He's very ill, in fact. I'm very worried about him."

"Is he going to be okay?" she asked fretfully.

"I really don't know, but if I can't break through to him, I'm afraid we might lose him."

"I knew it would break him," Robbie spat angrily. "I told them that, but they didn't care so long as they got what they wanted."

"Who did what to Xavier, honey," Dublin asked.

"William and that... that lady, Dr. Angelo. Dr. Angelo transfigured into..." she paused, looking apprehensively at Jeremiah.

Jeremiah immediately understood and his heart sank. His son had dealt with his mother's death once and now was forced to relive and cope with her death all over again. He sighed and looked at the tearful girl.

"Go ahead," Dublin prompted.

"Julia?" Jeremiah answered for her.

Slowly, she nodded.

"Jesus," Dublin groaned.

Jeremiah stood abruptly. "Thank you, Robbie. This is very helpful." He gave her a reassuring smile and looked at Dublin. "Thanks, Dub. I appreciate your help."

"Anytime, Your Highness. Let us know if there's anything else we can do," Dub said, standing and patting Jeremiah's shoulder.

"Thank you, old friend," Jeremiah said, shaking Dublin's hand before turning and exiting the Minnows's home. He marched purposefully down the drive toward the palace.

When Jeremiah entered the residence, Milton was waiting by the door, looking very distraught. Chilling screams from Xavier's room sent Jeremiah sprinting for the steps.

"The boy's been screaming non-stop for nearly an hour, Sire. Emma and I tried to calm him, but nothing would work. It's as if he's having a nightmare that he can't wake from. Emma went after Dr. Evans," Milton called to Jeremiah's receding back as he climbed the stairs three at a time.

"Okay, Milton. Send him up when he arrives."

"NO!" Xavier screamed, his voice hoarse. "MOOOM! GOD, NO! WHERE ARE YOU?"

Jeremiah burst through the door, but Xavier was nowhere to be found. "Xavier?" he called, panicking.

"No," the boy moaned and began sobbing.

Jeremiah scanned the room frantically for the source of the crying. Finally, he found Xavier huddled under his computer desk with his face in his hands. Jeremiah knelt in front of him.

"Son?" he said tentatively, but Xavier didn't acknowledge his father's presence; he continued to sob and began screaming again.

Jeremiah struggled under the desk toward Xavier. He

grabbed the boy and pulled him out from under the desk and into his arms.

"Son?" he whispered. "Xavier? Talk to me, boy."

Suddenly the sobbing stopped, and Xavier lifted his blood-shot, vacant eyes, but he did not look at the man holding him.

Jeremiah closed his eyes and concentrated. Xavier's developing blocking skills coupled with this self-induced oblivion made it difficult for Jeremiah to penetrate his thoughts. Finally, by concentrating on the thought and image of Julia, he was able to break through the barrier the boy had created. He entered a clouded, surreal state— where you're unsure if you're awake or dreaming. Xavier stood with his back to him. He seemed to be regarding a red door in front of him, and his head tilted from side to side.

"How?" the boy muttered to himself.

"Son?" Jeremiah whispered.

Xavier spun around, and his eyes widened the moment he saw Jeremiah. "Father!" he exclaimed, running into his arms. "Father! We have to help her!"

"Who, Son?" Jeremiah asked, hugging him.

"Mom! She's in there," he exclaimed, turning and pointing to the red door. "Only I don't know how to open it." The boy frowned dejectedly.

"Son," Jeremiah said softly, cupping the boy's chin and drawing Xavier's eyes to his. "We can't help your mother. She's not there. She's dead Xavier."

Xavier began shaking his head with disbelief. "No," he whispered, his voice cracking. "She's not. I've seen her. She's alive!"

"No, Son. She's not," he said kindly. "Xavier, the woman you saw was another woman transfigured as your mother. It wasn't really her. You know that. She's dead, Son. I found her and buried her, myself. She's gone."

Xavier gave a defeated look and slumped to the floor.

"No," Jeremiah said firmly. "You can not stay here; you must wake up, Son. Now, stand up and let's find our way out of this fog."

"No," Xavier whispered hoarsely.

"Are you defying me boy?" Jeremiah's voice became stern, and he lifted Xavier to his feet. "I am your father, and you will do as I tell you."

Xavier looked up at him angrily.

"Let's go!" his father demanded, pushing him toward the nebula behind him.

"No. I don't want to!" Xavier growled, fighting against his father's large body toward the red door.

"Stop it!" Jeremiah snapped, grabbing the boy's flailing arms and shaking him. "Stop it, right now! You're going back even if I have to drag you," he told him.

"No!" Xavier shouted, twisting out of Jeremiah's grasp and darting toward the red door. Jeremiah grabbed him and pulled him toward the shifting fog. "Stop! Father, no! Mother's there! No!" Xavier screamed, kicking him. "I hate you! I hate you!"

These words brought Jeremiah to a halt. He turned and looked down at the boy glaring up at him. "That's okay, Son. But, I love you. I love you more than anything in the world." He swooped down, lifted the boy, and carried him through the fog.

Xavier blinked several times, trying to determine where he was. His father's aftershave lotion drifted into his senses, and he felt his father's short beard tickling his cheek. Jeremiah's strong arms cradled him like a baby, and Xavier suddenly felt like crying.

"Father?" he rasped.

Jeremiah looked down at him. "Xavier! Thank God! You had me worried out of my mind. Are you all right?"

"Y... Yeah," Xavier muttered, burrowing his face into his father's chest, but he wasn't all right. He was far from it!

"Xavier?" Jeremiah whispered, lifting the boy's chin to gaze down at him. "Xavier, talk to me. Don't bottle it up, Boy. It doesn't solve anything. Please don't close me out, again."

300

Xavier's chin quivered moments before he burst into wailing sobs. "God, Dad! I real...really thought it...was h...her! I thought...we all could be...a family! A... r...real family that we n...never got to be! I really wanted...that! You, me, and...MOOOOOM!"

Jeremiah hugged him tightly and murmured, "I know. I know, Son. That's it. Just let it all out."

His father held him for a long time as the sobs racked his small body. He just couldn't seem to stop. Finally, the sobs waned, and Xavier sat hiccupping in his father's lap and listening to his father's heartbeat thudding against his ear.

Jeremiah stroked and kissed his head. "How do you feel?"

"Okay." He thought a moment and sniffed. "You came after me, in my dream."

"Yes, I did," he answered.

"You weren't very nice to me," Xavier said matter-of-factly.

"No, I wasn't. I didn't intend to be nice. I intended to get my son out of the trance he had placed himself in and being nice wouldn't have done that," he smiled briefly at the boy. He sighed and cupped the boy's face in his massive hands. "Are you sure you're all right?"

"Yes, sir. But, I sure am hungry."

Jeremiah laughed heartily and then, nodded. "The kitchen's closed, but I think your old man can whip up a couple of cheeseburgers."

* * * * *

Over the next couple of weeks, the Royal Guard investigated the passages and tunnels of the ruins. There was no sign of LeMasters or the others, but they did find the true Madam Bowerman in a locked chamber; she had been electrocuted to death.

The following week, Xavier returned to school. Sir Spencer had been promoted as the new Headmaster, which was well received by most students. Many believed it was like having a king running the school since he was King Wells's brother. Xavier's first day back was very awkward, and although Headmaster Spencer had informed the students during a school-wide assembly that the events from the past couple of weeks had not been Xavier but that it had been LeMasters impersonating the Prince, people still seemed to be fearful of Xavier. Most students wouldn't even look at him and skirted around him in the hall. The rest simply avoided him all together. Then, there were the insistent thoughts pressing in on him. Xavier had not intentionally set out to read others' thoughts, but their thoughts were so strong that they might as well have announced them over the school's intercom system. After encountering the twelfth skittish schoolmate, Xavier looked at Robbie, but her only response was a shrug.

Xavier sighed despondently. "Where're Court and Erica? I haven't seen either one of them since I got back. Are they mad at me? Are they afraid of me, too?"

"No," Robbie told him. "They know it wasn't you that did all those things. So, does everyone else. They'll come around."

Xavier nodded, and they walked on to Mathematics in silence. Erica and Court were not in the room, and when Xavier turned to Robbie to point this out, Ken Calhoun and Mac Clarke approached him.

"Hey, prince of cream puffs, I heard you went mental," Ken hissed as Mac chortled loudly behind him. The entire class became silent and tensely watched the confrontation.

Xavier glared at Ken. "You try watching your mom die a torturous death and have her reappear as if nothing happened. Then, you tell me if you can keep from becoming a little unglued!" he growled.

"Did you cry, Mama's boy? I bet you bawled like a baby when you saw your mommy again," he said, smirking.

Xavier looked at the boy before him with disbelief that someone could be so cruel. He stepped toward Ken his anger swelling. "I'd watch what you say to me, Calhoun. I may not be fully recovered! In fact, I may be on the brink of insanity. So, who's to say that I wouldn't lose it and send you flying across the classroom? Surely, they wouldn't blame me? After all, I've been through a very traumatic event!" He paused and studied the boy's tense face before him. "Nah, that's a cop out. I will not make excuses for my actions. So, I guess I'll just take my punishment like a man."

"Punishment? What punishment?" Ken grumbled stupidly.

Xavier smiled mischievously and said, "The punishment my father will have in store for me when I'm sent home for fighting." His swing was steady and true, and Kenneth crumpled to the floor, holding his eye. Mac backed away with his hands up, surrendering.

Sir Underwood entered the classroom and looked at Ken and then at Xavier.

"What's going on?" he drilled.

"Nothing, sir. The boys were just playing around, and Kenny slipped," said Maggie Applegate.

"Yeah, that's all. Ken was showing us how he got the better of William LeMasters during the rugby match, and he slipped," piped another student.

Sir Underwood looked unconvinced. He studied Kenneth who was getting to his feet, his eye already darkening into a shiner. "Is that right? Is that what happened, Kenneth?"

"Yes sir," he mumbled. "Just showing the Prince how I handled that imposter during a rugby match like they said." He glared at Xavier.

* * * * *

It wasn't until lunchtime that Xavier finally caught up with Court and Erica. Unlike his predecessor, Sir Spencer was very visible around the school. He even pulled a cafeteria duty. Xavier watched the new headmaster circle the tables, stopping occasionally to speak to students. Then Spencer looked up at him and nodded. Xavier smiled feebly before looking away and searching for Court and Erica.

"Come on," Robbie said, stepping up beside him with her lunch. "They're at the back table." She led him to the two children in the back of the cafeteria. As Xavier approached them, they looked up from an intense conversation.

"Hey," Xavier said unsure.

Court nodded to him, "Hey, X."

"Where were you guys? You missed mathematics," Robbie said, plopping down next to Erica.

"We had a meeting with Headmaster Spencer," Erica said.

"Oh! What did he say?" Robbie asked.

"Hey, X. How's it going?" Beck interrupted as he and Garrett settled themselves at the table, nodding to Xavier.

"All right. And you?"

"Brilliant!" He grinned and looked at Court soberly. "So? Did the Headmaster go for it?"

"Go for what?" Xavier asked.

Court looked at him and smiled. "We've been lobbying the school to allow us to play rugby in the spring league."

"What? What did he say?" Xavier blurted hopefully.

"He said that he couldn't hold tryouts all over again and the only way we could play is if we created a new team," Court told them.

"Are you serious? He'd let us do that?" Robbie grinned.

"Yes, he'll let you do that, Miss Minnows," Sir Spencer smiled down at them, "if you can find enough players to create a team. Do that before the end of the holidays, and I will allow it."

Court and Erica beamed up at him. "That's not a problem! We already have ten people willing," Erica chirped.

"Well then, I guess you better start considering names for your team." Sir Spencer smiled. Then, he looked at Xavier pensively. "Sire Wells? Telepathy lessons will be held in the headmaster's office from now on. Be on time."

"Yes, sir," he said.

Sir Spencer turned and strolled to another table.

"You know, with Sir Spencer as headmaster, it won't be easy to get away with stuff," Erica remarked, shaking her head gravely.

"What stuff?" Court snickered.

"Oh, you know, stuff," she said with a grin.

The group laughed heartily, and to Xavier, it felt like old times.

"So, who's agreed to be on the team?" Robbie asked.

"Well, the six of us, of course," Garrett announced.

"My sling comes off at the end of the week, so I'll be good as new to practice," Court said, waving his strapped arm.

Xavier felt the sting of guilt. His carelessness had been the cause of pain and injury to his closest friends.

Court seemed to have read his thoughts. "X, mate, it wasn't your fault. It wasn't you!"

"Thanks. But, it was somewhat my fault. I felt danger in the wood that night, but I chose to ignore it. If I hadn't, William would have never gotten the chance to hurt you," he grumbled. "Any of you!" He looked around the table with unwanted tears swelling in his eyes. He swiped at them hastily. "I'm really sorry."

"X! So what! It still wasn't your fault! We should have stuck together in the wood when he came. We shouldn't have left you in a position where William could capture you," Erica told him.

"Yeah, X. It wasn't you! How can you be responsible for what that maniac did! Let it go!" Beck hissed.

Xavier smiled feebly. At a lost of what to say, Xavier ducked his head, fighting the emotions ballooning inside him. They would always remain loyal to him, he realized. They were his friends.

* * * * *

"Now, tonight I want you to practice impediment with your father for at least thirty minutes. Understood? You still

305

have some deficient skills, and you need the practice. I trust that now you realize how important it is for you, of all people, to learn to block intrusions?" he asked roughly.

"Yes, sir."

"All right, then, you're dismissed," he said and began tidying up his desk.

Xavier stood and started toward the door, but he stopped and turned back to Sir Spencer. "Headmaster, may I hold a school assembly?" he asked.

"An assembly? Why?" Spencer looked up, shocked.

"I think I should say something about everything that happened when... Will... William..."

"I don't think that's necessary, Sire," Spencer interrupted.

"Yes it is. It's necessary for me," Xavier pleaded. "Please? Can I have it before dismissal today?"

Sir Spencer regarded him a moment and then nodded. "Okay. I'll call for the assembly fifteen minutes before dismissal."

"Thank you, sir."

As soon as the boy left the office, Sir Spencer contacted King Wells.

* * * * *

At the end of the day, the students began migrating into the gymnasium. Xavier wasn't exactly sure what he was going to say and stood fidgeting in the hall.

"Yo, Xavier!" Court called. Xavier looked up and found his friends approaching with broad smiles. "We came to offer some moral support."

"Yeah," Garrett added. "If there's anything you'd like for us to do, just say."

The group nodded in agreement.

"Thanks. Thanks a lot! I really appreciate it," Xavier said.

"Sire?" Maggie Applegate stepped forward, her gray eyes bright and clear. "Can I kiss you for luck?"

Xavier stared at her with an open mouth unsure of

what to say, but before he could answer, she leaned in and kissed him on the cheek. He felt his face grow flush, and his stomach did flip-flops. The group snickered.

"Xavier?" his father's voice came from behind him. Xavier spun as the other children gasped and sank to a knee.

"Father? What are you doing here?" he asked surprised.

"Please, stand up," Jeremiah said, addressing the other children.

The children rose and looked uncomfortably between Jeremiah and Xavier.

"Well, I think we'll go in and get good seats. Good Luck, Xavier," Court announced, patting Xavier's back, and the other children followed him into the gymnasium.

"Father? Why are you here?" Xavier repeated.

"Well," Jeremiah smiled, "the word's out that the Prince of Warwood just called for his first public assembly. I couldn't miss that; now, could I?"

Xavier smiled back. "No, I guess not."

"Prince Wells?" Jeanette whispered, poking her head out the gymnasium door. "We're ready."

"Thank you, ma'am," he said with a tremendous sigh.

"I'd like to provide you with some kingly advice, if I may?" Jeremiah asked, and Xavier nodded eagerly. "Be honest and sincere. Don't talk too long or you may say something that you'll trip over later. And, speak only for yourself. Don't apologize or make promises for other people," he told him.

Xavier nodded.

"Good luck, Son, and if it's worth anything to you, I'm proud of you," his father whispered, patting his cheek affectionately.

"Thanks, Dad," Xavier whispered.

Jeremiah froze and stared down at his son. "You called me Dad," he commented.

Xavier shifted uncomfortably under his father's elated

expression. "Yes, sir. It's okay; isn't it?"

"Is it okay?" Jeremiah repeated, beaming down at him. "It's more than okay. It's...it's wonderful." Jeremiah crushed Xavier in an enormous hug, leaving the boy coughing and laughing.

Father and Son entered the gymnasium together and were met by a sudden hush. Butterflies fluttered wildly in Xavier's stomach as he stepped away from his father and onto the stage. He watched as Jeremiah walked along the side of the gym, found a seat next to Spencer, and gave him an encouraging smile. Instantly, Xavier felt a little braver, more confident. Xavier took a deep breath and turned to address the crowd of students filling the gymnasium.

"My fellow students and friends," he began hoarsely. He cleared his throat and continued, "You may already know me; I'm Xavier Wells."

"Yeah, we know who you are, X!" a student hollered, followed by a soft chuckle from the crowd.

Xavier gave a nervous snicker before continuing, "Up until a few months ago, I grew up thinking that I was a normal, common kid. So, I guess in my heart, I don't feel that I'm all that special or much different than any of you. But, in the past few weeks, I've come to realize that by birthright, this is not true. I am a prince and my thoughts and feelings won't change that. I let my guard down and allowed an evil presence in the very heart of this kingdom. I felt the dangers around me, and I ignored them. That was very wrong of me. So, in the end, I had a hand in the chaos that William LeMasters created here. I apologize for that. I know he hurt many of you—some, my best friends. So, I promise to be more diligent and alert. I will never ignore my warning abilities in the future because I now realize that it's not just me who I put in danger when I do but all of us, the entire kingdom. As your prince and future king, it is my duty to protect our kingdom and its citizens. I am your prince; you are my loyal brothers and sisters. I will try to be worthy of the respect and honor that being your prince brings. So that one day, I will be a king worthy of you. Thank you." Xavier stepped away from the microphone and bowed.

The gymnasium erupted thunderously in cheers and applause. Many students jumped on top of their seats, yelling and clapping. His closest friends seated in the front row were loudest of all.

At the end of his son's speech, Jeremiah stood proudly and applauded. He looked at the boy who seemed so small to him and realized that he had just taken a giant step into manhood. It was a bittersweet experience.

Spencer leaned toward his brother and whispered, "That's some boy you've got there."

"Yes, indeed," he beamed. "He's made his father proud."

Jeremiah watched Xavier stride proudly from the platform and toward his friends in the front row who congratulated him and thumped him on the back. As the students filed out, many went out of their way to come forward to speak to Xavier, congratulating him and welcoming him home.

"So, it begins," Jeremiah whispered, smiling and watching as his son shook hands with student after student from an ever-growing line.

Coming Soon…

The Prince of Warwood
and the
Fall of the King

Xavier Wells is the happiest he's ever been in his life! He has friends who are loyal to him, he has a father who adores him, and he's the Prince of the empowered!

But, as Xavier develops new powers, he finds himself in mischief and a heap of trouble with the King. Subsequently, when Jeremiah begins a romance with Governor Yaman's niece, Xavier is beside himself with resentment and jealousy, and Father and Son find themselves at each other's throats.

Then, one night, a strange, deformed man appears at the palace and foretells of dark times lying ahead for the kingdom. Xavier refuses to believe the man's predictions until a disease begins to sweep through the kingdom. Soon, panic spreads as children begin to die, including someone close to Xavier. Regrettably, the disease is only the beginning of dark things happening in Warwood, and soon, the Prince, the King, and ultimately, the entire kingdom are in great peril.

Watch for it at